Diplomacy of Wolves

'Full of imagination, subterfuge, terror, and surprise . . . Holly Lisle's work has grown beyond my
wildest expectations.' Mercedes Lackey

'The magic and its transforming side effects
are exhilaratingly horrid; the novel ends with a
whopping cliffhanger. Whatever next? Highly
readable.' David Langford

'well-paced, absorbing and frequently exciting'
SFX

'A grand adventure' *Locus*

'Carefully crafted and well thought out . . . wonderful.' SF *Site*

Also by Holly Lisle in Victor Gollancz/Millennium

VENGEANCE OF DRAGONS
BOOK 2 OF THE SECRET TEXTS

DIPLOMACY OF WOLVES

Holly Lisle

The right of Holly Lisle to be identified as the author of this
work has been asserted by her in accordance with the
Copyright, Designs and Patents Act 1988.

This edition published in Great Britain in 1999 by
Millennium
An imprint of Victor Gollancz
Orion House, 5 Upper St Martin's Lane, London WC2H 9EA

To receive information on the Millennium list, e-mail us at:
smy@orionbooks.co.uk

A CIP catalogue record for this book is available
from the British Library

ISBN 1 85798 872 8

Typeset by Deltatype Ltd, Birkenhead, Merseyside

Printed in Great Britain by
Clays Ltd, St Ives plc

To Russell Galen,
my fantastic agent –
for standing by me through hard times and leading me,
through his encouragement, persistence,
and belief in me and what I could do, to better.
Neither this book
nor the world of Matrin
would exist without him.
Thank you, Russ.

Acknowledgements

My thanks to Peter James and Nick Thorpe, authors of *Ancient Inventions*, whose book proved a constant source of inspiration in the writing of this one; to Betsy Mitchell, my editor, whose incisive criticisms kept me on track, and whose enthusiasm for the story made the book fun to write; to Michael Watkins, for early technical criticism and the loan of books on dirigibles that made some of this project work; to Becky and Mark, for encouragement and support and carrying ten thousand glasses of ice water up the stairs for me after school and during summer vacation; to Matt, for love and support and many, many suppers.

DIPLOMACY
OF WOLVES

men forge swords of steel and fire;
gods forge swords of flesh and blood and tragedy.

Vincalis the Agitator

from *The Last Hero of Maestwauld*

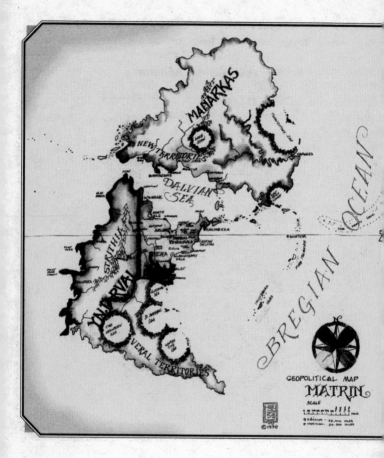

MABARKAS

NEW TERRITORIES

DALVIAN SEA

STNITHIA

PERA

ANDARVAL

VERAL TERRITORIES

BREGIAN OCEAN

EQUATOR

GEOPOLITICAL MAP
MATRIN
SCALE

©1990

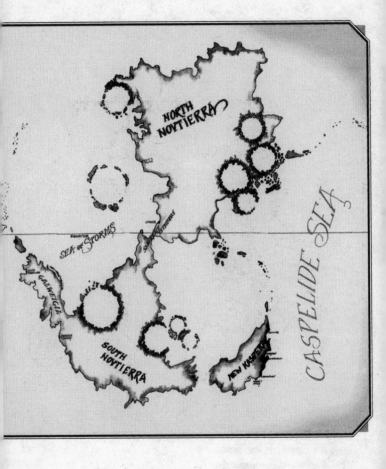

Chapter 1

For more than a thousand years, the Mirror of Souls waited for the return of magic that would awaken it and allow it to finish its work. It waited in a closed-off room on the side of a hill in a long-abandoned city, its existence forgotten on a continent where men had been replaced by the monsters spawned of a hellish war. It slept, oblivious to the passage of time, oblivious to the change that went on all around it, oblivious to the destruction of an old order and to the chaos that followed, and to the new world that rose on the ashes of the old. For more than a thousand years, the Mirror had waited in vain.

Now, though, it glowed softly, as faint currents of distant magic began to wash against it, and within the shimmering depths of its central well, shadows stirred. That far-off spellcasting – still too weak to rouse the lost artifact to wakefulness – sufficed to permit it to dream.

Within the reborn stream of magical energy, the Mirror began to dream of the past that remained its present. It dreamed of the ghosts of the great men and women held within its memory. It dreamed of a world lost and forgotten, of wonders no longer imaginable, of secrets buried in the rubble of a world that no longer existed. It dreamed of the task that it had left undone for a thousand years.

Undone. But not forgotten.

The Mirror yearned to waken, and to complete the task for which it had been created.

* * *

'Your job will be to keep her away from the men, Kait. Just until after the wedding. You know how Tippa is – and with the Sabirs getting a firm foothold into the Kairn Territories, we need this alliance.'

She had acknowledged her cousin's fascination with all things male, and the senior diplomat had smiled at her and patted her shoulder. 'This is your chance to prove yourself,' he'd said. 'Do well here, and the Family will place you in a regular diplomatic position. You'll have other assignments.'

He hadn't said, *Fail and you'll go back to your life as a decoration in Galweigh House*. He hadn't needed to. That was a given.

She would be secondary, of course. Tippa would have a professional chaperone from the Galweigh Family, and another from the Dokteerak Family; Kait would be a 'companion,' as far as anyone outside the Galweigh diplomatic corps knew. She would act as a fail-safe, nothing more, and while her chances of failing were slim, her chances of winning any recognition for competent performance – and with that recognition, a chance at a real diplomatic job – were even slimmer.

But this was her beginning. Her opportunity to serve her Family, and perhaps to win a place in the diplomatic corps. This was the opportunity she'd thought she would never – *could* never – have. Under no circumstances would she allow herself to fail, or even to consider failure. Though she stood in the breezeway with her head aching and her eyes throbbing, her pain meant nothing; the fact that her skin crawled and her gut insisted that something evil lurked in the party meant only that she needed to focus her attention, that she needed to work harder. She had her assignment and her chance. She would make it count.

So Kait Galweigh stood off in one corner at the Dokteerak Naming Day party and scanned the crowd while she pretended to sip a drink. The Dokteerak Family women in their gauzy net finery clustered beneath the broad palms in the central garden, chatting about nothing of consequence. Torchlight cast an amber gleam on their sleek skin and pale hair and made the heavy gold at their throats and wrists seem to glow. They were decorative – Kait's Family had such women, too, and theirs was the fate she so desperately wished to escape. The senior diplomats from both Families, Galweigh and Dokteerak, gathered in the breezeway that surrounded the courtyard, leaning along the food-laden tables, nibbling from finger servings of yearling duck and broiled monkey and wild pig and papaya-stuffed python, telling each other amusing stories and watching, watching, their eyes never still. Concubines flirted and primped, tempting their way into berths in the beds of the high-ranking or the beautiful. Dokteerak guardsmen in gold and blue propped themselves against doorways, swapping racy stories and tales of bravado with Galweigh guardsmen in red and black. Outland princes and the parats of other Families and their cadet branches drifted from group to group, assessing available women the way hunting wolves assessed a herd of deer.

In the salon beside the breezeway, dancing couples moved in and out of Kait's view. Tippa and her future father-in-law stamped and swirled among them, performing one of the traditional bride's dances, with, perhaps, a bit more enthusiasm than necessary. Kait watched the older man and wondered if the Dokteerak paraglese would be a threat to his future daughter-in-law's virtue. If he would, he wouldn't be a threat on the dance floor in front of his son and subjects, but Kait wondered at the wisdom of an alliance with a man who eyed his son's future wife with such blatant lust.

Both Tippa's Galweigh chaperone and her Dokteerak

one watched from the sidelines, and Calmet Dokteerak, the future bridegroom, danced with a series of gaudily dressed paratas. Things there remained under control.

The people she needed to watch were the parats. Like the one approaching her at that moment.

'Beautiful parata,' he said, 'please dance with me and be my flower of the evening. You are so beautiful, I cannot continue to breathe unless my air has first been kissed by you.'

Kait had heard variations on the same line half a dozen times already. As the night wore on, the protestations would become more passionate and more vehement. Also, she mused, more desperate. The concubines flocked to the older men and women – those with wealth and power, who could be expected to give fine gifts or even offer permanent positions in their Houses. The younger men, who had less to offer, could only seduce others among the partygoers if they hoped to round out their night with sexual amusements. Kait – young, unmarried, and acceptably attractive – had come in for a complete range of attempted seductions, and her patience began to wear thin.

'You'll have to find another flower,' she said. 'I'm afraid I've promised myself that I would bloom alone tonight.' She didn't even waste time on a smile. The parat, who wore the silk of one of the lesser branches of the Dokteerak House, blanched and nodded stiffly and walked away, the anger evident in his stride and the set of his shoulders.

He wasn't the sort who would interest her cousin Tippa, but there were plenty of others roaming the party who would. Kait discovered that while the parat had distracted her, Tippa had moved out of view. Kait stepped closer to the arches and almost tripped over the Dokteerak head artist, Kastos Miellen, who was demonstrating the workings of a charming mechanical playhouse to a pair of admiring Galweigh women. Kait apologized, backed away, and caught sight of Tippa, now dancing with her future husband.

She relaxed, almost amused by her paranoia. From a quiet place under the arches, she alternately watched the artist's tiny mechanical men and women moving across the miniature stage, and her cousin spinning and leaping on the crowded dance floor.

A plump hand settled on her shoulder and she jumped. She turned to the sun-browned, grinning man who'd come up behind her, and for an instant didn't recognize him. His scent tipped her off before she placed his face.

'Uncle Dùghall?'

'My Kait-cha. You haven't forgotten me.'

'It *is* you!' She hugged him hard and, laughing a little at her own confusion, stepped back to look at him. 'You've changed.'

He smiled. 'Age and women, Kait. Age and women – the first gives you wrinkles and the second makes you fat. Whereas you are more beautiful than ever.'

'So I've been told,' Kait murmured.

'I'm sure you have. The lads are out in droves tonight. But you're still alone. Haven't found one you fancy yet?'

Kait lowered her voice. 'Can't even look. I'm working.' She grinned then – her uncle was the reason she had any diplomatic assignment at all, however minor it might be. He had recommended her to the diplomatic services when she turned thirteen, and had insisted she be trained by the best teachers in the best classes. He had shipped her final two tutors to Calimekka from his post on the Imumbarra Isles himself.

He gave her shoulder a quick squeeze and leaned in close enough to whisper in her ear, 'Then you have an assignment.'

'Minor,' she said. 'But important to me.' She glanced in to be sure that Tippa was still behaving herself, then turned to her uncle. 'What are you doing here? I thought you

5

couldn't get away from the islands for this . . . that some holiday interfered.' She tried to remember the name of the holiday her mother had mentioned when reading Dùghall's letter to her, but failed.

'There are advantages to being considered a minor deity back home. I changed the date of the holiday, boarded a fast ship, and here I am.'

She hugged him again, and started to effuse about how happy she was to see him. But Kastos Miellen's miniature had caught his attention.

'Impressive toy, isn't it?' he asked her, nodding at the mechanical stage.

'Ingenious. And everyone seems to like it.'

He held up a finger, the way he always had when he was about to impart some tidbit of wisdom. 'Dokteerak hasn't forgotten the immortal advice of Vincalis.'

Kait raised an eyebrow.

Her uncle grinned at her. 'All your studies of diplomacy and you haven't read Vincalis the Agitator yet? That's criminal.'

'I don't think I've even heard of Vincalis,' Kait admitted, hoping that he was one of Dùghall's island diplomats, or someone obscure, so that she might have an excuse for not knowing his works.

'One of the Ancients. A troublemaker of the first water, by all accounts, which is probably why you haven't been taught him. I hear you have some talents in the direction of trouble yourself.' Dùghall didn't look at her when he spoke – he squinted instead at the artist and his mechanical marvel. 'Vincalis said, and I quote, "To the man of wealth who would be great, remember this – an artist is a better investment than a diplomat for three reasons: first, an artist, once bought, stays bought; second, you screw the artist instead of the other way round; and third, if you should find it essential to permanently dispose of your artist, the value of his works will increase, which no one will say of a diplomat."' He paused for just an instant, so that he could be sure she had a chance to let the words sink in, then guffawed.

Kait laughed with him, but even to her own ears her laughter sounded nervous.

Dùghall studied her face and his smile grew mischievous. 'I believe I've shocked you.'

'At first, I suppose. But Vincalis wasn't serious, was he?'

Dùghall shrugged. 'My dear, in the best humor lies the deepest truth, and Vincalis is as true now as he was more than a thousand years ago.' He smiled at her and then stiffened as his gaze moved past her and fixed on something in the courtyard. Suddenly he was as intent as a jaguar who'd spotted a fawn. The expression vanished as quickly as it had appeared, so quickly that Kait couldn't begin to guess what had caught his eye, but when he returned his attention to her again, his smile was apologetic. 'And now, sadly, I must move on. I see an old friend out in the courtyard, and if I don't hurry, she's sure to vanish.'

And before she could even give him another hug, or tell him how glad she was to see him, he was gone.

She glanced into the salon to check on Tippa. She didn't see either of the chaperones. Tippa's future father-in-law had vanished. Her future husband stood in the center of a circle of admiring women, none of whom was Tippa.

Tippa . . .

Kait felt her stomach knot. This was her chance to prove she could serve the Family's interests, and Tippa was nowhere in the salon.

Kait looked around the breezeway and out into the courtyard; a cluster of men parted, and revealed Tippa spinning in a circle on the arm of a tall, handsome young outlander dressed in Gyru-nalle finery, while two others, similarly dressed, looked on.

The couple stopped spinning and Tippa flung herself down onto a seat beside a fountain in one shadowed corner of the courtyard. Her companion said something too softly for Kait to catch over the crowd noise, and Tippa squealed with laughter. She took a tall goblet from one of the men who'd been watching her impromptu dance with his associate, and swallowed the contents in two hard pulls. At some point she had opened the outer blouse of her silk dress and pulled it back, revealing the filmy silk underblouse, which was tugged so low that Kait could see a new-moon sliver of one rouged nipple peeking over the scalloped hem. Very stylish . . . but not appropriate for a woman who was to marry within the week. Tippa's hair had come loose from its netting and hung around her face in wild tendrils. Her eyes were too bright and her laughter too loud. All three men clustered around her as if she were one of the party concubines, and not the bride-to-be of Branard Dokteerak's second son, Calmet.

And that would be an incident, wouldn't it? The drunken bride-to-be and three Gyru 'princes' caught together in some back room or stable stall a week before the wedding? Kait set her goblet on a marble rail and pushed through the crowd, abruptly and totally furious.

She caught her cousin just as the girl had begun to run her fingers along the lacings of the tallest man's shirt. 'Isn't he lovely?' Tippa asked as Kait's hand clamped around her wrist, and the man, who didn't look in the least drunk, said, 'Unless you want to join our party, little parata, just move on. But don't be spoiling our fun.'

The anger that was always in her, anger that sought to break free from the tight chains of self-control with which she bound it, slipped toward the surface. She turned from the Gyrus with difficulty. 'Tippa, we have to leave early. The Naming news from Calimekka will be arriving soon, and we need to be there for our devotions. The carriage is waiting.'

It was a lie, but it was at least a plausible lie.

Tippa, oblivious to the scene she was about to cause,

8

leaned forward farther, and whispered in Kait's ear loudly enough that Kait, the Gyrus, and probably most of the guests could hear, 'Then go back without me, Kait. I'm having a . . . good . . . a good . . . time, and I've made some . . . some nice friends. Aren't they cute?' Her smile when she leaned back spoke of too much wine as loudly as her whisper. 'They're Prince . . . um, Ersti, and Prince Keera . . . er, Meerki, and Prince . . . Prince . . . I can't remember. Ah, Prince Latti.' She smiled hazily. 'Right?'

'I'm sure they are,' Kait growled. 'But you will have to visit with these . . . royals . . . another time.' How could Tippa have gotten so drunk? The chaperones should have prevented that. And where were they, anyway? She hated sloppiness, but this suggested more to her than that.

And a prince's hand suddenly gripping her shoulder, too rough and insistent to be mistaken for anything but a threat, screamed to her that the incident had been planned. Somewhere. By someone. The man said, 'Leave her alone. We're having a good time. Just go back to your *Family*, where you belong, girl.' He spit out the word 'Family' as if it meant 'garbage.'

Kait's anger broke half of its chains, and she twisted out of the man's grip and turned to face him, and her fury (*or am I slipping . . . have I lost control?*) sent him a step back wearing shock on his pale freckled face. 'Don't press me,' she said, so softly that only the three Gyrus could hear her. She heard in her voice the dark timbre of that second self that begged to be set free. Her skin grew hot; it tingled over muscles that longed to shift and slip, over bones that yearned for violent force and violent change. She stood fast, permitting no flash of teeth, no growl, no tensing of muscle. She forced her anger to whisper, knowing that she dared not let it shout.

She stared, and all three Gyrus glared back at her. She felt the growl starting in the back of her throat, and the last

9

of the chains weakened. But the men saw something in her, something that warned them. All three backed away.

Furious, Kait turned on her cousin. She pulled Tippa's outer blouse closed, then grabbed her wrist and yanked her to her feet.

'But I don't want . . .' Tippa started to say, but stopped herself when the edge of Kait's anger seeped through the wine haze. Her eyes went round and her mouth clamped shut. She followed, unprotesting, as Kait pulled her toward the breezeway that led into the House, and eventually toward the grounds where the carriages waited.

Kait glanced back to be sure the Gyrus weren't following them. She didn't want to cause an incident; wanted no one dead, no difficult questions, not now when she was finally, finally on her own and working as a productive member of the Family. The three of them were huddled together, faces flushed and tight with anger. She tried to listen to what they were saying while still moving toward the door, and she told herself that was the reason she ran right into the short young man who stood near the archway. She hit him hard, but she was the one who staggered back – he was solid as a tree, and seemed to be as thoroughly rooted to the earth. She caught her balance. Tippa wasn't so fortunate; she tripped and went down. Both Kait and the stranger moved to help her. Kait took Tippa's arm but the man planted one hand on either side of Tippa's waist and lifted her to her feet. 'I'm so sorry,' he said, loudly enough that anyone who had seen the girl go down could hear him. 'I wasn't watching where I was going.'

Kait started to smile at him, appreciative that he'd made an attempt to cover her cousin's drunkenness to preserve her reputation, when she became aware of something noticeable only by its absence.

The ache in her head and behind her eyeballs was gone. The crawling sensation of her skin was gone. More, the pervasive sense of stalking evil that Kait had felt all night had been lifted and removed, like someone pulling a heavy counterpane off a bed. She felt better. Safer. Her volatile emotions, fed by the aura of danger that had surrounded her, calmed. She took a slow breath, and smiled at the man, and had the presence of mind to thank him for helping her cousin.

'Think nothing of it,' he said. He had a pleasant voice. A nondescript face, an ordinary smile, kind eyes; when Kait turned away from him, she was halfway to forgetting him already.

Then, three or four strides away from the place where she'd run into him, with Tippa dragging along in her wake, Kait felt the full brunt of crawling nighttime evil drop onto her shoulders again. The headache grabbed her; her skin prickled and she shuddered involuntarily, and she gasped from the pain. She wasn't prepared. Not prepared at all. The change caught her in the gut like the kick of a street fighter, and for just an instant she almost couldn't think.

Her first thought when she could breathe again was that the helpful stranger was the cause of the aura of evil that filled the night. Her second and more logical thought was that he was somehow immune to it – or somehow protected from it. She stopped, turned slowly, and stared at him. He looked back at her, and she could no longer understand why she'd thought him nondescript. She could still see that outer shell of inoffensiveness, but underneath she could see a man as complicated and fascinating as that mechanical marvel the Dokteerak artist had unveiled for the Naming Day party. Her expression told him something he didn't like, for the 'I'm no one of consequence' smile gave way to an expression of fear in his eyes, and a look of understanding that unnerved her. The fact that she had looked twice at him told him something about her. He knew. She didn't know what he knew, but she had to find out. If her secrets got out, they would kill her.

'Who are you?' she asked.

His eyes tracked from one corner of the courtyard to the other. 'No one of importance. Just a guest.'

'Tell me. I'll find out one way or another.' She didn't mean for that remark to sound like a threat, but the second the words were out of her mouth, she knew it did.

'You probably will.'

She moved back toward him, and seemed to step through a wall when she did. On the outside, her nerves screamed that something terrible waited to attack. Inside, the evil vanished as if it had never been. 'How do you do that?' She kept her voice low; she sensed that whatever his secret was, it probably wasn't one that he wanted bruited about to the world.

That weak smile again, and eyes that darted left, right, left, checking to see if anyone was listening. Or watching. He said nothing.

She had to know. She said, 'The wall around you. The one that keeps out the foulness of this place. How do you do it?'

His face went slack with fear then. A man with a knife held to his throat by a madman could not have looked more frightened. 'Not here,' he said. 'By all the gods, not here.'

'Your name, then. And where I can find you.' She narrowed her eyes. 'Don't lie to me. I can smell lies.'

He nodded. 'I have a shop in the west quarter. Hasmal's Curiosities. It's near the wall, on Stonecutter Street.'

'You're Hasmal?'

'The Third. I work for my father.'

Sons of shopkeepers rarely found themselves invited into the Houses of the Five Families. And if they did, they would be there as workers, not guests. Yet Hasmal the son of Hasmal, sipping at his wine, dressed in his Naming Day finery, certainly looked like a guest.

She tightened her grip on Tippa's wrist and said, 'I'll be by to talk with you tomorrow.' Then she turned, braced herself against the malevolent night, stepped out of his circle of sanctuary, and dragged Tippa out of the court-yard.

* * *

The paraglese of Dokteerak House, Branard Dokteerak, balanced the tip of his dagger on the corner of his desk. With his index finger pressing against the emerald in the pommel, he rocked it slowly back and forth, gouging a tiny scar into the wood. Across from him, standing next to the chairs because Branard had not bidden him sit, the Sabir messenger stared at the rocking knife as if he were a chick in its nest watching an approaching snake. The paraglese was aware of the Sabir's attention. He kept his own eyes fixed on the tiny chips of wood that he worked loose from the desk. He was waiting for the messenger to fidget, or sigh, or in any way express his impatience, but the man had been well trained. He gave away nothing. At last, Dokteerak, still watching his knife rocking back and forth, said, 'What do you have to say for yourself?'

The messenger said, 'My Family sends off the troops you requested; they will depart at the first light of dawn tomorrow, and the pigeon must have time to reach them if you have any last message you will send. They require any final information that you can give – anything that has happened that might change the number of troops required, or the route they must take, or the necessary supplies.'

The paraglese, disgusted, said, 'Anything that might change the number of troops required, eh? Well, what about this, then? My House is full to the rafters with Galweighs getting ready to celebrate the marriage of their damned daughter to my son. As host of this farce, my place is out there with them, acting the part of doting father and eager ally. Instead I'm in here with you, and you cannot think for a moment that one of their number hasn't noticed that. Further, if you're seen here and recognized, all our work will be for nothing. They'll call off the wedding, get their people back to Calimekka, and go on the defensive. If they do that, neither your people nor my people nor the rest of the countryside combined will rout them out of that House of theirs, and we will lose this fine opportunity – which the senior members of your Family and I have been planning for *three* years – to take it. Your presence here, and your demand for my presence here, could be the tiny breeze that topples our tower down upon us.'

The Sabir envoy spread his hands wide. 'My people required a final reassurance. My paraglese asks me to remind you that we risk more than you do, Paraglese Dokteerak – if we fail at this we risk Galweigh retaliation more than you do. You don't share Calimekka with them, whereas our House lies inside the same walls as theirs.'

'Indeed. But when this is over, we will share the city with you, and I ask you to remind Grasmir that he and I will get along better if I haven't lost the best of my fighters and my sons needlessly through his carelessness, or his impatience, or his pointless worrying.' He felt his anger getting the better of him. He shoved harder on the knife, and it dug itself deeply into the wood – he allowed himself no other display of temper. 'Nothing has changed. Nothing. Now leave before you give us all away.'

The envoy bowed gracefully and said, 'Enjoy your party, Paraglese.'

And then he was gone.

The paraglese sat staring at the closed door for a moment, and wondered if that hint of irony he heard in the Sabir envoy's last words was in the envoy's voice or in his own mind.

Chapter 2

The stone walls, rough-hewn and slime-coated, gleamed in the torchlight. The chill of the place, and the stink and the darkness and the skittering sounds of the rats, wore on Marcue's nerves even when all the cells were full and the men in them talked and quarreled and wondered about their futures. Now the dungeon was empty except for one prisoner, and that was a girl – a child, really – and she rarely spoke, but frequently cried. Her crying was worse than the rats.

She was crying at the moment.

'Your Family will ransom you,' he told her. He wasn't supposed to offer comfort to the enemy, but he had a hard time thinking of a little girl as an enemy, and an equally hard time understanding how his employers could justify treating her as one, to the point of locking her in the lowest dungeon in Sabir House for more than a month.

The girl said nothing for a few moments, but she did sniffle a bit and take a few slow, deep breaths, as if she were trying to get herself under control. Then she moved a little way out of the shadow that hid her and looked at him. 'I thought . . . I thought they w-w-would, too,' she said, and started sobbing again.

Marcue winced. Poor girl. She was so young and pretty, and so very helpless. And she obviously didn't understand how these things worked. Families didn't hurt little girls.

He had no compunction about holding warriors and diplomats in the cells. He didn't lose sleep when he had to kill one for trying to escape, either; the warriors and diplomats of the world had chosen to be where they were, doing what they were doing, and they knew the risks involved in their work. This girl, though, had been kidnapped from her bed while she slept, and had been dragged into this cell in the month of Brethwan, during the Festival of the Full Circle. And there she had languished while his employers and her Family bickered over the price of her return.

If I had such a daughter, the guard had thought more than once, I would pay any price for her safe return. But he had discovered long ago that the ways of the rich and powerful were not his ways. From everything he had heard, her Family was demanding not only her safe return, but also an exorbitant punitive payment to reimburse them for the anguish they had suffered from her kidnapping. He thought, though he hadn't dared to say it aloud, that her Family didn't know a damned thing about suffering if they could leave a daughter locked in a cell while they screamed for compensation.

The girl rose and came to the gate. Even dirty and unkempt, with the tattered blanket she'd been given wrapped around her delicate shoulders, she was impossibly beautiful. Dressed still in the silk pajamas she'd been wearing when she was kidnapped, she looked so fragile he wondered again how she had survived a month in the cold, dank, filthy cell.

'You could release me,' she said to him. Her little-girl voice was soft and tentative, and tinged with hope.

Her voice could have broken the heart of a stone, and Marcue was no stone. He looked at her sadly, though, and told her, 'That I cannot do, though if I dared, I'd do it in an instant.'

She gripped the bars and glared at him. 'Why *can't* you? You admit your employers have taken me wrongfully, and that their behavior is shameful.'

He'd said those things to her a few days earlier, and now wished he hadn't. He'd meant them; he thought what he'd said was completely true; but if she told any of the Sabir Family about his indiscretion, his head would be decorating a post at the west gate of Sabir House.

She leaned closer and her voice dropped to a whisper. 'If you helped me, you could have anything you wanted from the Galweighs.'

He moved toward her, though no closer than the line of the no-pass zone carved into the stone floor. He kept his voice low and prayed no one was listening. 'I know I could, but I still can't release you. Not for fear of my own life, but for the lives of my parents. Both my mother and my father work in the Sabir kitchens. If I set you free, whether I stayed on or ran with you, both of my parents would be killed the moment my betrayal was discovered.' He stopped and reconsidered. 'No, that isn't true. The Sabirs would torture them first, then kill them.'

She seemed to sag and shrink in front of his eyes. 'That's it, then. You were my last hope. And you say exactly the same thing as the other five guards who have watched me – "I'd help you if I could, but they would kill my family ... or my wife ... or my sister ...'" She looked, for just an instant, furious. 'I'd think, when the Sabirs told you what stories to tell your prisoners, that they would have told you to try to be a bit original.'

He was startled. She thought he was lying to her? He shook his head and almost moved across the line to explain to her, but remembered himself in time and kept back of it. 'Girl –' he began.

She cut him off. 'Danya. My name is Danya. I want

you to remember it, since you won't help me. Remember it, so that when they do whatever they're going to do to me, my face and my name will haunt you for the rest of your life.' She flung herself away from the bars, facedown into the straw.

He winced. 'Danya,' he said, 'you think we were all told to tell you a story . . . but that isn't so. How do you suppose the Families ensure the loyalty of their guards? Eh? Have you ever thought about that? They choose only those of us who have something to lose . . . someone, actually. And they make sure we know, from the day we don these uniforms, that our loved ones are the reason we were chosen to serve – and that they will be the price we pay if we fail.'

Danya rolled over and sat up. She glared at him and brushed loose tangles of hair back from her face. 'Perhaps that is how the *Sabirs* do it –'

Marcue didn't let her finish. 'Unless you have also spent time in the Galweigh dungeons, and have spoken to the Galweigh guards to be sure you know differently, assume the guard who watched over you was chosen the same way. Assume that when your Family discovered you stolen away, the person he once loved was murdered while he watched, and when she was dead, that he was killed, too. Loyalty can be bought and sold, child, and even given away for free . . . but fear can make the price of a man's loyalty higher than even the richest buyer could pay.'

The girl stared at him for a moment, horrified. 'My Family would never hurt Quintal. He has guarded me since I was born. And his wife and daughter . . . his daughter was my companion until just last year, and his wife works for our seneschal. They are a part of the Family.'

She leaned forward to hide her face against her thighs. She wrapped her thin arms under her legs and began to cry again. 'No one would hurt them,' he heard her insisting again and again.

'Oh, please,' Marcue whispered. 'Don't do that. I'm sure you're right. Your guardsman will be fine, and his family, too. Meanwhile, Danya, you're safe here. Your Family isn't going to let anything happen to you. They'll pay to get you out – any day now, someone will come down the steps to release you.'

She didn't raise her head. The guard could barely make out her reply, muffled as it was. He thought she said, 'It's *Theramisday.*'

And what did the fact that it was Naming Day have to do with anything? He asked her as much.

'Because,' she said, lifting her head, 'the Sabir diplomat who came down and talked to me just after I got here gave Theramisday as the last day that my Family could come to an agreement on the terms of my release. If the Sabirs didn't get what they wanted then, they said they would take it by other means, and my life would be worth nothing to them.'

The guard tried to smile at her. 'They always say things like that when they're dealing with each other. I can't even tell you how many threats I've heard the Sabirs giving . . . and you have to know the stories I've heard of the Galweighs are no better.' He shook his head and his smile grew more confident. 'But all those threats won't mean anything when it comes to you. What could they gain by hurting you?'

She gave him an eerie look, one that seemed to bite with knife-edged teeth straight through his skin and into his bones. That stare chilled him from the inside out, and made him wish that there were more people in the dungeon than just the two of them. Then she looked away and the awful feeling passed. She said, 'You'd be surprised.'

Perhaps I would after all, he thought, but he said nothing.

From far above, he heard the first soft, rhythmic thuds of boots on the curving stairs that led down into the dungeon. The hour was far too early for his relief to be coming, and too late for someone from the kitchen to be bringing meals for him and the girl. So then, who came?

Danya moved into the farthest corner of her cell and pulled herself into a tiny bundle, huddled behind a little pile of straw. She said, 'It's time for the bad news now. But perhaps you could still find a way to save me.'

The child was determined to get him killed. He shook his head.

She watched him, eyes like those of a fox in a trap – terrified yet cunning, too. 'I'd consent to marriage in my own right, if that's what you wanted. Even if you demanded both marriage and a name in the Galweigh Family, I could promise that, and you would have it. I will promise it. I do. If you'll just get me away from here.'

Her hand in marriage? He smiled sadly at her and said, 'How old are you, Danya? Not old enough to be thinking of marriage, I'll wager.'

She said, 'I'm eighteen. Old enough to give legal consent.'

She was eighteen? He wouldn't have guessed her age at more than thirteen, and she wouldn't have made a particularly well developed thirteen-year-old. If she was eighteen – and he wasn't sure he was willing to believe her about that – she might be in more trouble than he'd guessed. As a legal adult, she couldn't count on the safeguards promised to children by the Family treaties. As an adult, if her Family wouldn't ransom her and she couldn't offer her own ransom, the Sabirs really might do what they wanted with her.

But they would start a war if they hurt – or killed, but that was unthinkable – the daughter of a Galweigh. And none of the Families and subfamilies in Calimekka wanted a war.

Did they?

The footsteps grew louder. He thought he could discern three separate pairs of feet coming down the stone stairs.

'Save me. Anything it is within my power to give, you'll have.'

He felt her fear as if it were a blanket wrapping itself around him, smothering him. 'You can't guarantee the safety of my parents,' he said quietly. 'I'm sorry, girl, but I can't help you.'

She screamed – fear and rage, in equal parts. She ripped handfuls of straw from the floor and flung them at him. He drew well back from the line and steeled his face to impassivity. Above him, the pace of feet on stairsteps quickened. He grew uneasy. Perhaps she had reason to fear. Perhaps. But so did he.

The first man appeared from around the curve of the staircase. His long cloak, which swirled against his riding boots and billowed behind him, also effectively hooded his face from view, but Marcue knew him anyway from the ring on his right hand. A wolf's-head ring, gold, with tourmaline cabochon eyes that glowed in the torchlight, with a mouth opened in a vicious snarl. The wearer of the ring was Crispin Sabir, one of the Sabir Wolves.

A wave of queasiness washed over Marcue. The girl had reason to fear. Crispin Sabir was mad. Evil. Cruel beyond words, beyond human comprehension. If even one one-hundredth of the stories Marcue had heard about him were true, the man kept corpses in his quarters and planted them in his private grounds the way gardeners planted roses. Marcue had seen him torture a man once; that memory would never leave him. If he had known the girl would end up with the Sabirs' Wolves instead of with their diplomats –

'Why is she screaming?' Crispin asked, and Marcue swallowed and said quickly, 'She's afraid. She heard you coming down the stairs and she said something about this being Theramisday.'

'Theramisday. Gregor said he told her about that. I'm glad she remembered,' Crispin said.

The second man appeared as he said it, and if Marcue had been sick at the sight of Crispin, with the arrival of Andrew Sabir his heart sank, weighted with dread. Andrew Sabir. Better a visit from Zagtasht, god of the underworld. At least Zagtasht was sometimes known to show mercy. Andrew was a massive man, twice as broad through the shoulders as the leaner, taller Crispin, with a chest like a beer barrel; he kept his head shaved in the manner of the Sloebene sailors, with a single braid above his left ear; and he was ugly as red-eyed evil. He grinned as he caught sight of the girl, and said, 'Do you want me to shut her up, Crispin?'

'Not at all. Let her sing a bit. I like the sound of it.'

The third set of footsteps on the stairs approached slowly. Marcue heard a hissing slide, then a thud and a grunt, then the normal click of boot heel on stone. A pause. Then the sequence repeated. Over and over, louder and louder. And throughout, a curious scraping that he hadn't heard at all until the other two men were off the stairs.

Marcue shivered, and not from the chill and the damp. He'd heard stories of the creatures the Wolves kept hidden in their chambers. He'd heard, too, that they consorted with demons and monsters. And that shuffle-step on the stair (what was that scratching sound?) might just be a kindly old Family diplomat limping down to tell the girl her ransom had been met . . . but Marcue didn't think so.

'We have news for you, little Wolf,' Andrew said.

Crispin glared at him. 'Wait until Anwyn gets here. He doesn't want to miss this.'

Andrew laughed, a creepy high tittering giggle that made Marcue want to retch. 'News,' he repeated. 'But maybe Anwyn will want to give it to you himself. We'll all want to give it to you.' He giggled again.

The girl stood and faced the men. She wasn't screaming any longer, and Marcue could see no sign of tears. She'd drawn strength from someplace; she'd found a measure of courage from deep inside herself; now her chin went up and her shoulders came back and her body wrote defiance in the air with her every move. She glared at Andrew and said, 'So what is your news, Wolf?'

Crispin and Andrew both grinned at each other. As they did, Anwyn slouched into the dungeon. Marcue had thought from his name that he would be human. Anwyn was a good Parmatian name, like Crispin . . . or Marcue, for that matter. The thing that skulked into the dungeon wasn't human, though. He might have been one of the Scarred – one of the creatures from the poisoned lands whose ancestors, stories said, had once been men. If he was Scarred, however, he was from no realm that had ever traded in Calimekka. And if he wasn't one of the Scarred, then he was a demon from the lowest pit of Zagtasht's darkest hell. Long horns curled out from his forehead. His scaled brow beetled over eyes so deeply set they looked more like hollow sockets. His lips parted in a grin that revealed teeth long as a man's thumb and serrated like a shark's. He hunched forward, and Marcue could make out the ridge of huge spines that ran down the center of his back beneath his cloak. His hands were talons, though five-fingered, and while one of his feet fit in a man's boot and grew from a man-shaped leg, the other was a cloven hoof attached to a leg that, beneath a man's breeches, bent backward at the knee. That leg he dragged forward as he moved into the room.

Marcue longed to run. He kept himself where he was only by the fiercest exercise of will, and he knew that his terror showed plainly on his face.

The girl didn't flinch. She looked at the monster as if he were someone she had known and disliked all her life. Marcue couldn't even see fear in her eyes.

Well, he was afraid enough for both of them.

You should have helped her escape, a tiny voice in the back of his mind whispered. You are going to regret the fact that you didn't for the rest of your life. The name Danya Galweigh is going to ride with you into the dark halls of nightmare when you sleep, and perch on your shoulders when you wake.

The girl gripped the bars of her cell with slender, long-fingered hands and, in a voice that said without words that she was their superior and beyond anything they might do to her, said, 'You're all here now. Give me your news.'

The monster Anwyn said, 'Dear child, the diplomats still talk, and we will let them talk, of course – but they achieve nothing. Your Family is *most* unwilling to give us what we want.' He shook his head and looked from Andrew to Crispin, then back to the girl. 'And the work of Theramisday has come and gone, and no decision that we will accept has yet been reached.'

She frowned. 'But you said the diplomats are still talking.'

Anwyn smiled, and those horrible teeth gleamed. 'Well, of course. If we had given your people our actual deadline, they would know to be watching for our next move. As it is, they think we're still considering what they have to say, so they won't be prepared for our attack.'

Danya paled, and Marcue, pressed against the wall, ached for her. Her Family still thought they had a chance to get her back alive, when in fact she had become the trick that would make them vulnerable.

Danya Galweigh didn't collapse into tears, nor did she beg for mercy. She glanced at Marcue, then back at the monster, and said, 'So now I assume you have come to kill me.'

All three visitors to the dungeon laughed. The demon said, 'Lovely girl, we wouldn't dream of killing you. Yet. What a stupid waste of valuable resources *that* would be. How would we bring ourselves to kill someone so young and beautiful, so strong and full of life? No. We have a place for you among our number.'

'Indeed,' Crispin said, 'the central place of honor in the circle of the Wolves.'

That meant nothing to Marcue, but it meant something to Danya. Her facade of courage and impassivity crumbled, and tears filled her eyes. 'No,' she whispered. 'Please, no. Not that.'

Andrew tittered again. 'Well, not that right away. After you have been the guest of the Wolves, you won't be . . . well, you won't be the same, and we hated the idea of wasting so much prettiness. So for the next few days, you'll entertain the three of us. Just us.'

She backed away from the bars. 'Don't touch me.'

Crispin and the demon laughed, and Crispin said, 'Well, brother, I don't think she likes us.'

The demon said, 'She'll probably like you well enough. But I think I shall like her.'

Andrew said, 'Guard, give me the key to her cell.'

Marcue shuddered.

I should have helped her. I should have . . . I had the time. I could have made an opportunity. I could have done something. Maybe I still can. Maybe I can find a way to get her out and lock the three of them in there – I can run with her and my parents before anyone is the wiser. Galweigh House isn't so far . . .

'Let me open it for you,' he heard himself saying. 'The lock is stiff and tricky, and won't open if you haven't practiced with it a great deal.' His voice shook when he spoke, but he thought anyone's voice would shake on being confronted for the first time with a demon. And what he said about the lock was true, actually, though he took nearly three times as long unlocking it as he would have normally. His delay came partly because his hands were shaking from fear, but more than that, the whole time he was scraping the key back and forth, he was figuring out how he would get the men and the monster into the cell and the girl safely out. By the time the door screeched open, he thought he had found the way.

'There,' he said, and stepped back, keeping himself beside the door and leaving the key in the lock.

'Very good,' Andrew said. 'That did look very difficult.'

Marcue nodded and took another step back. He tried to catch the girl's eye, but she was looking at Andrew, who stepped into the cell first. Crispin followed, and Marcue wished with all his heart the second one in had been the demon. Crispin would have been so much easier to shove.

He watched both men close on Danya, and backed up another half step, hoping to spot the demon, who had inexplicably vanished. He felt his fear in the tightening of his gut and his testicles, in the pounding of his heart, and he thought, Come on! Come on! Move in front of me, you bastard, before it's too late.

Then he felt the point of a needle at his throat.

'It probably would have worked,' the demon said from behind him. He felt it rest one hand on his belly. The other tightened around his neck, and the monster picked him up, strangling him and dragging him backward at the same time. He kicked and struggled, trying to pull the hand away from his neck and finding that he might have

26

bent the bars of one of the cells with his hands more easily. He couldn't breathe at all, couldn't make a sound. The demon took him to the stone wall directly across from the cell (to the rows of manacles, why is he taking me to the manacles?) and released his throat just as the world was beginning to turn gray and his pulse was threatening to explode out the sides of his skull.

Marcue vomited and gasped in air, choking, his throat on fire, and the demon laughed. It grabbed one wrist and locked it into a manacle, then caught the other one. 'You couldn't have saved her, but you might have gotten all three of us into the cell.' The demon smiled at him (horrible smile) and added, 'But you think too loudly, and with your whole body. Not a good survival trait, that.'

Marcue became dimly aware that the girl was screaming. He looked past the demon to see her held between Crispin and Andrew. She was staring at him. Screaming for him.

The monster fitted his other wrist into the manacle, closed it. Locked it. Smiled at him.

Terrible, terrible teeth.

Terrible.

The girl, screaming, 'Let him go! Let him go!'

'We were just going to take her up to our quarters,' Crispin said from inside the cell. 'Just going to go on our way and leave you to your job. But, naughty lad, you let yourself think of a prisoner as something besides a prisoner, and you are going to have to pay for that.'

'I don't think,' the demon said, 'that he should leave life without at least a little entertainment, though. Do you, Crispin?'

'What did you have in mind?'

'Killing him slowly,' the demon said. 'Letting him watch us with the girl as he dies. So that at least he dies amused.'

27

Andrew giggled. 'Do it,' he said. 'Do it.'

The demon turned to face Marcue and said quietly, 'A voice speaks to each of us in the still silent places – a voice that tells us to stand, to have courage, to do what is right.' He smiled. 'And if we're very, very clever, we hunt down the source of that voice, and kill it.'

He dragged one dagger-tipped finger down Marcue's gut, and the fabric of his tunic fell away, and the link mail under it rattled. The demon clicked his tongue, and ripped the link mail in half from top to bottom. Sliced away the padded quilt shirt underneath. Exposed the bare skin of Marcue's chest and belly.

'Such smooth skin,' he said. 'Mine looked like that once. Enough so that I think I would have had to kill you anyway. I miss my old self.'

'Don't,' Marcue said. 'Don't hurt me. I didn't do anything.'

'You wanted to. Wanting to was enough.'

'You don't know that. You can't know what a man thinks.'

'I can. I *do*.'

'Let me go.'

'We're going to let you watch. The mating of Wolves – not a sight many men have ever seen.' The demon laughed, and dragged its claw down his belly a final time.

  white

    red

  pain agony pain

      terror and blood and stink and

      the incredible noise of screaming someone screaming inside his head and he wanted it to stop he called to the pain to kill him and it didn't

    the weight of something hot and slick and stinking sliding away from him, landing on his feet

    faintness, but faintness that abandoned him at the last

instant and left him to the cruel ministrations of the waking world

he kept on living

and a voice that cut through his screaming like that claw had cut through his belly, and silenced him.

'We can do much, much more to you without killing you outright,' Crispin Sabir said. 'So unless you want us to prove that, shut your mouth and watch. We're doing this for your benefit.'

Marcue opened his eyes. He didn't look down. He knew what he would see there, and he couldn't look. Couldn't. He couldn't keep his eyes from the scene in front of him, either. His supply of courage was gone. He hung in the shackles, his back against the wall, and watched, wishing he could die quickly, wishing he could die right away. He watched the demon and the two men who were no better than demons, and he tried not to look at the girl. He tried not to hear her. Because he lived to know that they had killed him, that he was a breathing dead man, and that was terrible.

Terrible.

But the things they did to her were worse.

Chapter 3

It was a scent in the hallway that did it, that almost threw Kait into an uncontrolled Shift; a scent at once as familiar as family and as alien as the far side of the world. One instant she was dragging Tippa down the long, empty side corridor toward the yard where the driver had parked the carriage. The next, she was leaning against a wall feeling her bones going liquid in her body, feeling her blood bubbling like sparkling wine, while exuberance filled her and colors and sounds grew sharper and cleaner and the very air she breathed became a rich, full-bodied, intoxicating beverage.

Tippa struggled to free her wrist from Kait's grasp, and bleated, 'Kait? Kait? What's wrong?' in that timid, frightened voice Kait loathed.

Kait wiped tears of frustration and longing from her eyes with the back of a hand, checking the appearance of the hand at the same time. Normal. Thank the gods, thank *all* the gods, it was normal. If she could just get herself under control, she might still be all right.

I want to run, she thought. I want to fly, to race against the wind; I want to feel my muscles burn from exertion, I want to hear my blood pounding in my ears. I want to taste the wind and feel the cut of the tall grass against my skin. I want to hunt. I want fresh, hot meat, the iron tang of blood – and she pushed what she wanted away from herself. Far away. Far down in the dark places inside, her hungers fought against her and she struggled to lock them away where they belonged. She said softly, 'I don't want any of those things. I want to serve my Family and earn my independence.' Her voice sounded raw, husky, far too deep. Bad. Very bad. Her vocal cords had already slipped. She turned to Tippa, and gripped both her cousin's shoulders, and stared down into her eyes. Tippa swallowed, looking suddenly sober and very frightened. 'Go to the carriage,' Kait said. 'Tell the driver to take you home. Wait with the Family – tell whoever meets you that I sent you because three Gyru princes were up to something and your chaperones had disappeared. I'll . . . be along when I can.'

Tippa shivered. 'Kait, what's *wrong* with you?'

'Nothing that I can't take care of.' She wished that were true. Control, always elusive, now felt as if it slipped through her fingers like quicksilver. 'Go,' she snarled. 'Run.'

Tippa stared at her an instant longer, then turned and fled. When she disappeared through the archway at the end of the corridor and thundered down the steps to the carriage, Kait moved to the first dark side passage she could find, hid behind an enormous statue, and sank to the floor. Her silk skirts rustled, and the laced bodice of the damned party dress grew looser, then tighter, then looser, then tighter.

Her blood pounded in her wrists, in her temples, behind her tightly closed eyes – her blood burned in her veins and fizzed like the water of a sacred spring. The unbearable desire grew worse. She smelled him, this stranger – one of her own, an adult male, in the prime of life. Like her, pushed too close to the knife edge of control; like her, hungry for a hunt. She opened her mouth and wrinkled her nose slightly and inhaled, and along the back of her palate she tasted the scents of him that were both wonderfully familiar and wonderfully strange. That bottled exuberance threatened to burst free, to become the wild exhilaration of total Shift.

She couldn't let it take her. She couldn't let that other Kait loose. Not in the Dokteerak House, not surrounded by hundreds of potential enemies. She had to stop herself, and fast.

His scent was like a drug in the air, like incense made of caberra spice, which clouded the mind and filled it full of visions; his scent could lend her knowing and almost willing toward her own destruction. First she needed to block that.

She had perfume. A little bottle, always with her. Stinking stuff, like all perfume – she hated it because it ruined the taste of the air the way spices and sauces ruined the taste of meat. But scents had caught her off guard before, and she'd learned. She pulled the little bottle of perfume from her waist-purse, slopped some of it onto a corner of her skirt, and wiped the reeking stuff across her nostrils and her upper lip.

The effect was jarring. Painful. Like being wakened from the midst of a pleasant dream by being pitched head-first into an icy spring. Her eyes watered and she needed to cough and sneeze at the same time, and she didn't dare do either. Her bones hurt. Her blood churned. The thrill of Shift cooled, but not pleasantly. Her skin became a layer of lead smeared over muscles that ached as if they'd taken a hellish beating.

I can hold the other back. I am in control.

I want to run

The world is cool, blues and greens and icy whites, silent and scented with flowers and spices. My heart beats slowly; my feet remain firmly on the ground; I seek tranquillity.

the world is red and hot and scented with earth and blood and the rich raw taste of meat and sex

32

I have given up everything for this chance to be human. I told my parents I could do this, I promised I could take on the responsibility, I told them if they wouldn't give me work within my Family I would find work outside of it where they could never be sure I was safe.

you're a fool

I'm more than you would let me be. I'm more than instinct, more than running and hunting and rutting. My parents sacrificed just to keep me alive to adulthood. They gave me the keys to be human.

you're Karnee . . . you're a freak . . . you're a Curse-touched monster and in the end you will never be more than an animal

Kait opened her eyes and looked at her hands. Human hands. She smelled the flowery stink of perfume, and ignored the salt taste of her tears on her lips, and the wet heat on her cheeks. She would not give in to the voice of the hated other. She could be more than the Curse-trapped beast she'd been born as. She would be more.

The cool smoothness of the polished marble wall felt good through the thin layers of her silk dress. She pressed back against the wall, catching her breath, letting the stone caress the skin at the nape of her neck. The crystalline perfection of the world that had been within her reach had been erased, swathed in the dull, lifeless tones that characterized everything when she came out of an attack. She was already drifting into the Crash phase. She felt the moodiness setting in. Not too terrible this time – the near-Shift hadn't materialized, and the price she paid for the wild, joyous abandon of Karnee was always proportional. But the Crash was coming, and with it the ravenous hunger, the lethargy, and the other symptoms. Worse, this time she would have to pay the price knowing that she would still have to deal with a pending episode . . . and soon.

This time she had solved nothing. She had simply

postponed the problem. Her body demanded the Shift once within each forty days that passed, no matter how inconvenient or dangerous such a Shift might be. She planned and she accommodated ... or she got caught out.

'... and in spite of that, you let him in here. Tonight.'

She raised her head and opened her eyes. Voices. From down the hall, hidden behind the closed doors of one of the rooms. She'd been hearing them for a while, but she'd been too lost in the morass of her own problems to really be aware of them.

'He insisted on seeing you immediately – said that what he had to discuss with you might alter the Sabirs' plans.'

Sabirs? Kait thought she recognized the first voice as belonging to Branard Dokteerak. The second she had no idea about, but if she was right about the first, then what in all the demon-spawned hells was he doing talking to *Sabirs*? Especially with the Dokteerak alliance to the Galweighs pending ...

'He wanted nothing more than my reassurance that we'd be ready to move the night of the wedding. Gave me some vague line about his people needing to know if anything had changed, if they were going to need more men or if they were going to need to bring them down by another route – but he didn't want *anything* real. He didn't have any genuine reason to speak with me at all, and less than none tonight of all nights.'

'Had I been able to force a response from him, I wouldn't have let him in to see you, but you said –'

'I haven't changed my mind, either. Until the Galweigh holdings in Calimekka are ours, we do nothing to anger the Sabirs. That includes using force on their envoys. Once we're firmly entrenched within the House, however, I want the envoy killed. He's Sabir, even if it is by distant blood, and he was disrespectful to me.'

A pause. 'I'll take care of that, Paraglese.'

'Good. Meanwhile I have left my own party and my guests, and I must give them an appropriate reason when I return – one that will stand up to scrutiny. Have any messengers arrived?'

'None.'

'A pity. That would have been the easiest of excuses. Well, then – who among our current list of houseguests have not attended my party?'

'Castilla and her children ... your nephew Willim, who has a touch of grippe ... the paraglese Idrogar Pendat –'

'Stop. Idrogar is here and hasn't shown his face at my party?'

'Just so. He arrived yesterday and is awaiting a moment of your time.'

'He's been causing me problems in the Territories. He wants more control over affairs in Old Jirin.'

'I must assume, Paraglese, that his mission this time will only be to continue with his earlier demands. He brings many bodyguards, but no gifts.'

Kait heard Dokteerak begin to chuckle. 'At last, a benefit from this long and expensive night. What apartment is he in?'

'The Summer Suite, in the North Wing. The best quarters for ... what I suspect you have in mind.'

'They are indeed. Please make sure my beloved cousin Idrogar's fatal illness doesn't inconvenience him too much. Or leave any marks on the body. We'll have to produce the corpse tomorrow for my story to hold ... but what better reason could any man ask to leave his own party, at least for a while, than an urgent visit to the bedside of a beloved and dying relative?' A pause. Then, 'Find out exactly what he came here for before he dies, Pagos. I don't want to destroy valuable information by accident.'

'As you will, Paraglese.' Kait heard the sound of stone sliding, and recognized it as the same sound that secret panels in Galweigh House made. The paraglese's man Pagos heading off to do his master's bidding, no doubt.

She had no time to get out of the hallway; the door at the end opened, and the paraglese came out. She couldn't see him from her position behind the statue, but she could hear his heavy footsteps and his labored breathing. He wasn't an old man, but he was a sick one.

He went past her without looking either left or right, turned down the larger corridor toward his party, and met a few guests there. 'My dear cousin came suddenly ill . . .' she heard him say, his voice dwindling as he moved away from her.

Kait waited another moment to be sure he didn't come back, then rose and slipped out from behind the statue, and hurried out toward the street. She had to get to the embassy to tell her Family what she'd heard. Keeping Tippa out of trouble was nothing compared to making sure the diplomats discovered the game Branard Dok-teerak was playing at, but just as important was deciding which member of the Family to tell. If she chose poorly, she would have the awkward task of explaining why she was able to crouch behind a statue at one end of a corridor and hear a conversation that took place behind heavy closed doors at the other end of it – and for that matter, she might have to explain how she came to be hiding behind the statue in the first place.

And even within her own Family, she suspected that if the truth about her got out, she would be regarded as an abomination by most of her clansmen, and as a dubious asset at best by the remainder.

* * *

The evil that seeped into the city of Halles and crawled through the streets and the homes had its beginnings in an ancient room deep in the heart of the Sabir Embassy, which sat at the far northern edge of the town. In the subterranean chamber, the Sabir Wolves moved through flickering light and the curling smoke of caberra incense, raising magic; they approached each other and then retreated in bewildering patterns, following the path of a complex design carved into the stone floor. Swirl and arabesque, move forward, move back, circle clockwise, counterclockwise; and all the while they whispered.

In the center of their path, a man branded with the mark of the convicted felon hung limp and unresisting against the bonds that bound him to the carved stone column. At the beginning of his ordeal he had sworn, he had begged for mercy, he had fought and screamed and cried – but the beginning of his ordeal was hours behind him, and he had nothing left in him with which to fight. He had withered to half his size, had sunk in on himself as the life drained out of him. Now he hung in silence as the Wolves moved around him. From time to time he roused himself enough to stare in terror at the shapes of ghostly others who trod the path between the men and women he knew to be there. Sometimes he heard other voices that emanated from the air around him. He didn't understand what he was watching, but he didn't need to understand to know that what they did was killing him quickly.

The Wolves paid little attention to him. Their focus was on the path, and on their precise placement on the path; they moved in relation not only to each other, but to their colleagues leagues away in Calimekka, who followed the footsteps of the path with them and who chanted as they chanted, linking the two places, raising magic.

A handsome young man stepped through the doorway into the room, and two of the Walkers looked up. He nodded to them. They kept moving around the path, but signaled to Wolves waiting along the wall, and as they reached the set point of a particular arabesque, each stepped off the path, to be immediately replaced by those to whom they had signaled.

The young man slipped out of the room and halfway down the corridor outside, where he waited. Both Wolves joined him there.

'How did it go?' The woman who asked the question, Imogene Sabir, was about fifty, with pale skin and rich golden hair just beginning to show some gray. Her eyes were slightly milky, and though she looked at the young man – her son – she gave the impression that she focused on him more by listening. She was nearly, but not entirely, blind; the magic that had stolen most of her eyesight had replaced vision with second sight, and she was satisfied with the exchange. And aside from the increasing opacity in her eyes, her visible Scars were still few enough that she remained beautiful.

'Dokteerak was furious that I showed up in the middle of his party.' Her son, Ry, had her slenderness combined with his father's height, dark gold hair he'd inherited from both of them, and a predatory cast to his features that was entirely his own. 'I wasn't obvious, but I know at least two of the Galweighs recognized me.'

His father, Lucien, smiled – a thin, tight-lipped smile that hid his teeth. 'Excellent. Were you overheard?'

'I can't be certain. I couldn't hear anyone outside the doors. Dokteerak closed them when we went in, and he had a man hidden behind a panel who made so much noise breathing and shifting from foot to foot that I almost couldn't hide the fact that I knew he was there. It shouldn't matter. If the Galweighs know I was in Dokteerak House, they'll get suspicious.'

His mother said, 'Hid a man behind a secret panel in the same room, eh?' She laughed. 'The Dokteeraks have no one like you or me, and do not, I imagine, believe that anyone like us could still exist in these days. I'm sure the two of them thought they were being quite circumspect.'

Ry started to agree with her, then stopped himself. He frowned and said, 'Now that you mention it, I should have realized that was wrong when I was there.'

'Wrong?' His father's voice grew sharp. 'What was wrong?'

'Mother said they have no Karnee. But I crossed through the garden behind a guardsman on my way to find Dokteerak, and I caught the scent of one of us.'

His mother said, 'You can't have. None of our Karnee were there, and the Dokteeraks have no Karnee. I know this.'

'One was there. I didn't have the chance to find her –'

'Her?'

'Yes. Female, young, a complete stranger . . .' He closed his eyes, remembering for an instant that bewitching scent that had caught at him as he moved between the milling mass of human sheep in the garden, and how difficult he had found it to keep moving, to follow the guard, instead of breaking free and finding her. Finding her. Gods, he'd almost slipped right then – she'd been at the edge of her control; he was due and probably overdue; and her nearness to a spontaneous Shift had almost taken him over the cliff with her. And wouldn't that have been a mess?

'She has to be one of the Galweigh Karnee,' his father said.

His mother frowned. 'We killed them all.'

'Evidently not.'

'They've kept her hidden, then – and if they could hide one from us, they might have hidden others.'

'Perhaps,' Lucien sighed. 'Well, she isn't hidden anymore. They've decided she's strong enough to take care of herself and they've realized how beneficial she can be to them. We'll have to kill her –'

'Of course. But we can do that during the attack –'

Ry looked from his mother to his father, and remembered that sweet, tantalizing scent, and cut them both off. 'Don't kill her. I want her.'

Both parents stared at him as if he'd gone mad.

'Be sensible. You couldn't breed her, Ry.' His mother rested a hand on his arm and turned her face up to his. 'Every child you had would be stillborn. And how would you keep her? She'd be forever at your throat, as dangerous an enemy as you could have.'

'We've found half a dozen young women who would serve as mates for you,' his father said. 'Choose one of them.'

'They're sheep. I don't want a sheep. I want someone like me.'

'Maybe you do, but you don't expose your throat to an enemy when you sleep. And how could you lead the Wolves when your father steps down, with such a consort as that?'

Ry said, 'I'll take my chances. Besides, you assume I'll receive the acclaim of the rest of the Wolves when Father wearies of leadership. But the Trinity already are positioning themselves to take over someday.'

Both his parents snarled, and his mother said, 'The day they take over is the day every decent Wolf is dead.'

Which was basically true. The Trinity – the cousins Anwyn, Crispin, and Andrew – were loathed by every Wolf who could call himself human with a clear conscience. Which didn't mean Ry had any desire to fight with them for leadership within the circle of Wolves.

But he had years yet to worry about that. His father was still hale and quick and powerful. Ry's immediate problem was finding a mate. He stood thinking about the young women his parents had presented to him. Girls who carried the Karnee strain in their blood in safely small amounts, but who had none of the Karnee fire.

Dull, passive creatures who simpered at him and tittered and giggled, and who owned not a single original thought among the lot of them.

He hadn't seen this Karnee woman at the party – he could tell she was young from her scent, but he couldn't tell what she looked like. She might be hideous. That wouldn't matter, though. Not if she was intelligent. Not if she was fiery, tempestuous, spirited . . . and she would be, wouldn't she? She'd survived. Her scent had been full of passion, full of suppressed rage, full of her curiosity and overt delight at everything around her – and even at that moment, well away from her, he could feel her tugging at him as the moon tugged at the sea.

He said, 'I'm sure you're right. She wouldn't be suitable.' And he excused himself. His parents returned to the path, and to building the power that they would have to have in the next week. He was not permitted to walk the path – those who walked the path became Scarred by it and had to hide themselves away. His work for the Family was still in the outside world.

And in breeding, of course. He stalked up the steep stairway, glowering. When he'd produced a suitable number of living heirs, he'd be pulled from whatever work he was doing out in the world and placed on the path with the rest of the wizards, and his world would narrow down to the research libraries and the artifacts that those who still went freely outside brought in, and to the making of dark magic.

His future had been determined by others from the time of his birth. Now, though, he sensed a different direction that it might take – rather, he sensed a direction in which he might *take* his future. The possibility of action and choice both elated and frightened him.

Chapter 4

Galweigh House covered all of the first peak along Palmetto Cliff Road, and its balconies, carved from the living marble of the cliff and studded with chalcedony and turquoise and set with glowing mosaics of colored glass, comprised the whole of the cliff face beginning after the soaring stone span of the Avenue of Triumph and only ending where Palmetto Cliff intersected with the obsidian-paved Path of Gods.

The Galweighs did not build the House, though they had added to it and decorated it – both the stained-glass panels along the balconies and the inlaid semiprecious stones were Galweigh conceits. The House predated its inhabitants by more than a thousand years. Once it had been a winter estate for a man of unimaginable wealth and power who had in his summers inhabited the city of St Marobas, far to the south. The man and his wealth were dust, and the city of St Marobas was a perfectly circular patch of water named the St Marobas Sea down along the eastern coast of the deadly Veral Territories, but the House survived. Over the course of a thousand years, its shining white balconies had lost some of their luster, and from time to time a stonemason had to be called in to repair a pillar or bearing wall that the jungle had damaged before the Galweighs found the House and claimed it, but those small imperfections only gave

Galweigh House character. It was the finest known surviving artifact of the Age of Wizards, and was of wizardly make and magical nature.

Part of its magic lay in its beauty, which was unsurpassed, and part in its vast size, which could only be guessed at. The Galweighs had not finished mapping the House, though they had lived in it for better than a hundred years. Some portions of it they knew well. The ground floor, which was the story that ran along the top of the cliff, had been mapped and explored and filled up; it was the floor that held the grand salons and the beautiful fountains, the vast baths, the exquisite statuary, the broad promenades, and the gardens both public and private. The first floor, reached by gorgeous curving staircases from any number of points on the ground floor, held rooms for business, courtrooms and holding rooms, rooms for private entertaining, classrooms for children, workrooms for adults.

The floor above that held the Family apartments, more gardens, and several aviaries, as well as a fortune in artworks both ancient and modern and an entire gallery of curiosities from around the known world. The Family, and the spouses and concubines of the Family and their children, and frequently their children's children, all lived there – over a hundred people when the place was emptiest, with plenty of room for more. The third floor was for the servants of the Family (as opposed to House servants, who lived on the first subfloor), and its apartments were as spacious and graceful and lovely as those the Family occupied. It was commonly known throughout Calimekka that the servants of the Galweigh Family lived better than the richest of men outside of the Family.

Two floors lay above the last of the occupied floors, testament to the grandeur that had been before the

Wizards' War, and to the promise, at least in the eyes of the Galweighs, of the grandeur that would be again.

The great House was ringed with massive walls of ancient make, high and smooth-sided as if formed of glass, harder than anything save diamond or the unrusting steel of the dead wizards, so that the people who lived within the upper stories of Galweigh House feared little, and had little reason to fear.

But the House had a second face and a second character, as some people do; a darker side hinted at in the secret passageways and rooms sometimes accidentally happened upon aboveground by a child at play, or by a servant intent on cleaning who pressed a secret panel or tripped over a slightly uneven flagstone. At those moments, the maps of Galweigh House grew by inches; and the Family sometimes acquired another oddity or two for its collections; and depending on the character of the passageway, and where it went, and what it disclosed, sometimes the servants acquired a new cleaning headache. Sometimes, one or more of them quietly disappeared, along with the news of their discovery, and stories circulated for a while among the staff about accidents.

That hint of darkness became more pronounced in the subfloors, which lay below the ground floor. The first subfloor held kitchens and pantries and servants' work halls, and seemed as comfortable and knowable as the aboveground floors. But below it lay ten more floors. There, the open, breezy beauty of balcony rooms carved along the edge of the cliff were characterized by their vast panoramas of the beautiful city that lay below, and occupied by downstairs servants and adventurous guests, by loud revelries and late-night explorations of uncounted types. Moving in toward the heart of the great hill, those rooms gave way quickly to halls lit only by torches even in broad daylight, and deeper in, to hallways left unlit, where light never reached and the last feet to leave tracks had become nothing more than dust on the floor some ten centuries earlier.

The secrets of the Galweigh Family resided, as most secrets do, in the darkness and the silence, in the unventured depths. The Galweigh Wolves kept themselves contained within the very heart of this darkness, ten levels below the bright and public world of the main Family, where not even the most curious of children dared to explore, and where not even the most ardent of young lovers dared tryst.

In the perpetual gloom of windowless rooms, in the stillness that was more than silence, the Wolves, who were their own law, and who were the secret and hidden power behind the Galweigh Family, kept the power flowing and kept their enemies at bay and humbled. They worked with ancient books and records, with instruments of their own devising, and with those that had survived a thousand years and a final war of unimaginable devastation. They studied the one forbidden science of the world of Matrin – the science of magic – and learned, and put their learning into practice in every way they could devise. They were the new wizards, and the unheralded kings, and the unworshiped gods.

Unhampered by the restrictions of society, equally unhampered by the restraint of conscience, they pursued every avenue of personal curiosity, indulging in experiments in every conceivable area of magic, and in doing so touched areas of pure good and pure evil. And like all wizards and all kings and all gods, they eventually came to discover that the pursuit of goodness imposed uncomfortable confinements, and the pursuit of evil for evil's sake became wearying after a while, and lost its novelty – but that the pursuit of power never failed to enchant.

* * *

Fog blanketed the city of Halles so that the dark

houses, shutter-eyes shut against the dark, became form-less cliffs; and taverns ejected their rowdy customers with a whisper, not a roar; and ghosts welled up out of the darkness from nowhere and vanished again, leaving only the faintest clicks and clanks to mark their passing. Kait moved along a narrow cobblestone street, noting the way the scents grew richer in the dark and the damp. She could have tracked any of the dozens of people who'd trod the streets before her by scent alone, and never mind that others had passed by long after them, and laid new scent trails over the old.

The moon rode overhead, fat but not full, casting murky light into the swirling mists – light that, fighting through the fog as it did, illuminated nothing. It glowed ahead of Kait and off to the right like a dull clot of turned milk viewed through cheesecloth. Sharply to her right, the rich stink of sewage roiled out of an open gutter. To her left and just ahead, the wine-and-piss stench pin-pointed a drunk curled up beneath mildewing rags. Somewhere farther ahead, meat . . . but overcooked. Her mouth hungered for the warm taste of raw meat – the wild Kait, the one she preferred to deny, had not been satisfied by the dainty foods of the Naming Day party, and growled dissatisfaction.

. . . hunting, running, fur and ripped and bleeding flesh torn from its fur-coated package and the first hard gush of hot, thick, iron-salt blood . . .

Ahead, three men waited at the mouth of an alley. They discussed their night's take in gloating tones, and Kait wondered, briefly, if the man under the rags who had smelled so strongly of wine had fallen there on his own or if the thieves had robbed him . . . had maybe killed him. She had not heard his breathing, she realized.

Deep inside, the darkness coiled tighter, urging her to confront the men, taunting her, naming her caution cowardice.

She clamped the rage tight. Moving silently, she crossed to the other side of the street; the fog hid her, and she passed the trio without any of them suspecting she had been near.

The slimy feel of evil that pervaded the night lay thicker in the direction she traveled. It became an added dimension to the fog, and for an instant she wondered about Hasmal son of Hasmal, and how he had kept the vile grasping tentacles of hatred and despair at bay.

She did not hold the thought long. The roads of Halles, narrow and twisting, full of dead ends and maze-like alleys, were at that late hour cheek by jowl with thieves, rapists, and other trouble, and required her full attention. She kept the moon in front of her, though twice she had to double back when she took a wrong turn. She knew by feel where the Galweigh Embassy lay; she simply did not recall the precise combination of roads that would take her directly to it. This city was not hers; she did not feel it the way she felt the streets of Calimekka. So she walked, patient. She didn't fear the night. She had little to fear; her eyes and ears and nose told her everything she needed to know to stay safe; and if by some chance she found herself trapped between trouble on two sides, she felt certain she could guarantee that her attackers never bothered anyone again.

She'd been tried only once, but that once had given her the courage of experience.

At the age of thirteen, when her parents first moved her into the Galweigh House from their secluded farm in the country, she'd been unable to sleep. So in the middle of the night, she got up to go prowling. Following her restless urges, and a nagging, tickling sense at the back of her skull that insisted something about the night was wrong, she'd slipped through the residential corridors and down a back staircase. She loved the House – loved its grandeur and its endless secrets, its immense age and

47

air of mystery – and she had quickly learned ways from place to place few others knew. Stalking by impulse, following instinct, she'd traveled downward, using every trick she shared with the House. She slipped through a hidden corridor, glided down a banister, skulked behind rows of statues, used the noise of the fountains to cover any hint of her approach.

One man down in a dark back corridor carried a lumpy bag over his shoulder, the bag human-shaped, human-smelling. Another man, redolent of blood not his own, crept behind him watching their backs. Neither spoke, and Kait could not identify their scents, but the blood she smelled belonged to her oldest sister. Kait heard no sound from Dulcie. Fear caught in her throat, and the darkness and the rage that always waited inside of her broke free. She remembered lunging at the men, her body ablaze with the Shift, teeth bared, lips curled back, the exultation of the glorious madness pulsing in her veins and the scent of her sister's blood sour in her nostrils. She remembered the satisfaction of rending and tearing, claws digging, teeth sinking in, the singing of her blood in her ears . . .

The sounds of screams alerted the guards. They came running, to find two men dead with their throats torn out, and Dulcie Galweigh unconscious and bleeding in a bag on the floor. When they looked further, they found the guards who would have been protecting the Family lying in a back stairway with their throats cut. The guards never found Dulcie's avenger. No one knew the meaning of the animal tracks smeared in blood across the pristine white floor. Among the House staff, rumors grew that the Galweighs were protected by a terrible ghost, that the spirit of a great wolf hunted the halls of the House seeking to avenge any hurt that came to the Family.

Neither Kait nor any of the other Galweighs saw fit to correct this story.

*　*　*

Dùghall met the carriage at the door. But only Tippa was in it, and Tippa wore the terrified expression of a doe that had barely escaped the ravages of a leopard. Dùghall's stomach twisted. Where was Kait? His heart thudded, and he felt his blood drain to his feet. In an instant, Kait in a hundred forms flashed before his eyes. Tiny Kait-cha with dark eyes and dark hair and flashing white teeth, grinning up at him from the floor where she played in her parents' country home – seven years old, or maybe eight, the first time he'd met her. Enchanting girl, like a wild creature all shy and curious, stepping closer bit by bit, ready to escape should she sense danger. And Kait running, hair flying behind her like pennants, out in the walled yard with a daisy chain around her waist. Kait at fourteen, astride a horse, urging it over a gate, the two of them sailing like a single bird through the air, then thundering across a meadow. Kait in a tree, calling down to him. Then Kait, older yet, staring wistfully out a window, yearning for places she'd never been. Kait suddenly angry, running from the room so fast she seemed to blur even in memory. And Kait at seventeen, overjoyed when he told her he'd convinced her parents that she would be a perfect ambassador for the Galweighs, that she could begin training.

And now Kait missing. And if anything happened to her, he could only blame himself. He should have pulled her out the instant he saw the treacherous Sabir stalking through the courtyard . . . but if he had, he would have blown his own cover, and he hadn't thought anyone would try anything against an ambassador – even such a junior ambassador – at such a public party, and on Naming Day.

He forced his mind to stillness. Maybe Tippa had some logical explanation for coming home alone.

'Where is she?'

Those bright, terrified eyes stared up at him. 'She . . . stayed behind. Something was the matter, but she wouldn't say what. She got so fierce . . . And the princes . . . they treated me nice, but Kait fought with them . . . and she made me come home on my own.' Tippa started to cry.

She stank of wine, and the flush in her cheeks and the brightness of her eyes told him how drunk she was. Chaperoned closely, she should never have been allowed to get drunk. And what princes had been nice to her? The Families held little regard for the pretenders after long-vacant thrones, and in Ibera any princes she was likely to meet would have been of that sort. Kait was a sensible girl – she'd seen trouble coming, and had pulled Tippa out of the party and sent her home.

Then what? Had she gone back to deal with the princes? A lone girl in a strange city, in the home of people who had been her Family's sworn enemies for more than a hundred years? Would she do a thing like that?

No. Kait was a sensible girl. Whatever had happened, it hadn't been that.

Tippa looked too drunk to be of much use, though for Kait's sake, Dùghall hoped she would be able to tell them something of value. He'd take her inside, rouse the embassy physick, and make the man give her something to sober her up. Meantime, he'd chase down the security staff and send them out looking through the streets. He couldn't get into the private parts of Dokteerak House – not without an army – and at this late hour, and with most if not all of the guests surely gone he wouldn't even be able to come up with a convincing excuse for getting inside the public part of the House. But he could send the

Galweighs' trusted men to look around the outside of it without being seen.

What it came down to was that he was severely limited in what he could do without taking a chance at giving away the one secret that he had to keep in spite of everything. Back home in the islands, he could have moved the earth searching for the girl without fear of reprisals. But in Halles, in an embassy that hired most of its household staff from among the locals, and that had surely acquired at least one spy, and probably several, he didn't dare. It wasn't even that he didn't want to end up with his drawn-and-quartered body hung on display in the city square, though of course he didn't. If his secret got out, though, he would risk exposing the Falcons, and he would jeopardize the Texts, and he would fail his obligations as a Warden.

If only he'd taken the time earlier to divine the location of a safe room, or, if none existed, to create one.

While he hauled Tippa toward the physick's quarters, he raged inside at how helpless he was. He would do everything he could – and everything he could wouldn't be enough to do the girl a single bit of good if she was in real trouble. From the way his skin crawled, and from the inescapable pounding of foreign Wolf magic in the air, he could only fear the worst.

Chapter 5

Kait recognized the street on which she walked. Two blocks, maybe three, and she would be at the embassy. Almost home, almost safe, almost where she could tell the Family about the Dokteeraks and the Sabirs. Perhaps within her room she would be able to leave behind the pounding threat of evil that hammered at her skull. Perhaps she'd be able to shake the feeling that she was being followed, that downwind of her something moved to intersect her. She'd stopped several times, tasting the air, and each time it brought her only the overripe scents of sewage and the unwashed bodies of drunks and whores still ahead of her; each time the wind, so often her friend, blew from the direction of home, and not the direction of whoever ... or whatever ... she sensed following her. She never heard anything suspicious. She never saw anything out of the ordinary.

But the feeling remained. Eyes watched her through the fog. Eyes saw her that were keener than her own.

Someone ran toward her. Focused on her – she knew this in her gut. Only in her gut. The rest of her senses were blind. But her gut told her enough. The running wasn't random, the feel of the runner's intent was, to her, the feel of a bolt launched from a crossbow, aimed at her heart.

Danger. Betrayal. Death.

She tucked the front hem of her dress into the bodice ties, where it brushed against the hilt of her hidden dagger, and ran down the nearest side street ... silent, hard, as fast as any man, all of her senses trained behind her to the one who pursued. Her only goal became the eluding of capture; her attention narrowed to the world of her pumping legs and arms, the placement of her feet in the precarious uneven streets, the evasion of obstacles that could slow her flight. Fear sent her blood singing through her veins again; Shift pursued her as swiftly as the runner who followed her every twist and turn, and who somehow, impossibly, kept up with her. Was he a hired assassin? A Galweigh-hater who had recognized her leaving the party, who was seizing an opportunity?

She ran left, right, left, choosing streets at random in the alien city. She toppled a drunk into the gutter in her haste; he cried out and fell, clinging for the merest instant to her skirt before she broke away. He cost her a step – perhaps a step and a half – in a race she was already losing. Her fear rose higher. She ran harder, fought Shift and the betrayal of her body that would mean, in such public places, her death. The fog that had been an ally became an obstacle, making each footstep precarious. She wanted to hide, to disguise herself as a part of Halles and not a thing apart from it; in the back of her mind, something whispered *people* and, frightened and pushed to the limits of her human body's capacity, thinking only of what was behind her and not of what might lie ahead, she made a mistake.

She smelled people above the fading scent of perfume on her upper lip. Many of them. *Men and women*, the back of her mind said, *that way*. She followed the scent to her right, down a twisting street that narrowed instead of widening.

She prayed that the walls of the buildings on either side of her would move away from each other again. That she would smell the movement of air that indicated an opening at the other end of this passage. She didn't. The air lay dead, the passage narrowed still further, until, if she had stretched her arms out straight to either side of her, she could have touched the walls. She heard the people ahead of her now. Laughing. Voices kept low, an edge to them, a feeling of caution. Man voices, but she smelled woman-scent, too. Touches of sex-musk on the air, the iron-metal tang of fresh blood. She lost the moon's light in the shadows of buildings, and only her Karnee eyes let her see well enough to keep running. Her pursuer never slowed. She heard him turn in behind her. How did he pursue her so closely? How did he follow her so well? She had no time to think of how.

Suddenly the walls to either side of her fell away, and she burst into the midst of the people she'd sought out. She was in a cul-de-sac; she crashed into two men; they caught her arms as they staggered to keep their balance; she rasped, 'Hide me.'

Behind her the sound of running stopped.

She saw then what she had run into. A woman crouched on knees and elbows on the paving stones, her wrists bound, a rag stuffed in her mouth, a man at her head with a knife at her throat, two others behind her. One kneeling; one standing. Her tattered, slashed bodice exposed her breasts, her skirt bunched around her waist. She bled freely from a cut down the cheek. A dead man dressed in the height of Halles fashion sprawled against the alley wall to the far side of her, his throat a raw patch of darkness against the bloodless whiteness of his skin. One man who wasn't taking turns raping the woman robbed the corpse. Kait heard the sounds of the contents of a purse being emptied onto stones; the unmistakable dull clink of gold, the rattle of jewelry. Six of them in all. Six murderers, thieves, rapists . . . and the woman. Another man moved out of the shadows and stepped in front of her, grinning. A young man, handsome, well-dressed, well-born. Round face, pale hair, pale eyes – he had the look of a Dokteerak heir, and she thought, So this Family entertains itself at the expense of its subjects, too.

The hands that held her arms tightened. 'Look what the gods sent to us,' the man to her left said softly, and the one to her right laughed.

Her blood fizzed, her bones tingled, she tasted metal in her mouth and heard the singing of her heart in her ears. Fear died, strangled by Karnee rage. Her voice grew husky as vocal cords slipped toward another configuration; her other self strained for release. With the last of her control, she said, 'If you want to live, let her go and let me go. You don't know what I am.'

Giggles from the men who held her. Raw braying from the men who were taking their turns at the woman.

The Dokteerak shook his head. 'Oh, help, she's going to hurt us –'

'– a pretty rich girl who ran down the wrong alley –'

'– Give us your money and maybe we'll let you go –'

'– maybe we'll let *you* live.'

'Not me. I'll bugger 'er when she's dead.'

Raw, hating laughter. More giggles.

The highborn bastard slashed her silk bodice open, ripped downward to her waist – for just an instant the blade nicked skin, and she smelled her own blood. He moved behind her, wrapped a hand in the coils of her hair, yanking her head downward and throwing her to her knees. Grabbed her dagger, pulled her dress off, slashed at the ties of her underclothes – lace breast binder, silk tie-string panties. Cut her again removing them . . . little cuts, the pain like bee stings, like a goad to the madness that enveloped her. Red hazed her eyes.

The other Kait sang in exultation at the lightning bolt of pure fury that tore into brain and gut. She twisted like a python in the hands of her captors, tasting in her mind the gush of blood, feeling the delicious crunch of bone and cartilage between teeth before she even had a man in reach. The hunt. The hunt. The kill. And that other Kait grinned, and a growl started low in her throat. Rage drove through all the barriers between Kait-the-woman and Kait-the-wild-thing. The growl in her throat grew louder. Naked in the embrace of the night, rational Kait lost herself to the exultant, joyous, buoyant, shivering other who wanted only to fight, to destroy, to tear and taste and slaughter in the heady, scent-rich darkness. She broke free, and spun around, and grabbed the nearest man with a hand that Shifted and re-formed before her eyes – a hand already covered by the silky, glossy, close black coat of Karnee, her fingers grown shorter and thicker, her tendons standing out, retractable claws stretched forward.

She laughed, and in that laughter nothing human remained. She growled, 'You're mine,' and leaped on top of him, two hands and two feet Shifted completely into four widespread paws in midair, spine stretching and flexing to give her a heavy, flexible tail. Her muscles bunched and burned and flowed under her skin, and the claw-tipped paws ripped through the rough cloth of the would-be rapist's shirt and she dug through the flesh of his chest as if it were butter, and darted her face down close to his, smelling on him the delicious stink of fear, hearing in his throat the start of a scream. Her grin grew wider as her muzzle stretched forward. Her teeth were daggers in her mouth. She bit down, crushing his scream before it was born, tasting the iron and salt of his gushing jugular against the middle of her tongue and feeling the steady spurts of his pulse against the roof of her mouth for only two bird-fast beats of his heart before she launched herself backward and upward in a twisting arc that brought her nose-to-face with the shocked young lordling.

She tore out his throat in passing, already on the way to her next meat before her paws hit the ground. She charged the third man who had held her. Tore into him. Brought him down.

She'd had the benefit of first surprise, and had taken the three, but the other four had regained feet and weapons, and now the odds were against her.

All four men moved through the fog to circle her, to surround her. Their swords pointed in, and she knew she was in trouble. Outnumbered, overmatched. In the fight between a beast and a man without a weapon, or with only a dagger, the odds lay in favor of the beast. Against four men with long blades, with murder in their eyes – well, there, the odds went to the men. And even as she thought it, one darted in at her and slashed with his sword, and she took a deep cut through her right shoulder and along her ribs.

She snarled and leaped in low, beneath the upswung blade, and lashed out at him with one paw. She connected across her attacker's knee and shin, but not deep enough, for though he shouted, he stayed standing. And she took another cut, hard into her left flank, because she had left her flanks unguarded and one of the men behind her had seized the advantage.

She twisted, snarled, and snapped but came up with only empty air as the second attacker stepped back and brought his sword to a defensive posture. He grinned; she could see his teeth flashing in the darkness. He knew they had her. She knew it, too. And she was afraid. She didn't want to die.

One of the blades wavered and she charged the man who held it, broke through his guard and dug into the softness of his belly with her claws, and he went down. But not without cost to her. She exposed her back to the

57

other three, and they charged in at her, and the nightmare bite of sharp metal scored the back of her neck and her other flank, and sought her vitals, though she twisted away before the blade found its target.

I'm going to die.

Here. Now.

And then the miracle happened. Something dark and big and terrible burst from the alley. The man who had his back to it screamed once, then went down and didn't rise. A looming shadow, fast and solid, ripped his throat when he fell, then slashed the next closest man. Kait didn't have time to watch the outcome of that second battle; she turned to face her only remaining attacker. One man, but that one remained armed, unhurt, wary. She feinted right, then left, faked a leap high in the air and when her enemy brought his weapon up, anticipating a gutting stroke, she lunged in low again. He wasn't as fast as she was, and she bit through his thigh, and leaped away before his blade could come down across her spine. He took her across the back of the skull, though, and had the blow carried more force, he might have taken her right there. She was lucky that he struck while off balance. As it was, she staggered and a million white lights sparkled behind her eyes and pain half blinded her.

Breathing hard, hurting and bleeding, she braced herself for the man's attack. But the stranger –

... he's Karnee, he's the one I smelled in Dokteerak House, he's the one who was following me ...

– the stranger charged the last of the criminals from behind, biting into the back of one leg. The man screamed and fell. It was over very quickly then.

Kait felt the heat of her Karnee metabolism burning her wounds closed. The shallow ones wouldn't even leave scars by morning; the deep ones probably would, but even those would be gone in a day or two. The blessing of

58

her curse, such as it was. She was a monster, but a monster who was damned hard to kill.

'We should leave,' the strange Karnee said. 'Guards will have heard the screams.' His voice shivered through her bones straight to her gut. Hypnotic. Growling, sensuous, full of passion and mystery – she turned away. He could not do to her what he was doing; he wasn't doing anything but standing there, bleeding, covered in blood, warning her of danger, and yet his voice was as powerful as a drug to her, as overwhelming as caberra incense or as his scent had been earlier in the night, in Dokteerak House. He was impossible, and so she turned away, and looked at the woman who huddled against the far wall of the cul-de-sac.

Terrified, clutching the tattered remains of her gown over her breasts, she stared at Kait and the stranger as if this night of hells had just spawned the greatest hell of all. And that was the worst of it. Kait had saved the woman's life, but because she was Karnee, she could expect only fear and hatred – perhaps even betrayal. Kait wanted to offer comfort, to help the woman to a place of safety, but she dared not.

So she glared down into the huddled woman's eyes and curled her lips back in a snarl that exposed every knife-edged fang. She growled, 'I know you. I know where you live, who you pray with, which streets you walk on. I've saved your life tonight, but I know you don't appreciate that boon from someone like me. So I'll warn you only this once – if you dare speak a word to anyone of what you saw here tonight, I'll find you in the darkness and you'll never greet another dawn.'

The woman had pulled the rag from her mouth with still-bound hands. She shivered, nodded, croaked, 'What shall I tell them, then?'

'That you saw nothing. That you struggled to escape, that those bastards hit you on the head, and that when you woke, you found them the way they are now. A word other than that will be your death – my promise.'

'I saw nothing,' the woman whispered. Tears gleamed on her face. 'I saw nothing . . . saw nothing . . . they hit me . . . I fell . . .' She whispered to herself, not to Kait.

Kait had other things to do. She dug among the corpses and found the remains of her dress and her underclothes. She located the slippers she'd worn, and the dagger she'd carried. Any of those things would betray her far more immediately than the woman could – the silks were woven by Galweigh weavers in the Galweigh pattern, the lace was Galweigh Rose-and-Thorn, the shoe buttons bore the Galweigh ring in gold, the dagger had both rubies and onyx in the hilt and the Galweigh crest on the pommel, and her name worked into the vines that decorated the crosspiece. Everything she owned would be mute betrayal, would bring soldiers and priests and blood-hungry mobs to her and to everyone she loved.

She bundled her belongings together as tightly as paws and claws were able, lifted the bundle in her mouth, and loped toward the alley. Obstacles remained – people in the streets, finding the embassy, getting past her own Family's people and inside. She had to clear her mind, to put everything that had just happened out of her thoughts, or she would not survive.

But the stranger moved beside her, silent and beautiful and bewitching. He picked up his own bundle halfway down the alley and loped at her side, until they reached a place where the moonlight lay across him like a kiss. Then he moved in front of her, turned, and stopped. 'I've spent my life waiting to find you,' he said.

He was huge, easily twice her weight, massively boned, sculpted by the hands of an artist who had loved him. His eyes, pale blue ringed around the outside of the irises with black, would be recognizable even after Shift – neither their exotic color nor their striking pattern would change. His glossy coat, copper striped with black, emphasized powerful muscles that bunched across his broad chest and steeply sloped shoulders and rippled in his haunches. His powerful jaws spread in a grin; his strong, arching neck tapered upward to a head as broad-skulled and sleek as any wolf's or jaguar's. Small gold hoops pierced both of his ears and the silver of a shield-shaped medallion gleamed from the point where his neck curved into his chest, suspended by a heavy silver chain. She could make out the crest on the medallion clearly: twin trees with curved branches intertwined, delicate leaves interspersed with the full curves of ripe fruit. The Sabir Family crest – a lovely design unless one considered that the Sabirs claimed one tree bore good fruit for the Sabirs and their friends, and the other bore poisoned fruit for their enemies.

And Kait was Galweigh, and thus was an enemy with five hundred years of Family hatred behind her. She was what she was because of the curse some Sabir wizard had put on her Galweigh ancestor; he was what he was because that curse, after it poisoned the Galweigh bloodlines, had rebounded on the man who cast it. Five hundred years of bad blood, and he said he'd been waiting his whole life to find her.

The worst of it was, the attraction she felt for him was so overwhelming and so total that she found herself wanting to believe him, and wanting to tell him what she was thinking – that she wanted him. Which of course was ridiculous; she couldn't desire him in any real way. She didn't know him, and if she did, she would hate him because he was Sabir. Never mind that he'd saved her life. He didn't know who she was, or he would have been, at that moment, at her throat.

He watched her, waiting for her to make the next move.

She dropped the bundle between her paws, pressing it

tightly so that she could pick it up again. Pretense would have to get her away from him. 'My thanks,' she said. Formal words, at odds with her incomprehensible feelings. She *knew* him somehow, though she had never seen him before in her life. The knowing was more than simple identification; it was the bone-deep knowing of one who has, coming around the corner of a crowded city street, rushed headlong into the arms of the man who is destined to be her soul mate.

My enemy. My soul.

Ludicrous. It made her want to laugh – and made her grateful that she didn't believe in destiny.

My soul. My enemy.

'Come with me,' he said, and his rich, rumbling subterranean growl made her own fierce Karnee voice sound soft and high-pitched. '*Be* with me.'

'I must go home.'

'But I want you.'

'The guards are already coming,' she said. 'Can't you hear them?' She thought she lied, but as she said the words, she realized they were true. The rhythmic tramp of footsteps – double-time, strides matching – moved up through the streets. And voices, still faint but moving closer. 'Break off! Search that alley! Faster, men, before we lose them!'

For an instant he hesitated. An instant only. Then he said, 'Find me. Please. Please find me.' And he picked up his own bundle in his teeth and turned, ready to run. She followed suit, and they raced toward the mouth of the alley together, claws drawn in so that they made no more noise in running than wind made moving across the cobblestones. Both cut sharply to the right as they came out into the street, moving uphill, away from the oncoming guards. For a short while they ran side by side, sometimes brushing each other, sometimes pulling away. Her muscles bunched and flowed, her spine arched and stretched, her body sang at the breeze that caressed her skin, sang with the joy of movement, and with the wonder of her nearness – however temporary – to him. The world was all her senses: sweet night scent, Karnee musk, the wetness of fog, green growing things far off and the food-scent of city vermin in the streets nearby; the steady rush of water from a fountain, voices calling from far away, the soft *thrup-thrup* of a nightbird hunting overhead; late moonlight falling like silver through the thickening curls of fog, the graceful lace patterns it cast through trees and buildings; the cool smooth roundness of the cobblestone beneath her feet, the damp fog condensing on her sleek fur, cooling her. The sting of her healing wounds, the fire of the air in her lungs, the joy of being alive. Later, and once again human, she knew she would feel horror at the slaughter she'd wrought. The ghosts of the dead men would haunt her dreams. Later she would grieve the actions of her monstrous half. But the Karnee Kait did not grieve. *She* felt glorious. Glorious. She was alive, and those who would have raped and murdered her were dead, and their deaths filled her with furious joy.

The strange Karnee turned away from her, left down a side road. She kept to the road she was on; she'd finally recognized where she was. She had chanced upon the combination of roads that would take her home. One block, one right turn, and she would come upon the high, spike-topped fence that separated the embassy from the city surrounding it. The Sabir Karnee was already out of sight, fleeing to his own safety; he would not, then, discover who she was. Good. She'd live longer that way.

She slowed to a lope, becoming wary. While she was in this form, her own people would be as deadly to her as any enemy. She dared not let herself be seen. She had to get past the guards, over the fence, up three stories of stone wall to the window of the suite where she stayed.

She had neither closed the shutters nor barred the window before she left for the party; the Karnee part of her chafed at the smell and feel of enclosed places, and the more she needed the Shift, the worse the feeling became. That was to her benefit. Nothing else was.

She crouched in the park across the street and watched the guards moving behind the fence. Regular movements; a sweep by two men, a short interval, then two men going across the grounds in the opposite direction. She'd watched them from above on other sleepless nights. The intervals at this early morning hour were shorter than they would normally be – more men were on the grounds, and they were more alert. No joking now, no banter as pairs crossed; they were anticipating trouble ... or her absence in the carriage that brought Tippa home, and whatever garbled story of trouble Tippa had managed to convey, had put the embassy on alert. Kait would have to be quick and precise to get past the guards. They never looked up at the walls of the house, though. So she had a second fact to her advantage.

She moved under cover as close to the street and the fence as she dared. Then she waited. A pair of guards passed. The fog would help hide her from sight, but would amplify any noise she made. The guards moved as far from her as she dared let them; their opposite pair already worked its way toward her from around the corner of the house, and the next pair of following guards from the first direction would not be far behind.

She raced across the street and bunched herself into the air, teeth clenching down on her bundle. Her body compacted and then uncoiled as if she were a spring. Straight up to twice the height of a tall man she soared, clear to the top of the fence. All four paws found purchase; her back arched high to avoid the impaling spike over which she swayed; her tail lashed behind her, keeping her balance.

From her left – 'Did you hear something?'

'Sounds like . . . like something shook the fence.'

'Yes. Ahead?'

'Can't tell. The whole damned fence rattled.'

They would stop and check. Maybe work their way back to her. She couldn't meet them, didn't dare let them catch sight of her. She gauged distances, then poured downward, liquid as a cat – though no one who saw her could ever have mistaken her for any sort of cat – and landed in the clipped grass on the far side of the hard path. The faintest of rustles when she landed; she heard it clearly, but the guards wouldn't. Their voices camouflaged the sound. One leap over shrubbery, several lengths of skulking behind plantings to bring her to the spot below her window, the merest instant to ensure that her bundle was secure and that nothing would fall to the ground and draw attention upward to her. A wait, as the next pair of guards moved past, their attention on the two men ahead of them, and on the fence. Good.

She climbed up the rough-cut stones to the window that let into her room, limbs spread wide to improve her balance, claws hooking around every projection, body tight to the wall. One moment of worry, heart-stopping, as just above the second floor she came clear of the fog. The moonlight would outline her clearly to anyone below – she was a gleaming black-furred monster on luminous white stone. But no one looked up.

She threw herself through the window and sprawled on the floor of her bedroom; there, finally, the rush of fear and desperation that had kept her going guttered out, and the Karnee beast gave way once more to the sense-dulled, guilt-ridden creature who could pass as human, but who could never he human.

Kait the woman washed away the blood left by Kait the monster as best she could in the darkness. She hid her bloody bundle beneath her bed, and tugged on a dressing gown. Then she fell into her bed, and into the world of nightmares and terror, where her victims' specters hunted and haunted her, where blood clung to hands, and where a destiny she did not believe in mocked her and whispered in her ear, *Your soul, your enemy; your enemy, your soul.*

* * *

Dùghall Draclas turned to the captain of the guards and said, 'I'm going to be useless if I don't get some sleep. Wake me the second anyone finds out anything. I'll be in my quarters.'

The captain nodded. 'You think this is like what happened to Danya, sir? That someone snatched her?'

'I think I don't know what to think. If this is kidnapping, we'll get the ransom demand soon. But it doesn't feel like a kidnapping to me. My gut says otherwise. And anything could have happened to her. She doesn't know her way around the city; if she tried to walk home, she could have wandered down into a bad alley and been robbed . . . or worse . . .' He turned away from the captain. 'I wish she'd told Tippa what she thought she'd found. Or why she was staying behind. Then maybe I'd know where to start looking.'

His people had already tracked down the princes who had schemed to get Tippa drunk so they could disgrace her and, through her, shame all of Galweigh House. They'd been part of a small band of the Gyru-nalle fanatics who thought a union of the Dokteeraks and the Galweighs would spell the end of Gyru-nalle independence in the disputed territories that lay between Dokteerak land and Galweigh land. All three were going to deny everything . . . until they discovered that they were being questioned on the disappearance of an ambassador and not on their plan to cause embarrassment to the Family. Had they been linked to the kidnapping of any

66

Family ambassador, every Gyru-nalle in the Iberal Peninsula would have been hunted down and slaughtered. The Families maintained their hold on the lesser people of Ibera with the iron-clawed grip of eagles, and had no respect for the crownless royal heads of long-dead empires.

So the Gyru-nalle princes talked hard and fast – with some encouragement from the embassy torturer – and Dùghall, after listening to the questioning, was satisfied that none of the three had anything to do with Kait's disappearance.

He walked toward his quarters, the weariness of a night spent anticipating disaster adding weight to every step he took. It wasn't enough that an ambassador was missing. It had to be Kait. He had too many relatives, and most of them he loathed. But Kait was the image of his favorite sister, Grace – delicate, dark, and beautiful, and with the spirit of a young lioness. He would grieve if anything had happened to her.

His path took him past Kait's room; on impulse he stopped outside her door. Perhaps he should go in and look through her things to see if he could find anything that might tell him what had become of her. He felt sure the search would be pointless, but the same gut instinct that insisted she hadn't been kidnapped told him he ought to look.

He glanced up and down the hall to make sure no one was watching. There in the empty hallway he felt he had a bit of an advantage; spies would find it pointless to hide in rooms and spy on hallways most of the time, since the business that would keep them in the embassy in the first place would almost always take place behind closed and locked doors. Nevertheless, he'd be a fool to betray the Falcons with such a simple gesture as opening a locked door. The hallway remained empty, though. He decided to take the calculated risk. He drew his dagger and made a quick, light slash across the index finger of his left hand – just enough to draw blood, no more. When the dark droplets welled to the edge of the cut, he murmured a few words, and a soft, radiant light coalesced around his hand. He touched the lock above Kait's door handle. A thought, a flicker of light from the tip of his finger to the smooth metal cylinder, and her door swung open.

She lay sprawled in her bed, in restless sleep, covers flung to the floor in a tangle, her nightdress riding up to reveal several long, freshly healed scars on the back of her right thigh, and smears of what looked in the dim light like blood on her leg, her hand, and her face. She whimpered as she slept and her legs thrashed; she breathed in short, hard gasps. As if she were running from something.

Dùghall frowned. He closed his eyes for an instant, and studied the faint glow of her form on the bed that his second sight revealed. Odd that in all the time he'd known Kait, he'd never seen that before. Odder that he'd never thought to look. The aura of magic lay lightly on her, and seemed to grow dimmer as he stood there. It wasn't Wolf magic, though, and it wasn't Falcon magic. She was the source of it, and yet she *wasn't*, as well. His frown deepened. Mysteries within mysteries – that she could get into her room past guards who were looking for her, that she had vanished in the first place, that she carried enigmatic scars, that a faint whisper of magic clung to her in spite of the fact that he *knew* her to be magically unschooled.

These were mysteries he would have to fathom. And quickly. But not so quickly that he had to disturb Kait's restless sleep. Perhaps he would discover something useful if he just waited.

He settled himself into the chair across from her bed, set a shield around himself that she would disturb the moment she woke, and let his head drop back. Within minutes, he slept deeply.

* * *

Hasmal trailed salt across the surface of the mirror with his left hand. It soaked into the line of blood that he'd drawn into a triangle. He sucked at his right thumb for just an instant to lick away the last traces of his blood – should he let any stray drops fall onto the mirror when he summoned the Speaker, he would find himself devoured. Or worse.

He whispered the final lines of the incantation:

> *Speaker step within the walls*
> *Of earth and blood and air;*
> *Bound by will and spirit,*
> *You must bide your presence there.*
> *Answer questions with clear truth,*
> *Do only good and then*
> *Return to the realm from whence you came*
> *And don't come back again.*

The salt on the mirror began to burn. The pale blue flames flickered for an instant, then settled into a steady glow. And in the center of the flames, a tiny light burst into life and shaped itself into a perfect representation of a woman, though one no taller than Hasmal's longest finger.

She stared up at him, long glowing hair blowing in a breeze that never traveled beyond the triangle of fire. 'What do you want to know?' Her voice was deep and sweet, softer than Hasmal's whisper, but not whispered. She spoke from unimaginably far away, over the incessant sobbing of the wind that blew between the worlds, and her words only reached him by the magic of her simulacrum standing on the glass.

Hasmal cleared his throat and crouched nearer the

69

glass, shielding the light it cast with his body. 'I met a woman tonight. She saw through my shields, though she should never have been able to do that. I told her my name, though I didn't intend to. She frightened me. She's not what she seems to be. Does she mean me harm?'

'No, though she will someday bring it to you anyway. You are a vessel chosen by the Reborn, Hasmal son of Hasmal; your destiny is pain and glory. Your sacrifice will bring the return of greatness to the Falcons, and your name will be revered through all time.'

'My sacrifice?' Hasmal felt his heart tie itself into a hard, small knot inside his chest. Having a revered name sounded good enough, but the people the Falcons revered tended to be dead, and worse, to have died badly. 'What kind of sacrifice?'

The woman waved a tiny hand, and in the flames Hasmal saw his parents being nailed to the Great Gate. Then he saw himself being beaten, tortured, and flayed by men wearing the livery of one of the Five Families; and finally standing skinless in the midst of the city of Halles while a crowd jeered and threw rotted fruit at him, and soldiers tied his limbs to four horses, then sent the horses galloping in four different directions.

Hasmal thought he might faint. He'd suspected he wasn't being asked to sacrifice a pure black goat, or even a bag of gold. But his parents' lives and his own . . .

The images died away, leaving the tiny woman looking up earnestly at him. 'Your deeds will make you beloved. You'll live on in the pages of the Secret Texts, and in the hearts of all Falcons forever after.'

Hasmal looked away from her, trying to erase from his mind the image of his skinless body being ripped into four pieces by the galloping horses.

I'll forgo the glory, he decided. I'd rather live in the present than on the pages of a book.

He stared down at the Speaker and shivered. 'Can I escape this fate?'

For an instant, he heard only the sound of that otherworldly wind. Then she laughed. 'You can always try.'

'How?' he asked.

But the fire on the glass burned low and all at once guttered out. The Speaker vanished, leaving the mirror bare of salt and blood.

He could draw more blood, summon another Speaker, perhaps get the information he desired. But the spell had cost him in energy. And worse, it had cost him in time. He might be able to control the energy of another spell, but he would never get back the time he'd lost.

The strange woman had said she would be coming to find him. His fate, and his and his parents' destruction, were linked to contact with her. He had no guarantee that he could escape the Speaker's images of doom; he'd been given no promise that he could spare his mother and father, either. But if he was not in Halles, the woman would not find him, and perhaps he would not be such a danger to them – or to himself.

He rose, tucked the mirror back into his case, and stepped out of the storeroom. Before she arrived, he needed to pack his belongings and leave. He dared not say good-bye to his parents – his father would demand an explanation when his solid, dependable, decidedly unadventurous son suddenly decided to pack a kit and hare off to destinations unknown. And if the old man ever suspected his son was fleeing his sacred duty to die for the Falcons, he would probably turn Hasmal over to the Dokteeraks, then nail himself and his wife to the Great Gate in penance. The elder Hasmal wouldn't approve of running away from destiny – especially not a destiny that furthered the aspirations of his beloved Falcons.

Hasmal the younger was neither so dedicated to that

ancient, secret order, nor so sanguine about his portended demise in its service. He packed a few necessary belongings, his magic kit, his copy of the Secret Texts, and what little money he had, and wondered not how he could serve, but where he could hide and how he would get there.

Chapter 6

In her sleep, Kait heard breathing not her own and felt eyes watching her. In spite of her dreams – dreams of running and Shifting – she became aware of a stranger who entered her domain. She fought against the pull of sleep, knowing that she had to awaken, feeling that while she lay unprotected someone was discovering her secret, but she could not break free of the tenacious depths of the Shift-fueled dreams.

The nightmares gripped her and tore at her. She saw the Sabir Karnee coming for her, and she fled, but he caught up to her. This time he did not come to rescue her from rapists and murderers; this time he came because he wanted her. He touched her and kissed her, and her mind cried out that her desire was a betrayal of her Family, that she should flee before she gave in to him. But she was weak. She did what she knew she should not do. She welcomed his embrace – and her Family died in droves at the hands of his Family while she fed her lust and ignored her duty. Then the dream metamorphosed, and she ran, wild and reckless, smelling the rich earth and the vibrant growth of jungle and forest and field, floating at incredible speeds with her feet never quite touching the ground. And all the while, something terrible pursued her. The scent of her pursuer rose out of the ground and poisoned the air she breathed. Honeysuckle. Sweet honeysuckle. It terrified her, though she did not know why. She careened along the edge of a cliff that appeared out of nowhere, and discovered in the same instant that she was running beside her cousin Danya. The two of them were girls again, exploring the grounds outside of the House, and she knew without knowing how she knew that the two of them had wakened something old and evil . . . and that the monster that they had awakened wanted to destroy them. Then the cliff fell away beneath them, and she and Danya fell silently. As she fell, Kait started to Shift again – terrified that her cousin would see her and discover the secret she fought so hard to keep. In spite of her attempts to control the Shift, her arms stretched into front legs, then thinned into wings . . . but she still fell. She dropped, helpless, into an abyss, and watched the ground loom closer and closer.

With a snap, heart racing, mouth dry, she was awake. She didn't move, didn't open her eyes – because someone *was* in her room. The scent told her that the someone was her uncle Dùghall; the irregular purring snores told her he slept in the chair next to the door. When had he arrived, and why had he chosen to wait for her to wake instead of waking her? And more importantly, what had she betrayed of her nature while she slept?

Her body ached, and she wished she could forget the disasters of the previous night. She wished she could forget the Sabir son.

She also wished she could get past Dùghall without waking him so that she could get something to eat before she had to answer a lot of questions. She was ravenous – her body demanded a price for its Shifting, for its rapid healing and tremendous strength and speed. It demanded food in enormous quantities; if it didn't get what it needed, it would drive her into despair, and then into a deadly, uncontrollable rage. The longer she waited to eat, the more out of control her moods would become. But the instant she opened one eye to survey the room, Dùghall woke as if he'd been slapped. His snore became a snort, his eyes flew open in bewilderment, and he shot upright, gasping.

And there went any hope of breakfast before the interrogation she was sure to face. She said, 'Good morning, Uncle,' and tried her best to look pleasant.

He required a moment before he remembered where he was and how he had come to be there. Kait could see the information filtering out of the dreamworld he'd inhabited and into his eyes, and she saw pleasure leave him by degrees, replaced by ... what? Worry? Fear? Anger? Whatever she saw there vanished beneath the diplomat's mask of calm before she could identify it.

'What happened?' he asked.

How much did she dare tell him? Dùghall wasn't the senior ambassador in Halles. He was peripheral to the embassy itself – he was important, certainly; in the islands where the Galweighs harvested their meager supplies of caberra, the natives worshiped Dùghall as a god and wouldn't deal with anyone else. He had power and prestige, and he represented the Family at the moment as a respected elder statesman. But he was not the head of the Halles embassy, and thus he would not be the man who would decide what to do about the Dokteeraks and the Sabirs. If she followed protocol, she would tell Dùghall she couldn't discuss the issue, and she would go upstairs to speak to Eldon Galweigh, to whom responsibility for the decisions would fall. But to Eldon Galweigh, she was a junior diplomat of no real importance. To Dùghall Draclas, she was a beloved niece and the young woman he'd sponsored into the diplomatic service. And Uncle Dùghall would be less inclined, she thought, to pursue difficult questions. So she said, 'First, I ran into conspiracy.'

He raised an eyebrow. 'The Sabirs and the Dokteer-aks.'

Kait should have been relieved that the plot had already fallen into the hands of those capable of dealing with it, but she was perversely disappointed. She'd hoped that, by telling the Family what she'd discovered and by thus saving them from betrayal and defeat, she could expiate the sin of desiring the Sabir Karnee. She closed her eyes. 'You already knew.'

'I recognized one of the Sabirs being led through the midst of the Naming Day party by an irate houseman. I have no idea what he was doing there.'

Kait met his eyes and told him. '*I* know.'

She reeled off the conversation she'd heard between the Dokteerak paraglese and his servant.

When she finished, Dùghall sat for a moment staring at her, his face pale and his lips and knuckles white. At last he said, 'Good gods, girl, that's a nightmare. They plan an attack during the wedding itself? Actual battle? I had thought at very worst the damned Sabirs were attempting to curry favor – perhaps arrange a marriage of their own to weaken our alliance.' He looked down at the backs of his hands for the longest time. Then, quietly, he said, 'If I can verify this, you will have obtained valuable informa-tion, Kait-cha. Tell me, how did you come by it?'

Kait had given the answer to that question plenty of thought as she made her way home the night before. She'd already fixed her lie firmly in her mind. 'I felt ill, and sent Tippa to the carriage ahead of me. I told her to go ahead home – she was flirting with three Gyru-nalle princes and somehow had managed to get herself drunk, and I didn't see any sign of the chaperones who were supposed to be with her. I wanted her out of the Dokteerak House before she did something stupid. As it was, I'm afraid it was a near thing.'

'I've . . . heard . . . from the princes already. Last night. Some colleagues of theirs on the Dokteerak staff drugged both chaperones and dragged them off, intending to make both women look like they'd indulged in too much of the Dokteeraks' wine and had been sporting with some of the concubines that were on hand for the evening entertainment. They hoped to humiliate our Family.' He waved her on. 'We've already dealt with that. Continue.'

She glanced at him sidelong, curious. In Tippa's condition the night before, she would have been able to tell him little that would have been useful; considering that, Kait found herself wondering if perhaps Dùghall's methods of acquiring information were as unconventional as her own. How had he known to go after the three princes? How had he managed to locate them? She leaned against the stone wall, pulled her blankets up around her shoulders, and said, 'I went down a side corridor, thinking I might find a fountain from which to draw a drink of water. I became dizzy, and leaned against a statue, and when the dizziness passed, I realized that I heard voices. I listened to what they were saying; I moved behind the statue to hide when I found out what they discussed was of interest to us. When the paraglese left, I saw him go.' She closed her eyes, remembering the pale, squat man who strode down the corridor past her, so close that she could feel the breeze when he passed. He'd looked remarkably like a toad, she realized. She glanced at her uncle. 'He ordered a visiting paraglese in from the Territories killed to give himself an excuse for leaving his party.'

Dùghall frowned, and for a moment she wondered what she'd said wrong. But he said, 'Damnall. That's one confirmation of your story. One of our runners came to the embassy not long after Tippa arrived to inform us that the paraglese Idrogar Pendat from Old Jirin died of a sudden fever last night. It doesn't fill me with joy to discover his death was . . . convenient.'

'You don't seem surprised.'

His thin, humorless smile wasn't comforting. 'I'm not. Pendat assumed that he would be welcomed into the Dokteeraks' House and kept safe because he was among his own Family. But new faces in any House create opportunities for many sorts of change, and if the visitor isn't careful, he often finds himself a pawn in another's game. Sometimes a dead pawn.'

'But he was *Family*.' To Kait, Family was sacred.

Dùghall said, 'Not all Families are like ours, Kait-cha.'

Kait nodded. She'd known the Sabirs were evil, and she hadn't liked the Dokteeraks much when she'd been introduced to them. She still found it difficult, though, to reconcile her hazy images of evil with the reality of a man murdering one of his own Family to provide a convenient excuse for missing a party. That gave a face to the word 'evil' that she would never have imagined on her own.

She tried to block out her hunger by concentrating on Dùghall. She knew she needed to stay on her guard. But the aftereffects of Karnee Shift would not be denied; she wanted food. Food. Dùghall seemed to blur in front of her eyes and his voice came from far away, as if he spoke from the other side of a long field.

'What happened to you on the way home?' he asked. 'I couldn't help but notice the blood on your legs and hand and face when I came in.'

Her hands flew to her face and she felt herself flushing. 'I thought I'd washed it all off.'

He nodded. 'So what happened?'

She hadn't had time to come up with a good lie for that. 'I was . . . attacked,' she said. 'While I walked home. Thieves.' She shrugged. 'I was lucky – I cut one

78

with the dagger I'd hidden in my skirt when he threatened me, and just then a stranger came along and chased off the others. I got a little bloody, but I was fortunate.'

'You were indeed. The streets of this city are dangerous. You could have had much worse happen.'

She nodded solemnly and said nothing.

'If I can confirm the parts of your information that we haven't verified yet, I'll pass it on to Eldon,' he was saying. She continued to nod, thinking more of what she might find to eat than of his words. But what he said next brought her attention back to the present. 'Meanwhile, we'll have to make an appearance at the Celebration of Names today. The Dokteeraks have a parade and some sort of festival in the main city square. I want you to come along – you did a fine job of protecting Tippa last night, but even more than that, you managed to be in the right place at the right time to get information that your Family desperately needed. I never attribute opportunities of that sort entirely to luck. There is always some skill involved. Perhaps you'll be fortunate again today. I'll see that you get a commendation for your work last night, by the way.' He studied the backs of his hands. 'Perhaps even a posting.' He glanced up, noted the delight in her eyes, and smiled. 'No promises on the posting, though, Kait. You're very junior.'

'I understand.'

He added, 'But about the celebration, be ready to leave by Stura. The ceremony begins at Duea, and we're to have places alongside the Dokteerak Family atop their old ruin of a tower.'

Kait wondered if she'd heard her uncle correctly. 'They're plotting to kill us all, and we're going to sit in their damned tower *with them* and pretend to enjoy their festival?'

Dùghall smiled broadly. 'Indeed, we are going to go and have a marvelous time. Further, we're going to be understanding and magnanimous about the unfortunate situation last night with Tippa and the princes; our chaperone failed as badly as theirs at protecting her, after all, and in these days reliable help is hard to find.' His eyes narrowed and something lethal crept into his smile. 'And while we play the fool, our people here in the embassy will be making sure that their plot against us turns around and bites them instead.'

He chuckled, shook his head as if the whole thing amused him, then rose to leave. 'Don't wear anything orange. These Baltos think it's an unlucky color the first month of the new year. You haven't eaten yet, of course.'

'No. Not anything.'

'You're hungry?'

'Ravenous.'

Dùghall opened her door, then turned again and said, 'You'll need to hurry. No time to go to the kitchen. I'll have the staff bring something up for you.'

'If they don't bring me enough, I'll devour whoever carries the food into the room,' she said, and perhaps some edge of her hunger crept into her voice, for Dùghall looked at her oddly. 'Tell them to bring me something meaty. And not that spiced meat they love so much here.'

He laughed. 'All grown up and you *still* hate spices? I'll just tell them to trot a whole lamb up to your room – you can have that as plain as you'd like.'

Still laughing, Dùghall stepped out the door and closed it behind him, then poked his head back in. His face still wore its merry smile, and Kait grinned at him. 'Forget something?'

'Nothing vital. How did you get into your room last night?'

She wasn't thinking clearly. Hunger had dulled her reactions. Worse, the question took her completely by surprise and his tone was so casual that she didn't sense the danger in it. She glanced at the window through which she'd climbed before she could stop herself. The logical lie came an instant too late, but she tried it. 'I came in through the front door, of course,' she said, but Dùghall's smile had vanished so quickly and so totally that she realized he'd been acting when he asked how she'd come in – that he'd been planning all along to ask that question, and that he had delayed asking her so that she would relax. So that she would think he had forgotten that she had come in without being seen or checked in at the gate.

He ignored her lie; instead, he came back into her room. Strolled to the window. Pushed open the shutters and leaned out and stared down at the ground. Her room was three stories up, and though the stone was unpolished, it offered no visible handholds. She knew what he saw, and she knew that a human woman could not have climbed up the wall and in that window. When he pulled the shutters closed and turned to face her, she couldn't begin to guess the meaning of the look on his face.

'We'll talk later, you and I,' he said. No trace of his previous good humor appeared on his face. But he didn't look angry, either. She couldn't read him at all. 'Meanwhile, eat and get ready to accompany me to the Celebration of Names.'

This time when he left the room, he didn't return. She stared at the window, hating the stupidity of her response and wondering if she had, with that single thoughtless glance, destroyed her chances in the Galweigh diplomatic corps . . . if she had betrayed herself . . .

Or worse, if she had betrayed her parents and sisters and brothers.

* * *

Dùghall hurried toward his room, lost in thought. Kait presented mysteries within mysteries, and he would have to take whatever time was required to divine the secrets

81

she kept hidden. The Family couldn't entrust its diplomacy to anyone who kept secrets from it – agents with secrets gave enemies easy tools for blackmail.

Whatever Kait was hiding, however, appeared potentially useful. If all her information about the Sabirs and the Dokteeraks checked out, she'd won the gold ball in the spying game, and he wondered how she had really done it. Mind-magic? Some form of invisibility? Access to an artifact that gave her new talents? Whatever she'd done, she'd be the best diplomat the Family had ever had if she could do it again.

Maybe she'd learned how to fly. That had been an impossible bit of wall she'd gone up – and with the guards doubled and on alert, he thought the invisibility theory gained another point in its favor, too.

Further, he didn't believe for a moment her tale of a minor attack by thieves and a rescue by a stranger. First, she'd had long scars on her leg and her hand, and blood all over her; a minor attack would have done less damage. Second, she hadn't managed to meet his eyes with confidence while she told him the story. If she was going to survive as a diplomat, he would have to teach her some of the finer points of effective lying.

Kait's secrets could wait, though, until he made sure that her information was sound. If the business between the Sabirs and the Dokteeraks proved to be true, she would be worth any time she took.

Dùghall went directly from Kait's room to his own, and once there made a show of stripping off his morning clothes and putting on the broad black silk pantaloons and elaborate red silk brocade robe that were his official garments as chief Galweigh ambassador in the Imumbarra Isles. He knew he was being watched – someone always watched his room from the hidden panel along the north wall. He'd discovered that the first night, and had pretended to remain oblivious. Knowing for certain that a spy was watching was almost as useful as knowing one wasn't.

Once dressed, he opened one of the half-dozen wig boxes he had in the room, pulled out an elaborately braided wig, and settled it on his head. From another box he pulled out the spike-adorned headdress that would hold the wig in place. He settled the headdress in place so that the rib bearing the seven spikes ran from ear to ear, wiggled it a bit to be sure it was firmly on, then drew out the tuft of beaded feathers that fit into the tip of each spike and slipped them into their sockets.

He'd not intended to go so formally attired to what was basically a semiformal event, but the wig, the headdress, and the brocade robe all had special character-istics about them that suited his purposes at the moment, and the spy would think it odd if he donned them, then took them back off again before going anywhere.

They were the clothes he'd prepared before he left the islands to attend this wedding. The brocade robe was lined with hidden pockets, and each of those pockets carried in it a packet of powders useful for the casting of spells, or a talisman already spelled for a specific purpose. He slid a hand into what looked like a decorative slit and felt along the beads embroidered just beneath the edge for a particular pattern. When he found it, he pulled out the silk bag tucked into the pocket beside it.

He opened the drawstring on the bag and pulled out a charming gold brooch – the design was a playful fox kit done in intaglio, surrounded by the seven ruby stars that stood for the seven major islands of the Imumbarra Isles, on a background of hundreds of tiny incised stars indicating the uncounted lesser islands. It was a very good copy of an official piece of jewelry, and the spell it bore had cost him a solid week of work, and more than a little of his own blood.

He affixed it to the central panel of his robe, and felt the wall of magic he'd created come to life. He smiled. The spy – sitting on the other side of that cunning peephole – would now see nothing more than what he'd been seeing and what he expected to see: a man getting ready to go to an important function. Dùghall's double would appear to putter around the room, riffling through documents, perhaps writing one of the endless correspondences that made up diplomatic life, but doing nothing noteworthy. Dùghall, meanwhile, went to another wig box, lifted the wig from the stand it sat on, and took the stand, dumping the wig back in the box. The stand, a head-shaped bit of carved wood, came apart in his hands when he moved a carefully disguised slider in the right jaw to expose a hidden recess, and pressed fingers simultaneously into that recess and against the left ear.

He'd hidden his divining tools inside: a bowl and stand for catching blood, a mirror for the flames, two powder brushes, sulfur sticks and warding powders, and a bloodletting kit he'd designed himself after wearying of the pain he got when cutting himself with even the best knife. He sat cross-legged on the floor and set the divining tools up, then fixed one of the hollow thorns into the glass vial, wrapped a rubber tourniquet around his forearm, and plunged the thorn into the first vein that rose to the surface, wincing as he did. Still not the most comfortable of methods, but infinitely preferable to the knife.

Blood spurted through the thorn into the bowl. When it covered the bottom, he marked the first circle of his blood on the mirror, letting it drip out in a neat, perfectly narrow line from the tip of the thorn. Then he sprinkled the warding powders into the cup, struck one of the sulfur sticks to make a flame, and lit the powders. While they burned, he hurried through his opening incantation with the speed of long practice.

A sympathetic fire sprang up along the circle of blood, and he drew a glyph within it that indicated the past. Then he murmured the name of the Dokteerak paraglese, and focused on the last time he saw the man at the party the night before. Dùghall dripped a little blood onto the mirror every time the flame began to burn low; he watched as the enemy paraglese talked with the Sabir emissary about his Family's destruction. He tried to follow the Sabir emissary back through the streets of Halles to wherever he was hiding, but magic blocked him from seeing the man once he was well away from the Dokteerak House.

It didn't really matter. What mattered was that he'd confirmed every word of what Kait had told him. The Dokteeraks and the Sabirs were in alliance, and the Galweighs were their target.

Chapter 7

Stolen horses made for uncomfortable riding. Hasmal cursed every ill-gaited strike of the beast's hooves on the stone road, and every nervous bolt at the sudden eruption of birds from shrubs or children from hovels. The horse, he had no doubt, belonged to none other than Brethwan, the Iberan god of celibacy and sex, of pleasure and pain, and of life and death – and was a harbinger of pain and death, and probably, if the state of his testicles was any indication, of long-term celibacy. Hasmal's sores had sores, and he hurt so much that taking short breaks to walk on the ground and lead the accursed animal no longer gave him any relief.

Which would teach him to live in a country watched over by Iberish gods, instead of the good Hmoth gods a man knew he could depend on. Would Vodor Imrish have permitted him to steal such a foul beast? No, no, and never.

Hasmal intended to get himself to someplace where the gods had a sense of decency about them – where he didn't constantly have the feeling that they were laughing at him or playing clever tricks at his expense. He heard the humans who still hung on in the Strithian lands had congenial gods, if amoral ... but perhaps gods who approved of thieving and whoring wouldn't look with too cold an eye on a Falcon, even one so far from where he belonged. So he would go to Strithia, then – a place enough like another world to suit his needs, yet still within his reach. A hundred leagues southeast to Costan Selvira, he could book working passage aboard the first ship leaving harbor for Brelst. Once in Brelst, he could sign himself aboard a riverboat going up the Emjosi River; traveling upriver, the boatmen always needed extra hands. Had he wanted to travel downriver, he would have had to pay passage, so luck favored his enterprise already. The less a thing cost, the more dearly Hasmal loved it, and the better he considered the omens regarding it.

And as soon as he was across the border into Strithia, he'd be safe. The woman who was his doom was Familied, he would bet his life. He *was* betting his life. She was probably Galweigh, if he'd read the woven pattern of her silk dress right, and she certainly stood well up the ladder of social rank. She wouldn't throw all that away by crossing the Strithian border to come after him.

Thus engaged in his thoughts, he allowed himself to forget the pain his razor-backed mount caused him; more importantly, he allowed himself to forget that he rode the Shatalles Forest Road. The former might have been a blessing, but the latter nearly became his death.

He trotted the execrable excuse for a horse around a sharp curve in the road, and suddenly men dropped out of the trees that tangled their branches across the road like a canopy – and the men held knives and wore rags and desperate expressions. His horse panicked and reared. Hasmal, because he was a poor rider and inexperienced, fell to the road. And just like that, a knife grazed his throat and all he could do while his horse galloped back the way it had come was sit very still, trying hard not to breathe too deeply.

'Your money,' the man with the knife at his throat demanded.

'I have none,' Hasmal said.

Several of the thieves laughed, and one said, 'You ride a horse, don't you? Your clothes are new and very fine, ain't they?'

And the thief with the knife at his throat said again, 'Your money.'

Hasmal swallowed hard, wishing he had taken the time to build a shield of nonseeing around himself before he left Halles – but that would have taken hours, and *she* might have come for him before then. For that matter, he should have made himself a permanent shield talisman long ago ... but he had always had tomorrow for such luxuries, and too many things to do today. So the talisman had gone unmade, and now he stood in need and helpless.

'I swear,' he said, 'I swear on my own soul that I have no money. Not so much as a dak.' And he thought of the bit of money he'd had, and of his precious magical supplies and his book, and his other clothes, all of it at that moment galloping away on the back of the damned horse, 'I stole the horse,' he said in a burst of honesty, then added an inspired lie. 'And the clothes, too.'

The men laughed at him, and the one with the knife at his throat said, 'He thinks he's hid it too good for us. Strip him – we'll find it soon enough.'

Four thieves held his arms and four his legs, and three more began pawing at his clothes. The one with the knife at Hasmal's throat snarled, 'Don't tear his clothes, you pigs. I want them.' Then he leaned in close to Hasmal and said, 'Even if you swallowed your money, I'll find it.' His smile was evil.

Hasmal sweated and shook. He had no chance of winning free of the thieves, no matter how hard he fought. They held him tightly and they didn't relax their guard or assume that because they outnumbered him he wouldn't fight. They were careful and cagey, and acted with a unison and a precision that spoke of long practice at their work. They were going to find out he had nothing on him, and then they were going to gut him to see if he'd swallowed his gold as some men were said to do before setting out over dangerous roads. And when they discovered he really did have nothing, the truth would come too late to benefit him.

One of the thieves finished going through his clothing. 'Nothing on him.'

'I reckon I'll have to gut you, then.' The men who held Hasmal tightened their grips, and Hasmal stiffened and squinched his eyes shut.

'Everything I had in the world took off with that damned horse,' he gasped. He expected the sharp fire of the knife in his belly at any instant, but nothing happened. He cautiously opened one eye and found all the thieves staring at him.

The one who had been on the point of gutting him said, 'You piss-brained *idiot*. Everything you had was on the horse? *Everything?* What were you going to do if you were thrown?'

Hasmal said, 'I didn't know the damned things were so hard to ride.'

The thieves guffawed then, and their leader shook his head and said, 'I almost believe you now . . . almost . . . 'cause who else would be so stupid that he wouldn't keep hisself anything in case of he lost his horse, excepting a man who never had hisself a horse?'

One of the other thieves said, 'Look at the raw spots on his legs. Looks to me like he really ain't never rid a horse before.'

Hasmal felt a moment of hope. He was naked, he had nothing, but if they didn't kill him, he might always find clothes to steal and food to eat and a place to sleep, and, given time and a few materials, he could spell himself some protection, find work . . .

But his hope died at birth. 'Still want to gut him?' another one asked, and the leader said, 'For what? To get blood all over my new clothes? Just hang him and be done.'

'Why hang me?' Hasmal asked. 'Just let me go. You don't need to hang me.'

'And let you go and tell a mess of guardsmen where we met you? Or how many of us they might catch out, if they came looking? I reckon not. We'll stretch your neck until you won't tell anyone anything. That'll do for our needs.' He turned to his men. 'Tie him and bring him.'

'Bring me?' Hasmal kept hoping that something might break his way; if they weren't going to hang him right away, perhaps he would get a chance to escape.

'If we strung you beside the road,' the leader said in a surprisingly patient voice, 'we'd as well as tell the roadsmen this was where we was. We'll take you into the woods a ways and do you there.' His voice said, *No hard feelings; this is just the job.*

Hasmal couldn't find it in himself to be understanding.

They walked a long way, dragging Hasmal between them – at one point, one of them explained without being asked that they had to walk so far because if the smell blow out to the road, that could sometimes bring down the authorities, too. He didn't say *the smell of the corpse*, but he didn't need to.

Hasmal realized that he was a walking dead man. He sagged at last, and quit hoping for an opportunity to present itself. He allowed himself to be dragged forward. He was sure he had ceased caring. Then he heard singing. He thought at first he heard the voices of the *karae*, prematurely beginning the dirges that would accompany him into the Darkland; however, the *karae* only sang into the ears of the dead, never the living, and several of the thieves had started at the sound.

'*Boesels?*' someone whispered.

Boesels were supposed to be great hairy man-eating forest creatures that lured travelers to their deaths by pretending to be humans. Hasmal wouldn't swear that no such creatures existed – after all, he had seen stranger things with his own eyes – but he had never heard of one being taken in civilized lands. And he'd never heard of them singing.

'Hunters, I think,' someone else suggested, keeping his voice down, too.

But the refrain of the song reached them then, and with it the sweet minor-key piping of a stick-flute.

'Khaadamu, khaadamas, merikaas cheddae
Allelola vo saddee.
Emas avesamas betorru faeddro
Komosum khaadamu zhee.'

'It's not either,' the leader said. He grinned like a leopard come upon unguarded goats. 'That's Gyrus, by 'Coz, and the first goddamned bit of luck we've had all day.'

Luck for the thieves – half-luck for Hasmal. The song was haunting, the singer's voice a rich and vibrant baritone that ached with pain and loss, but the only way Hasmal could have regretted hearing it more would have been had the thieves already hauled him by his neck up into a tree when it started. He knew at the same time that he had been granted both a possible reprieve from death and a likely sentence in hell.

When the thief had said *Gyrus*, he'd meant Gyru-nalles: the notorious Gyru-nalles, members of an entire race devoted to thievery of a high and organized order; known from the ends of Ibera to beyond as traders of horses and dogs and stones and rare metals; reputed as liars and pickpockets who claimed to have once been kings of all Ibera; and most importantly, whispered in the dark of night and behind the safety of barred doors as stealers of children and young women and handsome boys, as slavers with no scruples about where they acquired their human merchandise and no quibbles about where they sold it, or for what purpose. Men who dealt with the Gyru-nalles – unlicensed buyers who would buy unpapered, untaxed slaves – would do so, Hasmal thought, only because they wanted their slaves disposable. Hasmal knew worse deaths existed than hanging, and were he sold into the ungentle care of the Gyrus, he thought himself likely to meet one of those deaths at firsthand.

Not that he had any choice in the matter. The thieves dragged him forward again, and at a harder pace than before, and the leader began to whistle: a long, falling note, two short, sharp rising notes, and a trill. He repeated the call three times more as they hurried forward, and the fourth time added a bit of what sounded like birdsong, though Hasmal was city bred and couldn't begin to guess what bird that call might have imitated. When the thief fell silent, from the trees around them Hasmal heard movement where he had heard nothing before. A man stepped out from behind an enormous ficus – he was pale-skinned, blotchily freckled, and light-eyed. Red hair in hundreds of tight braids hung to his waist, and he wore his mustache braided, too, and tipped with gold beads. He smiled and gold teeth flashed in the forest gloom. He was a Gyru-nalle for sure. Hasmal would have wept if he hadn't thought doing so would make things worse for him. None of the other Gyrus who surrounded them stepped into view, but Hasmal knew they were there. And that they had arrows pointed straight at his kidneys, no doubt.

The Gyru hugged the leader of the thieves and said, '*Tra metakchme, baverras ama tallarra ahaava?*'

The leader laughed and clapped the Gyru on the back. '*Allemu kheetorras sammes faen zeorrae llosadee, vo emu ave. Haee tahafa khaarramas salleddro.*' He tipped his chin toward Hasmal. '*Tho fegrro awomas choto? Hettu!*'

Hasmal had caught a fair amount of that exchange – Gyrus traded antiquities, and he'd been hearing them selling to his father since he was old enough to walk. Shombe was not a tongue Hasmal ever thought he would hear while he was the merchandise being discussed, but then life was like that. The Gyru had said, roughly, 'Well met, you hoary bastard, and what have you brought to trade me?' And the thief, in dreadful pidgin Shombe, had answered, 'My brother, I found the most marvelous slave wandering on the road, and no one to claim him. So what will you give me? Come and let's trade.'

The Gyru sauntered over and stared down at Hasmal, and his eyebrows rose and his lips pursed. He walked around Hasmal, studying him from all angles, came back and crouched in front of him, snorted with disgust, and subjected Hasmal to the sort of concentrated visual inspection that would have made a stallion blush. At last he stood and turned to the thief. Still in Shombe, he said, 'Well, he isn't bad, I suppose. He has some muscle to him. I can't sell him to the dowagers, though, because he's hung like a gnat, and the boy-market won't care much for him, either, for the same reason.' The thieves giggled and laughter echoed from the trees where the Gyru's allies hid. 'About the best I can hope for is to sell him as a laborer, and those don't go for much.'

The thieves' leader glanced over at Hasmal. 'He says he likes you,' he said. 'He says if you futter any women, they will still be virgins afterward. He thinks owning you might give him a market in miracle babies.'

Hasmal didn't see any reason to let anyone know he

93

knew what the Gyru had actually said. In Iberan, he replied, 'Lucky, then, that no one is trying to sell you. I don't imagine dickless eunuchs would be worth anything to that market.'

The head thief glared at him, though the other thieves – and a few of the Gyrus – laughed. The head thief turned his back on Hasmal and said, 'Give me eight ros?'

The braid-haired Gyru rolled his eyes and held up two fingers. 'I could see my way to give you two.'

'That eats donkey dung. I want seven anyway, for all my trouble in getting him here.'

The Gyrus laughed again and the one who bargained shook his head. 'You want seven ros for that? *Phtttt!* I'll give you four, but I'll be lucky to sell him for that.'

The thief raised his eyebrows. 'Maybe miracle babies ain't worth much right now,' he said to Hasmal in Iberan. 'He wants you cheap.' Then in Shombe to the Gyru, 'I'll take six ros . . . and you're stealing my eyes and the food from my mouth to get him for a bargain like that.'

The Gyru grinned. 'I can't steal what you don't own. You can be lucky we don't take the lot of you and sell you all – I think that one is more a freeman than any of the rest of you. But because I like you and because we've done some business before, I'll buy your problem from you. For four and a half ros. No more.'

The thief flushed and frowned, and suddenly no one was laughing. He stood there for a moment looking like a man who wanted to fight, but with all of the Gyru's men still hidden in the trees, he would have been a fool to start anything. At last he shrugged and said in Shombe, 'Yeah. I'll take your four and a half ros.' He added in Pethca, one of the backcountry dialects of Iberan, 'And I hope your balls rot off, you stinking whoreson.'

No flash of comprehension showed in the Gyru's eyes. He opened a small leather purse that hung at his waist and with a smile counted out four silver ros and two small coppers. He dropped the coins into the leader's outstretched hand, bowed slightly to all the thieves, and, still smiling, beckoned Hasmal to follow him. The thieves who'd dragged him into the woods let him go.

For only an instant, Hasmal considered running. But in the trees above him and from the thick underbrush all around him, he heard the soft murmurs and faint movements of the Gyru's friends. He felt their stares, and he could almost feel their arrows piercing his body as he fled. Better to live, he thought, for tomorrow may bring freedom – better to live a hard life than to die an easy death. He stumbled a bit – his hands bound behind him threw off his balance, and his nakedness made fighting his way through the thorns and scrub brush and needle-edged palmettos more of an adventure than any man deserved.

He followed, wishing that he were a stronger man, or a faster or a braver one; wishing that he might suddenly be set free by a miracle or an act of the gods, knowing that he wouldn't.

He had only one pleasant thought that he could hold on to. At least he was well away from the woman who would have been his doom.

Chapter 8

The great square of Halles fluttered with ribbons and pennants and jangled with tambourines and mamboors and cymbals and gongs. The thronging lower classes danced in long, snaking lines up the broad main avenue toward the ancient obsidian tower in which the Dokteerak Family – and this year the members of the Galweigh wedding party who had already arrived in Halles – waited and watched. Kait thought the tower was interesting; it was certainly an artifact in that it predated the Dokteeraks and most, if not all, of the other structures in Halles, but no one would mistake it as the work of the Ancients. Where their structures, built almost entirely of white stone-of-Ancients, soared in delicate arches and pinnacles and bore no designs on their smooth, translucent surfaces, the Halles tower had been built out of black marble, with each stone dressed to fit perfectly against the rest and the topmost stones carved into fantastically hideous winged monsters. Time had marred them and worn some of the detail from them, but the pocks and moss only accented their terrible teeth and the mad expressions in their eyes. Who had built the tower? Kait looked down at the rabble below and thought their ancestors were unlikely candidates.

The crawling sense of blindly seeking evil that had set Kait on edge at the party the night before had, if anything, grown stronger. The entire city reeked of it. But her senses were dulled and the tension of pending Shift had been sated, and she was able to push the awareness of that evil to a dark corner of her mind, where she could ignore it. Having eaten a huge meal before she left the embassy, Kait wanted nothing more than to sleep; the inescapable weariness that always overcame her after she Shifted held her in its unrelenting grasp. But she had to stay awake; further, she had to be charming when what she wanted most was to rip out the throats of the lying Dokteerak bastards who surrounded her.

The paraglese, Branard Dokteerak, short and fat, with his long hair greased and twisted into beribboned ropes, walked over and leaned on the balcony next to Kait and didn't attempt to hide the fact that he was looking down the neckline of her dress to see her breasts. She kept her irritation hidden – after all, her purpose in attending the ceremony and wearing the revealing dress and associating with the lying, double-crossing connivers was to allay suspicion and to give her Family time to come up with a suitable revenge. Nevertheless, the paraglese was a loathsome toad and had Kait been able to do it without causing an incident, she would have hurt him.

'Lovely girl,' he said, smiling up at her. 'You're called Kait-ayarenne, aren't you? Daughter of Strahan Galweigh, if I'm not mistaken.'

Kait hoped she appeared sufficiently flattered by his attention. 'I am,' she said, 'though I must admit I'm surprised that you heard my name mentioned at all. I'm far too junior a diplomat to have been brought to your attention by my Family.'

'And far too exquisite a creature to have escaped my eye.' His smile stretched, making his resemblance to a toad startlingly exact. 'I confess that it wasn't in your role as diplomat that I heard your name. I saw you at my party last night, and thought that you looked very lovely, and I asked one of your people who you were so that I might come over and make your acquaintance.' His smile vanished, and he shook his head, eyes suddenly downcast. 'Unfortunately, before I could find a mutual acquaintance who could introduce us, I was called away to attend to a dear cousin who was taken ill –'

'Idrogar Pendat? I heard that he died last night.'

'Sadly, you heard right. His death came unexpectedly – he was a strong man, and in the prime of life, and though he had been ill, no one realized how terribly near death he was. My physick says he had some weakness in his heart, and that the heat and the dampness of the air here became too much for him.'

'I grieve with you in your time of loss, and commend your cousin's spirit to Lodan that she may treat him with kindness,' Kait said. That was the expected formula; she managed to say it as though she really meant it, however. She discovered to her amazement that she was enjoying the interchange; not speaking to the paraglese as such, because he disgusted her, but knowing the truth behind the lies that he told her and pretending that she didn't, and acting a part that made her someone other than who she was in order to deceive him. Unlike her lifelong charade to be human, she shared this charade with everyone around her. All of the people atop the tower were pretending – well, with the possible exception of Tippa, but Tippa was an idiot. Sweet, but an idiot.

For Kait, the conversation with the paraglese was a revelation. The creation of a Kait that did not exist – the living lie that had made most of her existence a study in guilt – now served a purpose. Through the years of pretense she had learned to act, and acting was part of diplomacy. And through diplomacy she could serve her Family and bring honor to the Galweigh name.

The paraglese smiled again, but sadly. 'You are as kind as you are beautiful. Which makes me all the sadder that when I returned to my party, I discovered you had already gone.'

She nodded, and conveyed disappointment of her own. 'The regrets are mine. But I had no choice. A few of your guests were bothering my cousin Tippa, as you have no doubt heard. I only attended the party as her companion – I had no choice but to take her home.'

For one unguarded instant, she saw shock in his eyes. He hid it quickly with another oily smile. 'The three guests have been apprehended, and are now in our care. The Gyru-nalles have plotted against the Families for years; this time, however, they were careless enough to get caught. All three of those so-called princes are to be executed today as part of our entertainment. The insult to your cousin – my future daughter – cannot be tolerated.' He gave her a long, thoughtful look and added, 'But I had no idea you were the one who took her home. The men, when we ... ah, questioned them ... they mentioned a terrifying Galleech of a woman who frightened them away from dear Tippa, but neither I nor anyone else could recall such a woman at the party. And seeing you now, I fail to see any resemblance to the Galleech.'

The Galleech was one of the five Furies, goddesses who predated Iberism – she was blue-skinned and fang-toothed, with ruby eyes that shot fire that consumed her enemies. She strode through the myths of Ibera like a one-woman plague, laying waste to all that enraged her.

Kait said, 'I'd hardly compare myself to the Galleech, though I do have a bit of a temper.'

The paraglese responded with a cocked eyebrow and a half-smile. 'Evidently.' He chatted only an instant more, then excused himself to visit with other guests.

Bemused, Kait watched him go. When he found out she was the one who stood down the three princes, the musky scent of attraction he had emanated while talking to her had vanished, replaced by a faint sweat stink of fear. Interesting. She wondered what the men had seen and what they had said that would create such a response in him.

Down in the square, the tail end of the parade came into view, and the peasants who lined both sides of the avenue began to cheer. Easily a hundred parnissas in the purple robes that they alone could wear on the day after Theramisday marched forward. On their shoulders the foremost carried a litter, and in the litter sat a woman wrapped all in cloth of gold. The new carais of Halles, the woman who had by oracle and lottery named the city's new year, waved to the cheering hordes. Kait leaned forward on the balustrade, interested in spite of herself. The choices of the gods in picking their caraisi never ceased to be surprising.

This woman appeared to be tiny and ancient.

Beside Kait, someone chuckled. 'Wait until you hear what she named the year.'

She turned to find Calmet Dokteerak, who was to be her cousin's husband within a week, standing at her shoulder. He was as clearly Baltos – with his white hair and ice-blue eyes and flat face and short, stocky body – as Kait, tallish and slender and dark of hair, and eye, was Zaith. He didn't yet look like a toad, but Kait could see signs that he would one day. A perfect young copy of his father. Kait tried to imagine herself married to such a man to seal an alliance, and she had to swallow her revulsion. Thank all the gods that her branch of the Family lacked the status to make such marriages an issue.

She smiled. 'We're almost Family already. You wouldn't keep me in suspense, would you?'

He winked at her. 'I think I could be convinced to tell you . . . if you gave me a little kiss. Seeing as we are almost Family.'

Like father, like son. The other Kait, the dangerous Kait, stirred in her sleep, dreaming of the slaughter and destruction of men who deserved it. The Kait who had won her place as a diplomat, however, smiled broadly and said, 'I would have given you a kiss without the excuse. I think my cousin is a very lucky woman.' She leaned toward him and gave him a brief but passionate kiss on the lips.

He flushed an amazing shade of red and rewarded her with a smile that almost made him likeable. Almost, but not quite. 'The new carais is a pig farmer,' he said, staring down at the procession that wended its way ever closer. 'And she named the year *My Glorious, Enormously Fat Pig Abramaknar*.'

Kait's laugh was genuine. 'Oh, no! A pig year. That's embarrassing . . .' She flashed a wicked grin at him and said, 'But we had worse once.'

He had regained his composure. 'Do tell.'

'Four years ago a girl of fifteen became our carais. On the day she added her yearname to the lottery, she'd had a fight with her brother. Her name was so terrible our family parnissa said all the parnissas lobbied the oracle to see if they might discard the name and draw out another. But of course they couldn't.'

'Really. I've never heard of parnissas wanting to change a name before. What was it?'

'Now we just call the year *Miracle Sword*, but his full name was *My Shit-Breathed Brother Gamal's Penis, Which He Has Named Miracle Sword, and Which I Hope Turns Green and Falls Off Because Gamal Is an Asshole*.'

Calmet giggled and his ears turned red. 'I can see why they would want to change that – yes.'

'That isn't the worst of it. The parnissas had a terrible time deciding which god ruled over the year. They finally loaded him off on poor Brethwan in his dark aspect, and decided he was to be an ill-omened year. We were all glad when he passed, not least of all the carais. She got tired of being linked in everyone's mind with the omens and Brethwan-Dark and her brother's penis. Probably especially that last.'

'I should think so,' Calmet said vehemently. 'At least with a nice fat pig, you know the omens will be good.'

Below, the parnissas had finished their instructions to the new carais. Now the crowd began to chant, first softly, then louder and louder. Kait caught what they were saying and winced. They shouted, 'Bring them out! Bring them out!' Traditionally, on the day after Naming Day, the parnissas executed criminals in public as a symbolic sacrifice of evil, to destroy evil influences for the coming year. The sacrifices were real crowd-pleasers, too, as the increasingly wild calls below demonstrated. Kait hated them, and had almost always found reasons to avoid them. But she wouldn't be able to escape the spectacle this time; if Calmet hadn't been at her elbow, she might have managed to slip away unseen. The paraglese's son, however, showed no inclination to move on to other guests.

'We have some excellent sacrifices,' Calmet said.

In the street below, first one horse-drawn cage and then another rolled into view. The cheering grew louder.

'You have a lot of people in there.' Kait could make out at least ten in the first cage; the first blocked the second so she couldn't see how many it held, but she guessed it would carry roughly as many as the first – why crowd one cage and not the other? Her stomach knotted; she'd hated the sacrifices in Calimekka, but usually only one or two criminals were offered, and they had always done such evil things that Kait had to admit their deaths served justice. But twenty people . . . she didn't know how she could force herself to watch twenty people die, no matter what evils they had committed.

'This isn't many at all. Last year we did almost a hundred, most of them by drawing and quartering. The people would be disappointed by such meager entertainment if we didn't have something really special for them this year. You talk about good omens . . .' He shook his head, bemused. 'I didn't think we would ever find anything like this again. And after the slaughter in the Blamauk Quarter last night . . . but you wouldn't have heard anything about that . . .'

He didn't finish his thought. In the square below, a dozen mounted guardsmen in the blue and gold livery of the Dokteeraks rode out from their station at the base of the tower; their black stallions pranced to the blare of trumpets. The horses wore not saddles but gleaming black harnesses that looked like they had been designed for drawing the plows of the hells' damned. To either side of the twin line of horsemen marched armed pikemen in squares five wide and five deep. The people in the square cheered louder.

Kait thought about feigning a fainting spell; it wouldn't be that hard, and she would be able to escape the gruesome spectacle that was about to play out in front of her. But any action of that sort would draw attention to her – and the wrong sort of attention – and one thing Kait had learned early in her life was *never* to draw attention to herself. She would stand fast. She would witness the sacrifices. And she would remind herself that the time she stood pretending to be a part of the crowd atop the tower was time that her Family was using to plan the destruction of the traitorous Dokteeraks.

Below, a sudden gust of wind swirled down the street, blowing leaves and trash toward the tower, and several things happened at once. The guardsmen's horses reared and shied. Their unexpected movement threw several of the pikemen to the ground, causing localized uproars. And a familiar, terrifying scent, borne up to the top of the tower by the gust, reached Kait's nostrils. She froze.

'Who are your sacrifices?' she asked quietly, though she already knew – if not by name, then by ties that ran deeper than mere blood.

Calmet grinned at her. 'I can't spoil the surprise ... but this is going to be marvelous.'

It wasn't going to be marvelous; it was going to be worse than anything Kait had anticipated.

The Dokteerak guardsmen had gotten themselves in order and were awaiting the arrival of the cages. Conversation atop the tower had died; the representatives of both Families aligned themselves along the balustrade so that they could watch the proceedings. The exception was Kait's uncle Dùghall, who appeared suddenly at her left shoulder.

She looked at him hopefully. 'We have to leave?' she asked.

He shook his head. 'I thought I would watch the entertainment with my favorite niece.' He smiled when he said it, but she sensed, or maybe just smelled, warning in his demeanor.

She forced herself to smile back. 'You know your companionship always brings me pleasure.' She glanced over at Calmet and was startled to find him moving away from her. For just a moment, anyway, she and her uncle were far enough from the others on top of the tower to have privacy.

He turned and stared down at the crowd, to all appearances as enraptured by the unfolding spectacle as the rest of the Family spectators. In a voice so quiet that she could barely hear him with her own extraordinary ears (a voice which told her more than words ever could have how severely her secret had been compromised) he murmured, 'I heard from the elder Dokteerak what this is to be. And while I don't know what I *know* about you, Kait, I know what I *suspect*. We can't leave for any reason; our every move is being watched. Are you going to get through this?'

She followed his lead, pretending to focus on the three princes she'd pulled Tippa away from the night before; pikemen were binding their arms and legs, one limb per horse, to the modified harnesses the stallions wore. She said, 'I've spent a lifetime maintaining appearances. I'll do whatever I have to do.'

The screams and pleas for mercy from the three men echoed louder in the square than the jeers and shouts of the delighted crowd. The head parnissa stepped up on a dais and gave a signal, and the crowd fell silent. 'Paraglese,' he shouted, and his voice filled the square and boomed up to the tower, 'on this first true day of the year of *My Glorious, Enormously Fat Pig Abramaknar*, I ask you what you say to these men.'

The paraglese took a deep breath and shouted down to the crowd, 'I say these things. For treason against the Families of Ibera, conspiracy, plotting to harm Family members, and the breaking of sacred trusts with the gods who find favor in the rule of the Families, I declare guilty by means of confession the Gyru-nalle men who declare themselves princes, and who are named Erstisto Ghost-in-the-Road, Lataban Too-Long-to-Home, and Meeraklf Three-Tunes-Waiting, and sentence them to death.'

The parnissa shouted back, 'Do you offer mercy or pardon?' Kait thought if there was any hope of mercy or pardon, the men shouldn't have already been tied to the horses ... but the crowds, who wanted their spectacle, didn't seem bothered by any qualms about the fairness of the proceedings they witnessed. Immediately they began to shout, 'No mercy! No mercy!'

The paraglese raised his hands, and the crowd quieted. 'No mercy!' he shouted. The roar of approval from the mob covered the order that sent all twelve horses lunging in opposite directions.

Kait clamped her jaws so tight the muscles in her face ached; she stared with outward impassivity as all three men tore apart.

She became aware of a hand on her wrist, and glanced at her uncle to see her own anger mirrored in his eyes. Realizing that she wasn't the only one who did not revel in the public sacrifices lightened a burden in her that she didn't even realize she'd been carrying. In something, at least, she was not alone.

Servants were cutting loose the pieces of the three Gyru-nalles; the guardsmen, meanwhile, had gone to the second cage. From it they drew a lone boy. He was no older than five or six, and he was beautiful, with a sweetness and an innocence that seemed to radiate from him. His clothes marked him as a merchant's son, and suggested that his family was well off. His cleanliness and the care that had been taken with his grooming suggested, further, that he was well loved. He twisted toward the people in the second cage, and Kait could hear his thin, terrified wail of 'Maman! Papan!'

She swallowed hard, fighting back the tears that she could already taste. Several of the parnissas took the boy from the guardsmen and dragged him to the center of the dais. The head parnissa drew a great jeweled dagger from within the folds of his robe and shouted, 'Paraglese, behold the monster!' He slashed the dagger down one side of the child's face, and a red line gaped open in the blade's wake. But not for long. The child screamed, and Kait felt his terror as strongly as if it were her own. And she felt the response, too – the scream that became a growl, the pain that set free the red-eyed, always-waiting rage, the sense of power as blood began to sing and bones began to flow and re-form and skin and muscles leaped to the glorious promise of Shift.

Then fingernails dug hard into her wrist, and Dùghall's voice in her ear murmured, 'Steady, girl,' and Kait drew back from a brink she had not even known she'd stood upon. Thank one and all the gods that she had Shifted the night before, or not all the calming voices in the world could have kept her from betraying herself. As it was, the rage surged through her, refusing to be leashed, as she stared down at the beautiful little boy who was no longer a little boy. His own Shift had thrown him partway into the four-legged form the Karnee curse bestowed, but only partway. His captors must have kept him hurt enough and frightened enough that he would have spent much of his time in a state of Shift; by doing so, they exhausted the fuel that fed the fire of Shift. He was a small boy, but he would have been dangerous for them to handle in a fully Karnee state. Half-Shifted, unable to go either forward or back, he merely proved to the paraglese that he was what they said he was. A monster. A beast.

The crowd rippled with excitement. This was better than pulling thieves apart, more thrilling than bear-baiting; one of their respected neighbors had hidden a monster among them, and the monster had been revealed, and with it the dirty secrets of a family that had become criminal. The head parnissa shouted up to the paraglese, 'That child is Marshalis Silkman's son, and each Gaerwanday for his first five years, another child was presented in his place to the god Abjan and the parnissas, so that his monstrous nature might be hidden. Paraglese, on this first true day of the year of *My Glorious, Enormously Fat Pig Abramaknar*, I ask you what you say to the Silkman family.'

'I say these things. For the breaking of oaths and the hiding of monsters in our midst, for the deceiving of both gods and men, for the endangerment of the public good, and for conspiracy against the Families of Ibera and the people of Halles, I find guilty by means of physical proof the Silkman family, and sentence every living member of the family, by either birth or marriage, in all generations, to death.'

It was the sentence Kait had dreaded for her own family; not her Family, for the Galweighs as a whole were immune to summary justice, but her *family* – father, mother, sisters, and brothers – because no single branch of the Family was so valuable that it could not be cut off if doing so appeased a mob or maintained the power of the Family as a whole.

'Do you offer mercy or pardon?'

'The gods themselves have judged this beast and his family. There can be no mercy, and no pardon.'

The boy wept. The family begged the gods to intervene. The guardsmen bound the boy to the horses. The mob screamed its delight.

The horses leaped forward.

Chapter 9

Half a dozen young men leaned elegantly on pillars or draped themselves across the white stone benches that decorated the tavern courtyard. A single barmaid, her face flushed and her eyes worried, brought them trays of ale in flagons and platters of fried pork strips and fried bread, but her mind obviously wasn't on her customers, or on the sizable tip she might reasonably hope for; every time she heard cheering in the distance, she cringed. When she had delivered the last of the refreshments Ry Sabir had requested, she asked, 'Will you be needing me for anything else?' She was a typical peasant, her mind on the religious festivities she was missing.

Several of the men laughed coarse laughs, but Ry silenced them with a wave of his hand. 'No. Go. Enjoy your festival. Give my regards to the gods,' he added as she slipped through the arches of the breezeway and vanished.

'We could have had fun with her.' The man who spoke wore two vertical scars on his cheeks like badges of honor. His shirt, of the sheerest and most expensive red silk, was so transparent it served only to emphasize the powerful, lean lines of the torso beneath; his leather pants, oiled to a shine, limned the rest of him in equally sharp detail. His black slouch boots and wide-brimmed scarlet velvet hat and the careful weaving of cloth-of-gold ribbons through his long blond braids declared him a dandy, but only a fool would mistake him for a weak one. His name was Yanth, and he was rich, and a member of one of the cadet branches of the Sabir Family, and for most of his life he had been Ry's best friend and closest ally.

Ry shrugged. He was so tired he ached, and was still starved and testy as he always got after a Shift. If it hadn't been for the festival, he would have spent the day in bed, demanding the servants bring him food. But the festival gave him the chance to speak alone to his lieutenants, away from the Sabir Embassy and *also* away from any spies that might listen in a place like the pleasant outer courtyard of this small public tavern and inn. 'True. But then we wouldn't have been alone.'

'What fun is being alone? You have something better for us than a pretty girl?'

'I need your help.'

Ry's five lieutenants glanced at each other with expressions that ranged from curiosity to surprise to caution.

'You know you have it without asking,' brown-haired, green-eyed Valard said.

'Not this time. What I want goes against the Family's orders. You have to decide whether you'll help me or not; I'm not going to tell you that you owe me this, because this could break me with all of them, and maybe you, too.'

Now he could tell they were really curious. He'd never gone against anything his Family told him to do, and they knew it.

Yanth stopped leaning against the pillar trying to look like life bored him, and sat on one of the stone benches. Just sat; didn't drape himself, didn't worry about present-ing his best profile to the passageway in case some lovely young thing might come in. He leaned forward, elbows on thighs, frowning. 'I can't speak for them, but I'm still with you. Not because I owe you, even though I know I do. Because you're my friend.'

Valard nodded. 'Same for me. You lead, I'll follow. Doesn't matter where or why.'

Broad-faced, pale Trev spoke up. 'I suppose I want to know that we aren't talking about an overthrow first. I can't put my family at risk with something like that.' Trev had two younger sisters for whom he would have moved the world. And while Ry knew that in all other ways he was as loyal and as devoted as either Valard or Yanth, he also knew that Trev would never do anything that would put his sisters into the slightest disfavor. He was of a lesser family, and hoped to see them both marry well.

'Not treason,' Ry said. 'But not something that will make you beloved in the House, if your role in it should be discovered.'

Karyl, Ry's cousin and older than all the rest of them by a few years, gave Ry a thoughtful look. 'If you're about to do something stupid, I suppose I ought to be along, if for no other reason than to pick up the pieces and return them to your mother when the worst happens. So count me in.'

Ry laughed. Leave it to Karyl to maintain the darkest possible perspective.

He turned to Jaim, who had said nothing so far. That was typical of Jaim – slow to commit, but even slower to concede defeat once he had committed. Ry felt if he could enlist Jaim's assistance, he would guarantee his own success. 'How about you?'

Jaim smiled his slow smile. 'I want to know what we're going to do before I say yea or nay.'

Ry chuckled. So typical of Jaim. He was their voice of reason, the one who advised caution, the one who always saw weaknesses in plans before anyone else, and who usually already knew how to find a solution before anyone else had defined the problem. Ry *wanted* Jaim with him.

'I'm going to steal a girl that the Family wants killed.'

Now the eyebrows did go up. 'A girl? Whatever for? The Family is always throwing them at you, and you *never* want to catch,' Karyl said.

'This one is special.'

'She'd have to be. You've refused most of the beauties in Calimekka.'

Yanth was grinning. 'We do have to wonder what makes her so special.'

And that was the question Ry couldn't honestly answer – not because he couldn't trust these five friends with the truth, but because he didn't know what the truth was. How did he explain to them that the Galweigh woman he had met the night before had moved into his mind, and that even though she was nowhere near him, he could still feel the heat of her body pressed against his as they ran together after the fight; how could he admit that his thoughts were no longer his own? How could he make them understand that somehow he sensed where she was if he closed his eyes and thought about her; that he could feel her anger at that moment at some injustice which, in ways he couldn't quite fathom, was linked both to her and to him? He sighed. 'She's . . . like me. And she's Galweigh, which is why they won't let me have her. And it's why they want her dead.'

Now they were frowning at him, not so amused by the idea of his risking his relationship with the Family over a woman. Yanth said, 'Like you in what way? Reckless? Bull-headed? Stubborn?'

'Karnee,' Ry said.

The silence that followed that blunt reply stretched, while Ry's lieutenants stared at each other. It kept on stretching, as one by one they turned from each other to look at him.

'Karnee,' Yanth whispered.

The silence fell again.

Finally, Jaim sighed. 'It won't be like catching a normal girl. If we do anything wrong, she'll destroy us. I'd hate to stand against you with a dozen armed men; I don't imagine she will be much weaker. Considering that she's survived this long.' He sucked in a breath, then blew it out. 'One moment of carelessness is all it will take . . .' He looked down at his hands. 'And I'm guessing that you mean to grab her when we take Galweigh House.'

Ry nodded. 'I thought that in the confusion we would have the best chance to get her out without anyone realizing what we were doing. I can't steal her before then without risking the Family's plan to take the House, and if I wait and try to find her after, she's likely to be dead.'

Yanth said, 'So we're going into the House during the invasion, just as we'd planned, but instead of rounding up the Galweighs and taking them prisoner, we're going to search through that whole enormous place for one woman.'

'Right.'

'One woman who knows the lay of the House, who isn't going to want to come with us, and who just happens to be one of the more efficient killing nightmares we're ever likely to meet.'

'Right.'

Yanth nodded. 'I only wanted to be sure I understood.'

Jaim sighed. 'Well, put that way, I don't see any way that I can refuse. Without my planning, none of you will live past the first rush. So I'm in, too.'

Everyone laughed. Laughing came easy, Ry thought, when all the danger and all the trouble lay in the future, when the six of them had nothing to do but drink and eat in the pleasant shade of the palm trees, with the sweet scents of jasmine and roses in the air. But all five of his friends had just volunteered to die for him, if dying was called for, and he couldn't allow himself to forget that, or to overlook how much it meant.

'She's staying at the Galweigh Embassy right now. They'll move her back to Calimekka before the wedding, of course, along with all the rest of the noncombatants. Before then, we have to find out who she is.'

Yanth groaned. 'You don't know her name?'

Jaim sighed. 'And if we don't know her name, how are we to find her?'

'I'll show you what she looks like.' Ry was nervous about doing so – the showing was only a small magic, and nondestructive, but until now, not even his best friends knew of his involvement with magic. They knew of his Karnee curse; he'd Shifted in order to save Yanth's life once, when both of them had been younger, and reckless, and woefully outnumbered. The magic, though, he'd kept hidden, afraid that there were some heresies so grave that not even best friends would forgive them.

Which only proved to him how mad he had become. He was going to betray the one secret about himself that he had kept hidden at all costs, and he was going to do it to try to save the life of a woman who had been born his enemy. Who was still his enemy. A woman he had every reason to hate.

Why didn't he hate her?

He wished he knew.

He sprinkled caberra powder on the ground in a circle, and his friends all stared, bewildered. He murmured his incantation, and sliced the palm of his left hand with his dagger, and dripped the blood into a tiny circle within the circle. He called on the link he felt inside of himself, and summoned the only image of her that he had – bleeding and half-exhausted and covered with blood, still in her Karnee form. He closed his eyes and drew the image close, recalling as he did her scent, the sound of her voice, and the incredible, impossible way her mere presence made him feel. He did not call last night's image into the circle – instead, he called on the inexplicable bond he felt between the two of them, and focused on her as she was at that moment.

He heard a gasp, and opened his eyes, and drank her in. She stood in the center of the circle he'd cast, staring at something in front of her while she leaned against the parapet of the tower in the center of Halles; the black carved stone monster glowering just beneath her was unmistakable. Her straight black hair blew like a silk pennant behind her. She wore a deep blue silk gown, elegantly cut in the Calimekkan style that had not yet come to backwater cities like Halles. She looked the highborn and delicate daughter of power; she did not look like a woman who had killed an alleyful of murderers and thugs the night before. In his first glimpse at her in her human form, he fell more completely under her spell. He knew he had to have her, or die trying. She was exquisite, beautiful . . . forbidden. But not so forbidden as the manner in which he had conjured her image.

His friends – his lieutenants – seemed frozen in time; silent as ice statues, they stared at the shimmering image, their eyes huge and shocked. Slowly, one by one, they pulled their gazes away from the bewitching, ephemeral, softly glowing image of the woman and looked to him. Ry looked for their rage or for signs of betrayal, but instead he saw only wonder.

'How . . .?' Yanth whispered.

For the longest time, none of the other four said a word. Then Jaim added, 'I don't care how. Could you teach me?'

That broke a dam, and his friends' words rushed out. They wanted him to do more magic; they wanted him to show them how to do what he knew; they wanted to be a part of this beautiful, forbidden world that he had revealed to them; and they didn't care that the knowledge he had was knowledge men had died to rediscover, or that it had been lost for a very good reason, or that they would be executed in the public square if they were ever caught. They didn't intend to get caught, and in the meantime the wonder of it held their imaginations and promised them secrets and a world beyond the everyday. They wanted that world. And they were willing to overlook any sin, any crime, were willing to promise almost anything, to gain access to the door that would take them there.

'We'll help you get the woman,' Yanth said, summing up for all of them. 'But promise that you'll teach us magic in return. As a favor to your loyal friends and your unquestioning allies, just give us that boon.'

For what they were offering to him – their lives, their honor – he had to offer suitable recompense. He had thought of land and additional titles . . . but they had the right to request the favor they wanted most. And he would not refuse them. He agreed.

* * *

'I didn't think I was going to make it through that.' Kait paced from one end of the narrow library to the other. Numb and sickened and still enraged, she fought the demon inside her that begged for a chance – just one chance – to destroy the monsters who had ordered that nightmare slaughter of innocents.

All through the ceremony, Dùghall had said nothing. He'd stayed by her side and headed off anyone who seemed to want to talk with her, though he didn't seem to be doing anything at all; he'd kept her calm and he'd gotten her and Tippa back to the Galweigh Embassy at the earliest possible opportunity. When he brought her to the library alone, though, Kait knew he wanted to talk. 'You did make it through,' Dùghall said. 'Now you have to let it go. You still have a part to play, and the Family needs you to play it without stumbling. Especially ...' He stepped into her path and brought her to a standstill, and stared into her eyes. '*Especially* since your information checked out exactly. The Dokteeraks and the Sabirs are plotting against us, exactly as you told me. You have certain ... talents, should I say? ... Yes, talents ... that make you irreplaceable to your Family.'

Kait held her breath, then released it slowly. 'You need to know what I am, Uncle.'

'I've figured it out – at least I think I've figured out some of the difference in you. Sooner or later, perhaps a few others of the Family will need to know. But you need not think your differences make you anything but an asset to us. You're a gift, Kait. You're beautiful, you're intelligent, you're charming, you're educated ... and your special talents allow you to do things other people can't.' He patted her arm. 'You were a marvelous child – never afraid of anything. You're becoming a magnificent young woman. But more than that, you can become a weapon for the Galweighs unparalleled by anything the other Families can bring to bear against us.'

Kait raised her eyebrows, thinking of the Sabir Karnee. If Dùghall didn't know he existed, he didn't realize exactly what the Galweighs were up against. 'That's all I want. It's all I have ever wanted – to serve my Family. I want to do anything I can to protect them from their enemies. To repay them for protecting me, and giving me the chance to take a place among them.' She paused and looked beseechingly at Dùghall. 'But maybe I don't have the right to risk Maman and Papan by staying with the service,' she said. 'Maybe I don't have the right to serve, because more people than I will pay the price if I fail.'

'Sit.' Dùghall pointed to the high-backed carved chair nestled into the corner beneath one of the library's leaded glass windows. He settled himself into its twin, and only when Kait was seated said, 'You serve the Family; that is duty. You do so without endangering the lives of *your* family; that is both obligation and act of love. But the needs of *the* Family must come first, Kait-cha. I have lived by this dictum, as you must: "You are born to greatness, but greatness must be re-earned in every generation. Your life —"'

Kait cut him off. '"— is an extension of the lives of my ancestors, and a bridge to the future, and as such my life can never be wholly my own, for my every action reaps yesterday's fruit and sows tomorrow's seeds."' She quoted Habath solemnly. 'I *know* my duty.'

'Then no more uncertainty about whether you do right to serve. You have been chosen; you must serve.'

'My comment is that I was not chosen by those who knew the truth about me; I question that I would have been asked to serve if the truth were known.'

'And that you reached adulthood alive so that you could be chosen, what of that? I do not question too closely the value of miracles — the gods guide our feet down mysterious paths; I chose you, but I think now that my choice was better than I had previously thought, rather than worse. No matter what anyone else might think. I'll keep your secret to myself for now; I don't trust everyone in the Family to know a boon when one is given.'

Kait laughed at that. 'I don't trust *anyone* in the Family to keep me from the horses in the square, to tell you the truth. Except my family and you.'

'Nor should you. Remain circumspect, and I'll make sure that you receive assignments suited to your peculiar talents.' He leaned back and laced his fingers together. 'And speaking of your talents . . . what are they, exactly?

I've already figured out that your hearing is better than mine, and I know that you can climb sheer walls that I would have thought impossible to breach without hammers and pitons. But why can you do these things?'

Kait said, 'I'm Karnee.'

Dùghall looked at her thoughtfully for a moment, and let out a slow breath. 'I thought that might be it. For that reason I warned you of the boy they executed today – I'd heard ... rumors ... before we left the embassy that such a creature had run wild last night and had been apprehended in the early hours. I doubt the boy was the cause of those deaths in the alley.' He arched a thoughtful eyebrow in her direction. 'So the Family curse has not yet abated.'

'I would seem to be proof that it hasn't.'

'To what degree are you affected? Improved hearing, improved sight, increased lust and vigor, added strength?'

Kait's laugh this time had no humor in it. 'All of those benign things, and all of the foul ones as well. I'm fully Karnee, like the child who died in the street today. I Shift when I'm angry or overcome by other emotion, or when I've gone too long without Shifting; I'm both woman and monster in one body, and the part of me that knows joy and pleasure without regret is not the woman, but the monster. When I'm Karnee, my blood sings out for other blood, and for the hunt, and for rutting, and I'm without mercy, and without remorse.'

'There are times, child, when both mercy and remorse are curses, too.'

Kait frowned. 'Maybe so. But the human part of me carries the remorse for both parts – and seems to carry it in double measure.'

Dùghall nodded and leaned back in the chair, and templed his fingers in front of him. '"In order to live with ourselves, we accommodate who we are with who we wish to be. If we are to know happiness in this short life, we do it without lying to ourselves, and we remember to be kind." Vincalis again. I really must find you a copy of *To Serve Honorably* when we get back to the House. It and the Secret Texts will be essential to you. Simply essential.'

Kait said, 'I'll read both if they'll help me serve the Family better.'

'They'll help. Of course if you really want to serve the Family, find the Mirror of Souls for us.' He laughed when he said it.

Kait didn't get the joke. 'The Mirror of Souls? What's that?'

'A myth, I think,' Dùghall told her. 'We've found several references to it now in the oldest books we have, and of course the Secret Texts speak of it.' He sighed. 'Supposedly, it's the greatest artifact of the Ancients. From the best translations we've obtained, it seems to have been a device that called the dead back from the grave and returned them to the world of the living. Imagine being able to bring back to life all of our dead relatives.' He shook his head, bemusement clear on his face. 'We could overrun the Sabirs and Dokteeraks and Masschankas and Kairns in days and take control of Ibera. And that would be the end of the wars and the slaughter and the struggle.'

'You sound like you think such a device might exist.'

'Do I? Forgive an old man's wistfulness. I *wish* such a device existed – if the Galweighs alone could obtain it, of course. But in spite of the several references to it in the ancient literature, I believe that, had it ever existed, it has long since vanished from the face of the earth. And I number myself among the cynics, for I don't believe it ever existed. Such magic would be . . .'

He sat forward and smiled. 'Forget my musings, Kait. How childish of me to fill your head with the fancies of the Ancients. You don't need any such silliness. Concentrate on keeping Tippa out of trouble, and make sure she doesn't suspect the Dokteeraks' treachery, or she'll give us all away. She's a sweet child, but far too naive.'

'I'll make sure she thinks everything is still fine. How long will I have to keep up the pretense?'

Dùghall's grin was predatory. 'You and I and Tippa will be leaving for Calimekka by airible four days from now, at predawn.'

'That's the day of the wedding.'

'Yes.'

'What about everyone else?'

'Most of them will be gone by tomorrow. The last few will leave the day after.'

Kait winced. 'The Dokteeraks will notice.'

Dùghall laughed. 'That's the beauty of this. The airibles have been bringing in a steady stream of "wedding guests" since we got word home yesterday . . . but they aren't truly wedding guests, of course. They're soldiers in wedding dress, many of them disguised as women to make up for the few swordswomen and female archers we have. And the embassy staff has been traveling back in the supposedly empty airibles, disguised as ballast. The three of us can't leave until the last minute because Tippa and that rodent Calmet have the sunset purification ritual the night before the wedding, and I have to stand witness, and you're to chaperone again. But we'll have an airible waiting for us when we return to the embassy, and veiled soldiers will attend the wedding in your stead, and my replacement shall wear a hood.'

Kait smiled, and for the first time that day the smile felt genuine. 'Then the wedding won't be what the Dokteeraks are expecting.'

'Far from it. When it's over, the Galweighs will be the only ones celebrating.'

Chapter 10

His horse – well, even in the most liberal terms he couldn't truly call it his horse, but it was the horse he had stolen – stood in the makeshift paddock with the Gyrus' other beasts, contentedly munching on hay. He recognized both the animal's speckled hide and the curving brand on its right flank . . . and he thought, too, that he recognized the vindictive gleam in its eye. Hasmal saw the animal when his guard took him down to the stream to wash himself; the Gyrus kept the horses both downhill and downstream, by which they showed more concern for sanitation than the designers of the city he'd lived in. He didn't give any sign to the guard that he recognized the beast; reticence seemed the best course of action to him. But inwardly, he was elated. If the Gyrus had found his horse, perhaps his belongings were somewhere in the camp, too. Perhaps he could find a way to recover them.

The Gyru camp covered the north slope of the low hill it occupied, from the long crest down to the stream that meandered through the trees in the valley. Hasmal guessed more than a hundred of the Gyru wagons sat there, though he couldn't be sure, because the forest was thick enough that as he got a clear view of some of the wagons, others disappeared, and the wagons themselves, beautifully painted with scenes of forests and meadows, had the unnerving tendency to blend in with their surroundings. Still, he had a rough count, which was good enough to tell him that the Gyrus outnumbered him by at barest minimum fifty adults – so he could give up any plans of overpowering guards and fleeing.

Too, he knew his strengths, and he knew his weaknesses, and he considered himself intelligent enough not to mistake one for the other. Born a city boy, raised in civilization – where water came to his home via the aqueduct and where people cooked food indoors in fine brick ovens, and where they washed in public baths instead of a river – he did not think for an instant that he would be able to escape through the forest, eluding his pursuers and surviving the dangers of the wild. The wilderness was not his strength.

Guile and caution were, though, and with guile and caution, he would get himself out of his mess.

His guard didn't seem impatient with the time Hasmal was taking with his bath. He sat on a fallen tree and grinned, his crossbow steady on Hasmal's chest. The crossbow made Hasmal nervous; nevertheless, the guard had treated Hasmal well, made sure he got plenty of food, and let him walk around the thorny underbrush instead of pushing him through it. Since Hasmal still didn't have any clothes, that last consideration meant a great deal to him.

'Kind of you not to mind my taking the time to get clean,' Hasmal said in Iberan. He and the guard were playing out an elaborate game, in which the guard pretended not to understand a word of Iberan, and he pretended he'd never run into Shombe. They pantomimed when they wished to communicate, and spoke into the air in asides to the gods at other times, each attempting to get the other to be the first to reveal secrets.

Hasmal scrubbed with the soap the guard had given him, appreciating the lather on his skin as much as he appreciated the feel of running water on all those places yesterday's horseback ordeal had left aching. 'Those bastards who grabbed me yesterday dragged me through every patch of filth and thicket they could find between the road and the place where they met you folks.'

The guard kept grinning; he made no sign that he understood a word that Hasmal said.

Hasmal relaxed into the water. It wasn't as clear as aqueduct water; and it was colder, but at the moment it felt good enough. 'I don't imagine you have any idea what it feels like to be sold,' Hasmal continued. 'To be a free man running away from omens that spell your death, and to be captured by thieves, and to have them decide to hang you because you don't have anything to steal, and to have them decide, when the rope is already around your neck, to sell you into slavery instead so they can make some profit off of you.' He shook his head, ducked completely under the surface of the water long enough to thoroughly wet his hair, and came up to begin lathering. 'The bastards stole my clothes and left me naked, too. Didn't even throw me a few rags so I could cover myself. Still . . . being a naked slave is better than being a dead freeman.' He finished lathering, rinsed, and stood.

His guard, still grinning, threw him a towel so coarse and crude that in the bathhouses of Halles, it would have been used for nothing more lofty than knocking the dirt off shoes. Hasmal wasn't sure whether he was supposed to dry himself off with it or wrap it round his waist, and decided, since his guard offered neither suggestion nor pantomime, to do both. The women in the camp had gotten a few giggles out of his nakedness when he'd paraded by them on his way down to the stream; if he could skip a repeat of that experience on the way back, he thought he would.

'I'd give anything to get my things back and get out of here,' Hasmal said. The guard pointed up the hill. Hasmal started walking. The rough forest floor hurt his feet, but he felt almost cheerful after the bath and with the towel to keep him from being completely naked. 'You'd probably want me gone, too, if you knew the sort of trouble I'm likely to become. I'm under a curse – a doom tied to some Galweigh woman. I want to put as much distance as I can between the two of us, before something terrible happens. It's sure to happen to me, but the oracle didn't say there wouldn't be trouble for anyone around me.'

The guard led him back to the tent where he'd been kept. He left the towel – something good – and didn't put Hasmal's hands back into the stocks in which he'd had to sleep. Something else good. He did still put the metal ring around his neck, and he did attach it to the chain that attached to the stone ball that rested in the center of the tent. Hasmal didn't fight this indignity any more than he had fought any other. He let happen what was going to happen, and then he settled in to wait. He was good at waiting.

The sun followed more than half its path across the sky, and the noises in camp changed in character and volume. Hasmal heard shouting and the stamping of horses and creak of wagons, and he wished he could see what was going on. Finally someone came back into the tent, but she wasn't his guard. She was a woman of, he guessed, middle years, though she had aged extraordinarily well. She dressed in loose leather pants and a gaudy silk shirt, the costume favored by Gyru women, and she wore a heavy gold torque around her neck and rows of gold beads in her braided hair. In her youth she had been, he had no doubt, a stunning beauty, and even though time had added lines to her face, and streaks of gray to her fiery hair, it had not been able to erase her loveliness. All it had done was add character – something he always found lacking in the faces of women his own age. He smiled at her out of reflex. She was the sort of woman who would have caught his eye in any circumstances, and these difficult times made no exception.

She studied him, thoughtful. He continued to wait, sensing in her presence the shifting of his fate. Finally, she said, 'You're a strange sort of slave. You haven't begged for your freedom, yet you claim to be a freeman; you have not threatened us with doom if we do not release you, yet you claim to be under a curse. You haven't tried to reclaim your horse or your belongings, yet Ffaunaban says you saw your horse tethered among ours.'

'So Ffaunaban does speak Iberan.'

'As well as you speak Shombe, unless I miss my guess. We told him to find out what he could about you. You were most obliging. And, I might add, most unlike our usual slaves.'

Hasmal smiled but said nothing. Politeness, gratitude for kindnesses done, and a bit of information dropped in the right ears at the right time never failed to yield action. He could only hope that it was the right sort of action.

The woman waited, too, as if expecting him to say more – perhaps to protest his status as slave, or to ask if he could have his belongings back. When he remained silent, she rewarded him with a brilliant smile of her own and arched an eyebrow.

'Excellent,' she said. 'You honor yourself with your silence.' Then she said something that shocked him to his core. '*Katarre kaithe gombrey; hai allu neesh?*'

They were the words of greeting used among the Falcons; words from a language mostly lost in the destroying tempest of time, but kept alive by the brethren sworn to uphold the secrets of the past and to work toward the prophecies that would better all of human-kind's lot. His father had taught him that they meant 'The falcon offers its wings; will you fly?'

He responded as his father had taught him. '*Alla*

126

menches, na gombrey ambi kaitha chamm. I accept, and for the falcon's wings I offer my heart.'

'Well met, brother,' she said. She leaned over him and unlocked the ring that bound him to the stone. Her heavy braids brushed against his naked shoulders, and her sweet, faintly musky scent filled his nostrils, and he was suddenly more grateful than words could express for the coarse towel still wrapped around his waist. 'We have things we must discuss. Please come with me.'

As quickly as that, he found himself a guest of the Gyru-nalles instead of a slave. She led him out of the tent, and he saw that the wagons were lined up, and that people were tying spare horses to the backs of the wagons, and that outriders already moved along the enormous train, shouting orders.

She showed him into a beautifully painted wagon which she identified as her personal residence. A driver already sat on the high crossplank, reins in hand. She waved to him and shouted something in Shombe, then ushered Hasmal into her home on wheels.

He was immediately enchanted. He had never seen the inside of a Gyru wagon before, and he hadn't imagined how delightful such a tiny space could be. The structure formed a single room, with a stone-polished, close-planked wood floor and a painted wood ceiling high enough to permit him to stand upright easily. A padded bench seat ran along one wall below a genuine glass window, and along the other wall were a pantry, a built-in floor-to-ceiling bank of drawers, and between them another window and an area for food preparation. The front of the cabin was given over to a deep closet with a ladder that ran up one side to a loft, which a thick down mattress and several cushions completely filled.

She had everything anyone really needed, he thought, and she took it with her everywhere she went. For a moment, he was envious.

Then she moved one of the cushions on the long bench seat, and lifted the hinged lid of the compartment beneath. From the storage space, she pulled out a pair of worn, dark green leather pants and a dove-gray silk shirt. She tossed them to him, and he put them on, conscious that she was watching him. They didn't fit him too badly, considering that Gyru men were, on average, tall and lean, and he was short and muscular. The clothing was very fine – better than what had been stolen from him the day before.

'Whose are these?'

'Yours, now. They once belonged to a . . . friend . . . but he has since moved on.'

'Thank you, then . . .' He paused. He didn't know her name. '. . . Lady.'

'Never a lady,' she said with a chuckle, 'though always a woman. You may call me Alarista.'

Which wasn't her name, he knew. Gyrus never gave anyone their real names – they felt possession of the real name gave one access to the soul. He nodded. 'Alarista. You may call me Chobe.' That had been his nickname as a child, and would not cause him to commit the social error of forcing his real name on her, thus making her partly responsible for his soul whether she wanted to be or not.

When he'd dressed, she sat him down and offered him a drink she called *kemish*, which she told him was made from the seeds and fruit of the cocova plant, and from red peppers and ground dried fish, and which tasted bitter and spicy and fishy – it was the most noxious thing he had, in fact, ever been asked to drink. His people made confections from ground cocova and honey that were sweet and smooth and marvelous; he'd never imagined anyone would find a way to make cocova taste terrible. Still, he was a guest, and more importantly, the guest of a fellow Falcon, and as a guest he swallowed the noxious stuff and smiled and pretended he loved it.

When they'd finished their drinks, she finally got to what was on her mind.

'When you told Ffaunaban about the curse you were under, I told him that was nonsense, and that you were just trying to tell him something that would frighten him into letting you escape. But I couldn't permit such an assertion to go unverified.' She smiled at him.

'Of course not.' He waited without adding anything about the curse, because she was going somewhere with this, and anything he added would only take away from the information she gave him.

'I did a divination. What I saw was . . . frightening.'

He kept waiting. Maybe she knew more than he did. Maybe she would tell him what she'd found.

She sighed. 'We can't keep you with us, as much as I would like to; I've never had the opportunity to meet a Falcon from outside of my own people. But the doom you carry on you will, according to my divination, swallow us in order to reach you.' She sat looking at him, her hands folded primly in her lap, her head held high. 'We have always made a point to offer sanctuary to those oppressed by the forces in power. But the forces that want you . . .' She shrugged delicately. 'Not even I could suggest that my people stand between you and the gods.'

He hoped she would say more, perhaps tell him specific details of the doom her divination had foretold, and why it had fallen on him. But she had taken his route of silence; she watched him, and now she waited.

'Then you intend to release me? To set me free?'

'In a fashion. We've sent pigeons to our agent in Costan Selvira, and passage has been arranged for you aboard a ship. We're breaking camp now – we're going to take you there, give you back your belongings, see you aboard the ship, and watch until it leaves the harbor.

Once we're certain that we have sufficient distance between you and us, you may do whatever you wish; until the time that your ship leaves harbor, however, either a guard or I will accompany you.'

'Then I'm a prisoner.'

Her laugh was as lovely as her smile. 'Well, you aren't a slave any longer, and I'd rather you considered yourself my personal guest, but if you decided to try to . . . ah, escape my hospitality before you sailed with your ship' – she shrugged again, a movement that he noticed did interesting things to her breasts – 'my people would be forced to shoot you before you ran ten steps.'

'Why? Why not just return my horse and my things to me and let me leave?'

Her laugh this time was heartier than before, and the corners of her eyes crinkled with merriment. 'Because – and you will pardon my frankness, please – I don't think you have either the sense or the skills to get yourself as far away from my people as I want you to be. You apparently have neither the ability to ride a horse nor the woodsense to know when you're riding into an ambush, and I think, for all your intelligence and whatever skills you do possess, that you'd end up someone else's captive before you'd gone a furlong.' She leaned forward, and her silk shirt gapped enchantingly over her bosom, affording him a clear view of her right breast and most of the left one.

Hasmal was having a hard time feeling indignant.

'So you are going to make sure I end up a long way from here.'

'As far as the sea and the ship will take you.'

'I suppose I can't complain. I'd planned to do something similar; as long as I leave my doom behind, I'll be content.'

She hadn't moved, and he became aware that he'd been talking to her chest. He flushed, looked into her eyes, and

realized that she knew exactly what he'd been looking at
. . . and that she seemed amused by his scrutiny. He
stared down at his hands, feeling like an oaf and an idiot,
and to change the subject, asked, 'What am I to do in the
meantime?'

She didn't answer him. After a moment he looked up
to find an enigmatic half-smile on her lips and a
smoldering look in her eyes. Her voice dropped to a low,
husky purr, and she said, 'I imagine we can think of
something.'

Chapter 11

Kait walked down Freshspring Street with Tippa at her side and a retinue of soldiers disguised as servants and minor functionaries at her back. They were ostensibly on a mission to buy additional silks and glassware for Tippa's trousseau, but in fact were simply out to be seen, to convince the Dokteeraks and the Sabirs that the Galweigh Family suspected nothing and would walk into the wedding trap when the bells rang in the station of Soma the next day.

Tippa, poor dim child, still suspected nothing. She'd been told that her parents and the other notable members of the Family would be arriving by airible that night, after the dedication service, and that those who had arrived so far were simply distant relatives from Goft and the colonies. She accepted the whole tale as sacred writ, and tried to spend time meeting these 'relatives,' much to everyone's chagrin. So Kait got the twofold job of keeping her out in the public eye and away from the newly arrived soldiers, who needed the time to finish going over strategy.

Thus this buying expedition, which had resulted in the purchase of five bales of sapphire-blue silk, and the order of a hundred ruby-red spun-glass goblets at a price Kait couldn't begin to believe, and the acquisition of a set of silver decanters shaped like leopard cubs that Tippa declared 'precious' and that Kait found ridiculous. Thus, also, Kait acquired a blinding headache that came partly from trying to push away the incessant pounding waves of evil that had grown worse instead of better since the night of the Naming Day party. In part, however, she thought the headache had to be from hunger; she'd had only a light morning meal, and that had been at sunrise. Already the Invocation to Mosst was ringing through the streets, and the sun, directly overhead, beat down on her.

The fragrant smells of meat and bread and pies and a multitude of other delicacies filled Freshspring Street from one end to the other; the silk houses and metal changers and craftsmen's shops shared the narrow street with bakeries and fish houses and mead brewers – and Kait, smelling the various offerings, thought that if she didn't get something to eat soon, she would go mad.

'Wouldn't you like a pie?' she asked Tippa, who had already turned her nose up at python-on-a-stick, and whole roasted parrots beautifully braised in their own juices and stuffed with corn and sweet yams, and a peccary stew that had smelled like heaven to Kait.

Now Tippa sighed that pained sigh of hers that indicated she thought herself surrounded by idiots. 'Cousin, don't you see? I can't eat food from these places. I'm to be an adrata in this city, and I may someday be paraglesa. You should know that I can't allow myself to eat street food like a commoner.'

Kait, eyeing a beautiful rolled-crust mango pie that sat on the counter of one of those common cookeries, was not about to be put off yet again, and for no better reason than that eating common food was below the station that her cousin wasn't going to attain anyway. So she said, 'One of the things I've learned in the diplomatic corps is that if you would be truly beloved by all the people, you must find ways to make them believe you care about

133

them. And what better way to begin showing that you care than by sharing their food without shame?'

Tippa frowned down at her feet, and Kait could see her lips moving. Finally she looked up. 'You're certain that eating the street food won't make us seem . . . base-born?'

Kait schooled her face to sincerity. 'I'm positive.'

A pause. Another sigh. Then, 'Very well. We'll all eat. I was a bit hungry.'

So they waited in line behind the workingmen and the merchants and the salesgirls, and they bought two of those beautiful pies, and the soldiers got themselves pastries. Then they visited another shop, where they ate stuffed parrots. After that, a meadery, where they indulged in strong red mead served in containers made of the leaves of bassos trees, curled and sealed with wax to form hollow cones. Kait thought the idea of disposable cups wonderfully clever – it was the first thing she'd seen in all of Halles that had genuinely impressed her. Finally, just before they reached the last silk shop on the street, they stopped at an icery.

The shopkeeper bowed graciously and asked them what they would have. Ice was even rarer in Halles than it was in Calimekka, because it had to be brought in not only from the mountains, but overland as well, and the prices marked on the man's board were astronomical. Still, the heat of midday made frozen confections irresistible to both women – and Kait, in a moment of largesse, bought her cousin and herself plus all of the mock functionaries and mock servants little bowls of shaved ice flavored with fruit juices and honey. They stood against the building savoring these treats and trying to stay out of the sun when Kait suddenly became aware that she was being watched. She stiffened slightly but managed to avoid giving any outward sign that she knew what was happening – she and Tippa were supposed to be drawing attention, of course, but this was different.

He was somewhere in the crowd. The other Karnee. The one she had met and wanted.

She had been at least slightly aware of him since the moment they had parted. She could tell through stone walls when he paced outside the embassy, hoping for a glimpse of her. She could feel her heart begin to race sometimes in the middle of the night in acknowledgment of nothing more than his existence. She felt herself drawn to him, as if he were a lodestone and she were iron; something beyond her reach and her understanding made her desire him even though she knew that her desires were a betrayal of her Family's well-being. He was a hunger that she dared not confess and dared not sate; he was both potion and poison, and even the contemplation of indulging her craving felt as compelling and as unforgivable as Shift.

Now he was close to her – not within smelling distance, or perhaps just downwind – but close enough that she could feel this other hunger building inside of her like a madness. Animal passion, she told herself. Karnee lust, the weakness of your inhuman other self. Don't give in to beast behavior.

The lust raged unabated.

And for the thousandth time since the night of the party, she thought of Hasmal son of Hasmal, and of the wall of peace that he carried with him. For the thousandth time, she chafed at the presence of the inescapable others; she had never had time during the daylight hours to make good on her promise to find him. She suspected her uncle's design in that fact, and not just bad luck – though Dùghall had not asked her what else had happened before she arrived at the embassy and climbed the wall that night, she thought he suspected more went on than she'd admitted. And he seemed determined to have her observed to ensure that nothing else happened without his knowledge.

Now, though, with Tippa and the soldiers with her, Kait wondered if she might suggest a side trip to Stonecutter Street, to Hasmal's Curiosities, on the excuse that she had heard of something fabulous there that she wanted to buy for Tippa as a gift. She caught the attention of Norlis, who was the embassy master sergeant dressed up today as a junior undersecretary. He came to her side and in a low voice said, 'My thanks, lady, for the ice. It was very fine.'

She smiled. 'A recognition of the . . . ah, the suffering you have done today.' Tippa would never have dared speak to a master sergeant in the same tones she employed on junior undersecretaries, and Norlis and his men, so disguised, had found themselves the targets of several petty tongue-lashings. Soldiers attached to Families held high rank and positions of great esteem, and Family members treated them with the respect any sensible person gave to those who, in moments of crisis, stepped in to save one's life. Mere household staff hadn't earned such respect and usually didn't get it.

Norlis flushed and shrugged. 'It's been a long morning, and difficult, but . . . all for a good cause.'

'I have a request. I've heard that wonderful gifts might be found at a little shop on Stonecutter Street.' She stared off to one side and frowned, as if struggling to remember the name. 'Had . . . Har . . . something Curiosities.' She met his eyes and smiled triumphantly. '*Hasmal's* Curiosities! That's it! I'd like to go there before we return to the embassy, to buy something special for Tippa and her new husband.'

Norlis shook his head slowly and stared into her eyes, trying to figure out what she really wanted. Well, of course he knew that the wedding present story was a lie, because he knew as well as she did that there would be no wedding. But the expression on his face led her to believe that he would not have been enthused about her request no matter what excuse she had given. He said, 'I know more or less where that is . . . but I could never take you there. It's a dangerous part of the city; people dressed as well as we are go missing there in broad daylight, and the fact that we're traveling in a group would be no protection.'

She raised her eyebrows and silently mouthed the words, *But you're soldiers.*

He pointed to his belt, where only a poniard hung. She realized he carried no sword; none of the soldiers carried a sword. After all, what household servant could afford a weapon of war . . . and what could he hope to do with one if he had it? She felt a wave of pity for the warriors dressed in the functionaries' red-and-black fusses and frills – they must feel naked without their blades and their own uniforms, which were designed for ease of movement, not to show off the fine curves of their calves and shoulders.

On Freshspring Street, a block from the embassy and in an excellent neighborhood, the group had no real worries. Kait and Tippa carried only the smallest amount of actual cash – like the rest of the well-born, Tippa purchased the things she wanted with a letter of credit. Robbery would be a futile gesture, a fact even the poorest city inhabitants knew well. Kidnapping, though, was always lucrative, and with the soldiers mimicking functionaries even to the arms they carried, the group would be easy targets for a gang looking for such opportunities, if they were to allow themselves to get too far from home or to wander down the wrong streets.

But she had to find Hasmal, to discover his secret for keeping the evil of the world from touching him. This was her last chance; when she and Tippa returned to the embassy, they would immediately begin to prepare for the dedication service. They would be under constant supervision until the moment they returned once again to the embassy, which would not be until the station of Telt, when the sky was fully dark and the Red Hunter joined the White Lady in the sky. And then she and Tippa would be hustled onto the last airible leaving Halles, and they would lift into the blackness, and Hasmal and his secret for peacefulness would be lost to her forever.

She had to find him, and she could not. She knew she could order Norlis to take her there, and he would be duty-bound to follow her orders and to protect her with his life . . . but Family did not recklessly expend the lives of loyal soldiers. Kait had her duty, too, and it was to accept Norlis's warning for her own safety and to protect Tippa. Kidnappings forced the Family into a position of weakness; look at poor Danya, still not ransomed while the Sabirs dithered over sacks of gold and inches of boundaries like matrons over fish in a market, and the Galweighs tried everything they could think of to get the kidnappers to accept some sort of deal and send her home.

She looked away, toward the western wall of the city, where Hasmal went about whatever it was he did during the day, and then she hung her head. She would have given almost anything she had to get his secret; she would not, however, chance ransoming her Family's strength and honor.

She looked back at Norlis and said, 'Then let's go to this last silk market for Tippa. She hasn't managed to buy everything in the town yet.'

Norlis said softly, 'If there is something in particular you would like to get, I could go there once I'm off duty and purchase it for you.'

'No. I just wanted to look around. But thank you for offering. You're very kind.'

Norlis smiled and turned away, and Kait closed her

eyes for just an instant, feeling the inescapable evil that pounded at her skull, and the Sabir spy watching her and lusting after her as she lusted after him, and she mentally said good-bye to Hasmal and his secret, and to the possibility that she would ever find the sort of peace and self-control he carried with him.

She wondered briefly if he even remembered her. Then she got back to the business at hand.

* * *

Hasmal, finally over the seasickness that had kept him in his tiny cabin for days, sat on the aft deck of the small Rophetian merchantman. Out of the way of the sailors who scrambled up and down the riggings, he enjoyed the pleasant breeze and the clear air and wondered why the ship seemed to be sailing steadily northeast.

True to her word, Alarista had put him on the ship with orders to the crew that if he tried to get off, they were to kill him. She'd paid one-way passage for him to the Kander Colony on the other side of both the ocean and the world. The ship was supposed to already be heading there to trade silk and glass and grain for caberra spice. Alarista had given him his belongings and a final, passionate kiss, and had told him she would miss him like she'd never missed anyone in her life. And then she had walked away without even looking back, and the ship had sailed, and he had discovered that he didn't have much stomach for the sea.

Well, maybe he would never make a sailor, but he still had a sense of direction, and he knew that the ship had been heading due southeast when they sailed from Costan Selvira. When he tried to ask the captain or the crew why they had changed headings – for he had lost an unknown number of days lying in his hammock, too sick to move – they made the sign of the viper at him and quickly spit on the deck to ward off evil. He'd finally given up asking. He worried about the ship's change of direction, though, and the fact that he was the only passenger, and the fact that everyone without exception regarded him with dread. He knew that they had found out about his doom – no doubt one of the Gyrus had let it slip – and he wondered if he was to be dumped into the sea and left for the sharks and the sea monsters.

The cry of 'Land!' brought him out of his reverie. He looked to the horizon, and to the northwest made out a low black smudge, like a line of clouds rising along the horizon. He squinted, and the line stayed a smudge, but after a while time brought into focus what his eyes could not. A large point lay before them, flat and green, with the land falling back to either side; the place had seemed tiny from the distance but grew as they drew nearer, until he wondered if he looked at a large island or the leading edge of a continent. Three of the soaring white towers that marked the work of the Ancients stood above the trees; he imagined that they were used as lighthouses. The merchantman cut sharply east and sailed some distance off the coast, running parallel with it. The wind hummed through the ropes and snapped the sails as the crew lowered the largest of them and raised smaller sails instead. The captain shouted his directions, the sailors shouted their replies, and everyone acted as if Hasmal didn't exist.

Before long, a town rose into view to Hasmal's left; plastered houses painted vibrant shades of red and yellow and purple, with bougainvillea climbing the walls, sending cascading blossoms of fuchsia and lavender and crimson over the curved-tile roofs. Monkeys clambered over the houses and bounded into the palms and banyans and swung from the feathery fronds of date palms and shrieked; a flock of parrots screamed overhead; gulls spun in lazy arcs around the merchantman's mast and pelicans trawled in the ship's wake. People thronged the streets, most of them dressed entirely in white, so that they seemed to glow in the tropical sun. The merchant-man heeled over suddenly and headed due north around a point that Hasmal hadn't seen because the long line of coast behind it hid it, and a mass of tiny islands off to Hasmal's right slid into view, while to his left he discovered a beautiful harbor, in which berthed easily fifty sailing ships of every imaginable description, their bare masts rising like a denuded forest. Among them, cockboats and row-boats and lean outriggers and cata-marans slipped from ships to shore and back, ferrying passengers and cargo.

The merchantman's crew furled her sails and dropped her anchor, and the tempo and mood of the ship changed; it became slower and darker, and somehow ominous. In that lively, lovely place, Hasmal thought fear should be an obscenity, but he was afraid.

The captain came back to him and said, 'Get your things. You leave us here.'

The look in the man's eyes didn't encourage questions, and Hasmal didn't ask any. He ran below, grabbed the single bag that held his artifacts, his clothes, and his few other belongings, and scurried back up the ladder, in time to see four of the crewmen hoisting the ship's longboat over the side. The captain was waiting for him. He said, 'Go with them, and don't give them any trouble. You're lucky I didn't drown you the first night out; the only reason I didn't was because that band of Gyrus did me a favor once, and they asked that you be treated well. But favor or no favor, your trip with me ends here. I'll rot in Tonn's hell before I'll drag you and your curse clear across the Bregian Ocean and chance the sinking of *my* ship.'

Hasmal didn't have any money, any place to stay, or even any clear idea of where he was; he thought perhaps he might be in the Fire Islands, or perhaps up along the Lost Souls Coast. But he didn't protest. As much as he would have been happy to find himself in Kander Colony (which along with being clear across the world had the advantage of being settled by Sabirs – sure promise that his trouble wouldn't follow him), he would get himself to land wherever he was and take stock of the twin blessings of being alive and of being farther from the Galweigh woman than he'd been before.

He got into the longboat, rode in silence across the water to the shore, and at a sign from one of the crew, jumped into the water when it was knee-deep and waded to land. The four men in the longboat immediately began rowing back to the ship, and by the time he'd found a comfortable observation spot on a stone pier, the merchantman's sails were already flying again, and it was headed back out to sea.

He sat watching it until it disappeared around the point again; his sense of loss seemed stupid to him, but he couldn't deny the feeling. That ship had been a tie to his old life and his old self, however tenuous, and when it sailed away, it left him wondering who he would become, and what he would be.

At last, though, he stood; his leather pants were still damp, and he needed to find fresh water so that he could clean the salt out of them before they dried and cracked. He needed to make arrangements for a place to stay, and for some way to earn money. He needed to find a place to eat, too; his stomach, freed of the rolling of the sea, began to announce to him that food had been scarce of late and would be appreciated.

And he needed to find out where he had come to ground. That last would be the easiest problem to remedy, if he could find someone who spoke Iberan and if he was careful how he asked the question. He didn't want to start out his new life the way he'd finished his old one, as a man commonly known to be under a curse. He thought for a while about innocuous reasons why he might have been put ashore with no money and with no idea of his location – it took him a while, but at last he concocted a story that he thought would serve.

Then he located a Rophetian sailor standing by the pier, both arms around a white-dressed girl, and went up to the man.

'My comrades threw me off my ship,' he said. 'I thought I had sure luck with the bones, and at the last throw the goddess deserted me, and I ended up owing more than I had . . .' He sighed and grinned. 'And I've been drunk the last five days, and I don't know where I am.'

The sailor laughed, white teeth flashing behind the thick black beard. 'The bones and the mead have landed more than one man on strange soil,' he said, 'but if you're an ass, at least you're a lucky ass. You're a stone's throw from civilization. This here's Maracada, on Goft.'

'My thanks,' Hasmal said. He managed a smile that he didn't feel, and walked away without stumbling, and looked for a place where he could hide. He fancied he could hear the gods laughing at him; Goft was a big island – perhaps thirty leagues in length – but it wasn't big enough. A narrow strait separated the island from the mainland, and on the other side of that strait lay Ibera, and no more than twenty leagues from there lay Calimekka. The home of the Galweigh Family.

He was closer to disaster than he'd been in Halles. He needed to find another ship, and he needed to get himself to sea, and he needed to do it fast.

Chapter 12

Darkness, the hard cold blackness of the station of Huld, when the presence of light and warmth seems like a dream that will never come to pass. Kait stood beside Tippa in the courtyard, watching Dùghall pace. Tippa kept sobbing, 'How can I not have a wedding? I'm to get married today!' and neither Kait nor Dùghall had the patience to explain anymore that she was to have been murdered at her wedding along with the rest of the Family. The last airible should have already arrived, should have come during Telt, and had not. Something was wrong, and the three of them were going to be trapped in an enemy city in the midst of war. Kait kept very still, watching the sky, listening for the airible's engines, for the soft thudding of the pistons and the beating of the rotors against the night air, but the beast inside of her already tasted panic and wanted to flee. To run, to go to ground, to hide.

The Galweigh soldiers responsible for catching the airible's tethers held their pose, torches lit, waiting along the line of fire that marked the embassy landing field. They would catch the tethers and pull the airible down to anchor; at least, they would if it ever arrived . . .

Kait fingered the hilt of the longsword at her hip and tried to keep the monster inside of her still; tried to figure out what she could do to keep Tippa and Dùghall safe;

tried to think not of becoming the Karnee creature, but of staying human and helping her Family as a human. But the walls of the invisible cage constricted, and her heart raced and her senses grew sharp with incipient Shift – and it was only then that she heard the steady, metallic *thupp, thupp, thupp* of the airible over the normal noises of the night.

'It's coming,' she said, and a murmur ran through the line of soldiers; they heard nothing, and said as much.

Dùghall turned and stopped pacing and looked at her. 'You're sure?'

'I hear it.'

'Good.' He nodded. Waited a moment, and another, while to Kait's ears the noise of the engine became impossible to overlook. But only when still another moment had passed, and the sound she heard began to drown out the background sounds of Halles with its predawn racket of peddlers and tradesmen rattling through the streets, did the first of the soldiers stare at her and say, 'By the gods, I hear it, too.'

Karnee ears. They were their own betrayal. She told herself to be more careful about her timing in admitting what she heard. At another time, in another place, perhaps revealing her acute hearing might be her death.

The noise of the airible grew louder, then yet louder, and suddenly Kait could make it out against the sky, its shape a darker blackness that blotted out the stars. This time she said nothing, uncertain if human eyes would be able to mark the form so soon, and not wanting to seem a woman of too many miracles in one night.

A moment passed, and one of the soldiers said, 'There! Against the Shepherds.' He pointed north by east, to a constellation high in the night sky. The airible moved across those stars, blotting them out, and the rest of the soldiers nodded and bent to the groundlamps that would mark the readiness of the landing field. They put their torches to the lamps and, as the flames in the green glass lanterns flickered one by one to life, doused the open flames of the torches in the buckets that lay alongside. The airibles no longer used gaimthe, the burning gas, to fill their large balloons, but the fuel the engines used was flammable and dangerous, and the practice of never permitting open flame around an airible remained.

The field, lit only by the row of green lanterns, looked eerie. The grass of the field seemed leached of color, and the people in it looked like week-old corpses. A chill crawled down Kait's spine; the ghastliness of the scene seemed an omen to her, as portentous as the pulsing, unending waves of evil that rolled over Halles, or the inescapable certainty that the Sabir Karnee wanted her and was coming for her. She pushed it out of her mind; the airible dropped with surprising speed, and ropes snaked down out of the sky. The soldiers caught them with practiced hands and looped them around huge wooden pulleys anchored deep into the ground, and began winding in the rope, straining against the huge cranks.

Within moments the airible hung just above the ground, tugging at its moorings. In the green light, the red and the black of the Galweigh crest blended on the garishly green-smeared silk of the airible balloon, rendering the whole an illegible blob. Men and women dropped out of both hatches in the long, enclosed basket, landing on the ground below with the soft clanks of muffled armor. The pilot appeared in the front hatch last of all and said, 'Quickly, quickly, we must go. From the air I can already see the leading edge of dawn in the east.'

The soldiers hoisted Tippa into the hatch, and then Dùghall; Kait refrained from jumping and allowed herself to be unceremoniously shoved upward. She was grateful that she wore sensible traveling clothes – sturdy boots and heavy leather pants and a cotton blouse with a wool tunic – instead of the delicate silk dress that Tippa had insisted on wearing. Entry into an airible was never a graceful thing, and even less so when in such a hurry. While she still lay on the basket floor, Kait heard the whine of the rope paying out, and felt her weight press her tight to the floor; they were rising fast, shooting upward so quickly that her eardrums felt as if they would burst.

Dùghall said, 'Why were you so late?'

Kait sat up. The pilot, a Rophetian named Aouel, didn't turn from his stopcocks and his rudder wheel. His back to all of them, he said, 'We had a foul crosswind in the midsky that blew us south of course before I could rise out of it, and when I did, I found myself in a headwind that I fought all the way in. If you want the good news with the bad, though, we'll have the same east-running wind all the way back, and this time it will speed us on our journey.'

'I thought you weren't coming,' Dùghall said.

Aouel glanced quickly at Kait, and as quickly made the look take in the three of them. 'I would have flown through Tonn's hell itself to get to you,' he said.

Which Kait suspected to be true; Aouel was a longtime friend of hers, since the day when she had wandered onto the airible field on the House grounds in Calimekka at the age of thirteen, and he had shown her the miracles of airible flight for the first time. In secret, in the following years, he had taught her to fly the smaller of the airships – those, like this one, that could be handled by one person. The two of them had discussed her dreams and his, and had remained in each other's confidence even when Kait had been sworn into the diplomatic service and her time had ceased to be her own. The Family would have been horrified; a girl of Galweigh breeding and future high position learning the trade of a sailor, even a sailor of the air? A woman who would one day negotiate the fate of the Family the confidante of a Rophetian commoner? Unthinkable.

As Kait was wont to do, she had cherished the friendship and guarded it as she guarded her own dark secrets and, giving a nod to Rophetian theology, had decided the Family could go to Tonn's hell if they couldn't understand what Aouel meant to her.

The airible rose higher and the first flat gray light of dawn that edged the horizon to the east suddenly illuminated the inside of the cabin. No sight of the sun yet, but it wouldn't be long. Kait shivered at the narrowness of the margin of their escape; below, in the darkness that still blanketed Halles, eyes watched the sky, waiting for the first beam from the sun to fall across the top arch of the stone tower in the city square. That light would herald the arrival of the station of Soma, and start the ringing of the single alto bell that would mark the greeting of the new day and launch the 'wedding' processions from Dokteerak House and the Galweigh Embassy into the streets. And would culminate in the destruction of the Dokteerak Family, and perhaps a large part of the Sabir Family as well.

For an instant, staring into that pale light, Kait saw a reflection of the lean, hungry face of the Sabir Karnee, and for an instant she felt his touch. And in that instant, her traitorous heart hoped that he would escape destruction.

* * *

The first beam of sunlight struck the top arch of the black Tower of Time through cloudless skies, and at once the bell ringer filled the air with the single, repeated tolling of the station of Soma. First station of morning, the First Friend of the New Day.

As if the gates of the Galweigh Embassy were linked to the bell, they swung open at the first note, and ten trumpeters and ten drummers stepped into the street.

They were gorgeously dressed in the Galweigh red and black, their faces covered from forehead to nose with fringes of gold beads, their instruments poised at the ready. Behind them came ten handbell players, and behind them, ten wood-flautists, and behind them, fifty dancers.

The bell of Soma rang seven times, and the last note hung in the air, and the musicians waited – still, poised – until the final shivering whispers died away into the morning hush. Then, at a spoken signal from someone still in the compound, they launched into the Wedding Dance. The dancers leaped in the street, catapulted themselves into the air, and launched into great, rattling flips and clattering spins. The heavy fringes of beads rattled like another phalanx of drummers on their metal costumes. The dancers carried curved swords that they swung at each other's legs with blinding speed and jumped over as they moved forward; they shouted the names of the god of the week, who was Duria, the spinner, and the god of the day, Bronir, who was the god of joy – and they never missed their footing. Graceful, glorious – they presented a grand and noisy spectacle.

The sides of the streets all the way from the embassy to the Dokteerak House were already lined with working-men and women dressed in their finest clothing, out to see and be seen. The paraglese of the Dokteeraks and the city's parnissas had already jointly declared Durial Bronirsday a holiday, and the common people of Halles were determined not to miss an instant of the grand wedding parade that had come to amuse them; free entertainment came hard in the city, and not often.

Behind the acrobatic sword dancers came the jugglers; oddly, all of them juggled flashing swords, three at a time. The folk who lined the streets murmured to each other that the trick wasn't so much – everyone knew jugglers never used sharpened swords. But everyone agreed that the way light caught the edges of the false weapons made them *look* sharp.

The concubines followed the jugglers. They flirted with the crowd as they swayed forward, waggling their hips, jutting their breasts, seeming a bit uncomfortable in the unaccustomed covering of their wedding finery.

The people of Halles had hoped for trained tigers next, or perhaps for some of the weird beasts that inhabited the Scarred lands, but none were forthcoming. Instead, sixteen powerful litter bearers in full dress uniform brought out the first litter, in which sat a handsome man and a rather sturdy-looking woman, both oddly dressed in heavy cloaks, with the customary beaded fringes covering their faces from forehead to upper lip. Behind this first litter came a seemingly endless succession of others, each litter gaudier than the last, each couple swathed and veiled in more or less the same manner. Crimson and black, a sanguinary Galweigh river studded with flashes of gold poured forth from the embassy, and in that outpouring the breathtaking gleam of gemstones seemed as common as mere stones in the bottom of an ordinary river. Glittering faceted rubies and cabochon onyx on everything; studding the litters, the litter bearers, the bride's family. A few of the more knowledgeable marked the unending flow of gemstones as almost surely glass, but even they had to admit the glitter made for a gorgeous spectacle.

A choir of male singers accompanied the last litters, those of the ambassadors, the Galweigh paraglese, and finally the bride. They sang the standard selection of wedding songs, dedicating the marriage to Maraxis, the god of sperm, seed, and fertility, in whose month the wedding took place, and dedicating the bride to Drastu, the goddess of womb, eggs, and fertility.

As was customary, the bride was completely veiled; the younger married women in the crowd tried to make out the lines of her face beneath the swaths of red silk and the gold-beaded fringe (for seeing the eyes of a bride before her wedding was supposed to be an omen of fertility in the coming year) but had to content themselves with responding to the generous waving of her jewel-studded hands. *Those* gems, everyone agreed, were real. The Hallesites passed rumors back and forth about the bride. She was beautiful and kind, she had taken a meal in the street, eating common food, she had been generous with gifts and money to those she'd encountered in the streets. She had good wide hips, excellent for bearing babies. Breasts big enough that those babies would have plenty of suckle. She wasn't clever or witty and hadn't seemed terribly ambitious – always a plus in a woman who would be the bride of a second son.

Altogether a fine young woman – that was the common consensus. Perhaps too good a girl for their paraglese's second son, who had the reputation throughout the city for being spoiled, and something of a shit.

Another batch of sword jugglers and musicians followed the bride's litter, but they weren't any great surprise. As wedding parades went, the people decided, this one hadn't been bad. A few tigers, less clothing and more cleavage on the concubines, and perhaps a couple of fire-eating midgets and it would have been perfect.

* * *

In the White Hall of the Sabir House in Calimekka, brilliant morning sunlight slanted in through colored glass windows, throwing harlequin patterns of tinted light across the carved white marble floor so that it looked like a field of jonquillas and rubyhearts and bluebells bursting out from beneath a sudden snow. The delicate vaulted arches of a vast stone canopy soared over the circular stone room, and the ceiling curved with them, echoing back every soft sound born within the room's confines. In this beautiful sanctuary, the Sabir

Wolves walked the final arabesques of their power-building spell, joined by arrivals just in from Halles – Imogene and Lucien Sabir, the head Wolf and his consort. The Wolves murmured in unison, their voices joined by the ghost-whispers of their distant colleagues who moved – insubstantial and only half visible – along the path with them . . . and perhaps joined by other, stranger spirits as well.

The scent of honeysuckle suddenly filled the room from nowhere, and as it did, all whispering and treading of the path and steady chanting ceased at once, as abruptly and as completely as candles snuffed out by a sudden draft. On the path, the Wolves in the chamber and the ghostly images of Wolves that walked with them from Halles and Costan Selvira and Waypoint halted as one, feet solidly planted on the worn stone lines, heads turned toward the central pillar – which was not carved stone, as the pillar in Halles had been, but solid gold. The air, tinged with spicy curls of caberra incense and with the thickening sweetness of the honeysuckle, and with malevolence, shimmered expectantly. A voice spoke clearly into the mind of each Wolf: 'The time has come – let the sacrifice begin.'

Something pattered softly across the room, unseen but felt by the Wolves nearest it as pressure in the chest, as icy air that stirred not one hair on a single head when it moved by; and all breathed in the cloying honeysuckle reek that thickened, tainted suddenly with the underlying stench of something long dead and rotting.

Silence. A sense that more than the Wolves within the room waited – that other, older eyes watched, that other ears listened. The walls of the sanctuary sighed, then murmured on their own; words in a long-forgotten tongue that might have been full of meaning or might have been the babble of some long-dead madness.

Further silence.

A moment passed, and another, and then a third. Then the faintest of drumbeats rippled through the air. One, then another, then a third, ghostly, drummed by something that was not and had never been human, pulsing through the air, increasing in speed and strength as they increased in volume. The sound was the starting of some monstrous heart that gathered resolution and power as it moved nearer the source of its lifeblood: the White Hall and the center of the Sabir magic. That beat moved nearer, and still nearer, became louder and more forceful. Quickening as it moved nearer. Nearer.

The Wolves stared straight at the pillar, eyes never wavering toward the room's single arched doorway, through which the roar of that hellish heartbeat now ripped and raced like the pulse of a stag pursued by wolves.

A girl appeared, hanging in the air, floating in the embrace of nothingness. Her long black hair had been braided with elaborate attention to detail and woven full of flowers, so that, as she floated through the patterned sunlight, she seemed for an instant to be another flower in that stained-glass garden, an ephemeral creation of light and shadow.

She should have been beautiful; her delicate cheekbones, fine lips, straight nose, and large, slanting eyes were perfectly shaped. Her hands, resting folded in her lap, were works of art. Beneath the gauzy whiteness of her gown, her small, perfect breasts curved away to a slender rib cage and a tiny waist.

She should have been beautiful. Surely, she had once been beautiful.

But the deadness of her expression, the unnatural pallor of her skin, and the faint tint of bruises imperfectly covered by powders and creams, and revealed by the sharpness of the morning light, gave her the ghastly appearance of a corpse animated by something other than life.

Three pairs of eyes glanced away from the pillar long enough to study the girl – to be sure that the signs of days and nights of torture and rape and degradation were sufficiently hidden by the makeup and fine clothes to ward off censure or punishment. Crispin, Anwyn, and Andrew then looked to each other from their places on the path, all of them disturbed that Danya didn't look as convincingly pristine as she had when they'd prepared her in their quarters. Crispin gave the faintest of nods, though – affirmation that if her appearance caused a commotion, he would be the one to deal with it. With no other sign, the three of them returned their gazes to the pillar.

The girl floated in the cloud of frigid, honeysuckled air to the center of the room, where invisible hands lowered her to the ground and held her against the golden column with an unbreakable grip. She shivered with each beat of the phantom drum, but otherwise gave no sign of life.

The drumming died into silence and the room sighed again, the walls breathing softly, whispering unintelligible things. The Wolves beneath did not permit themselves to be distracted by the murmurs; they immediately set to the task of casting the spell into which all the preparation had gone. Years of research, more years to cull the proper spell from Ancient texts and reform it from the old tongues of wizards into the rich, rolling Iberan language, months of power-building, hundreds of lesser sacrifices, the kidnapping of a young and powerful enemy Wolf, a delicate diversionary plot and the commitment of all the Sabir Family resources, in both material and manpower – all moved at last to this single time, this single place, this single irrevocable irretrievable opportunity to annihilate the Family's hereditary enemies, the Galweighs, from Calimekka. No faltering now, no going back, no second thoughts. The dead were in attendance; the living must act.

In unison the Wolves began the chant.

Chapter 13

Something's wrong,' Kait said.

Dùghall looked up from patting the sobbing Tippa. 'Wrong in what way?'

The feeling of all-pervasive evil had, in the last few moments, grown unendurable. Kait felt it as nausea and joint pain and a pounding headache behind her eyeballs, and as the crawling of thousands of invisible spiders up and down her spine. 'I've felt something evil in Halles since the night of the Naming Day party,' she told him, 'but now I feel almost as if it were going to . . .' She frowned. 'As if it were going to burst.'

Dùghall turned to Tippa. 'Lie down, child, and breathe as slowly as you can. You'll feel better soon.' He waited until she curled up on the velvet-upholstered bench, then came over and sat next to Kait. 'You've felt the presence of *evil*. And you feel it now.' He frowned, but to Kait he also had the scent of excitement about him.

'Yes.'

'*How* do you feel it?'

'I don't know how. I just do.'

'That isn't what I meant to ask. Describe the sensations by which this evil tells you of its existence.'

Kait nodded, understanding. 'First as pressure against my skin. And tingling along the back of my neck. A sort of . . . of *greasiness*, I suppose, that seemed to move around and through me. Now . . . I feel as if my eyes are about to explode from my head, and I want to vomit, and I hurt everywhere.'

Dùghall's eyes were wide. 'Yes. Yes. And the sensation of greasiness?'

'I still feel that, but everything else is so much stronger that it doesn't bother me as much.'

'Yes. Precisely. Tell me . . . have you had dreams recently?'

'Nightmares. Every night. Monsters chasing me, and death everywhere – I haven't had a good sleep since we got to Halles.'

'Just so.' Dùghall had begun to grin. The scent of excitement around him intensified. 'I'm going to do something. Tell me what you feel.'

Kait waited. Dùghall sat with his hands clasped on his knees, eyes squeezed tightly closed . . . and did nothing. And then, suddenly, Kait's headache was gone, and the nausea and the pain with it. She felt wonderful – as wonderful as she had the moment she ran into Hasmal. Perhaps even better, since her discomfort and anxiety had been so much worse to begin with.

'It's all gone,' she said. 'All the evil, all the pain.'

'Marvelous,' Dùghall murmured, so low that only she could hear him. 'This is simply marvelous, Kait-cha.'

'Why?' She kept her own voice pitched nearly as low and soft as his.

'What you sense is magic being worked. I must assume that no one taught you to do this . . .?'

'No. Of course not.' Bewildered, Kait stared at her uncle. *Magic?* She sensed magic being worked? But no one did magic – its practice had been forbidden ever since humans had climbed out of the rubble left by the Wizards' War and set about rebuilding the world. 'Why would you say I felt magic?'

He took her hand and held it between his own. 'Don't

think that because it is forbidden, magic isn't practiced. Or even that it is solely the tool of evil. If you can sense it, girl, you have the potential to use it. And you could do good things with it – magic was once one of the paths to enlightenment.' He sighed. 'Even being able to tell when you are around magic, though, will be invaluable to you as a diplomat in the Family's service. We always need to know when our enemies and allies have capabilities that we don't.'

Kait considered that for a while. Magic was heresy of the worst sort; doing magic was worse even than being Karnee. If she could sense magic, did that mean she was doing magic? Was she guilty of this further heresy in spite of having never sought it out?

She probably was. It didn't matter. She could only die once, and the automatic death sentence she carried just by being Karnee couldn't be made any worse if she added a cartload of other sins.

Dùghall seemed able to follow the tenor of her thoughts, for he said, 'You think about it and discover that things can't get any worse for you, don't you?'

'That's exactly what I was thinking.'

'Well, now I'll tell you how they can get better. You must let me teach you how to tap your talents with magic. Once you know how to use the forces all around you, you'll be able to avoid the pain you feel when you are close to those who are working *darsharen*, which is the magic of Wolves, and the sort of magic that is making you feel sick. And with *farhullen*, which is the magic of Falcons and a force for good, you will be able to overcome – and even prevent – some evils. Your ability to serve the Family will increase beyond your imagining.' As he told her this, his face lit up as if he were a boy receiving a great gift, and he radiated scents of pleasure and excitement.

Kait remained cautious, though his enthusiasm allayed

most of her misgivings. Everything Dùghall had ever done with Kait had made her life better. She trusted him. So she asked, 'If this is so – if magic can be used for good and not just for evil – why is it forbidden?'

Dùghall made a disgusted face. 'Because the parnissas would rather forbid what they don't understand than learn how it might be of value if it were permitted. This is, I think, a characteristic common to those who seek public power. Willful ignorance and endless laws become the replacement for self-education and self-restraint, because ignorance and laws are easy.'

Kait despised the parnissas. If ever they discovered what she was, they would demand her death that same instant. Her parents had risked their own lives for five years substituting another child for her in the inspections on the Day of Infants. Yet she had done nothing to deserve death; and she could not forgive the parnissas for enforcing the laws that demanded it. 'Teach me,' she said. 'I'm quick, and I work hard. You'll find me an eager student.'

'We'll start tomorrow.' He smiled, then looked over at Tippa. She was sitting again, and sobbing twice as loudly as she had been before, and now she was rocking back and forth, too. His smile tightened and Kait could see strain in his eyes. 'Meanwhile, I can see that your cousin feels she's not getting the attention she deserves. Excuse me while I tend to her . . . or else I suspect she'll resort to tearing her hair and clothes and wailing like a war mourner.'

He moved to her cousin's side and left Kait to contemplate magic and what it meant to her, and to her world.

* * *

'Sacred is the binding of two lives, sacred the bond between two families, sacred the promises made this day.' The parnissa who presided over the wedding shifted

159

on her dais, and the morning sunlight caught her hair and spun a silver nimbus around her head. She smiled down at the veiled bride and bridegroom who stood before her on the rise at the north end of the basin. She smiled at the representatives of the two Families, the ranks of blue and gold filling the stone risers on the west side of the amphitheater, and the wall of red and black that rose to the east side. She even deigned to smile briefly at the troops of entertainers who crowded all the way around the rim of the amphitheater, though most parnissas would have not noticed them; the gods had nothing to say to their sort on these occasions.

Norlis, the embassy master sergeant, was playing the part of Macklin Galweigh, father of the bride. He watched the swordswoman playing the bride slide her right hand slowly into the deep folds of her skirt. He forced himself not to stiffen and he kept his breathing easy in spite of himself, and in spite of knowing that the same anticipation ran through the veins of every other man and woman in the Galweigh troops. Almost . . . almost . . .

Jerren Draclas Galweigh, commander of the troops, shifted on the hard stone riser. He sat just to the left of Norlis; he was, because he was slender and shorter than average, dressed as a Family woman. Norlis heard his breathing quicken.

Almost . . . almost . . .

And above, the extra ranks of swordsmen and archers, in their disguises as jugglers and concubines, made ready without being obvious about it.

The parnissa raised her arms over her head, her hands forming the symbols of the sun and the earth. 'As the sun feeds Matrin, so the man feeds the woman. As Matrin gives life to the universe, so the woman gives life to the man. You are equal and from this day forth you shall stand together, paired, two made one and stronger than any three.'

The battle hunger pounded in Norlis's veins, tinged with the sharpness of fear. Inescapable, the fear – that death could be such a familiar face and still be such a stranger, that it waited for him and for the rest who sat in the sacred basin – and yet he lived for moments such as these, when he became more alive than he ever was elsewise. He waited, watching the lemon lizards skittering through the grass below him, their bright yellow bodies gleaming in the shortening rays of the tropical sun . . . gleaming as bright and metallic as the tiny glimpses of armor reflected back at him from the Dokteerak side of the amphitheater. He smiled at that. Tradition gave the bride's family the eastern side of the basin, and tradition this time meant that the enemy would have the sun in their eyes at commencement of the battle, and that their stray movements now revealed their treachery, at the same time that the long shadows on the east side of the basin hid the Galweigh readiness to attack or defend. Norlis smelled the sweat of the men and women all around him who roasted as he did in battle armor disguised beneath wedding dress. He listened to the drone of the parnissa, and the murmurs of the audience, and he felt the sun on the back of his neck send trickling beads of sweat down his own spine, beneath the scale mail and the padding and his sodden clothes, to where he couldn't get at it. So good to be alive and so dear, when all those sensations could be snatched away from him in an instant.

'And do you, Tippa Delista Anja na Kita Galweigh, accept with honor this man, and pledge your faith, in the sight of the gods who bless all true unions?'

'My honor on his good faith, now and always,' the impostor said.

Almost . . . almost . . .

'And do you, Calmet E'kheer na Boulouk Dokteerak, accept with honor this woman, and pledge your faith, in the sight of the gods who bless all true unions?'

If the Dokteeraks were to go through with their treachery, they had to act or be forsworn before the gods.

And Calmet Dokteerak, who was ready to break his troth to humankind, evidently didn't extend his treachery to double-crossing the gods. He ripped off his groom veil to reveal a helmet beneath. 'I do not!' he shouted, and pulled a dagger from its hiding place beneath his short cloak at the small of his back. 'Die, you stupid bitch!'

Tippa's stand-in had her blade in hand before anyone from either side could move, and Calmet's hand and the dagger it had clutched lay on the stones, drenched in blood.

'To arms,' Jerren Galweigh shouted, and suddenly the circle around the top of the amphitheater was ringed with red and black, and a rain of arrows poured from both sides into the western risers.

All became chaos, but chaos with direction. The gold and blue Dokteeraks, well led, charged up the western risers to engage the archers there in close combat; the plan would have been good, but the archers fell back and gave way to the ranks of swordsmen who had been dressed as jugglers – elite fighters with tremendous skill with their weapons. Meanwhile, the Galweighs in the east risers swarmed down and pinned the enemy between themselves and the other flank of the attack.

The Dokteerak troops, who had expected no more resistance than could have been mustered by any wedding crowd, died in heaps and piles. Outnumbered and unprepared to meet battle-hardened warriors, shouting for reinforcements that never arrived, they fought well, but not well enough.

The two flanks of the Galweigh army forced the survivors down to the floor of the amphitheater and back toward the cowering parnissa, who screamed of heresy and abomination, and who remained untouched by both sides because to kill the sacred hand of the gods would bring down curses on the slayer's family for uncounted generations. So the bodies piled around her, most of them garbed in blue and gold. But not all, of course. Not all.

Norlis saw friends fall, and grimaced, and drove harder into the diminished ranks of the Dokteerak troops. His blade shone as red as his clothes, the blood runnels full of gore. For Kait, he thought, because he admired the Galweighs, but he secretly loved Kait. For Kait, because these bastards would have slaughtered her and all her Family.

For Kait.

Then there were no more enemies to kill – there were only surrendering soldiers begging for their lives. Jerren Galweigh mounted the dais and raised his still-bloody sword over his head. 'We triumph!' he screamed. 'To the city, where we will claim what has become ours.'

The roar of cheers. Norlis shouted with the rest, yelling his throat raw. Then movement overhead caught his eye. An airible sailed slowly over the amphitheater, and faces turned upward to watch it. Odd – he'd thought all the airibles were back in Calimekka. A second moved into view behind the first.

He frowned. Many of the troops still shouted and cheered on this unexpected air support, but the airibles didn't look *right* to Norlis. The enormous white envelopes seemed both too short and too round somehow. Their lines were oddly lumpy, their engines sounded both too loud and too rough, and the shapes of the gondolas beneath –

The surviving Dokteeraks started grinning.

Faces peered out from the tops of the gondolas, and a sudden chill gripped Norlis. None of the Galweigh airibles had open gondolas anymore, did they? But the

Galweighs were the only Family in Ibera who had airibles – or the engines that made them move. Those were secrets from the ancient past, and guarded as closely as the Galweighs guarded their lives.

But the airibles came on, and they were not Galweigh airibles. The watching men overhead waited until they had drifted closer; then hoses poked over the gondola rims, and in the next instant a rain of something stinking and wet and green and sticky doused him and everyone else in and around the amphitheater.

'Run!' Jerren shouted, but he hadn't caught on quickly enough. Not quickly enough at all. While the green rain still fell, archers from the second gondola began shooting flaming arrows into the crowd, and into the stinking deluge. The green liquid caught, and suddenly the sky rained fire, and around the amphitheater hundreds of men and women blossomed with flames.

The airibles turned sideways. Norlis, not yet burning but trapped in the center of flames, by all rights should have thought of nothing but his own onrushing oblivion. He did remark the airibles, though, and he recognized, when it was far too late to do him or anyone else any good, the crests painted on their suddenly visible sides. Sabir Family. Flashes of forest green and silver, the design twin trees laden with silver fruit.

The other half of the betrayal – and a betrayal not just of the Galweighs, but of the Dokteeraks, who had considered the Sabirs allies.

All of us burn together – Galweigh and Dokteerak alike, Norlis realized. And the Sabirs, who crossed us and double-crossed them, win Halles. And what else? With all of our fighting forces here, and all of the Family in Calimekka . . . do they win Galweigh House as well?

Then flames and smoke and screaming swallowed Norlis.

*　*　*

The long shadows in the courtyard of Galweigh House turned the manicured grass into rough-cut velvet in the places where the morning sun reached over the wall. Humid air, the temperature already rising, intermittent breeze catching and rattling the palm fronds around the House and bringing distant wind chimes to invisible life. A pretty morning that promised to give way later to a hot and possibly stormy day. The serving girl picked her way along the path to the guardhouse at the gate, carrying one tray on her head and one in her arms, both laden with food.

One of the guards saw her coming and ran out to relieve her of the heavier of the two trays.

'Thank you. I'm sorry I took so long.' She smiled up at him. She was attractive – wide smile, even teeth, eyes that crinkled at the corners when she grinned. A lot of cleavage – which she had gone to some trouble to show off.

He laughed. 'We were beginning to think Cook wasn't going to feed us this morning.'

The girl shook her head. 'You should know I wouldn't let you go hungry. When have I ever not gotten your food to you?'

'True.' One of the other guards opened the guardhouse door and sighed. 'Truly, Lizal, you are a vision to a hungry man like me.'

'Of course I am. But not because you lust after me, you goat. You only love me for my sweet rolls.'

All the men laughed. One said, 'You didn't really bring sweet rolls, did you?'

'I did. That's what took me so long. I couldn't steal enough for all of you until she left the kitchen for a moment.'

The man who had helped her carry their meal into the guardhouse said fervently, 'I'd marry you for real if you'd have me.'

The woman they called Lizal laughed. 'But I wouldn't. So your virtue and your honor are intact.'

She stood chatting with them while they ate, as she did every morning, watching them devour the corn flatbread and pudding and fried plantains, and especially the stolen sweet rolls, with bright, intent eyes. When they'd finished, she told them if she didn't get back to the kitchen, Cook would have her hide. She said the same thing every morning, and as they did every morning, the men laughed and patted her round rump, and told her they would marry her if she wanted and tried to tempt her into staying longer, into going to bed with one or all of them, and into various other indiscretions.

As always, she smiled, made vague promises that she would consider their offers, and left.

She didn't go back to the kitchen, however. This morning she walked back down the path toward it, but ducked behind some tall shrubs the instant she was out of direct sight of the guardhouse. There she stripped off her Galweigh livery and put on a grubby plain brown smock and patched homespun skirt and shabby leather sandals – clothing that made her look almost like a poor peasant. She disarranged her hair and rubbed dirt into the creases of her hands and underneath her fingernails, and rubbed more dirt into her feet and lower legs. Now she looked exactly like a poor peasant. Disguise completed, she gathered up two small bags, one that clinked heavily when she moved it, and a larger, lumpier one that did not, and, with them in hand, moved behind the line of shrubbery until the guardhouse was once again in sight. From her screened vantage point, she watched and waited.

For a short while, she heard only the normal conversation between the guards. Then she heard groaning, and vomiting. More groaning. Then, after what seemed like forever, silence.

She rose, walked back to the guardhouse, and looked inside. The guards all lay on the floor, some across others where they had fallen. Their backs arched, their arms pulled straight back at their sides, rigid as boards, their necks stretched backward, their eyes bulged out and their tongues protruded.

The poison her Sabir employer had given her certainly looked effective. Two sweet rolls each, and not a one of the men was still breathing.

'No mess, no fuss, no bother,' she murmured. Not much mess, anyway. She did watch where she put her sandaled feet as she clambered over the bodies. She pulled the lever that released the weights that lifted the portcullis gate (struggling a bit, because it was surprisingly heavy), and set it into the locked position. Then she walked out to the gate and to the obsidian-paved Path of Gods, where she bowed to the first of the men in dark green and silver who waited. 'The guards in the guardhouse are dead. Everyone else is alive – the Galweighs are too active this morning, and I was afraid one of them would come across the bodies in the kitchen if I poisoned the other kitchen workers.' She handed him the smaller bag. 'All the copies of the House keys that I could get my hands on are in here, as well as the best copy of a map that I could steal. The majority of the Family is on the second floor right now, in their quarters. A few are still in the main salon on the first floor. None, as far as I know, are on the ground floor.'

'And below?' Ry Sabir asked.

'I don't know who might be there. If you have to go below, you'll have trouble. There are . . . things down there that frighten me. You can hear them moving, and sometimes you can smell them . . . but they're always in the dark where you can't see them.'

He nodded, but didn't look worried. 'We'll manage. You know where to go?'

'I do. My passage has been arranged?'

'Yes. I think you're too cautious – you could have a place in Sabir House if you wanted it. You've served us well.'

She shook her head. 'You aren't planning on killing all of the Galweighs, and they may come to figure out who was the spy in their midst. They can be . . . vengeful.'

'As we all can if we're crossed.' He smiled slyly. 'Have a good voyage, then, Wenne.'

As the girl turned away from the cliff and hurried from Galweigh House, Ry Sabir, with map and keys in hand, led his lieutenants and his Family's troops into the enemy domain. The girl had been right – the servants were concentrated on the ground floor, and the showing of swords convinced most of them to surrender quietly; the efficient slaughter of the few who dared resist convinced the rest. From there, Ry broke the Sabir troops into five groups; they rushed both main sets of stairs and the several servants' staircases to the first floor simultaneously, and caught several more servants on the way. In the salon, almost all of the Galweigh Family waited for news of the battle in Halles. The Galweighs, caught unarmed and unprepared, gave no more trouble than the servants had – they surrendered in exchange for the promise of their lives. As easily as that, the great House fell.

Ry handed over control of the main troops to his father's chosen commander, and drew his colleagues aside. 'She isn't with them; we're going to have to search the House for her.'

'We could wait for her to come to us.' Jaim, uncharacteristically, was the first to speak.

Ry shook his head. He was both too excited to wait and too afraid that something might go wrong. His father's men didn't intend to honor the guarantee they'd given the Galweigh Family; as soon as the cleanup crews were sure the captives were all in one place, the Family – excepting a few individuals who could give useful information – were to be put to the sword. Lucien Sabir wanted no bold rescues mounted by the branches of the Galweigh Family in the Imumbarra Isles or Goft, or in the far colony settlements of Icta Draclas or the North Shore, and he reasoned that none would be if all the Calimekkan branch were dead.

'We have to find her now,' he said. 'Now. It's desperate.'

Yanth said, 'I'll follow where you lead . . . but where in this vast place *will* you lead?'

Ry closed his eyes and tried to locate the woman. In the House, her belongings and objects in which she had invested a part of herself surrounded him. He felt their faint glows in all directions, pulling at him. Too, his own fear and excitement pressured him to act quickly, now that his moment had finally come, before something could take her from him permanently – and both fear and excitement clouded his senses. Adding to that difficulty was the overwhelming force of magic gathered and aimed at the Galweighs but not yet discharged – that seemed to thicken the very air he breathed, and to make him feel as if he were running uphill through deep mud. He couldn't get a clear fix on her. In several places in the House, however, he felt her presence most strongly, and at least all of those were in the same direction. 'Upward,' he said. 'She's got to be somewhere above us.' He ran for the nearest stairs.

* * *

The Galweigh Wolves chanted in darkness, building a crushing blow against the Sabir Wolves – one that would strike them just as the Galweigh forces in Halles would surely defeat the combined Dokteerak and Sabir forces. Drummers at the four corners of the enormous work-room pounded out four separate rhythms that wound over and around and through each other, talking back and forth, moving like smoky voices in and out of the joined voices of the wizards who spun the destruction and death of their hereditary enemies out of syllables and will. No fires illuminated the windowless room, yet there was light – a soft glow that flowed around the sacrifices who begged for their lives in their cage in the center of the room. And there was, uncharacteristically, the smell of honeysuckle, at first soft and seductive, and then increasingly strong, and laced with scents of death and decay.

Baird Galweigh, much-Scarred head of the Family's Wolves, threw his head back and howled the final words of the spell of destruction . . . and as he did, he felt ancient minds brush against his, and ancient ambitions shiver against invisible bars. Fear curled in his gut, but he had faced more than fear in his lifetime, and the promises of his enemies' destruction sang louder than the warnings his gut gave him. He brought the spell to its conclusion, supported by the will of the rest of the Wolves.

Lightning crackled in the room, running from the floor up the walls, streaming across the ceiling, heading toward the Sabir compound, seeking the magical high ground the spell had made of the Sabir Wolves. The Galweigh Wolves braced themselves and turned their attention to their captives, held in the center of the room – captives meant to handle the *rewhah*, the equal force of negative energy that would rebound from the spell just cast. Any part of the *rewhah* that they didn't absorb, the Wolves would have to take. And any magic that the Wolves had to absorb would Scar them.

The pressure built in the room, and built, and built, and Baird crouched lower and lower, mimicking in an unconscious physical display the magical preparations his body made to ward off the coming blow.

Abruptly the lightning reversed course and poured into

the captives, directed there by the Wolves. The fierce will of the wizards held the magical backwash on the screaming captives while the energy twisted and mangled their bodies. But suddenly the lightning spread, and burst free of the bounds, and poured over the Wolves, too, twisting them and melting them and reshaping them as if it were fire and they were wax.

The captives exploded in balls of light, vanished in clouds of dust.

The lightning kept coming, and the Wolves began to fall to the floor – writhing, dying. Baird, in a last moment of clear thought, realized that the Sabir Wolves had chosen to attack the Galweigh Wolves at the same moment the Galweigh Wolves had attacked them. He hoped their *rewhah* was as uncontrollable; he hoped their death toll was as high.

But the last stimulus to touch his dying senses was not a sense of pain and fear in the Sabirs. It was the reek of honeysuckle so strong it seemed a blanket suffocating him to death.

Chapter 14

Energy sang through the White Hall as the attack spell shattered the Galweigh Wolves, and the Sabirs braced themselves against the return blow. At the central pillar, Danya Galweigh screamed and writhed, her body absorbing almost all of the magical backlash. Her form changed from lovely to hideous as foul magic poured through her; she sprouted horns and spines, grew scales and fangs and claws, then shed them for worse and more hideous things; always she melted and twisted obscenely. But the Sabirs had guessed her strength and her resilience well, and she buffered them from the deadly *rewhah* energy, while the Wolves, by spreading out the slight overflow among themselves, prevented any one of their number from taking heavy Scars.

What the Sabirs hadn't figured into their careful calculations was a simultaneous attack from the Galweighs, and when that spell hit their sacrifice, the combined forces of it and their own *rewhah* broke free of the confinements of their spells and the buffer of the girl. Danya Galweigh sizzled for an instant, and black lightning coalesced around her; the air filled with smoke and the sickening scent of decay; she screamed so loudly and with such terror that her throat sounded like it was tearing itself apart. Then thunder crashed inside the White Hall, and the girl vanished utterly. And the combined magic of spell and *rewhah* smashed down on the Sabir Wolves, unbuffered, undirected, and raw.

Those quickest to understand what was happening – the senior Wolves and the unholy triad of Andrew, Anwyn, and Crispin – quickly shifted the brunt of the streaming hell of power onto the younger, weaker Wolves. Thus they survived, though even they bore fresh Scars. Those who were neither so quick nor so ruthless died horribly, melting into inhuman forms, changing and changing until the mutations became too many and too lethal to survive, begging as they writhed for rescue, collapsing with their pleas unanswered.

The walls of the White Hall began to scream – the babble of a thousand voices, of a hundred long-dead tongues. Clearly, the survivors heard the sound of a door opening, though the White Hall had no doors. Light shimmered, laughter echoed amid the thunder and the lightning, and for an instant the scent of honeysuckle became so thick it was suffocating.

The surviving Wolves fell unconscious to the floor, overwhelmed by the force of whatever it was that had come through that otherworldly door.

* * *

Almost home. Kait watched the great city slide beneath the airible and wondered if she would have time to visit with her sisters and brothers before she received her next assignment. She smiled out the window, her mind already racing ahead to the visit – Drusa was pregnant and Echo had just had a baby, and Kait, who would never dare have children of her own, loved to feel the movement of new life in her older sister's belly, and loved to feel her younger sister's son grip her finger with his tiny hand.

Almost home. Tippa had finally stopped her wailing; Dùghall had promised her a trip to his islands as consolation, and her choice of the best Imumbarran weaving. She napped. Dùghall stretched out on one of the velvet-upholstered benches, reading.

Below and well to her right, she saw the first glimpse of the House. Its ivory walls surrounded emerald lawn like a ring around a jewel. She sighed. Almost home ... to sisters and brothers and endless cousins; to laughter-spiced meals taken at the long tables; to talks with her mother as they sat by the fountains or walked through the hanging garden in the morning; to evening discussions of city policy and trade and politics with her father and uncles; to familiar books in the library and the familiar smell and feel of her bed, her sheets, her room.

She anticipated her return, and wondered if she would be so homesick after every assignment, or if leaving would get easier with time.

Her head began to ache again.

She blinked, and rubbed absently at her temples. She closed her eyes.

The pain got worse.

Dùghall groaned. Kait sat up, frowning, and said, 'Uncle? My head –'

The blinding pain took her by surprise. She clutched at her pounding skull and cried out, as wave upon wave of fire-hot agony drove sight from her eyes and threw her, helpless, to the airible floor.

The pressure doubled, and doubled again, and at last blackness swallowed her.

* * *

Aouel pulled the valve chain that shifted the ballast toward the airible's nose. Calimekka slid by below; the starkness of the gridwork of streets and the shadow-outlined pattern of red and brown tile roofs contrasted with the rampant jungle greenery that burst from every tiny square of unwatched earth, and with the colorful rush of people and animals filling the avenues and alleys. Already he could see the front face of Galweigh House carved into the side of the cliff, and the sleek, translucent curve of the walls around it. He loved the calm of the air, the distance from the noise and bustle of the city, the feeling of being part of the world that hurried below, yet apart from it and superior to it as well.

He let his concentration drift to thoughts of the newest airible, already under construction on the Galweigh airfield in Glasmar, and the improvements in lift and speed he'd heard boasted of it; he'd done no more than install himself as imaginary captain of it, though, before a groan, a thud, and a scream, all in quick succession, destroyed his fantasy. He grabbed his dagger and turned, expecting to find Dokteerak stowaways, perhaps – but he could see no sign of danger. Kait lay on the cabin floor, unmoving. As he hurried to her he could see that her chest still rose and fell. Sweat beaded her unnaturally pale skin, and beneath her closed eyelids, her eyes darted from side to side.

'What happened?' he asked Dùghall. But though Dùghall remained in his seat and his eyes stayed open, the ambassador didn't answer. Instead, he leaned against the velvet cushions, his face as pale as Kait's, seeming to see and hear nothing that went on around him. He trembled and pressed his hands to his ears as if to block out some unpleasant sound.

Aouel looked to Tippa, who stared back at him. 'What happened?'

'I don't know,' she said. She'd just woken up. Her eyes were red and swollen from all the crying, and she looked frightened. Still, she knelt by Kait and checked her pulse, then checked. Dùghall's. Aouel had always thought her empty-skulled, but perhaps she'd inherited a bit of the Family's sense after all. 'I was asleep, and I heard a shout.'

Aouel glanced toward the airible's controls. It maintained the gentle downward spiral that he'd set for it. He had a moment before he was needed back at the controls. So he tried to rouse Dùghall, who appeared to be less affected by whatever had happened. He shook his shoulder, then jerked his hand back as, for just a moment, an eerie faint green light illuminated Dùghall's body. The light vanished so quickly Aouel could have tried to convince himself that he'd imagined it – but he didn't think he had.

In any case, Dùghall groaned and clutched his head, and opened his eyes. 'All those voices . . .' he whispered.

Then his eyes met Aouel's. 'Kait?'

'She hasn't moved,' Aouel told him.

Dùghall massaged his forehead. 'Take Tippa to the front with you. Land us as quickly as you can.' Dùghall gave Tippa a hard look. 'You, as soon as we land, go inside and find your cousin Tammesin. Tell him I need help out here. Don't say a word about what has happened. Not a word. Nothing about Kait, nothing about me fainting, only that I need Tammesin's help out here. Do you understand?'

Tippa nodded.

'Go, then.' He turned his attention to Aouel. 'Have we much longer until we land?'

'No.'

'Good. Land us, then get me some help for the girl. Make sure that idiot Tippa doesn't go shouting all over the House that something has happened to Kait. This was . . .' He frowned and lowered his voice. 'It was an enemy attack. It has the feel of Sabir work, but there's more to it than that. Something dangerous is going on, and until I've had the chance to speak to the paraglese, we need to keep it quiet.'

Aouel felt sick. Sabir work – and it had affected Kait badly. He wondered how much danger she was in. He ran to the front and took up the controls again – the airible had drifted south of its destination, but it had not gone badly out of range. He'd have to circle around and come at the landing ground from the north, which would be awkward. Most of the regular landing men were in Halles with the rest of the soldiers; an unpracticed crew composed primarily of householders would be bringing him in, and they wouldn't be looking for him to come from the north.

On this day, he wasn't supposed to announce his arrival – the removal of the Galweighs from Halles was supposed to have been accomplished with stealth at both ends of the journey. Under other circumstances, he would have circled overhead until the landers saw him and came out to bring the airible in. These were not normal circumstances, however. He had strict instructions to get on the ground as quickly as he could.

So he pulled the cord that sent air screaming through the valves of the airible's ready alarm. They would hear that alarm inside the House, on the grounds . . . and yes, probably all the way to the Sabir compound, two hills away. To Tonn's hell with all of them, and anyone who complained of his actions.

By the time he'd fought the airible into position, the lander crew was on the ground. He skipped protocols and brought the airible down as fast as he could, dropping the mooring ropes well before any of the men could hope to catch them. Some might tangle . . . but enough wouldn't.

'Be ready to jump the second we touch down,' he told Tippa. For a wonder, she didn't quibble about muddying her skirts or skinning her knees. Partly to keep her calm enough that she wouldn't do anything stupid, and partly to reassure himself, he said, 'I'm sure Kait'll be fine,' though he wasn't sure of any such thing.

'She'd better be,' Tippa said softly. 'She risked her life for me, standing against some Gyru princes on Naming Day night. And Uncle told me she's the one who discovered the Dokteeraks' plan to kill me today. I'd be once shamed and once dead without her.'

The landers were slow to the winches and sloppy with the ropes, but Aouel had expected nothing better. He closed down the throttle that fed fuel into the airible's engines and let the landers do their work, never mind that they did it poorly. He got down into the gangway with Tippa, so that he could assist her to the ground – he couldn't expect the tyros manning the ropes to know assisting the Family passengers was their job, too.

So when the airible stopped descending and he opened the hatch, he wasn't prepared for the sight that greeted him – a line of Sabir archers hidden from the air by the overhang of the House's first-floor balcony, their bows drawn and their arrows aimed at the landers; two more archers, these not dressed in their Sabir livery, with their arrows trained on Tippa and him; and a handful of rough-looking swordsmen in Sabir livery who came running toward the airible gondola.

Aouel didn't think; he shouted, 'Dùghall – Sabir!' at the same time that Tippa screamed.

The Sabir troops grinned, and the archers drew their bows tighter.

'On the ground,' one man shouted. 'Both of you. Now. Or we'll kill the girl.'

Aouel swallowed. He lowered Tippa to the ground, then jumped down himself.

'Who else is aboard?'

'The ambassador. Dùghall.'

'That's all?'

'Yes,' Aouel lied.

The swordsman turned to Tippa. 'That the truth?'

Tippa nodded.

The swordsman glanced at Aouel, his eyes taking in the livery, the braided black hair, the bead-trimmed beard. 'You're the pilot of that thing, right?'

Aouel nodded.

'And Rophetian?'

'Yes.'

'Rophetians are all right, and we can use a trained pilot. You'll find a place with us.' He gestured to two of the other swordsmen, and they moved to Aouel's side, efficiently took his weapons away from him, and pulled him out of the way of the gangway.

The swordsman turned back to Tippa. 'And who are you? The little bride-to-be?'

She nodded.

'Another damned Galweigh. We have more of you people than we need . . . but I'm sure the men will find a way to make your wedding day memorable.' He laughed and grabbed her arm, intending to shove her toward more of the Sabir soldiers.

It happened so quickly that Aouel almost missed it. The Sabir's fingers wrapped around Tippa's upper left arm. Her right hand whipped out of the folds of her skirt and her dagger flashed across his throat before he could raise his hand to block it. Blood gouted from the wound in a pulsing stream, spattering the girl's face and her hands and her dress. In the same instant that the swordsman's fingers began to lose their grip, two arrows sprouted from Tippa's rib cage as if by magic, and she stared down at her chest, her expression shocked and disbelieving. She turned to look at him, eyes round; she looked so much like she wanted him to explain, and her mouth opened, and he would have sworn she was going to ask him a question. Then she sagged, and the life went out of her eyes, and she fell across the downed swordsman.

Then Dùghall appeared in the gangway, and looked down at the body of his niece, and dropped heavily to the ground. 'I'll see that you pay for that,' he told the archers. They laughed, and one drew back his bow. But another of the swordsmen snarled, 'Put that down. He's the one we were to get, you ass,' and the archer relaxed the tension on the bowstring.

Aouel thought, yes, they would want Dùghall. The Imumbarra Isles were the heart of the Galweigh caberra trade, and if the Sabirs wanted to take that over, they would have to find out what he knew, and perhaps work out a deal with him. He was, after all, one of the Imumbarran gods.

And the Sabirs weren't fools; they would want the spice trade. So for the time, at least, Dùghall would be safe.

He avoided looking at the ambassador, afraid that his eyes might show too plainly the question he wanted most to ask: *What did you do with Kait?*

He might find out too soon – several of the swordsmen were clambering aboard to search the gondola. He stood, forcing his face to remain impassive, hoping that Dùghall had hidden her, wishing he could sneak just a quick look at the diplomat but not daring even the most hurried glimpse.

He prayed for the safety of his friend, and stood sweating in the hot sun, and finally the Sabir soldiers came back to the gangway and said, 'All clear. Found some mail and some silk and a couple of silver bottles shaped like cats. Nobody else in there, though.'

As the soldiers force-marched him and Dùghall toward the House, Aouel almost smiled.

Chapter 15

The sound of voices yammering unintelligibly inside his skull finally brought Ry around. He opened his eyes, intending to demand silence of the people making all the noise – but only one person sat beside him. That was Yanth, and Yanth dozed on a chair, a bandage covering part of his head.

The voices shouted louder – not from another room or from far away, but from right inside his head. Three of them, two men and one woman, argued in the most heated and scathing tones, but while he could make out each syllable of each of their words clearly, he couldn't understand anything they said. Further, he couldn't even identify the language they spoke – which seemed to him both terrible and strange. As a Sabir, trained from birth to both diplomacy and magic, the languages of Ibera – both living and dead – kept few secrets from him. He spoke most of the living languages fluently and could at least follow basic conversations in the rest. Of the dead languages, he had solid knowledge as well; most of the surviving works on magic were written in the five major tongues of ancient Kasree, which had been Ibera and Strithia and part of Manarkas before the so-called Thousand Years of Darkness.

Yet he recognized nothing of the conversation that went on inside his skull save the tones of rage.

He pressed his fists against his temples and tried to remember what had happened. He and his friends had been running up the stairs. Something had exploded inside of his head – tremendous pain and noise had blinded him and driven him to his knees. The world had filled with the scent of flowers and rot.

And beyond that . . . nothing. Nothing.

What time was it? Where was he? Where were the rest of his friends? How long had he lain insensate? And what had become of the Galweigh woman in the meantime?

He sat up. The voices fell silent, but he didn't have the feeling that they had left him. Only that they waited for something. It was madness to believe he heard voices in his head, except he didn't believe himself the sort to go mad.

In a chair next to the cot on which he lay, his best friend slept. Ry said, 'Yanth, wake up.'

Yanth stirred, groaned, and opened his eyes. 'My head pains me,' he said, then focused on Ry. 'Gods, you're finally awake . . .' He frowned and rose from the chair in a jerky, almost panicked motion, and backed away. 'Or are you?'

Ry had no patience with nonsense. 'Of course I'm awake. What a stupid question.'

'If it were a stupid question, I wouldn't have a gash in the side of my head, and poor Valard would not be curled in the next room with his arm broke in two. We mistook you for awake once before, and you attacked us.'

Ry winced. Perhaps he *was* the sort to go mad; he remembered nothing of the incident, but he would not disbelieve Yanth.

'What happened?'

'What do you remember?'

'Going up the stairs in Galweigh House. Some sort of

explosion, and a terrible smell. Pain. Darkness. Then nothing.'

Yanth sighed and settled himself back into the chair. 'There was no explosion in Galweigh House. No smell, no noise. You were running ahead of us and suddenly you dropped to the floor and held your head. Your eyes were open, but you said nothing to us, and no matter what we did, you would give us no sign that you heard. We tried everything we could think of to wake you, but at last we realized nothing we knew to do would help, so we carried you down the stairs again. We left your father's man in charge with explicit instructions that if a girl like the one we were looking for showed up, he was to save her for you. He said he would. His men were already killing the nonessentials by then and dragging out the bodies to be burned, but he said he would watch for such a girl, and that he would not permit her to be killed. We tried to take you home for help . . . but . . .' Here his face clouded, and he fell silent.

'But what?'

Yanth said, 'I wanted one of your Family's physicks to see you, but none were available. Something terrible happened to your Family.'

Something inside of Ry knotted, and he swallowed. 'What sort of terrible thing?'

'The physicks don't know. One of your younger cousins went to the White Hall. He told the physicks that something had drawn him there. He found many of your relatives . . . dead . . . and many more . . . ah . . . changed, the physick told me, but he would not tell me how.'

'My parents?'

Yanth seemed to shrink. 'Your mother is badly injured, though she lives. Your . . .' He sighed deeply, and said, 'I'm sorry, Ry. Your father is dead.'

Ry paled. His father had led the Wolves, and through

them the entire Sabir Family. If his father was truly dead, then leadership of the Family came open. And the new leader would be chosen by maneuvering among the strongest of those who survived. The maneuvering would likely kill as many as the disaster had, though in cleverer ways. 'How many others are dead?' he asked. 'And who still lives?'

'I don't know. The physick I spoke to spared me only the time he needed to look at you and tell me he could do nothing for you, and that further he had others in desperate need of his services. I found out about your parents and the little I did hear while he checked your breathing and your heart, and then he told me to take you away from the House and hide you someplace safe, because he didn't know what had happened to your relatives, but he could not promise that it would not happen again. And until any of the survivors of the White Hall could wake up and talk, he told me to assume the worst.'

'Was it some trick of the Galweighs?' Ry mused, but of course it had been some trick of the Galweighs. They had discovered the Sabirs' true plan for their destruction and had countered it.

No, that wouldn't answer it. If the Galweighs were to blame, their corpses wouldn't be burning in piles on the grounds of Galweigh House. The Dokteeraks? No again. They had no Wolves among them – the Sabirs and the Galweighs alone among the Five Families knew the old magics, or dared to use them. Yanth hadn't said Ry's relatives had been attacked by magic, but the physick would never have dared admit that to someone who wasn't even Family, much less a Wolf. He had told Yanth those who survived the attack had been changed, though – to Ry, who had seen the Scars wrought by spell rebound, nothing more needed to be said. And nothing but magic could have destroyed his father and injured his mother in the same attack. Nothing else – he was sure of that.

Not the Galweighs. Not the Dokteeraks. He couldn't entirely rule out a play from the inside – he would have no trouble believing, for example, that his cousin Andrew and his second cousins Crispin and Anwyn would kill off whatever relatives they could in order to take over leadership of the Family among themselves. The only problem with that theory was that neither they nor any other faction that he was aware of currently held a majority among the Wolves. No one within the Family would be able to muster the sort of magical support it would take to subvert the energy of a spell against the other Wolves in the Family – and to attempt a takeover without a majority would be suicide. Crispin, Anwyn, and Andrew weren't suicidal. That he was sure of.

So the destruction had come from another player. A *powerful* player. Who, though? And how? And what did this other player hope to gain?

* * *

They're dead, Kait. They're all dead, and you will be, too, unless you get away from this place.

Stifling air and the stink of alcohol. A soft, heavy weight that covered her entirely and pushed her to the ground. Her head pounded, and her eyes refused to work. The voice inside her head would not be still; she wanted to return to the comfort of darkness, but some woman she did not know insisted on talking to her.

They're all dead – the Sabirs are burning their bodies now. You could smell the fires if you got up.

She blinked, but what she saw with her eyes open remained the same as what she saw with them closed – exactly nothing. The perfect blackness of blindness swallowed her. Something bad had happened. Something had taken her out of the security of the world she had known; something had changed the rules of the world as

185

she understood it; something dangerous had opened a door and stepped through it.

She recalled pain, and a sweet, rotting odor. She closed her eyes and pressed her fingers to her throbbing skull, and tried to recall as much as she could of those last moments. The feeling of growing evil that had been so strong at the Dokteerak party, which had worsened in the following days, had abruptly overwhelmed her in the air above the ground; and for just an instant she had felt the elation of a beast caged that had at last broken free of its bars; and then she had, impossibly, smelled some sickeningly sweet smell – and what had it been? The name eluded her, but she would recognize it again if she ran across it. And then an insane babble exploded in her skull, as if a thousand madmen began shouting all at once, each trying to get her attention, and the pain of that bedlam drove her into the dark escape of unconsciousness. And now?

Airible fuel, she realized. The alcohol smell was airible fuel. She was still on the airible, but no longer in the passenger part of the gondola; instead she lay in the space just to the fore of the fuel chambers, tucked under folds of emergency cloth kept on hand for en route repairs on the airible's outer skin.

Someone had hidden her. Had the ship landed safely, Dùghall would have carried her to a physick – or taken care of her himself, knowing what he knew. Instead, she had been carefully placed in concealment in a part of the ship that was easy to reach from the passenger section, but intentionally difficult to find. Further, she'd been hidden *within* that carefully chosen hiding place, which implied that whoever hid her expected hostile others to perform more than a cursory search.

Which they did, the unidentified woman said. She spoke inside of Kait's head, which made her either a sign that Kait had gone mad, or a sign that the world had.

Kait, who didn't consider herself prone to the weaknesses embraced by many of the women of her class, preferred to assume the latter.

For the time being, she would accept the presence of the stranger in her head. She offered information, and Kait needed information. Once Kait reached safety, she would question the other woman's presence, and her identity, but at that moment, simple curiosity was a luxury that Kait couldn't afford.

'So they searched the ship for me,' she whispered.

For anyone who was left. They got the other three.

'And who are *they*?'

You already know that.

Yes, she did. 'When you woke me up, you said the Sabirs.'

Yes.

That made sense. They were the only Family who would dare attack the Galweighs on their own ground; they were the only ones so evil or so desperate to expand their power that they would take such a risk. Apparently they'd succeeded.

So hostile forces held the airible. Kait ran her left hand along her thigh and felt the comforting shape of the sword pommel. Armed in human form, she might successfully protect herself without the dangerous exposure of Shift. She had at least some hope of vengeance. She listened, and was rewarded with muffled night sounds and distant but unintelligible voices, and the creak of the airible as it tugged against the mooring ropes.

She squirmed out to the edge of the bale and breathed slowly. The stink of the fuel got worse, but the air instantly became cooler; a more than even trade. She heard breathing just above the trapdoor that led into her hiding place – rapid panting interrupted by soft whuffles. 'Who's out there?' she whispered, and received a low whine and a moment of soft scratching at the trapdoor in response.

A friend of yours, the woman said. *He jumped into the airible when everyone else was gone, and has been lying on the door ever since.*

Kait's skin crawled. 'Gashta?'

The whining became louder, the pawing at the door more insistent.

The old friend was a wolf, a sometimes-comrade of the hills with whom she had run deer and peccaries when in her Karnee form. She had saved his life once, and he rewarded her with a loyalty she didn't think existed in humans. He was, however, no pet, but a fully wild wolf who ran the mountaintops through and around Cali-mekka, and she could not understand how he came to be aboard the airible. Either the ship had come down somewhere outside the walls surrounding Galweigh House, or the walls themselves had been breached and something had drawn him inside.

Out from under the piles of cloth, her eyes had adjusted to the dim light. She'd been unconscious for a long time. Night had fallen; otherwise, light-prisms that ran all along the top of the work areas of the gondola would have brought in daylight.

What should she do? Attack whoever she found outside the airible and kill as many as she could before she died? Try to escape to bring help? Or to raise an army to attempt retaking the House? Or should she surrender and die without a fight?

'"Before action, discern the situation,"' she murmured. Some of Nas Madible's wisdom – and unlike her uncle Dùghall's beloved Vincalis, the Family as a whole held Madible's works in high regard. Her tutors ground him into her skull from the moment she began diplomatic training.

Discern the situation. The stranger said the wolf was

the only one except for Kait aboard the airible. So she should be safe for the moment. She brushed her fingertips lightly over the hilt of her sword, seeking reassurance, then pushed up on the trapdoor. Gashta resisted only for an instant, then moved off. She slid the trapdoor out of her way, vaulted into the passenger compartment, and pushed the door back into place. While she crouched beside it, Gashta nuzzled her, licked her face, and whined again.

The stranger had been right. No one occupied the compartment. Now, though, she could hear more clearly the voices on the ground outside. And she could smell something that the fuel stink had completely covered: the rich, roasting-pork scent of burning flesh. Human flesh. She'd witnessed the burning of a Scarred spy in Calimekka's Punishment Square as part of her diplomatic training. What she smelled then, she smelled again.

They're all dead, the stranger had said. She'd been right about everything else so far. The Sabirs were out there burning the dead bodies of her relatives. So Kait had to entertain the possibility that she was the last surviving member of her Family.

No. She couldn't think that. Despair was too close, and her chances of survival slim enough even without it. They're *not* all dead, she told herself. If I act well, and quickly, I'll save some of them.

Before action, discern the situation.

She stood, and Gashta growled.

'Hush,' she whispered, and drew her sword. First she had to find out where she was.

She crept to the airible's windows and looked out. And her heart nearly broke. The airible was moored on the landing field of Galweigh House, and even from where she watched, she could see that the great gate stood open – that gate which had, in her memory, never stood open for more than the time needed to permit passage of any approved entrant. She could see the gate clearly in the dancing light of the flames from a massive pyre that burned beside it, and she could see, too, the pyre. And the black silhouettes of the bodies that fueled it. And outside the edge of the flames, soldiers. Sabir soldiers, with the twin trees of the Sabir crest clearly outlined on their cloaks.

Galweigh House had fallen.

She swallowed the tears that came, and she and the wolf crept out of the airible and down onto the airible field. She took her sword and killed the two men who guarded the field – silently, without either warning or remorse. The House lay under heavy guard, and she knew that no matter how swift or fierce she was, she would not be able to rescue any survivors alone. She could choose to die with them, or she could find help.

Goft lay only twenty leagues to the north and east, and the city of Maracada held one of the Lesser Houses of the Galweighs, Cherian House. The Family in Cherian House traded, and held tremendous riches, and owned an armada of ships and men by the hundreds who would be strong and fierce and able to fight for what the Family had lost. She had to reach them.

You haven't much time, the stranger said.

Kait already knew that.

The airible was the way to reach Goft, of course, but without a crew of men to cast off the mooring ropes smoothly, she had a problem. She had to get off the ground and obtain some height before the Sabirs noticed her. She lay in the dew-damp grass beside the wolf, watching the men who moved back and forth in front of the flames tending the fire. She studied the round lines of the airible as it tugged against the mooring ropes in the breeze. She tested the wind. She frowned. Too much of it to loosen the ropes one at a time; if she did, the airible would swing around and face into the breeze, or perhaps even unbalance and hang tail-up – and she would be discovered.

There was a way, of course. The Galweighs and their researchers and implementers held both the secret of airible construction and the secret of the great engines that powered them. According to her father, a single Ancient manuscript, which survived through the whole of the Thousand Years of Darkness, came to rest at last in the Family's hands – full of secrets, that manuscript, many of which it still kept locked within cryptic comments and diagrams for machinery whose uses no one in these latter days could discern. But the House artisans and inventors, moved to a safe, hidden location, had pried out the facts about powered flight one by one, and had at last succeeded in giving the Galweighs wings. And for the last ten years, the Galweighs had guarded those secrets jealously. Should any airible fall into enemy hands, the pilot knew to release a hidden lever that would break off all the mooring ropes simultaneously at the envelope and cast the ship loose. It would still be flyable, though not landable – the pilot would have to survive a crash once he found a place away from the enemy to bring the ship down – but keeping airibles out of enemy hands meant more than retrieving a single airship.

Kait knew where that lever was; she had some experience flying the ship; she could get herself to Goft. Getting safely to ground once there held its own risks, but she would deal with them when she got that far.

She ran her fingers along the wolf's hackles, wondering why he'd sought her out, and how he'd found her. She could not take him with her, but she feared to leave him within reach of the Sabirs. When she began to creep back to the airible, though, he solved her dilemma for her; he licked her nose once, and bit very gently on her ear. Then he growled, rose, and trotted along the wall toward the gate. She watched him for just an instant and realized other wolves waited at the gate for him.

She wondered if she would ever see him again. Then she crawled along the ground to the gangway of the airible, launched herself up and into it as if she were wolf herself, and quickly slid her hand under the polished wood of the control console to the hidden lever. She jerked the lever, heard for a fraction of an instant the whine of cables slipping, and felt the jolt as the airible leaped upward in an unpowered, awkward lift – and then the wolves began to howl.

Breezes that blew along the clifftop buffeted the airible; Kait feared that she would strike the trees or the wall before she could rise above them, so swiftly did the airible move across the ground. Miraculously, though she felt the gondola scrape along the top of the wall while the airible shuddered, she lifted free, and floated upward into the blackness of the night.

Below her the city blinked and shimmered with the soft illumination of countless thousands of candles glowing forth from countless thousands of windows; with the brighter fires in the lamps set by the lamplighters each night as twilight fell; with the sharper glow of the gas flames in the foundries where, even after dark, men toiled and sweated; and . . . with the stark bonfire that sent its greasy coils from the grounds of Galweigh House down into the already smoke-scented city below, taking with it much of her Family.

But not all. Not all. She would not let herself believe the voice of the stranger in her head, the voice that said *All gone. All gone.* She would make the Sabirs pay for the life of each loved one they took from her. She swore by all her gods that she would destroy them, or die in the attempt.

Chapter 16

Dùghall permitted himself the smallest of smiles when the wolves began to howl. He tightened his fist over the cut in his palm; the tiny magical spell that had drawn them to the fire hadn't been as difficult or cost as much as he had anticipated. His call had been general – to any creature that would slip within the walls of Galweigh House and watch Kait until she got safely away, then signal her escape. He'd expected a bird – birds responded well to him. But the wolves answered first, and seemed eager to come, as if they were familiar with the House and its confines . . . or with Kait. He didn't let himself worry about the strangeness of that. The night was full of magic, even yet, and as a Falcon he knew that all forms of life responded in their own way to it, and for their own reasons – but that those summoned from good responded with good. They wouldn't hurt her.

And their howling let him know that she had somehow managed to get herself to safety outside Galweigh House's walls. While curious about how she'd managed it, he wasn't surprised. That image of the wall she'd climbed in Halles remained clear in his mind.

With her safe, the time arrived for his next move. He continued to lie on the floor, feigning sleep; the Sabir guards had locked him and the other 'valuable' Galweighs, and such technicians and artists as they'd found, in a windowless inner chamber on the fourth floor. Two – the House seneschal and a brawny distant cousin of Dùghall's – lay dead in a corner from injuries they had sustained in an attempted escape. The guards had refused to summon medical help for them while they lived, and had (to Dùghall's relief and the rest of his companions' dismay) refused to remove the corpses when they died. Their bodies lay in the corner next to him – he'd bedded down within reach of them by choice.

Dùghall sent cautious mental tendrils out and touched each of the room's living inhabitants. Most slept deeply. A few drifted between sleep and wakefulness. Only one other than himself lay awake. Dùghall repressed a sigh and, with his tiny spare dagger, which had escaped the guards' careful search – for what guard would think of checking in the tuck beneath the roll of fat on a middle-aged diplomat's belly for a knife no bigger than a thumb? – he reopened the shallow cut in his palm and dripped his blood onto the floor, and summoned for the one who lay awake and the few who drifted or fought nightmares a peaceful, restful sleep.

He tried no such trick on the guards who sat outside the door, laughing at each other's stories of the women they'd raped and the loot they'd stolen that day. First, the Sabir men wore amulets made by some Sabir master which protected them from minor magics. Second, he *wanted* the bastards outside the door. It was the best place for them.

When he was sure he alone among the room's inhabitants remained awake, he sat up and crawled between the two corpses. He reached out and touched their cold bodies, feeling for their hands. When he found them, he placed both on the floor in front of him, fighting the stiffness that had set in. He would get no blood from them; he would have to make the offering one of flesh. Flesh would make the spell stronger, but also harder to control. And the taint of wild magic that still pervaded the House and the city gave him pause. No matter how pure his casting, no matter how entirely defensive its character, the wild magic could add an uncontrollable twist to it that could send it back to attack him and his, and the strength of flesh magic could make it deadly. But he could do nothing and condemn the few survivors of his Family to death and worse – or he could make the attempt at their salvation, knowing death and worse might still be the result.

In his favor, the Sabirs had burned the other Galweigh corpses. And they would have, he felt sure, removed their own dead to Sabir House; until the Sabirs could consecrate Galweigh House to their own use, any other action would be heretical. An offering of only two corpses would be a meager number for what he needed, but if any in the fire lay even partially unburned, they would add strength to the sacrifice. And the fact that only a few corpses lay within the House's walls would keep the strength of the spell within bounds he might hope to control if it ran amok.

Such a delicate balance – the narrow strait between not enough and too much. He pursed his lips and began.

First he cut the corpses' hands across the palm and pressed the cuts together. He lay his own bloody palm across the top of the two dead hands and whispered:

'By the blood of the living
And the flesh of the dead,
I summon the spirits of Family
Who have gone before.
Without the walls of this room
But within the walls of this House

Enemies have come
And killed,

Have plundered
And pillaged,
Have conquered
And claimed.

Come, spirits of the dead.
All dead flesh within the walls of Galweigh House
I offer as your payment
If you will chase beyond the walls of this House
All alive beyond the walls of this room.
Harm none; draw no living blood;
Inflict no pain.
I ask not vengeance;
I ask only relief.

By my own spirit and my own blood
I offer myself as price to ensure
The safety of every living creature,
Friend and foe,
Now within the House's walls
Until this spell is done.
So be it.'

A cold voice, distant as the dark realm between the worlds yet close as death itself, murmured in his ear, 'We accept.' The finger of a spirit traced a line along his cheek, and a tongue that existed nowhere in the physical world licked the blood from his palm. Something sighed. Something else chuckled. The hair on the back of Dùghall's neck prickled, and icy sweat dripped from his upper lip and his forehead, slid down the furrow of his spine, and slicked his palms. He had never before summoned the dead. He hoped fervently that he never would find the need again.

Then the corpses began to glow, softly, from the inside, as if they were fat-bodied candles with the wicks burning deep in their hearts. Soft and red they shone, their light burning brighter as the bodies became ever more translucent, and then transparent. Dùghall felt the magic rising, strong as a river. But the force of the spell far exceeded what he had anticipated. How many dead had lain within the House's walls? Had that current of wild magic taken hold? He could not find the place where the spell drew extra strength, but while he sought for it, desperate to control the wildly growing pulse of energy, the magical river rose to the flood point, to the place where he might have had any hope of calling it back, and then beyond.

He closed his eyes and prayed that he had cast his spell without a trace of hatred, without any secret desire for the destruction or death of his enemies. If he had not, those enemies would surely die – but so would he and everyone in the room with him.

* * *

Hasmal rolled in the berth on the ship, restless, wakened yet again from nightmare-wracked sleep by the sound of laughter. And once again the laughter hung only in his memory, tinkling and feminine, never touching the world he inhabited.

In his dreams the creature who mocked him hovered over him, her hair red as rubies, her wings flashing and sparkling like gems in brilliant sunlight, her delicate body no bigger than his hand. She was a creature of the spirit world – the same spirit world he had invoked in seeking to escape his doom. One of her kind had told him to flee. His later spells and auguries had led him to this ship, to a captain who needed a man who could work metal and repair things.

The previous shipwright had arrived in port with too much money and too little sense, and had gotten both drunk and in trouble. The captain, when hiring Hasmal, clearly stated in his terms that he would not bail his men out of prison (which was how the job came to be open in the first place); Hasmal, who didn't drink and whose entire existence at the moment focused on keeping himself out of trouble, saw no problem in this. He'd been working for the past few days on getting the ship seaworthy, and the captain had spent the time (though so far without success) hunting for a cargo. He assured Hasmal that the *Peregrine* never waited long in harbor and that they would surely sail within days.

While not as good as being at sea, that promise seemed sufficient to get Hasmal out of harm's reach. But the spirit laughter rang in his dreams, and interrupted his sleep, and as he lay there in the darkness he wondered if he ought not flee upland, away from people, to hide in the dark wet jungle.

His castings were clear – tossed bones, the cards, and even a solitary late-night check with another of the blood-conjured spirits reassured him that he was where he needed to be. No matter how nervous he might become, this was his right path. His ship. The *Peregrine* was a form of falcon . . . as he was a form of falcon – and wasn't that a sign in itself? One falcon would fly the other falcon away from danger and destruction.

He settled down again in his berth and listened to the comforting creak of the planks and the lap of water against the hull. Sweet, soothing sounds that promised imminent escape and glorious freedom. He drifted to the edge of dreaming, to the twilight land between waking and sleep. And there the winged spirit sat, cross-legged in the air, a wicked grin on her face, waving her fingers at him.

Miserable beast. He strengthened his shields, drawing energy from the bay beneath him and the currents of air around him and spinning them into another layer of the wall that kept out evil and made him seem to be no one – a man who made no impression, left no mark, captured no one's fancy – and that gave him silence. Blessed silence. The spirit, walled out of his mind, vanished. After a while he slept.

* * *

Get up! Get up or you will die!

A man, by turns annoying and angry, shouted at her from somewhere in the distance. The girl curled tighter into a ball and tried to shut his voice out; it was bringing her to wakefulness, and though she could not remember why, she knew she didn't want to wake up.

At least move beneath the trees, where you'll have some shelter! Move! Move, girl! You cannot die on me now!

Her body hurt, but not in ways she understood. She didn't feel attached to the hurts at all. She recognized pain, but it didn't seem to be her pain. It occurred in places that her body didn't have. It hurt *wrong*, though she could not quite comprehend how that could be. She seemed to have been inserted into the body of a stranger, and the stranger's body didn't feel things the way she felt them, or smell things the way she smelled them, or hear things the way she heard them.

Vaguely, she knew that she was cold. The air smelled wrong – sterile and empty. All her life, her world had been scented by the lush growth of the jungle, the rich dark earth scents, the profuse perfumes of flowers, and the thousand colliding odors of the city of Calimekka, and now all of that had been erased and replaced with nothingness. The cold didn't bother her as much as the emptiness of smell . . . and of sound. She heard wind whistling and moaning, and from time to time a distant, sharp cracking, and nothing else.

Get up! Please get up! I can't let you die, girl. We need each other, you and I.

Almost nothing else, then. *He* hadn't left her yet. Why hadn't he? He was a stranger. She'd never heard his voice before. In fact, she'd never even heard a voice like his before. He spoke with a faint accent, but one unlike anything in her experience. And she thought she'd heard all of them. She opened one eye.

Whiteness assaulted her. Something had erased the world, leaving her in a place as empty as a sheet of vellum untouched by the scribe's pen. Impossible. If she rubbed her eyes, they would work again. She tried to do just that, but when she moved her arm, a monstrous clawed hand moved into view and reached for her. She screamed and tried to scrabble away, and the white ground gave way beneath her and beside her, and turned to powder that blew into her nose and her eyes and her mouth, stinging where it touched, and melting, and tasting like . . .

Snow.

She dropped into a deep drift of it, realizing as she did just what it was that surrounded her. This was the snow that merchants brought from far in the south and sold by the cupful in the open market. She had never imagined the world being covered in the stuff – in her mind, those merchants had always had to dig for the precious delicacy, mining the earth for pockets of it the way miners dug out opals and emeralds. Here lay a fortune in snow, so deep the pocket she stood in reached from her feet to her neck, stretching away as far as the eye could see in all directions. She turned, looking for anything else, and at last circled around to see a small copse of trees not too far away. Endless wind had bent them until they hunched over like tired old men carrying firewood on their backs. Their leaves were needle-shaped and short; they were green, but the green looked dreary and dark to her eyes.

She could not see the source of the voice that had so insistently harassed her until she woke; neither could she see any monster. In fact, in the whole world she seemed to be the only living creature. She wondered where the monster had gone, or the speaker; she wondered if they were one and the same. 'Where are you?' she shouted, and immediately, as if from inside her head, the voice she'd heard before whispered, *Shhhhh! They'll hear you, and you aren't ready to face them yet.*

She whirled around, but nothing was behind her. Keeping her voice down because she didn't like the sound of 'they'll hear you,' especially not when said with the frightened tone the stranger used, she said, 'Don't hide from me. Come out and let me see you.'

I . . . can't come out. And you can't see me. I'm trapped in a place where I've been kept prisoner since . . . well, since long before you were born. I can only send you my voice, but not into your ears. I speak to your mind, though I can see things through your eyes, and hear things through your ears.

Danya frowned, and lifted a hand to brush blowing snow from her face. And once again saw the hand of a monstrosity coming toward her face. This time she didn't scream. Bits and pieces of memory were starting to come back to her – she began to recall being in a dungeon for a long time, and then being kept prisoner in the rooms of her Sabir torturers. Yes. Those days blurred into an endless pageant of humiliations and degradations and pain. They had ended, though; she no longer lay chained to the floor. Something had happened recently – something had taken her from the three of them, but that something had been worse than what they had done to her . . .

Then she had it. The memory returned, and she wanted to scream, but did not. Instead, she stared at the hand. Her hand. Tiny dark copper scales covered it like armor, right to the fingertips that terminated in hard, black, curving talons. The scales moved up the arm, becoming larger and lighter in color, so that at the elbow they were a bright copper, and at the shoulder, where spikes of bone or horn jutted from above and below the joint, they were pale, almost tan, but still with the same metal sheen. She moved the hand and its twin to her face, and closed her eyes so that she didn't accidentally scratch them out, and she felt her face. Nothing of the woman she had once been remained. She now found a sharp crest of bone running from the top of her skull down to the much-widened space between her eyes. Her nose swept forward, as long as one hand, part of a lean muzzle. Her teeth felt like daggers – rows of daggers. More spikes erupted from the angle of her jaw on either side of her face – a face now entirely covered by tiny, pebblelike scales.

Not until her fingers tangled into a heavy braid of long soft black hair did she begin to weep. The hair, now wet and in some places frozen, felt no different than it had before she served as sacrifice to the Sabirs. Before their magic Scarred her. The hair was still human, though she would never again be.

Ignoring the voice that implored her to move to the relative shelter of the copse of trees, she dropped to her knees and covered her eyes with her hands and sobbed. The invisible stranger kept telling her if she didn't find shelter, she would die. That suited her perfectly. She wanted to die.

Cold tears clung to her face and froze. The bitter wind howled around her and began to cut into her. In the distance, so far away that it might almost have been another voice of the wind, something screamed. Her heart howled out its pain and grief for all that she had lost and all she would never have again. She fell toward voluntary oblivion, looked at the darkness of surrender and easy death, and almost ... almost ... almost let herself tumble in.

Then, slowly, her sobs grew softer, and her tears fewer. Danya lifted her head and stared out at the bleak expanse of nothing that lay in all directions. Hellish nothing, empty of all she had once loved. She had lost her Family, her world, her friends – and in this twisted body she wore, she had to acknowledge that she had lost them forever. She could never go back and be Danya Galweigh, Wolf of the Galweighs, again. Her Family had not rescued her, had not ransomed her, had left her in the hands of enemies, and she could not and would not forget that. She had suffered in the hands of her captors, and she had expected to die many times, and wished to die many more. She hated the monsters who had tortured her. She would never escape the sounds of their voices, the feel of their touch, the bitter vision of their faces.

But she was alive. She was alive, and she was free, and no matter what the Galweighs had not done, and no matter what the Sabirs had done, she was now in a better position than any of them. Because she was alive, and they could not know that. And she knew who they were. And she knew where to find them.

And she would find them, no matter how long it took, no matter what it cost, no matter what she had to do. She would find the people who had abandoned her, and those who had tortured her, and those who had sacrificed her, and she would make them pay.

She stood, and shook the snow from her body, and lifted her head. Let them lie in their warm beds, safe in the comfort of their ignorance. She was coming.

She was coming.

Very good, the voice of her unseen ally whispered in her thoughts. *Very good indeed. I thought you were strong enough to survive. If you desire revenge, I will do everything in my power to help you get it. Anything, Danya. But first I suggest we get you to shelter, and perhaps food. Because you won't be able to make them pay if you die here.*

'You can get me to shelter?'

I can direct you. I am limited in what I can do – but I have ways of finding things.

'Why would you?'

Silence for a moment. Then, *Because I know what happened to you. Because I know what that's like. Because I didn't survive the things that happened to me. You wouldn't be wrong to never trust anyone again, but I can tell you that I've been where you are now, and I have more reason than you could ever believe to help you get what you want. You can help me, Danya – and I can help you.*

Danya considered that. She did not know how the spirit had found her, or why; she knew nothing of the person he had been. She did know, though, that she had no other allies, and was unlikely to survive to find them on her own.

'Lead me,' she said. 'I will follow.'

Chapter 17

Once in the sky and safely away from Galweigh House, Kait confronted the stranger who looked through her eyes, listened through her ears, and smelled the damp night air through her nose. The stranger kept silent, so that only the sense of presence and unfamiliar weight and the stranger's occasional restless shifting inside the recesses of her mind convinced her that the silent, watchful presence was not a figment born of imagination and the day's burden of grief and horror.

Kait started the engines in midair once she was sure she was well past the point where any of the Sabirs might hear them. She fought the tailwind that kept pushing the airible north more than west. And when the airship was securely en route to Goft, she said, 'Now you can stop hiding and tell me who you are. And *what* you are.'

The stranger in her mind sighed. *Does it matter? I can help you.*

'It matters. Are you a demon of the sort which possesses people and drives them to speak to the air and foam at the mouth? Or are you a god who wants to require a task of me? Or are you something else?'

Nothing so grand as either a demon or a god. My name is Amalee Kehshara Rohannan Draclas.

Kait froze when she placed the name. 'You're my

great-great-great-great-great-grandmother?' Amalee Draclas was a martyr, dead nearly two hundred years, and
victim of none other than the Sabirs. Her torture and
murder, according to Family history, had been carried
out in front of the walls of Galweigh House, in full sight
of her husband and children.

Yes.

Kait didn't know what to say.

You doubt *me.*

'Yes.'

*You'd be a foolish girl if you didn't. I can prove who I
am to you, though. And I can help you get revenge on the
Sabirs.*

That her many-times-great-grandmother would want
revenge on the Sabirs, Kait could well believe. But that
she should appear as a voice in Kait's head . . .

*Magic released me from the place where I had been
imprisoned since the day the Sabirs murdered me. I have
no body, of course. But I remember who I am, and my
life before I was killed. And when I was released, I
sought out a descendant. You were the one that survived.*

'That makes sense, I suppose, though I never truly
believed in spirits that visited the living. I always thought
the dead went between the worlds and were reborn into
new bodies and new lives.'

*Your theory isn't too far from the mark . . . unless
sadistic torturers trap the spirit and cage it. I would
surely have lived again before now, had they not done
what they did to me.*

Kait recalled the mayhem that had pushed her over the
edge of the abyss into unconsciousness. *Many* voices had
fought for her attention. Some of them – no, most of
them – had been frightening.

I wasn't the only spirit so trapped, Amalee said. *And
some of those with whom I've spent the last thou – . . .
ah, two hundred years were evil. Truly evil.*

206

Kait accepted that explanation. 'What happened to all those others?'

Amalee didn't answer.

'Grandmother . . . what happened to all those others?'

The response held an air of weary sadness. *I don't know. They might have gone between. Or . . . perhaps not.*

Amalee didn't want to talk after that, and Kait needed to concentrate. The island of Goft made for a difficult target on a dark, windy night.

And later, as she watched the lights on the Goft coast slide nearer and then drift slightly to her left, that difficulty became worse. Her fuel supply was dwindling rapidly, and she needed to come around into the wind so she could hold the airible steady while she jumped into Maracada's bay. One engine sputtered and died; the airible hadn't gotten its ground maintenance when it came in at the House. The other three engines were starting to choke and miss, making the sounds they made when the fuel began running out. She had only gotten to Goft because of the assistance of the tailwind. Facing a headwind, she would have been engineless and adrift long before. Now Maracada's harbor lay beneath her, but she felt sure she would only be able to make one pass over it before the fuel and her luck ran out. She needed to get out of the airible quickly.

She frowned and tugged harder at the rudder pull. At the same time, she shifted the ballast forward and nosed the ship down toward the surface of the water. She wanted to bring the airible as close as she dared before she brought the nose back up and released it to the wind. If she had to, she could crash it into the bay and sink the airible before she swam away, but Maracada was full of strong swimmers and divers and salvagers, and someone might dredge up the engines or the envelope and make use of the Family's secrets. Far better for Galweigh interests if she could set the ship adrift on the easterly wind and let it crash into the trackless expanse of the ocean. No one would find it then.

She edged the rudder over farther and the airible tracked south to southeast. The full reach of Maracada's bay spread out beneath her, crowded with ships, lively still with lights; in spite of the darkness crews ferried cargo in to shore or out to their ships in longboats or hurried to or from their liberties on land. She dropped closer to the surface of the water, and pulled the hatch open. She didn't want the airible to strike the masts of any of the ships that lay in the harbor. To prevent that, she would have to act quickly. She checked that her dagger and her sword were both strapped tightly to her sides; she tightened the laces on her boots. She had to bring the ship as close as possible to the surface of the water, then nose it back up again sharply, and jump before it rose too high. She was a strong swimmer, far stronger than any normal human, and the surface of the bay looked calm enough; she didn't fear that her clothes or her weapons would drag her under. She had quick enough reflexes to get out of the ship before it rose too high. But she was tired and her head hurt, and the pain and grief of the day's events had caught up with her. She stared down at the rippled mirror of water below her and wondered how bad it would be to sink to the bottom of the bay and never rise.

I've heard it's a painful way to die, Amalee said. *And while it would solve your problems, it wouldn't do anything for your hopes of revenge.*

True enough. Kait resented her dead ancestor's intrusion into her thoughts, but part of her was perversely grateful that she had been forced to face reality. Dead, she could do nothing to help any survivors, nor could she avenge the dead. She'd wanted to serve her Family. Now she was more than a very junior diplomat. Now her Family needed her desperately.

She set the airble on the course she'd planned, steeled herself against the momentary paralysis of fear, and jumped as the ship began to soar upward. She'd judged her moment well – she fell clear of ships and dinghies and other obstacles – but she'd failed to anticipate the effect that dropping from a great height onto the surface of the water would have on her. She smashed into the bay as if she had hit dry land; the rock-hard water slapped her and slammed her and the shock stunned her. Then the bay swallowed her, and she felt herself slipping beneath the surface. The water closed over her head.

Both her mind and her dead ancestor screamed, *Swim, damn you! Swim!* but Kait could not. Her body refused to respond. She was drowning and she knew it and she could only sink deeper into the swirling currents of the bay. Her lungs burned as she breathed in water.

Her body, even in its stunned state, responded to that threat. It brought out its ultimate weapon. Kait felt a subdued fire along the sides of her neck, and without realizing the moment that it happened, she found herself breathing the salt water of the bay. She blinked, and discovered her eyes could make out shapes underwater even in the darkness. The Shift was only partial; her last Shift had been too recent, perhaps, or the shock of hitting the water prevented her body from doing more. But the Karnee reflex was enough.

She could breathe, and after a while she could move, and after an even longer while, she managed to swim to shore. She dragged herself up onto a part of the sandy beach away from light and motion and humanity. When the Shift subsided and she knew she could walk among people again without drawing death down upon herself, she got up and brushed as much sand from her clothes as she could, dried both her sword and dagger on her shirt, and walked through the town and up the long hill to Cherian House, where her Family in Maracada resided.

She had to wait with the guards at the gate of the House while someone who could vouch for her could be found and brought out. The someone, when he finally came, was a distant cousin of about her age who had joined her in Galweigh House for a year's worth of diplomatic classes before he returned home and took up his duties as a trader. His name was Fifer, and Kait had always thought him both homely and dull. Time hadn't done much to improve him.

He stood inside the gate and studied her with sleep-bleared eyes. He didn't offer a smile or a greeting or give her any sign that she was welcome. He simply stared; then sighed; then turned to the night gatemaster and said, 'Yah. She's my cousin. You can let her in.'

'Hello, Fifer,' she said.

'You have no more sense now than you had before,' he told her. 'This is no hour to disturb a House. I've had to wake Father so he could greet you. And you look appalling.'

She didn't explain to him; she wouldn't get his sympathy even if she told him what had happened, and didn't need it anyway. She would hope for better treatment from her uncle.

Fifer led her through the House into audience with her uncle Shaid, who was paraglese of the Family in Goft. When he'd delivered her, he stood by the door, waiting to be released, a courtesy his father pointedly ignored.

The Goft paraglese seemed unrelated to his youngest son. Handsome, smiling, and affable, he greeted her in the house library with a glass of wine, some corn tortillas, and a bowl of fresh fruit one of the servants was finishing laying out as Kait came in. He appeared undisturbed that he'd been dragged from bed at such a dreadful hour.

'Kait, dear child, you look like death. And why hasn't my son taken you to get fresh clothes? I would have waited to see you.'

Kait took the proffered glass of wine and sipped slowly. 'I'm fine, Uncle,' she said. 'What I have to tell you is more important than a change of clothes or a shower. Those will wait – the news I bring should not.'

He showed her to the seat nearest the food and settled across from her. 'Then tell me, dear. How did you end up at my door, and in such a state?'

She told him the entire story, and watched as he grew pale. When she was finished, he leaned back in his seat and closed his eyes. 'Ah, gods. Galweigh fallen, and the Sabirs ascendant in Calimekka.' Tears glistened at the corners of his tightly closed eyes, which he knuckled roughly away. 'And of the war in Halles? Have you word?'

'No word. Dùghall, Tippa, and I left before daybreak of this day just past, before the battle was to begin – and I've already told you of our arrival in Calimekka. I had no way to get news before I escaped.'

He rubbed his temples, sighed, opened his eyes. 'Perhaps we have not lost the day there. Support from that direction would be helpful.'

Kait thought of the men and women in Halles who had served her Family so faithfully, and bit her lower lip. 'The Sabirs knew we would be back in Calimekka with our defensive forces away; they were ready for us in the one place. I have to assume they were ready for us in the other.'

'Then we must act as if no help will come from the west.' He frowned. 'A challenge, and a trial . . . Well, we shall triumph somehow.' He straightened his shoulders and smiled grimly. 'Kait, I must think tonight on how I'll implement the rescue of any survivors, even before I consider the retaking of the House and the destruction of the Sabirs. Go shower and rest, have the night staff bring you something from the kitchen if you're still hungry, and I'll be sure you're sent fresh clothing. Tomorrow when you wake, meet with me and we'll discuss the layout of the House and anything else you can give me that will help us going in. I haven't been to Galweigh in years, and though Fifer has, I'm afraid he hasn't demonstrated such powers of observation as would make me want to base a battle plan on his recommendations.'

He rose, and she rose, and, as she did, she heard a soft shuffling behind the wall of books nearest them. Shaid took no notice of the sound, and Kait wondered if his ears could hear it. Someone stood behind that wall, and had been very quiet there for all the time she and the paraglese had spoken, or else had just arrived. She wondered which.

'Fifer, give her the Ambassador's Room, please. That is well away from the busy parts of the House; she'll need a good night's sleep, and I would not have her disturbed. We'll have much to do tomorrow, she and I.'

'Yes, Father.'

Shaid hugged her tightly. 'Kait, my condolences on your losses. We have all of us lost much tonight, but I know you've lost more than most. I want you to know that I'll do everything in my power to bring the bastards to justice for what they've done. Not just for the Family, but for you as well.'

'Thank you, Uncle,' she said, and bid him good night, and followed Fifer out the door.

It closed behind them, and as it did, Amalee said, *Wait. You haven't heard enough yet.*

Kait thought fast. She caught Fifer's sleeve and said, 'Hold up, would you? I have something in my boot. Stay just a moment; I don't think I can stand to walk another step without getting it out.' She leaned against the library wall and began tugging at the wet leather . . . but slowly.

Inside the room, she heard the soft groan of a secret door sliding open. And Shaid's voice saying, 'That confirms the rumors, then.'

'Rather neatly. One survives to tell the tale. What do you intend to do?' The other voice was female; the accent highborn, the tone cultured, the attitude coldly amused.

'Wait, of course. See what the Sabirs intend to offer in the way of prisoner exchanges, see if we can work out some sort of deal with them – and eventually retake the House, of course. Not soon.'

'Which shall make having the girl around uncomfortable, I should think. She's sure to want to mount a rescue immediately.'

'I would rather,' Shaid said softly, 'let the Calimekka line of the Family die out entirely. With our bloodline in primacy, we stand to gain legitimate claim to the Calimekkan estates, and we no longer have to have approval for our proposed trade routes. And we can do as we will with the colonies. If even one of them survives, of course, their whole line maintains primacy.'

Kait tugged the boot free and made a show of feeling around inside of it while Fifer fidgeted, deaf to the conversation behind the door.

'Then you don't intend to let the girl worry you about a rescue.'

'The girl? What girl? She must have died in an airible crash, or drowned in the sea, or been waylaid by bandits, for she certainly never reached here.'

'Very wise, Shaid. Very wise. Shall I attend to the matter for you?'

'Personally. The fewer people who might remember her, the better. I'll make sure everyone else who saw her come in is given special assignments until we can be sure the rest of the main line is dead.'

Kait pretended to find a stone and put it in her pocket.

She started putting the boot back on again, and again made the process look difficult.

'Now?'

'No. Not until she's in the room. Fifer will come back and tell us when she arrives. I don't want any, ah . . . disturbing noises that might later recall themselves to someone's memory. And no one else is currently on the third floor.'

Kait gave the boot a sharp pull and it slid onto her foot. She had no idea who the woman in Shaid's confidence was. She thought, since she knew her death had been planned, that she could probably protect herself from that first attack. However, she would still be where she wasn't wanted, and where she could not get help. She would lose time, and she couldn't fight off the whole House if Shaid was determined to see her dead. Uncle Dùghall had been right in telling her that outsiders in a House offered opportunities, and need not expect a warm welcome.

Uncle Dùghall . . .

A tear slid from the corner of her eye and she brushed it roughly away. She would live, and she would avenge the people she loved, even if she had to do it alone.

Now, though, she had to do the unexpected. And she thought, since Shaid had been kind enough to hand over one of his sons to her, the present would be the best time for a surprise.

'I'm ready,' she said. 'Would you mind taking me by the kitchen first? I'm starved, and I'd love to take some food up to my room with me.'

Fifer regarded her with blank eyes. 'You can call to the kitchen from the room and have something brought up to you.'

'I'd rather eat on the way. I haven't had any food since the day before yesterday.'

He sighed. 'It's late and I'm tired.'

'*Fi*-fer. I had to steal an airible, fly it here, then swim to the House from the bay. I bet I'm tireder than you are. Besides, I'm the one who found you when you got lost in the lower levels of my House. You at least owe me a few favors.' She tried to give him a teasing smile, though after what she'd just heard, all she could feel was rage.

The stupid eyes regarded her with distaste. He sighed. 'The kitchen.'

'Yes. The kitchen.'

He dragged down one hallway, took a cross-corridor, and trudged down a spiraling back stair lit intermittently by oil lamps, sighing on every other step.

They went down two stories without speaking to each other. No servants passed them in all that time. Finally Kait asked, 'What floor is the kitchen on?'

'Ground. Of course. We're almost there.'

Kait casually rested her hand on her dagger. The next moment would tell a great deal. The archway that would lead to the kitchen appeared to their left, but it didn't lead directly into the kitchen. Instead it led into a hall. A dark, empty hall. Good. The stairs did not end at the ground floor, but continued downward. Kait fell half a step behind Fifer and wrapped her left hand over his mouth. With her right hand, she pressed the dagger to his throat. 'Listen carefully,' she said, 'and don't make a noise. I don't like you, and I like you even less now that I know your father intends to have me killed tonight. But I won't hurt you if you do as I tell you.' She tightened her grip to emphasize her Karnee strength, and felt the struggle go out of him. 'You understand me?'

He nodded. He breathed fast, and she could hear his heart racing. 'Where's your treasury?'

He mumbled something, but of course with her hand over his mouth it didn't come out clearly. She said, 'Point.'

He pointed down the stairs.

'Take me.'

He went. Funny how he didn't sigh constantly anymore. Maybe he was no longer sleepy. The stairway ended in a metal-ribbed stonewood door. The door had no latch and no handle, no keyhole and no window. She knew of such doors – Galweigh House's treasury had one just like this one. The person who opened the door had to slide fingers into the correct series of holes and push the latches aside. Pushing even one wrong latch released the knife mechanism that neatly cut off every one of the fingers just below the knuckle. Very effective at keeping people out, those doors.

'Open it,' Kait said.

'Mmmm mmaaaahhh,' Fifer said, shaking his head.

Kait pressed the edge of the dagger against his neck hard enough to blanch the skin. 'You can't? Of course you can. Or, at least, let's hope that you can. I can't let you go or you'll make noise or run for help. If I have to deal with the door, I'll need both my hands free, and I'll have to kill you first in order to have them free. Then I'd still have to cut off your hands so I could have something to push into the holes, because I'm not going to use my own fingers. I would rather not kill you – I would rather not have to kill *anyone* . . . else. But if it comes down to you or me, cousin, you need not ask which way the bones will fall.'

She tightened her grip again, and he groaned.

'You going to do what I tell you?'

He nodded.

'Then do it.'

He rested his hands along either side of the door, and slid each finger slowly into one of the depressions. He took his time, and Kait didn't hurry him – while she knew the combination to her father's treasury door, she wouldn't want to have to stick her fingers into it in a hurry, either.

Fifer swallowed so hard his body shook, and pushed the levers simultaneously, and after an instant Kait heard a click from inside the wall. Fifer removed his hands, and the door rolled silently into the left wall.

Kait stepped on the heel of Fifer's right boot and said, 'Pull your foot out of it . . . slowly.'

He wriggled a little, but removed the boot. Kait shoved it into the opening, right against the groove where the door would slide when it closed. Then she forced her cousin into the treasury.

As soon as they stepped across, the vault door slammed closed behind them, but it didn't close all the way, thanks to the boot. The insides of treasury doors required a different combination, and Kait didn't want to take her cousin back out of the vault with her. As long as the door remained wedged open, she wouldn't have to.

They stood to one side of a wonderland where neatly sorted jewels in glass cases rose from floor to ceiling, and stacks of bars of precious metals towered so high and so wide they created walls of their own, and banks of wooden drawers lined one wall, while beautiful embroidered silks and stacks of Ancients' books and carvings in ebony and amber and ivory sat collecting dust on shelves along another. 'This is very easy,' Kait said. 'I need money, and not even very much.'

Fifer pointed to the wooden drawers.

'Fine.' She marched him in the opposite direction. The shelf that housed the embroidered silks had ceremonial robes folded to one side – and the ceremonial robes came with belts. She pushed Fifer to the floor, drew her sword, sheathed her dagger, and took a couple of the belts. As soon as he was tied and gagged, she hurried over to the drawers.

The wealth of a small nation lay within them. Coins of gold and silver lay in heaps and piles, sorted by denomination and issuing mint: gleaming hexagonal

Dokteerak daks; tree-stamped Sabir farnes; Masschanka robans; Kairn slaudes; Galweigh preids; and from outside the realms of the Five Families, monies from the Strithian empire, the Manarkan Territories, and places unknown to Kait – monies stamped with the visages of the Scarred and their world. Enough money lay in those drawers to let her raise an army of mercenaries a thousand times over. She would hire from the colonies if possible, from allies if available. From foreigners if necessary.

Don't waste your time trying to find mercenaries, Amalee said. *I'm telling you, the Family is dead. But you can bring them back.*

'From the dead?' Kait blurted.

I know of an Ancient artifact that will let you . . . ah, resurrect them.

'From the *dead*.' She recalled Dùghall's amused speculation about the existence of such an artifact – the Mirror of Souls – and his comment that its existence was almost certainly a myth.

He was wrong. The Mirror of Souls exists, and it works. Get enough money to hire a ship and a crew that can sail you north and east across the ocean, and I will take you to it. You want to help our Family, then get the Mirror.

North and east would take her across the Bregian Ocean. Few ships made that crossing, and the lands on the other side were mostly unexplored.

But if her ancestor was right and she had a chance to bring her Family back . . .

Her Family. The Family that she'd believed so much better than the Sabirs or the Dokteeraks, the Kairns or the Masschankas. Her Family, with an uncle who had turned on her as quickly as that Dokteerak paraglese had turned on his relative – and for what? Because she stood in the way of his ascension to Galweigh House. And more power. And more wealth.

She'd always been told, and had always believed, that loyalty among Family members came above everything else – that it was the very essence of what being Family meant.

She sagged against the wall, for the moment all the fight gone out of her. She felt tears start down her cheeks; she tasted their salt, and remembered her mother's warm arms around her when she'd cut herself. Remembered the comfort of her father's voice, calming her down and helping her find her way to her humanity when, Shifted into Karnee form, she had to hide away in the dark places in the House, after they first moved there from their country home. She'd been so afraid then. Afraid that someone would see her, discover her secret, kill her as that child in Halles had been killed. But her parents had saved her. Over and over, they had saved her life. And her brothers and sisters had helped her, and she had survived to earn the chance to repay them.

Except she was too late.

No way to repay the dead. If she listened to Amalee, she would only be deluding herself. At best, the Mirror of Souls was a thousand years lost, and irretrievable. At worst, it was a myth. The Sabirs and their treachery were real. The Goft Galweighs and *their* treachery were real, too. And she couldn't even get her revenge on the bastards who'd destroyed everything she had ever loved in the world, because the surviving members of her Family would pay the spawn of evil their own souls to feed their lust for Galweigh House and the power it represented, and the treasure it housed.

All her life, her Family had been everything to her, because she'd been so sure the Galweigh name was synonymous with everything which was good, and just, and right in the world. She'd been wrong to believe. There was, she discovered, Family – which was a political thing and knew no loyalty – and *family*, which was a thing of blood ties and love, and for which she would gladly have given her life.

And if the only chance you have is a bad chance, is that not still better than having no chance at all? Is it, Kait? Think, girl. If the Mirror of Souls is lost forever, you have lost nothing that you had not already lost. But if it exists, and if you can find it, you will regain something you could have in no other way.

Kait stood straight and brushed her tears from her cheeks with one sleeve. She would have given her life for any of her family. She would *still* give her life. For even the slender chance that she might see her mother and father alive again, and her brothers and sisters . . . If she could hold on to the hope that her uncle Dùghall would once again tell her his bawdy islander jokes and quote his obscure philosophers . . . if she could even dream that one day beloved Galweigh voices might ring again through the halls of the House . . . for that, she would sail the almost-uncharted ocean, trek across the wastes of Scarred lands. For the lives of those she loved, she would risk everything.

Maybe she couldn't believe in Family anymore. But she would never stop loving her family.

The muscles of Kait's jaw clenched so tight they burned. If she wanted the chance, she had to act. Fast. She started filling a small leather bag with gold. She attached one bag of gold to the belt beneath her tunic, and started on a second.

Good girl. I knew I could count on you. Now, then, once you get your money, steal one of those books on the shelf – the older, the better – and flee this place. When you're safe, and we've told some greedy captain the lie that will get you berth and allies in finding the Mirror, I'll give you the proofs you want about me. Only get to safety first.

She filled and hid the second purse. Then she dumped a

handful of silver coins and a few bronzes into her pockets – a woman who showed gold in the wrong places wouldn't live long.

Finally, she dug through the Ancient books until she found one so old she couldn't even recognize the letter forms.

That one will do.

Kait didn't know why she would need it, but better to have and not want than to want and not have, as Wain Pertrad wrote. When she had what she needed, she mockingly saluted her cousin and fled.

* * *

Dùghall's spell spun itself into life. Down in the black heart of the silent House, the bodies of the dead Wolves glowed, casting light in their secret chamber – a chamber which would afterward be undisturbed by light for long years. Their radiance cast amorphous, shifting shadows, then dispelled all shadows in a burst of brilliance that seemed to destroy all darkness. But the bodies, devoured entirely by the spirits of the dead, disappeared without a trace of dust or ash, as if they had never been. And darkness claimed the room once more for its own.

In other rooms in the dark labyrinth between the main House, long-forgotten victims of violence, scattered suicides, and two small children who had wandered too far and never found their way back to the realm of daylight before starving cast their own small shadows before disappearing. Rats and cats and mice and snakes who had found dark corners in which to die sparkled like stars for an instant, then were gone forever. The meat in the House's cold room vanished in like manner, as did food left uneaten that waited in the trash bins for disposal. The graves of the dead Galweighs in the Family boneyard lit up inside, though no one could see. And out on the grounds proper, the embers of the fire that had burned the dead glowed more brightly for a moment. And two brilliant lights out on the landing field where the airible had waited showed that it had escaped, before ensuring that the fate of the two men who had been guarding it would never be known.

When the last of the lights died away, an instant's hush fell over Galweigh House. The guards and soldiers and officers looked at each other, words lost to them. And in that hush, the spirits of the dead reached out and touched the living.

* * *

Trev leaned against the stone wall in the hallway, staring at the door his searching had revealed. The passageway behind it led into darkness, a blackness that his lamp refused to illumine. His skin twitched as if touched by a thousand cobwebs, and sweat dripped from his forehead down his nose and beaded on his upper lip. An instant before, he'd seen the reflection of pale red light from beyond the point where the passageway twisted; in the instant that his eyes had registered it, it had vanished.

Something waited down there. Something bad, that knew he existed, and that now hid in the darkness, waiting for him to move into reach.

Why go on? Ry's woman wasn't in the House anymore – Trev would almost have staked his life on it. After Ry had that seizure, he'd volunteered to stay behind to look for her, but the longer and harder he looked, the more certain he became that she was nowhere in reach. Why keep looking? He couldn't say. Maybe secretly he wanted to earn more of Ry's admiration, or to take Yanth's place as his closest confidant. Maybe underneath everything, he hoped for advancement as Ry advanced in the Family. Though he despised such base motives in others, he had to admit they compelled him as much as friendship for Ry. Maybe more.

The darkness ahead of him seemed to deepen, to gain

weight and presence, and Trev swallowed hard. He wouldn't live in Galweigh House if the Sabirs made him paraglese of it. The damned place felt alive to him, as if it were watching every step he took.

You can't take her home with you even if you do find her, he told himself. *You try, and she'll Shift and slaughter you.*

The darkness began to whisper.

Sibilant almost-formed words caught at the edge of Trev's hearing. Pattering in the blackness, and dry squeaks, as if rats, pressed to dust by the weight of the thick dark, came at him to protest their fate. A draft of dank air brushed his cheek, and he stepped back, away from the door, caught off guard by the faint, unpleasant carrion reek it carried.

Wait, the darkness whispered, and he didn't know if he heard the word or only imagined it.

She wouldn't be in there.

He closed the door and slowly backed away, keeping his back to the wall so that no one would surprise him. His lamp cast long and dancing shadows, and he wished that dawn would come and chase them away. Whispering began behind him. He spun and squinted into the dark. Saw nothing. Heard the door he had closed open behind him. Jerked around, sword raised, lantern lifted so that he could make out the outline of his enemy.

Saw nothing.

But the carrion smell bore down on him, a moving wall. Nothing in front of him. Nothing behind him.

The cold, damp hands of nothing reached through his clothes to his skin, stroked him, prodded him. The long-dead voice of that nothing murmured, 'You belong to me,' and this time he could not doubt that what he heard, he heard with his ears and not with his imagination. What he felt, he felt for real. He flailed out with his sword, but his blade found no resistance in its arc to the floor, and steel rang hard on stone, and the shock of the blade striking ran through the palm of his hand and up his wrist, and he cried out. Lost his balance. Dropped the lamp.

It smashed to the floor, and for a moment the oil burned brightly in its puddle on the stone, and he leaped back to escape its spread. Carrion arms caught him. Held him, while the flames guttered down to blackness, and the darkness that was more than the absence of light descended with full fury. A carrion body that he could not touch, could not hurt, though it could touch him, pressed flesh to his flesh, and the corpse chill of it and the stench of it flowed through him. He believed he would die. Too frightened to make a sound, or even to move, he wished that he could faint and find that the sun would wake him in the morning, in his own bed, the victim of nothing more than too much wine and a too-vivid dream.

'Mine.'

Lips moldy and rotting brushed against the nape of his neck, and fingertips that alternated putrefaction with bony fleshlessness caressed his chest, his belly, his cheek, his back.

'I've waited for you for so long . . . for so long . . . for so long . . .'

She wasn't there. Nothing was there. But he could not break free, could not flee, and could not fight, and his sword dropped from nerveless fingers and clattered to the stone. His feet left the ground as she lifted him into the air and bore him off – blinded by the impenetrable blackness that surrounded her, by the fact that the only noise she made as she moved was a soft rustle that might almost have been the sound of a long-vanished silk skirt brushing the floor. He lost any sense of direction, of place. He did not know if she traveled up with him, or down, or for that matter which of those two things would be more frightening. He was the captive of death itself, and he could not think or reason or plan beyond that fact.

From the floors below him he heard screams and the echoes of screams. They got closer, became louder; did he move toward them, or they toward him?

The all-enveloping blinding blanket of darkness, the fetor, the fear, the screams of countless unseen others – they were the walls and floor and ceiling of his world, the perimeters of his existence beyond which nothing else was.

Then they were gone.

He lay on a bed of stones, breathing cool, clean air scented with morning dew and loam, and the sounds that surrounded him were the moans and sobs of others, but also the sounds of a city moving to life in the time before the break of day. Human shouts, good-natured or angry, and carts and beasts of burden in the streets, and farmers bringing livestock into market someplace below. In the valley. In the world beyond Galweigh House.

His eyes cleared, the unnatural darkness erased in an instant. He rolled to his side; sat up; looked around. He sat in the middle of a graveled road, surrounded on all sides by the Sabir troops who had taken Galweigh House, and by the officers who had led them, and by the Family who had come to direct the taking of the spoils. The road and the grassy berm to either side could have been a body-strewn battlefield, except that none of those who lay stunned and in shock seemed to be harmed. Before him, the road twisted into moonlit jungle. Behind him . . .

He turned, and saw through the frame of palms and many-trunked strangler figs the edge of the wall of Galweigh House, and a part of the gate the Sabirs had paid so much to get opened. It slid shut as he watched. Leaving him and the rest of the conquerors once again locked beyond the impenetrable wall, and the House in the hands of the dead.

Chapter 18

The woman who walked into the tavern where Ian Draclas sat sipping bitter mango beer with three outrageous liars caught his attention more for what was wrong about her than what was right. She strode to the bartender without bothering to acknowledge the interested glances she got from the men at the tables, which was odd enough; most of the women in the tavern at that time of night wanted the glances, and the money they could make from the men who gave them. Additionally, this woman looked like she'd been dunked in a well, then dipped in dirt; but nothing about her said 'poor' or 'in hard times.' Her clothes, entirely wrong for the area and the time of night, were outdoor garb made for protection from the elements and for durability. He studied them with a practiced eye; they were *well* made. Absolutely top quality. As were the sword she wore at one hip and the dagger at the other.

Her bones were delicate, her hands slender and long-fingered but strong-looking, her wrists thick enough with muscle that he suspected the sword was no decoration conferred by her Family status. And she was lovely, though her beauty hid itself behind her tangled hair and water-damaged clothing. Even the way she stood and walked spoke clearly to him of breeding. He would guess she belonged in the highest echelons of local society – in the parlors and salons of the Families, dressed in diaphanous silk, sipping nectar. She no more belonged in a dockside tavern than . . . He smiled inside, considering, and arched an eyebrow. She no more belonged than he did.

An enigma. He did love an enigma. His smile moved to the outside as, with a brisk nod, she turned away from the barkeep, scanned the room, and looked straight at him. She turned once more to the barkeep, said a few words, got a nod in affirmation, and began working her way through the tables toward him.

'. . . an' all three of them were begging me, but I . . . I . . . wanned 'em hungry . . . if y' unnerstan' me . . . so I . . .'

Ian decided a liar telling his tale of sexual adventuring with three Manarkan princesses was less compelling than a dark-eyed enigma. 'Later,' he said, and left them. Meeting her in a slight clearing between two tables, he said, 'I saved you the trouble of presenting yourself at a table full of boors. From the look of you, your night has been interesting enough already.'

Her half-smile of agreement never reached her eyes. 'Captain Draclas?'

'I serve you.'

'I'm given to understand, by some asking about, that you not only have a fast ship available for hire, but that you might not be averse to a rapid departure . . . and perhaps even, if the incentive were right, to sailing light.' She kept her voice low and her eyes focused on his face. He found her intensity unnerving. Deliciously so.

He nodded quickly, so slightly that only she could see it. Then he spread a drunken grin across his face and said, 'Why din' you say so, Leeze?' He let his voice sound a little too loud, a little drunk. 'If you need a place to sleep for a night or two, I'm . . .' He giggled. 'I'm sure we can find you a bed . . . *someplace*.' He looked around the room, trying to catch the attention of the men at the tables; they reacted by turning away, envious, or by hooting encouragement. Ian grinned and swaggered; he slid an arm around her waist, neatly catching her sword between her thigh and his as he did. Better, should anyone come asking later, that they not remember that sword. 'Outside,' he said under his breath.

She slid her own arm around his back, and dragged her fingers from the nape of his neck down between his shoulder blades in an intimate gesture that felt entirely too good. Almost as loudly, and in an accent he would have sworn was born and bred dockside, she said, 'Should'na say such things t' a good girl like me, you. I'm na' that kinda girl.' She managed a predatory smile and a laugh as professional as any in the room. She squeezed his buttock, and they walked out together. The attention of the room no longer fixed on either of them, since the nature of their association had been classified, in the minds of the other patrons, as business of a personal kind. Nothing worthy of further thought.

Outside, the act dissolved like a spun sugar treat in summer rain. The woman pulled gracefully out of his reach, turned to him, and smiled – this time a genuine smile. 'Nicely done. You think well under pressure.'

'Necessary in my line of work.'

'Reassuring to one in my position.'

'And what position might that be?'

Her teeth flashed – the grin broad and dangerous. 'There are some powerful people after me for a manuscript that I . . . acquired. Bought. From a dealer. These people got hold of information regarding the contents of the manuscript, and now they want it – and me with it.'

She was lying. He could see it in her eyes. He know it as surely as he knew the sun would rise soon. She hadn't gotten her manuscript from any dealer – she'd stolen it. And why would a woman who gave every indication of being Familied steal a manuscript of any sort? Why not buy it? Hells-all, why not simply command that it be given to her, for that matter? If she was of Family, she had that right. An enigma within an enigma – and only one way he could see to solve the puzzle. Ask. 'So what's in this manuscript that people want so much that they'd come after you?'

Her voice dropped to a whisper and she moved closer to him. 'The location of an undiscovered Ancients' city.'

Taken aback, he laughed. 'There's no place left on this continent to hide such a city – at least, no place that you or I could reach. Maybe in Strithia, or deep in the heart of the Veral Territories . . . but I'll not go there for any treasure.'

'Agreed. But it isn't on this continent.'

His heart started to pound. 'Where, then? Manarkas?'

She smiled. 'North Novtierra.'

He took a step back from her and stared, his heart skittering at the thought of such a treasure. 'North Novtierra?' Virgin land – unclaimed, uncharted, ripe for the taking. Hard to reach, hard to explore, vast beyond all imagining. Three months of sailing just to get there – and that wouldn't include any time crawling up and down the unexplored coast trying to find her city. No doubt a hundred undiscovered Ancients' cities lay within the fertile, forested slopes and broad plains of North Novtierra. A man could spend a lifetime trying to find just one, and fail. But if this woman knew the location of such a place . . .

Ah, shang! Such a place would be worth the risk of life, fortune, Family – anything at all – to the finder. With the fortune this woman could make from the spoils of an untouched Ancients' ruin, she could buy herself the paraglesiat of one of her Family's smaller cities . . . have enough money left over to build a solid standing army . . . take any technology she acquired from the site and either develop it herself or use it as leverage to an even higher position of power . . . One good city could take her into otherwise unreachable spheres of power. Make her the equal of any paraglese in Ibera.

Of course, what would be a treasure for her would be a treasure for anyone else involved, too, including him. She didn't strike him as stupid, so she knew that. He wanted to know what she'd done to protect her interests. 'North Novtierra. That's half a world away, and a hellish dangerous voyage into the bargain.'

'Yes. But your ship could make the trip. It isn't a coast-hugger. I checked.'

'You're right. It isn't. And it's seaworthy, and fast. Right up there with the newest caravels in the Family fleets. And I've crossed the Bregian before – I could probably get you there. But what's to prevent me from taking the treasure and stranding you once we arrive . . . or, for that matter, from dumping you overboard once we're well at sea and finding and claiming the city for myself?'

She chuckled, and something terrifying crept into the sound. The hair on the back of his neck stirred, and his gut twisted. 'You wouldn't want to try stranding or dumping me, Captain. I assure you I can take care of myself. As for you using the manuscript to find the place, you couldn't unless you happen to be a Family translator, and unless you happen to specialize in the Ancients' languages, and unless you can specifically read Tongata Four in Brasmian script. I'm betting you can't. Further, I'm betting that you won't find anyone else besides me who can. As far as I know, I'm the only one who has deciphered it.'

He could no more read Tongata Four than he could flap his arms and fly. And wouldn't know Brasmian script if someone tattooed it on his nose. Which made her as valuable to him as the city itself – and guaranteed her safety at least to the city. Which she obviously knew. Beyond that . . . well, he thought he believed her when she said he would make a mistake trying to strand her. *Why* he believed, he couldn't say. Perhaps it was the danger in her smile.

Abruptly what she'd told him fitted together, pieces of the puzzle falling neatly into place; in that moment he *knew* not only how she'd come upon the manuscript, but who she was. She hadn't bought the thing, of course; however, she hadn't stumbled across it accidentally and stolen it on a whim, either. She was one of her Family's lesser daughters, relegated to the dry and dusty translation of Ancient archives, pushed aside because her branch of the Family lacked sufficient pull to get her a good marriage or a good post. She would have been just a link between the will of her Family and the craftsmen and artists who used her translations to re-create Ancient technologies. She'd been given a manuscript to translate; had come, at some point in it, to a mention of the location of a city that she felt would be both reachable and worth finding; and because she had ambition and a hunger for a life better than the one she'd landed in, she'd leaped at the opportunity, snatched the manuscript, and fled into his life.

Which, of course, she would never admit.

He liked her. By all the gods, he liked her. She reminded him of himself. Even that dangerous little burr in her voice when she told him that trying to get rid of her would be a bad idea appealed to him. He decided that if – no . . . *when*; after all, why not have faith in his windfall? – he decided that *when* they found the city, he wouldn't waste his time trying to dump her or kill her. Why kill a woman worth marrying? Marrying power, after all, was more efficient than earning it.

And she was a *good*-looking woman. From her height and coloring and build, of either the Galweigh or Kairn

Families, and since she was on Goft, he'd bet Galweigh. Galweigh would be very good, if she could win her bid for power. Even a moderate position in that Family was worth a paraglesiat in the Dokteeraks or the Kairns or the Masschankas. The only other Family equal to the Galweighs was the Sabirs. Sabir would have been bad – he had solid reasons for avoiding them.

He regarded her with proprietary pleasure. His future wife. His future ticket into wealth, power, luxury. No sense letting her know he'd undertake the trip for free to have the opportunity to win her and through her claim her city. He needed to let that part unfold slowly. So he gave her his best hard-nosed trader impression and said, 'What's in it for me?'

'The transit fee there – you give me a reasonable price and I'll pay it. A fair percentage of the cargo we find – I'll make it worth your while. My patronage on any return trips. A place in . . .' She reconsidered what she'd been about to say, and smiled and shrugged. 'Well, let's say for now that anything else I can offer would be even more speculative than the city and the cargo. But as I said, I'll make it worth your while.'

He nodded. 'For the transit fee . . .' He didn't want to ask so much that she couldn't pay it, and how much could she possibly have, anyway? But he didn't want to ask so little that he raised her suspicions. 'Ten solid large. Up front.' It was a lot, but it was also within reason for the distance and the danger of the journey.

She winced.

He waited. If it was too much, he'd see it and lower his price a little at a time.

She sighed, stared at her feet, finally nodded. 'You have a preference for any one mint?'

'The Dokteeraks cut their gold coins with silver sometimes – don't pay me in stamped daks. Farnes and preids spend best, but gold is gold.'

She nodded. 'Done.'

Well enough. She didn't argue, so he might have gotten more. Still, if he got the city, what more did he need? 'So what must I know to get us out of the harbor alive?' he asked.

She didn't waste his time pretending she didn't understand what he meant. 'We need to move fast and we need to leave a false trail. We can't supply here if you aren't already stocked. Mentioning what we're looking for or where we're looking would probably be fatal.'

He shrugged. 'I figured that. Anyone in particular you need to avoid?'

Her laugh was so harsh it startled him. 'If you maintain close associations with the Five Families, don't mention me, eh?'

Now he truly was startled. 'All *five*?' Not even he had managed to get himself that deeply into trouble.

'To Galweigh, Sabir, and Dokteerak, my life is . . . forfeit. To Masschanka through their association with the Sabirs and the Dokteeraks, probably the same. And Kairn, through their alliance with the Galweighs, might also take me in for any offered reward. Avoiding all five would be best.'

He felt a measure of admiration at that. He didn't know *anyone* who could honestly claim to have made enemies of all the Five Families. 'I'll do my best.'

'How early can you be ready to leave?'

'Meet me on the beach by the wharf as the bells ring Huld.'

The woman looked at the sky, and he saw her picking out the White Lady from the other stars, and measuring her distance from the horizon. The Red Hunter, which would signal the passing of the station of Telt and the arrival of Huld, would not join her for some time.

'Well enough,' the woman said. 'That will give me time to do the few things I must do.'

She was already gone when he realized he didn't even know her name.

* * *

'He believed it.' Kait hurried down to the beach. She had nothing she needed to do so much as she needed to keep out of sight, and by the wharf near where she had dragged herself ashore she'd seen plenty of cover.

Of course he believed it. Tell anyone an implausible lie and build a plausible diversion behind it; he'll almost always dig through the implausible lie to your diversion, think he's found the truth, and fail to look further. Amalee chuckled and changed the subject. *The captain certainly was taken with you.*

Kait reached the beach and moved to a line of low shrubs and grasses that lay north of the wharf. 'It's because I'm Karnee. His interest didn't have anything to do with me.'

Amalee stayed silent while Kait found a comfortable, hidden vantage point from which to watch the wharf and settled into it. Once she'd stilled, though, her ancestor said, *What do you mean, because you're Karnee? You're lovely. He couldn't have failed to notice that.*

'Trust me, it wouldn't matter. One of the effects of the curse is that the Karnee attract members of the opposite sex and of their own sex by some sort of . . . I'm not sure . . . scent, maybe. Like flowers attract bees, I suppose. The bee doesn't desire the flower, and humans don't desire the Karnee – they both just want the thing that makes the scent. The effect was well documented four hundred years ago.' Kait sighed. 'My parents managed to secretly gather copies of everything that was known about my kind. They had me read them so that I would understand what I was.'

She didn't bother to add that they had done so at terrible danger to themselves. Or that they had given her every advantage they could to help her survive in the world, risking their own lives and the lives of all their other children in the process. She had known love in her life; her parents and her surviving brothers and sisters had loved her, without question or reservation. She would simply never be able to find such love again.

So all men want you.

'Most. And many women. The effect seems to be stronger on men. Some people seem immune to the scent. Or drug. Or whatever it is that I give off. Not many, though.'

A long silence. Then, *Oh, that would be delightful.*

'You think so? Imagine knowing that no one who wanted you actually wanted *you*. That wherever you went, men and women would approach you, court you, want to bed you . . . and that if you could get rid of your scent, and dump it on a dog, they would abandon you and court the dog. *Now* think how delightful it would be.'

And do you ever bed them?

Kait wondered if the woman had been such a prying nuisance in life. Could explain why the Sabirs sacrificed her.

'Sometimes,' she admitted. 'Another curse of being Karnee is the insatiable appetite. For everything. Sex included. I fight the appetites. Sometimes I lose the fight.' When she did, sex always felt hollow. Empty. A loveless, passionless exercise, in which she constantly had to guard herself against the excesses of pleasure that could throw her into Shift. She came away from each encounter with nothing but guilt and a desire to avoid the next. But like Shift, the sexual hunger of Karnee could only be held in check for so long. Longer than Shift itself most times – that was inexorable as the tide. But sometimes the beast inside of her would not be denied.

Kait yawned. Sitting and waiting began to feel like a mistake. How long had it been since she'd slept? That interlude of unconsciousness didn't seem to have helped – she'd woken from that tired and drained. Fear and rage and hope had kept the weariness at bay while she'd tried to find a way to help her Family, and then to save her life. Now, however, the exhaustion that weighted her limbs and dragged at her eyelids became unbearable. Sleep beckoned; a god to be embraced, desirable beyond all imagining. She settled lower in the sand, and discovered that one of the branches of the shrub directly behind her curved in an arc that would support her head.

Amalee was oblivious to her weariness. She was nattering on about being Karnee. *How marvelous. An enormous sexual appetite and an unending supply of people to fill it. My dear, I wish I'd been born Karnee. All of that power ... all of that control ...*

Kait felt a moment of sympathy for the long-dead Sabirs who'd sacrificed her ancestor. If the woman were alive, she thought she might have been tempted to follow the same course of action. She yawned again, and realized that her eyes had fallen shut – she had no idea how long they had been that way. She forced them open. 'Can you stay awake if I sleep?'

Child, I haven't slept in a th – in two hundred years.

'Can you wake me when we have to leave if I am asleep?'

Yes.

'Good. Then be quiet until the town rings Huld. I'm exhausted.'

Huld. Of course. A pause. *And how do they ring that now?*

Kait sank into welcome darkness.

Kait? How do they ring Huld now?

She fought the embrace of the dark god a moment longer. 'The same way they always have.'

The pause she got was not encouraging.

'Three bells. Different tones. You'll hear them.'

Odd that her ancestor didn't remember that. Perhaps nearly two hundred years of being dead made you forget things.

The dark god brushed her cheek with his lips, and she lost the thought in the feathery comfort of sleep.

Chapter 19

The last of the screams had died away not long ago. Silence owned the House for the moment. Dùghall rose and tapped the airible pilot, Aouel, on the shoulder. 'They've fled,' he said. 'But we're going to have to get outside and close the gate before they return. Can you kick the door open?'

Aouel, haggard-faced and sleep-drugged, struggled with Dùghall's words. 'Fled? The Sabirs? Why? Are you sure?'

'I don't know why, and we don't have time to figure it out. They all started screaming and ran away; they aren't out there now; we have to get to the gate.'

He could have opened it himself with magic, but he couldn't have explained to the other survivors *how* he got it open – and he didn't want to do anything that might link him with the suspicious disappearance of the two bodies from the room, or the flight of the Sabirs from the House.

On the other hand, the method by which a big, strong young man would go through a locked door was understandable by everyone. Nothing suspicious about it. And Aouel used that method. He ran at the door and hit it with his shoulder. It shuddered, but held. He hit it again and again; after six or seven solid crashes, the frame splintered around the catch and it burst open.

The noise woke the other sleepers. Dùghall told them only, 'The Sabirs ran away.' Then he ran out into the hallway and trotted toward the stairs that would take him to the ground floor, and eventually to the gate, following Aouel, who, being younger and in better shape, didn't have to go slowly to keep from jostling his belly uncomfortably. Behind them, Dùghall could hear the other survivors coming out, chattering to each other about what could have possibly made the Sabirs leave. Good. They could puzzle out some answer to their miraculous rescue while he wasn't present.

He followed Aouel, who charged through the House and out onto the grounds, tore through the gardens and across the manicured paths and the exercise grounds and the airible ground to the guardhouse by the gate. He managed to keep the younger man in sight, though sometimes only barely. He made it past the shrubs in time to see the gate close.

He smiled, bending over with his hands on his thighs, wheezing. Closed. His left palm hurt like the very hells. His lungs burned. The world faded in and out of a gray haze filled with tiny points of light. His heart felt ready to explode out of his chest. It didn't matter. None of it mattered. If he'd been missing legs or arms, that would have suited him fine, too. The Sabirs were out. Gone. Beaten again.

Aouel crunched up a graveled path between flower beds and stopped at his side. 'You going to die on me, old man?' He sounded like he was breathing hard, too.

Dùghall raised his head. 'Not today, young rooster. Not today.'

'Good. Because there's something you need to know.'

Dùghall straightened and looked up into the Rophetian's frowning face. His momentary feeling of triumph melted away. 'What?'

'She took the airible.'

This made no sense to Dùghall. He had, in the back of his mind, registered the fact that the airible was gone, but he hadn't considered what it might mean. Aouel apparently had. 'Who . . . who took the airible?'

'Kait.'

Dùghall snorted. 'Nonsense. You have to realize that she couldn't have taken it. Even had she known how to fly it, she had no ground crew to release the ropes – and where would she hope to take it or land it? The bastard Sabirs took it, and I hope it crashes with them and they burn to cinders.'

Aouel didn't look at all convinced. 'Kait took it,' he insisted.

'How, son? How could she have?'

'Look on the ground over there.' Aouel pointed, and Dùghall saw ropes still locked through the landing winches.

'They cut the ropes.' He chuckled. 'They cut the ropes.' He could just see those idiots struggling to get the airible off the ground, and he smiled. 'If the Sabirs cut the airible's ropes to take off, they'll dance Brethwan's jig getting back to the ground in one piece again.'

Aouel was shaking his head. 'The ropes weren't cut. The Sabirs would have done anything to get the ship safely from here to their House. The ground crew would have walked there through the city if they had to. Those ropes were intentionally released, and only Kait would have done that.'

Dùghall crossed his arms and waited for the explanation that was coming. The explanation he knew he wasn't going to like.

'There's an emergency lever hidden in the pilot's cabin,' the pilot said. 'It releases all the landing ropes at the same time – a feature the crafters built in just in case one of us ever found ourselves overrun by enemies when we landed.'

Dùghall frowned. 'You could have pulled that lever and gotten us all off the ground yesterday . . .'

Aouel shook his head. 'Had I been in the cabin, I would have. But Kait had taken ill with that spell, remember. Tippa and I were already in the hatch, ready to run for help for her. And the Sabir men threatened to kill Tippa if I moved anywhere but out of the airible.'

Dùghall remembered. 'Yes. That seems so long ago, but you're right, of course. About that, anyway. As far as this nonsense of Kait taking the airible . . .'

Aouel rested a hand on Dùghall's shoulder and said, 'She knew how to fly it, Parat Dùghall. She knew where the hidden lever was, she knew how to operate the lifters and the engines, and she had flown that particular ship several times.'

Dùghall could do nothing but stare, speechless.

Aouel saw the look and winced. 'I taught her myself,' he added.

For the longest time, Dùghall could think of nothing to say. Finally, however, he managed to croak, 'Why?'

Aouel shrugged. 'She wanted to learn. And she was quick, and clever, and . . .'

Dùghall felt his knees sag. 'Then she isn't hiding somewhere just outside the gate.'

'No.'

Dùghall had been so sure that at least one of the people from the Family that he truly loved was safe. Now he knew nothing. 'What emergency features did the crafters build in to land the ship, in the event that you had to release the ropes?'

Aouel pursed his lips. 'We weren't to land it. If we used the emergency release, we were either to get it to friendly territory and crash it within our own grounds, or we were to fly it out to sea and sink it.'

'And there are emergency boats aboard for such an eventuality?'

'We . . . ah . . . were always given to believe we would . . . ah . . . go down with it, so to speak.'

'You're telling me she has no way to get safely to the ground.'

'None. At least none that can be assured. The best she can hope for is that she will crash in friendly territory, and that the crash won't hurt her too much. But if the ground crew didn't refuel the ship when it landed – and I cannot imagine that they would – she may not be able to get to friendly territory.'

Dùghall glared at the pilot, and thought of Kait. She could have been an extraordinary diplomat, he thought. She could have done wonderful things for the Family. Or beyond the Family. She had been special. Now he could only assume that she was dead, and that her promise had died with her.

'I should have you hanged,' he told Aouel. 'I won't. The Family has lost enough people. But Kait's death is on your hands, and I will remember. And someday I will hold you accountable.'

* * *

The ship no longer rocked gently from side to side; instead, it surged and plunged, as if climbing one hill, sliding down the other side, and climbing the next, over and over. Hasmal's hammock moved with a life of its own. For a moment he puzzled over the change. Then a contented smile spread across his face as he realized what it meant. The *Peregrine* had put out to sea and was on its way somewhere, and anywhere would suit Hasmal just fine because it meant that he had finally escaped.

He pulled on his shoes and dashed up the companion-way to the main deck. A low line of islands lay off to the left, but the *Peregrine* sailed in a clear sea. The captain leaned against the tiller, eyes squinted into the low morning sun, a contented half-smile on his face. Several sailors, including the Keshi Scarred crew who hadn't dared show their faces abovedecks the whole time the ship lay in Iberan territory, draped themselves in the ratlines, enjoying the stiff breeze and the sunshine. Hasmal sensed their joy at being free again, and understood it well. He shared it himself.

He walked aft, and nodded to the captain. 'So we got our cargo.'

The captain smiled. 'And got you out to sea promptly, just as I promised. You wanted to be at sea awhile, you said. You should be pleased with our destination.'

'Really?'

'I should think. We're sailing all the way to North Novtierra. I hope you had everything you wanted with you – we won't be doing more than *looking* at land for a very long time.'

Hasmal laughed out loud. 'Good news,' he said. 'Ah, Captain, you cannot know what good news that is.' He settled against a rail and stared down at the rushing water.

'Thought you'd feel that way, even though you never said what it was you were . . . avoiding.'

The captain didn't say 'running from' but Hasmal heard the words anyway. He shrugged and told a half-truth. 'Nothing extraordinary. A woman. Expectations. A future I didn't fancy.'

Ian Draclas laughed out loud. 'I didn't think when I took you on that you had the criminal eye, Has. Many a good man has taken to the sea to escape a woman. Truth be told, my first voyage was for that very reason.'

Hasmal glanced up at him, curious.

'A young girl took a liking to me, and told her ferocious father that I'd taken her maidenhood, and that she wanted to marry me rather than see me hanged in the city square. I . . . ah . . . I thought a girl who would lie like that to her father would lie like that to her husband, and besides, I had no wish to settle down to life as an apprentice to a shopkeeper, no matter how fine his wares or how rich his coffers. So I found a berth aboard a ship heading north, and I never looked back.'

Hasmal nodded, thinking of the doom he had finally averted. 'There are fates worse than marriage or death, but those are bad enough.'

The captain laughed.

Hasmal closed his eyes and felt the warmth of the sun on his face and smelled the richness of the salt air and realized that he could breathe for the first time since that night that he'd cloaked himself in magic and crashed the Dokteerak Naming Day celebration because he could. Free, free, and free; he'd broken from his doom, escaped his unwanted fate, won his battle. And if he was on a ship bound for gods-knew-where, and if he hated the ocean, and if he got sick from the constant motion, no matter. He would pay the price to be his own man.

Vincalis, the ancient poet, philosopher, and patron sage of Falcons, had once said, 'The Art chooses the moment and the man, and rides that man like a nag until he bursts his heart and dies; only the fool ventures within magic's grasp without good reason.'

Maybe I'm a coward, but I have no wish to die for the Falcons. I'll not be magic's horse again. And I'll never again tempt fate for the sake of curiosity, Hasmal told himself.

He had convinced himself on Naming Day that he had good reason to slip unnoticed within the walls of Dokteerak House; Stonecutter Street, indeed the whole of the Bremish Quarter, was alive with rumors of preparation for war among the city's Family, and with stories of foreign messengers representing not one but two enemy Families, and with speculation that the upcoming wedding was not all it seemed on the surface, he thought he did himself and his family a service. And the city itself stank with dark magic. So he had invoked Falcon magic in order to observe the byplay of the Families – telling himself all the while that self-preservation and not idle curiosity impelled him – and by doing so he had wakened the interest of the other world in him, and tied himself to those Families and events, and had only narrowly averted binding himself to their doom.

'Don't play on the gods' playing fields – you won't like their games, and in any case, they cheat.'

Vincalis again. Words to live by.

I've learned my lesson, Hasmal prayed. Thank you, Vodor Imrish, for gentle kindness in delivering your good Hmoth boy from the hands of the meddling Iberan gods. I promise I'll never mistake prying for self-preservation again.

* * *

Kait had no idea how long she'd slept. She only vaguely remembered Amalee waking her to get her aboard the ship she'd hired. She remembered even less of paying the captain, explaining that she had no gear, and moving into her cabin. That she had succeeded in doing all those things, though, was evident. She lay in a comfortable bunk in a clean, tiny cabin, on top of the covers and still with her boots on. Her clothes were a wreck. She wished she'd had a chance to buy new ones, and to acquire a few other supplies while she was at it; she could only hope that Captain Draclas had women among his crew, and that one of them might be willing to sell some of her things to Kait to cover her until their next harbor.

Feeling better?

Amalee's 'voice' startled Kait. She jumped, and her long-dead ancestor laughed.

'I'm fine,' Kait muttered. 'I wish you wouldn't do that.'

I'm sure. But you can't imagine how lonely I've been. It's wonderful to have someone to talk to again, and it's wonderful to be heard.

Kait stretched, yawned, and sat up. The cabin smelled of oak and cedar, of wood polish and candle wax; it held an aura of honest hard scrubbing – its soapstoned floor gleamed white as bone, and its worn sheets and carefully darned blanket were spotless and scented with alaria and lavender.

Don't you want to talk? I have so many things to tell you –

'Frankly, no. In the morning, I want to be alone with my own thoughts.'

It's well after midday, and probably not long before sundown.

Kait unbraided her hair and wished she had a convenient place to wash it. Though no longer damp, it still had that unpleasant, heavy, gritty feel that came from having soaked in seawater.

'How about this, then? I *like* being by myself, and I have things I want to think about alone. So go away and don't talk to me until I ask you to. Whether it's morning or night.'

A gentle tap sounded on the cabin door. Kait froze.

'Parata? Are you awake?'

'I'm awake,' Kait said.

'Do you have company?'

Kait rubbed her hand over her eyes and sighed. 'I was – talking to myself. I woke out of sorts.'

'I'm your cabin girl. May I come in?'

'Enter.'

The door opened. Kait wasn't prepared for the creature who presented herself for inspection. Of the Scarred, Kait had only seen those who trespassed the borders of Ibera and were executed in Calimekka's Grand Square. Always she had seen them from a distance, and more often than not, she had looked away. She had never been within arm's reach of one; for that matter, had never expected to be.

And here stood a creature Scarred beyond anything Kait could have imagined, and the creature identified herself as Kait's cabin girl. In Ibera, the girl would have been criminal by virtue of her existence – which proved, Kait supposed, that they weren't in Ibera.

Matrin's Scarred came in two varieties – those like Kait whose Scars were hidden, either all or part of the time, and those like this girl, who wore theirs for all to see. The girl would come from an entire tribe of creatures just like her, a tribe that was only one of an unknown and perhaps unknowable number of similar tribes. The visibly Scarred were sometimes called the Thousand Races of the Damned. They came from the twisted lands surrounding Wizards' Circles; ancient magic run amok had ripped the humanity from those who, a thousand years earlier, had inhabited those lands. Ancient magic had twisted the survivors as it had twisted the lands, and in doing so had given birth to numberless races of monsters. Monsters barred from Ibera, the last home of humanity.

Kait vaguely recalled that captains were by law rulers of their ships and that as long as they and their crew were aboard those ships, all aboard ship were subject to no law but the captain's . . . but the fact that an Iberan captain would hire on Scarred crew had never even occurred to Kait. She had thought of Captain's Law as simply a matter of maintaining discipline over crew, not as truly setting up a foreign country within tiny wooden confines.

Kait stared because she couldn't help herself; because she felt herself confronted with heresy; because she felt herself a hypocrite for being herself a creature of heresy and still being shocked; because she didn't know what else to do.

The girl, caught under her gaze, lowered her head and whispered, 'If you are displeased with me, I can leave.

There are others who can take care of you who are not . . . what I am.'

What you are . . . Kait thought, disgusted with herself. What you are is an honest version of what I am.

'Please come in,' Kait said, making her voice gentle. 'And please forgive my rudeness. I have never seen one of the Scarred before – you simply took me by surprise. I did not realize any of the Scarred could be so beautiful.'

And though she had managed in her words to smooth over her rudeness, Kait realized she'd spoken nothing less than the truth. The girl *was* beautiful. Her eyes, enormous and pure jet-black, gleamed in a face as shiny and iridescent as the carapace of a beetle or the body of a hummingbird – in the sunlight that backlit her, she looked like a gemstone. Though her face shimmered mostly in purples and blues and greens, she wore highlights of ruby red and gold across her high cheekbones and long, delicate chin as she turned to pull the door closed. Once out of the sunlight, most of the iridescence vanished into a black as rich and pure as that of her eyes. Eyebrows formed of some wispy, delicate white stuff so light the faintest hint of breeze or even breath moved them arched above those bottomless pools of eyes; they seemed alive. The girl had braided the outer ends of the eyebrows where the hair grew long; the braids hung on either side of her face down to the angle of her jaw, the ends adorned with tiny polished beads and wrapped feathers. Her hair had the same almost magical life as her eyebrows. It was equally white, and caught up in one thick braid that she'd draped over a slender shoulder and tucked into the belt at her waist, looping it there like coils of rope. Hard not to wonder how long that hair would be unbraided, or to imagine what it might look like unbound. Amazing stuff. And her ears – Kait had seen their equal in the does and stags she'd hunted in her Karnee form. Same size, same shape, same ever-mobile nervousness; ears affixed to the sides of a face that they dwarfed. The nose was sharp-tipped, wide of nostril, mobile. The mouth – wide also, with full lips curved upward at the corners.

The girl's body, hidden beneath the draping folds of her white flax shirt, gray pants, and soft-soled boots, was impossible to guess at, other than that the arrangement of parts was more or less like a human's, and that there wasn't much to it.

The girl, for her part, studied Kait with the same intensity that Kait studied her. They sized each other up for a long moment. Then the Scarred girl tipped her head at an angle, and frowned slightly, and said, 'You aren't like the rest of them.'

Kait felt her heart pick up its pace at those words. 'No?'

The girl smiled, revealing a row of very white, very pointed little teeth. 'No. You are . . .' She shrugged and the corners of her mouth twitched, as if she were amused by the enigma presented. 'I don't know. Somehow you are more of a predator. Like me. Somehow. Please don't be offended. I would never say that you were . . . of my kind – I know that in your world that would be a deathcrime. But you have the smell of the hunter about you. And the mannerisms of the hunter *and* the hunted.'

Kait nodded. Predators knew each other, and the girl was right. Kait *was* a predator, and denial on her part would do more to arouse the Scarred girl's curiosity than to quell it. 'I often hunted when I was at home. Deer, mostly. Sometimes other things. Now there are people after me, so I have truly become hunted. Your senses are good.'

The girl smiled. Accepted the compliment, and perhaps the explanation, though something in her eyes made Kait think she considered it incomplete. Still, politely, she said, 'I thought as much.'

Kait changed the subject. 'And you were listening at my door.'

'Oh.' Those huge eyes went rounder. 'Yes, well. Not really listening at your door – I simply hear very well, and the captain told me I must take you, when you woke, to the ship stores. He'd stationed me outside your door with that charge, because when you came aboard you carried no baggage, and he said he'd laid in a few things you might need. Clothes, toiletries, personals – you're to have your pick of what we have, and then I'm to take you to the shower and let you change. I'll clean the clothes you're wearing for you while you're at dinner. I think they aren't as damaged as you might believe, though the dye in your vest will probably have to be redone.' She glanced at Kait's feet. 'And those boots . . .'

'Don't worry about the boots. With some leather oil and some hard wax, I'm sure I can work them back to something respectable.'

The girl nodded. 'I'll be sure you have what you need.'

'You're the one who cleans this room, aren't you?'

'Yes.'

'It's wonderful. If I could ask you one thing, though . . .'

'Anything.'

'In the sheets, the alaria . . .'

A quick smile flashed across the girl's face. 'It's too sweet for your nose, isn't it?'

'Yes.'

'For mine, too. It isn't a predator scent. It covers too much.'

Kait nodded. 'I like the lavender, though.'

'As do I. Very clean. Not very concealing. The diaga – but, no, you are diaga, too.' She frowned, a delicate operation that set her eyebrows dancing. '*Most* of your kind like the alaria. But I won't use it for your things. Just the lavender.'

'Thank you.'

'Are you ready, then? To go get some new things and take your shower and go to dinner? You're to sit at the captain's table tonight.'

'I'm almost ready. Tell me your name first.'

'The passengers always call me Girlie.'

'But that isn't your name.'

'No. But my name is hard to say.'

Kait waited.

The girl trilled her tongue, the note going from low to high and ending with a soft whisper.

Kait had always been good at imitating sounds, and years of studying the other languages of Ibera had sharpened both her ear and her tongue. 'Rrru-eeth?' she said.

The girl laughed, and the laugh was as musical as the name. 'That's it exactly. Exactly. Not even Jayti says it so well.'

'Jayti?'

'My lover. He's diaga, but he's wonderful. You'll come across him sooner or later; he's one of the sailors.'

Kait nodded, thinking that for a human man to have a sexual relationship with a Scarred woman would be an immediate sentence of death by torture and mutilation for both Rrru-eeth and Jayti should the fact and either of the participants ever touch land in Ibera at the same time. So she wasn't the only one on the ship keeping deadly secrets.

They went to the storeroom. Kait found clothes there that fit her – plain working clothes, sturdy enough for her needs, if not of the quality she'd known all her life. Sword oil and a whetstone and cleaning rags. Personal items. She restocked, and Rrru-eeth took her to the tiny shower, and she bathed in little spurts of cold water, and washed her hair, and dressed in the new clothing. Both women returned to Kait's cabin long enough to put all of her new things in the drawers built into the bottom of the bunk and onto the shelves at the foot of it. Then Rrru-eeth took Kait to the galley, where the captain and the crew were gathering for dinner.

There Kait discovered that miracles sometimes happened – and better yet, that they sometimes happened to her. Hasmal son of Hasmal sat at the long trestle between a crew member so Scarred Kait could not tell whether it was male or female, and a lean, hard-eyed woman who had one hand on his forearm and who seemed to be regaling him, nonstop, with some story he didn't wish to hear.

Rrru-eeth caught Kait's indrawn breath and expression of delight, and said, 'An old lover?'

'Simply an acquaintance, but one I'd hoped to get to know better . . . before circumstances changed. I never thought I'd see him again. Now . . .' She couldn't hide her smile. 'Excuse me for just a moment.'

Hasmal didn't become aware of her presence until, standing directly behind him, she said, 'Hasmal son of Hasmal, if ever I thought the gods might like me, that moment is now. Imagine finding you here, of all the places in the world.'

He turned, and in the first instant she could see that he didn't recognize her. Easy enough to understand; he'd seen her only briefly, and then she'd been dressed for a party, and in the company of her younger and prettier cousin. She decided she must not have made much of an impression on him. Then, in the second instant, the flash of recognition widened his eyes and drained the color from his skin. He said, 'You!' in a voice she would have reserved for a meeting with a walking corpse. His eyeballs rolled up in their sockets so that she could plainly see a rim of white underneath each. His muscles sagged, and he flopped like a child's rag moppet, and slid under the table before anyone could catch him.

Bewildered, Kait looked at the pale lump of him that lay under the table, and then up to the crew staring at her from every other seat in the galley. The captain had apparently witnessed the entire exchange; his expression was complex, but the clearest emotion Kait saw there was bemusement.

She held out her hands, palms up, and tried to find words. None came.

Ian Draclas came over and pulled Hasmal out from under the table, and made sure he was breathing. Then he glanced up at Kait. 'I would not have thought that you were the one. When we've eaten, please come with me to my cabin. You and I need to talk.'

Kait nodded, still speechless. She was the *one*? *What* one? And why had Hasmal reacted with such ... such terror, for certainly she could find no other word ... to her presence? She had been delighted to see him. Pleased that there was someone on board that she knew, even though she didn't know him well. She had certainly been hopeful that he could teach her that trick of his for creating a wall of peace around himself – the same one that Dùghall had replicated just before disaster struck.

She frowned, and while several of the sailors carried Hasmal out of the galley, she took her seat next to the captain.

Dinner was a hushed affair.

* * *

In the long ward, in the cloud-dimmed light of late afternoon, the Wolves who still survived lay separated by cold white rows of narrow, empty beds. Ry stood next to his mother, who still lived, but who now had no sight at all, and whose Scars would have given a younger Ry screaming nightmares. Might still give him nightmares, he acknowledged, though he kept his horror and his revulsion from his voice when he spoke to her.

'Who still lives?' she asked him. 'Your father?'

'No, Mother. I'm sorry . . . but he did not survive. Nor did Audrai,' who had been his older sister.

'Elen?'

'Of course. She's fine, and if you wish, I'll tell her you're ready to have her visit you.' Elen, seven years younger than he was, would not even be old enough to train with the Wolves for another two years. She hadn't been in the circle that day, and so had been, like him, completely spared.

His mother showed neither pain at the loss of her husband and elder daughter, nor relief at the survival of the younger. She had never pretended deep love for her children or for Lucien, and she didn't pretend it at that moment. Her concerns were with succession; with the direction that the Wolves would take now that Lucien was gone, and that was where she focused her attention. 'Who looks to have the best chance of leading the Wolves?'

'That you could accept?' Which wasn't what she'd asked, but Ry wasn't ready to deal with the question she'd asked just yet. He sighed, looking down those nearly empty rows. So many dead. Uselessly, pointlessly dead. 'Tomey will be well soon.'

'Tomey is both weak and stupid.'

'Tomey is pliable. Not stupid. With your support, he could be encouraged in an agreeable direction.' 'Agreeable,' of course, being defined as what his mother wanted. In all the years that Lucien held the leadership of the Wolves, that had been the definition of the word, and Imogene would not care to have it changed at this late date in her life.

'Stupid. He'll never take the leadership.'

And that was probably true. Tomey was not stupid; in fact, he had a remarkable sense of self-preservation that would likely keep him far from any power struggles. Ry shrugged. Considered others his mother might not object to. 'Gizealle is badly Scarred. She'll live, but her injuries are as deep as your own. She's going to need time.'

'She might make a successful bid for power.'

'Eventually. She's more likely to support her brother's bid.'

His mother sucked air through her teeth and hissed, 'Andrew lives?'

'The whole of the Trinity lives. Andrew thrives. His Scarring was minimal; he has already returned to his apartments. Crispin was somehow untouched on the outside, though the physicks say he bears internal Scarring. Anwyn also lives, though barely. Of the survivors, his Scars are worst, though even before the disaster he bore more marks than most.'

His mother rested one twisted hand over blind eyes and groaned. Though they might not have had support for a bid for power while his father lived, the Trinity – or, as the three cousins were called behind their backs, the Hellspawn Trinity – would likely be able to coerce a fair amount of backing from the Family's new, weaker configuration. Especially since those most established in the topmost ranks of the Wolves' circle were either dead or terribly damaged.

'You'll have to make your own bid now,' his mother said.

Ry had known the conversation would turn in that direction. It had been as inevitable as sunrise, as summer rain, as death. Before he went in to visit her, he'd tried to think of any way he could stop her before she started, but there was no way. His fate was sealed the moment his father died and the Trinity lived; his mother would either bind him to a course he did not want, or else he would defy her and the Family will and end up shamed. Perhaps even disowned.

'You're the one who wants to lead,' he said softly.

'*Your* ambition, *your* heart's desire, *your* skill. Why not make the bid yourself?'

'I wasn't born Sabir.'

'You've led the Family – in fact, if not in name – for twenty years. You still carry the Sabir name. Most of the Wolves will follow you. The few who don't you'll drag into line. Or disown.'

She forced herself into a sitting position, and he cringed. Her deformities became more clear and more terrible once the sheets fell away. 'If I were still Unscarred,' she said softly, 'with my sight, with my strength, with my beauty, even then they would not follow me. None but a Sabir-born has ever led the Wolves. None but a Sabir-born ever will. This is the truth that I have come to know and come to hate in all of these years – and that you, too, must accept. I am the only Wolf living who can truly lead the Family as it needs to be led. But you are the one who must stand before me and appear to lead. They will accept you, Ry, as they never will me. Your place is at the head of the Wolves. Your time is now.'

He crossed his arms tightly over his chest. 'And what of your insistence that I father a horde of children before I stand in the circle?'

Her face tightened. 'Too late for you to take a bride. I always told you that you needed to be thinking of the future. But no matter. You must have bastards running around all over Calimekka. Claim the most promising of them, and bring their mothers into the Family. If the mothers are disgraceful, we'll keep them out of sight until we can dispose of them entirely; if they're reasonably acceptable, we'll make them paratas. Either way, we'll legitimize the children and make them your heirs.'

He smiled, knowing that she couldn't see his face, but knowing that she would hear the smile in his voice. 'I have no bastards, Mother. I have fathered no children, legitimate or otherwise.'

Anger flashed across her face like lightning; there and gone, but threatening to return at any instant. He didn't care. 'Are you sterile?'

His smile grew broader. 'Not that I know of. I've simply been careful.'

She knotted the covers in her hands. Her ruined face darkened with rage – rage at him, that he had let her down by failing to plow the fertile fields of the women that had been presented before him, and probably rage at the universe that had deprived her in one stroke of her beauty, her strength, and her power. 'Then Elen will bear children to carry on the line, and either she or they will take your place when you can no longer hold it. We have no time now for you to decide you want the children you didn't want before. The place at the head of the Family is open, but the fastest and the strongest and the smartest will fill it. And that will be you.'

'With you behind me.'

'Yes. You don't have the experience to hold the position on your own.'

He didn't have the experience to hold it at all. And he wasn't his father, to welcome living under his mother's control for the rest of his life. Even if he had never met the Galweigh woman, he would have fought being pushed to become the true head of the Sabir Family. With her on his mind, though, the entire thing became unthinkable.

'No,' he said. 'I can't.'

'I didn't ask you if you could, son. I told you that you would. We cannot permit the Trinity to take over the Wolves, and you at least will have my backing and the heritage of your father's reputation to back you up.'

'I can't.' He sighed, and said what he really meant. 'I won't.' Then he told her a lie with the merest hint of truth in it. 'The Galweigh Karnee sailed northeast. I've heard rumors that she goes to raise an army of the Scarred to bring against the Family. I am leaving to stop her.'

His mother lay back in the bed, and all emotion erased itself from her face. 'Nothing you can do is as important to the Family as taking your father's place.'

'I wasn't asking your permission,' he said. 'I came to visit you to tell you good-bye. Nothing more.'

She held herself still and silent, and he wondered how much that show of self-control cost her. She never was a woman who kept her feelings hidden. He waited, knowing that she would not let him leave unless she had the final word; he waited, too, because even if he could not say that he loved her, he still respected her. He owed her the show of respect that she had earned by her position over him, both as his mother and as the longtime leader of the Wolves. He waited, and she let him wait.

At last, however, she said, 'You are decided that you will leave?'

'I am.'

'And you are taking your friends with you, no doubt.'

He lied to her again, in spite of his respect, in spite of the honor she deserved, in spite of his yearning to keep his integrity. One lie made the next easier. 'My friends were killed in the battle at Galweigh House. I travel alone.'

No emotion on her hard face. 'They died in the service of the Family. Their own families will gain the honor they won. As for you . . .'

More silence.

Ry stood, feeling the tension in his shoulders. He'd done the best he could for his lieutenants; all of them had insisted on going with him in pursuit of his obsession. They would not share his shame, nor would their families suffer his mother's vengeance. But if she could vent her fury only on him for his disobedience and disloyalty, she would punish him all the harder.

She coughed. Cleared her throat. 'As for you, if you leave, do not come back. The Sabirs will beat off any pitiful army of the Scarred that girl raises without assistance from you. If you leave, you will become *barzanne*, and all hands of this Family and the allies of this Family will be turned against you. Your name will be removed from the Register of Births and you will cease to exist as a Sabir. Further, I will curse you, and will carry my curse to circle, and the curse we will bring to bear on you will be that of walking death – we will crush your spirit and steal your life, but your corpse will never rest. This, my son, I swear – if you will not stay and take the place of honor you deserve within this Family, you will cease to exist.'

Worse than he had feared. Worse than he had imagined. To be made *barzanne* was to be declared not human. He had thought she might disown him; he had been prepared to some degree for that. But to realize that she would take from him his right to existence within any part of Ibera – that she would, in effect, declare him a target for every assassin and bounty hunter and unscrupulous profiteer – because he would not bow to her will, stunned him. He tried to imagine being marked. Being hunted. Or fleeing outside the realm of Ibera, never to return.

To his knowledge, no mother in Ibera's history had ever declared her son *barzanne*. Such a declaration was irrevocable. Once it was approved and made public, he would be walking dead for as long as he eluded capture – then dead. Then, if Imogene succeeded in the final part of her oath, dead walking.

He closed his eyes and the girl he sought came within his reach once more. He could taste salt spray on his lips and smell sea air. He could feel the warmth of late-day sunshine on his upturned face and the roll of a deck beneath his feet. If he listened, he could hear the rich timbre of her voice, though he could not make out the words she said. She moved farther from him with every breath he took, and his body burned for her. His mind burned for her.

But . . . *barzanne*.

He had thought himself brave. He had thought himself unstoppable.

I was wrong, he realized.

'I'll stay,' he told Imogene. 'I'll do what you want me to do.'

A ship lay in harbor, his friends already waiting on it, supplies laid in. It would not sail, or if it sailed, it would do so without him.

Chapter 20

The captain's cabin – small but private, elegantly appointed, furnished in rare and exotic woods inlaid with bone and semiprecious stones, draped in sheerest silks. Gold gleamed from odd corners: a small cat idol with jeweled eyes that perched in a nook of the writing desk; a medallion on an interwoven chain of heavy links that hung from an ebony hook; three signet rings in a partially open jewel case. Casual signs of wealth and success, more obvious but less telling than the row of books neatly shelved above the bunk: a well-bound edition of *Two Hundred Tales of Kaline* sitting next to the translated *Philosophies and Meditations* by Oorpatal, and beside that, lives of Braliere, Minon Draclas, Hahlen, and Shotokar.

Kait took the room in with a practiced eye, and came to some conclusions that would have discomfited the captain, had he known of them. She decided that he was of high, possibly Familied, birth; that he was well educated but rebellious, perhaps an enemy of the privileged world that was his birthright, that he was vain and ambitious, that he indulged in piracy when more honest work failed to come his way.

'I can't permit my shipwright to be distressed,' the captain was saying. He paced the short path in front of the chair in which he'd bade her seat herself, his hands tucked behind his back, fingers interlinked, head down. 'He's vital to us on a long voyage. When we're out to sea, we have to be able to make our own repairs – on the ship and its fittings, on the crew's belongings ...' He shrugged. 'Occasionally we need to fabricate some new thing for a special situation. In any case, I can't afford to have Hasmal threatened or distressed in any way. I'm not sure what your previous relationship was –'

Kait held up a hand. 'A moment, Captain.'

He paused in his pacing and looked at her.

'I cannot even claim to have properly met Hasmal. I know about him only these things: that he dealt in rare and ancient artifacts, that he was at a party I also attended, and that he was helpful to me and my cousin at that party. I never saw him before that night. I never saw him after, until today. I wanted only to thank him again for his assistance – my cousin became very drunk and behaved badly, and he helped me get her out of the building without drawing attention to her condition.' Not the whole truth, but surely close enough.

The captain slid his hands into his pockets and leaned against his locker. 'Then why did he faint when you spoke to him? I was under the impression that you had attempted to coerce him into marriage. Perhaps that you had threatened to claim assault on your maiden virtue unless he capitulated.'

Kait's shocked laughter erupted without warning. 'My *maiden virtue*? Dear Captain, any *assault* on that was years in the past and is best left buried there.' She took a few deep breaths, giggled, shook her head disbelievingly. 'My maiden virtue, if we're going to be so ... polite, was disposed of in a wholly voluntary and mutually agreeable manner and has not troubled me since. Nor have I ever felt the need to bother the disposer of it with threats; I am not yet ready to give up my autonomy to marriage and its rule by committee. My freedom was too hard-won.' The last of her amusement died away, replaced by puzzlement. 'As for why Hasmal fainted . . .' She turned one hand palm up and shrugged slightly. 'You know at least as much as I do.'

They studied each other, looking for cues.

'His reaction worried me,' the captain said. '*Worries* me.'

'Of course. It shocked me. But I don't know what caused it.'

'Your appearance caused it.'

Kait sighed. 'Unless he succumbed to poison at that exact instant – which seems unlikely – I'm inclined to agree with you. But I truly don't know why.'

Draclas frowned suddenly. 'That . . . the manuscript you mentioned . . . you say he was a dealer in antiquities?'

'So he told me at the party.'

'You didn't by chance . . . *buy* it from him, did you?'

'No.'

'A dealer in antiquities . . .' His frown deepened. 'He demonstrated his smithing to me before I took him on. His skills were excellent. But he claimed previous experience aboard ship. I had no reason to doubt him . . .' He stared down at his feet, speaking more to himself than to her. When he looked up again, it was to ask her, 'Where did you meet him?'

Kait considered her answer for a moment. She didn't want to be too open about her past – her presence in Halles, if Draclas kept current on events, could help him pinpoint who she really was. But lies were hard to control, and lying about where she met Hasmal seemed risky, especially since she didn't know why he'd reacted the way he did when he saw her. 'In Halles,' she said.

'Halles? That's nowhere near the coast.'

'That's where I met him. He told me he worked with his father acquiring and selling antiquities. That's all I knew about him, except that both he and his father were named Hasmal.'

Draclas settled onto the edge of his bunk and gave her a hard look. 'Halles. Why did you pause so long before telling me that?'

'I'm not sure how much I want you to know about me. I was trying to decide if letting you know I was in Halles would tell you too much. I decided that it didn't.'

He snorted. 'That sounds honest enough, anyway.'

'It is.'

'We're going to have a hard time being friends, you and I, if you don't trust me.'

Kait arched an eyebrow. 'If *I* don't trust *you*? Captain, I suspect you have many more secrets than I do.' She glanced around the room, letting her gaze settle on the various treasures casually displayed. 'I think that for now, at least, you and I would do well to keep our own confidences; I don't think you'll be any more eager to tell me your deepest secrets than I'll be to tell you mine.'

She smiled when she said that, and he responded with a smile, but she didn't miss the wariness that crept into his eyes. Certain she'd hit her mark, she rose. 'If we're finished here . . .?'

He rose, too. 'I'd like to be your friend, Kait. You seem like you could use a friend.'

'Perhaps I can. But not just yet. We'll be . . . associates . . .' She tested the weight of the word, and decided it suited her needs. 'Yes. Associates. For a time, at least. We share common goals, and possibly a common outlook. Friends, though . . . we'll see. Friendship takes time.'

He opened the door of his cabin for her, and she stepped out on deck. She walked to her own cabin, the pressure of his stare tickling along the back of her neck until she let herself into the room and closed – and locked – her door.

* * *

Hasmal crouched in his room, glaring at the Speaker who had come to his summons. 'She's here. *Here*. You knew this would happen. You *lied* to me.'

From within her wall of blue flames, the Speaker chuckled. 'My *sister* answered your call, and she told you only the truth.'

'She told me that I could escape my doom.'

'No. She told you that you could try.'

'If I had stayed at home, I would have been safe. Instead, because of what she told me, I traveled half the length of Ibera and ended up trapped on a ship with the woman I tried so hard to avoid.'

'If you had done nothing you would have been safe. But your safety is irrelevant to the larger scheme. While you have been trying to hide from your destiny, and unintentionally wrapping yourself deeper in it, whole worlds have stepped into the fray that is building.'

Hasmal clenched his hands into tight fists, but forced himself to breathe slowly and to let his anger drain away. 'Why did your sister mislead me? Why did she lead me to believe I needed to flee?'

'Because you have something to do, Hasmal rann Dorchan, that will change your world, and affect ours, and perhaps even others more deeply embedded within the Veil. If you escape your fate, these worlds will be the worse for it. You matter, mortal, in a way that few ever matter – and while no one and no thing can force your actions along the right path, my sister could, and did, steer you in a direction that seemed most beneficial to us at the time.'

'What am I expected to do?'

'That isn't the question. Your path is never cast in iron, your future never certain. The question is, "What *may* you do?" And even that I cannot tell you, not because I wish to taunt you, but because I do not know. I only see the branching paths that mortal lives can take, and the ways they flow together and apart. I can see that you and Kait Galweigh, the woman you fear, have a powerful future if you are together, and that the two of you may do great good, or great evil, but that you will succeed at nothing if you are apart.'

'But she'll doom me and all I love.'

'Your association with her leads to doom, and pain, and grief. Perhaps to great victory . . . and perhaps to your death. But all men die, Hasmal,' the spirit said. 'Few ever live.'

He sat in silence, watching the spirit disappear back into the Veil from which he had summoned her, watching as the last traces of cold flame burning on the surface of the mirror flickered out.

The coldness inside of him spread from his core – from heart and gut and spirit – out to his fingers and toes. His flesh prickled, and he shivered, though the air in his room was stuffy and hot. She had quoted Vincalis at him, in what he was sure was an intentional paraphrase. The original speech had been:

All men die, Antram. All men age and wither and creep at last into their dark graves, and from thence into the flames of Hell or cold oblivion, as their theology dictates. But to only a few men do the gods give a task, a burden, a road to greatness that can, if they take it, raise them above the thick clouds of complacency that blind most eyes and plug most ears. To only a few men do the gods give true pain, which removes the bloated cushion of softness and brings sharp awareness of the preciousness of life; which raises up heroes and strips cowards naked before the world. You, Antram, will do great things. You will see, you will feel, you will breathe and touch and revel in each moment you are given. And you will suffer great pain. And someday, whether soon or late, you will die.

But all men die, Antram. Few ever live.

* * *

In Calimekka, in the center of Sabir House, in a silent room that opened onto a balcony that hung above a jasmine-scented garden, Ry Sabir paced. The room lay in darkness – not even a single candle burned – but that mattered little to him; he saw very well in light so low that normal men would have been blind. Back and forth along the tall bank of glass-paned doors he stalked, oblivious to the sweet scent of the night air, oblivious to the gentle breeze that set the gauzy drapes billowing.

He was lost in the prison of his own mind, held to the pillory of the words he had said and the words he had left unsaid. And he could not find peace.

'Wait for me,' he'd told Yanth. 'I must attend my mother, to at least try to make her understand. But whether she gives me her blessing or not we'll said tonight.'

And to Trev, who ever feared for his sisters, 'I promise you that your sisters will in no way be dishonored by what we go to do. I won't let that happen.'

To the captain of the Sabir-owned ship, 'I'll pay you double your yearly wage, and a gift on top of that, if you'll take me and my lieutenants wherever we need to go, and get us there safely, and not ask questions. This is Family business, and dangerous; you have my word as Sabir that you will have the honor of the entire Family for the service you do us.'

And to his mother, 'My friends were killed in the battle at Galweigh House. I travel alone.'

And again to his mother, 'I'll stay. I'll do what you want me to do.'

Betrayal, the breaking of his word, the destruction of his honor upon a half-dozen rocky shores – no matter which way he turned, he would be lying to someone. Trev and Valard and Karyl and Jaim and Yanth had become, by his utterance, dead men, unable to return to their city or their homes under their own names; his mother would honor her word to treat their families well only if they were never seen again. When he'd faced an unknown journey, when he'd been sure he had the strength to defy her, his lie had seemed the only way that he could keep his promise to them not to drag their families into dishonor. He had intended to come back in glory, so that all would be forgiven.

And the captain who waited for his arrival at that moment, certain that his future was assured because he served a Sabir who had vowed no less . . . what of him? Ry had promised him the honor of the Sabirs, and if the man were to tell any of the other Sabirs what he had been waiting for, they would undoubtedly treat him as the accomplice of a traitor.

Only wild success in a journey that goes I know not where, and serves I know not what purpose, can give that man all I promised him, Ry realized. I intended to find a way to make good on the promise. But now?

What of his own cowardice in the face of a threat he thought his mother would never make? Cowardice . . . he could call it nothing but that. She had held *barzanne* over his head, and he had capitulated; he could have taken his honor with him into exile, but instead he had given her his word that he would stay and uphold his duty as she defined it. His word. What worth did that have? What value would it ever have again?

A pity he wasn't dead. No one maintained expectations of the dead, or held them to their word; they became exempt from every promise they'd ever made.

A pity he wasn't dead.

Such a pity.

He stopped pacing and moved to the balcony. Out in

the courtyard, in the beautiful night, only animals moved. He could smell them in the breeze: the mingled scents of cat and dog and peacock; the faintest hints of mouse and sparrow and owl; the musky perfume of the two fawns who would grace the courtyard until they became too large and unruly to live there, and who would then grace a banquet while replacements brought in from the wilds became the new living ornaments. Leaves rustled, and the cat caught a mouse, and Ry listened to the frantic squeaking, quickly silenced, and smiled slowly.

Better he were dead. Even better were he murdered and his body never found. Best of all if evidence existed that his death had come at the hands of the Hellspawn Trinity, for such evidence would turn Family sentiment against the trio's bid for power harder and faster than anything else could. Murder had always been a way to forward one's cause in the Family, but to be sloppy enough about it to get caught at it – no. The removal of one's obstacles, if one wished to maintain respect, had to be accomplished with finesse. A certain grace. An air of . . . mystery.

He could vanish, Ry realized. He could forward his mother's cause by doing so, or at least become an embarrassment to her enemies. He could find the woman he sought, and perhaps find the thing that she sought at the same time.

You can do all of those things. But only if you act quickly. Your opportunity will be lost if you wait until morning.

That pressure in his skull was back, and with it the mental itch. He stiffened. The stranger's voice had returned to his mind. This time it was only one voice, but he did not welcome one outsider into the privacy of his thoughts any more than he welcomed the babble that had erupted when he first woke after the Sabir Family's disastrous attempt to take Galweigh House. He was a Wolf, and no Wolf would tolerate such an intrusion. He began to spin the magic that would force the intruder out, but as he did, the stranger stopped him with a soft phrase. *Careful, little brother. You're clever, but you haven't seen what I've seen.*

Ry froze. 'Identify yourself,' he whispered.

How many dead older brothers do you have?

'I suppose that depends on how many mistresses Father had that Mother never found out about, and how careless their bastards were.'

Half a dozen that I know of. But I didn't say half brothers.

'You're Cadell?' He didn't believe it. He couldn't. That babble of voices in his mind when he first woke up after the debacle at Galweigh House had been in some language he'd never heard. This voice spoke clear, unaccented Iberan. And what would his dead brother be doing inside his thoughts?

It would take too long to explain, and we don't have much time.

'We have enough time for you to prove who you are.'

We do. I am – or was – Karnee, like you. We shared both a room and a bed until my death. When I left that last day, I had the feeling I might not be coming back, and I left my medallion, which you even now wear around your neck, for Mother to give you. And when you were four, I carried you across Red Bridge on my shoulders every time we had to cross it because you believed a man with purple eyes lived underneath it, and every time we got near it you insisted he was staring at you.

Ry remembered. Tears started in his eyes, and he closed them. 'I've missed you.'

And I, you. But if you don't hurry, you're going to lose Kait. And you don't dare lose her. This is important, little brother. *More important than anything you've ever done, and maybe more important than anything you'll ever do again.*

Ry was puzzled. 'Who is Kait?'

Kait Galweigh. A picture formed in Ry's mind: the compelling creature he'd first met in the back alley in Halles, whom he had viewed standing atop the tower there watching the executions.

'Fine. You know her name. Tell me, why is it so important to you that I find her?'

Because she knows where to find the Mirror of Souls. And she's set sail to get it. I'll tell you why the Mirror is so important later. For now, suffice it to say that it must not end up with any Family but the Sabirs.

'I've heard a legend about it.'

Not important. Just go. Trust me, little brother. You have no spare time. Do what you have to do to get away from here. And we can discuss the importance of all of this when you are at sea. Agreed?

'Agreed.'

Ry turned his attention to the staging of his own death. Carefully and quietly, he rearranged the furniture, over-turning a chair, breaking one of its legs, pulling the covers off the narrow bed and dragging them partway to the door. He took out pen, ink, paper, and blotter from the desk that sat against the north wall and wrote the beginning of a note:

Esteemed Uncle Grasmir,

I have accepted the burden of my Family respon-sibility; after discussing the matter with Mother, I feel as she does that my bid to lead the Wolves will be most beneficial to meeting the Family's needs and goals. Though I do not seek this position gladly, for I have neither wife nor child and will be barred from such once I begin to walk the circle, I feel I am the most likely candidate to prevent Crispin, Anwyn, and Andrew from taking over.

With that goal in mind, may I ask for your support, as paraglese as well as beloved family member? I'll need your

He let the letter stop in midsentence, blew on it to dry the ink, and dropped it down between the wall and the desk, making sure that an edge with handwriting on it showed clearly. Whoever discovered the blood and the disarray of the room would bring in the Family, and Grasmir would insist upon an investigation. The letter would point blame or at least suspicion in the direction Ry desired, while the signs he left behind would make everyone sure he'd been murdered.

He drew his knife, dipped the blade in the wine bottle he'd been drinking from – for everyone knew that a blade soaked in spirits prevented the spirits of sickness from entering the body – and sliced into his arm. The pain woke the Karnee madness in him, and he growled as he let his blood pour onto the floor. He smeared it on his hands and grabbed the blankets, then left trails on the floor as if he'd been dragged by his feet. He soaked the broken leg of the chair in his blood, getting most of it on the very end of the leg. Then he pulled out a few strands of his hair and soaked them in blood and caught them in the splinters. He thought that would give anyone enough to go on.

He let himself skirt the edge of Shift. He didn't *need* it yet, not in the way he would in another half month, but he was in enough pain that the changes came readily. He felt the fire flow into the wound and sighed. It healed itself as he crouched there, waiting. Then he pushed himself further and deeper into the Shift, letting the hunger build. He stripped off his clothes as quickly as he could and bundled them tightly together. With them he bundled his letter of credit (worthless if he were *barzanne*, equally worthless if he were dead; but he and the ship would be well away from Calimekka before the news of his death had a chance to affect credit), his rings, his purse, and his dagger and sword. In the little time he had, he made the bundle as tight and neat as he could.

Once he was fully Shifted, he leaped out onto the balcony and climbed up the wall, digging claws into the spaces between stones, hanging on to the bundle with his teeth. When he reached the top, he ran along the roof tiles, compromising between speed and stealth to get himself to the north end of the House. There, the wall lay less than a man's height from the roof, and the jump down, though not easy, would be more easily accomplished than elsewhere, and with less chance of his being seen by the guards or servants.

Once he was safely outside the wall, he found a dark, deserted alley, and there he relaxed and calmed himself until he was able to welcome back his human form. He dressed, strapped on his weapons, and stepped out into the street again.

A worried Yanth met him on deck. 'I thought you'd been killed on your way here, or that something had kept you from coming.'

Ry hugged his friend and sighed. 'More truth to all of that than you'd believe.' He watched the sailors raising sails while the captain stood at the helm. Both tide and a light breeze favored their departure, but wouldn't for much longer – if he'd taken any longer to figure out what he had to do, his delay might have cost them half a day, and that half-day might have cost them everything. 'But I'm away, and we're free to carry out our voyage.'

'She understood? I'm surprised.'

'She didn't understand. But there are other ways of

reaching an objective. I chose one of them. The dock log didn't list this voyage in my name, did it?'

'The captain did what you told him – registered out in the name of C. Pethelley, Merchant, cargo of fruit and equipment for the colonies.'

That was a relief. Sometimes people forgot details when it came time to act, but Ry had chosen the captain as much for his reputation for intelligence under pressure as for his equally solid reputation for discretion. 'Then we sail away happily and find Kait.'

'That's her name?'

'Kait Galweigh.'

Yanth grinned. 'Makes her a little less magical, an ordinary name like that.'

'Not to me.'

'I suppose not.' He shrugged, and his smile was unapologetic. 'So where is your Kait going?'

'East by northeast right now. We follow.'

Yanth chuckled. 'East by northeast. That's vague enough to point us at the tip of one continent and the whole of a second ... and the second almost entirely unexplored. Plus all of an ocean, and not a friendly ocean, either. I hope your nose is working well, or we'll have a long search ahead of us.'

'Which will give us enough time for me to teach you those few tricks of mine you wanted to learn, and for you to teach me that dagger move of yours that disarms the opponent; I've long envied that move.'

Yanth's face was a study of conflicting emotions. 'You want to start that tonight?'

Ry was tired enough that he thought he would be able to sleep through the night and all of the next day as well, and already ravenous from his brief Shift. 'Not tonight. Tonight we'll sleep. Tomorrow, or maybe the day after, will be soon enough to be industrious.'

* * *

Dùghall frowned over the oracle cast on the table. Had it been any less clear, he would have been tempted to use his own blood to summon a spirit to confirm its message. He could find no room for doubt, though, in the pattern made by the silver coins spread across the embroidered silk *zanda*. In the quadrant of House, the terse message of two coins: *Flee* and *Betrayal by trusted associates*. In the quadrant of Life, the equally terse *Present danger*. The quadrants of Spirit and Pleasure lay empty, while the quadrant of Duty held the complex message *Home* overlapped partially by *Seek new allies* and conjuncted with *Keep your own counsel* and *The gods intervene*. Wealth, Health, Goals, Dreams, Past, Present, and Future all lay empty, and he could not remember having seen such a strange throw in his entire life. The coins that should have landed within the empty quadrants had, to a one, rolled on their edges to fall outside the embroidered periphery of the *zanda*, where they gleamed on the black silk, haunting him with their silence. *The gods intervene*, indeed.

He'd planned to stay on in Galweigh House, to assist with the Family's business until the survivors of the massacre pulled themselves together and put the House back in order. But as he stared at the *zanda*, he realized that would not serve. He would have to pack a small bag, leave without explanation, and put as much distance as he could between himself and the rest of the Family. And he would have to do it immediately.

Betrayal by trusted associates. That distressed him. Which associates? His personal staff, who had come with him to Calimekka? His aide, who had served at his side for most of his life? The Family members whose lives he had saved when he routed the Sabirs? The pilot? Who would betray him? And why?

Certainly not all of those in the House with him were traitors – he knew there were those among the survivors who would help him, who would do what needed to be done with him. But what he could not know was who they were, or who they were not. And the message on the *zanda* told him he was not to try to sort them out. He would leave silently, immediately, as if he had been spirited away, and both the guilty and the innocent would remain behind to wonder what had become of him.

He fixed the placement of the coins on the cloth in his mind, then brought his arms up in front of him and pressed his palms together and pressed the heels of his hands to his forehead. With eyes closed, he released the energy he'd drawn around himself to cloak his activities, murmured his words of thanks to Vodor Imrish, patron god of Falcons, and added the subtle plea that this newest demand for his services would spare the lives and honor of any loyal members of his staff who were left behind.

Then he gathered up such of his belongings as he could carry in a small pack on his back, spun around himself a guise that said, *I am only someone beneath your notice, and someone you expect to be here*, and he stepped out into the hallway.

He would flee, he would seek new allies, he would keep his own counsel, and, for the time being at least, he would head home to Jeslan, in the Imumbarra Isles, alone and without questioning the orders that had sent him there. He had known from the day that his mother initiated him into the Falcons that the gods had a special mission for him. He had waited all his life to find out what it was, and he had begun to believe that the early oracles had been wrong, and that he would be only another Keeper of the Secret Texts, and that in itself had been special. He'd tried to convince himself that it had been all.

Now . . .

Now . . .

His gut told him that his moment was coming. That the world had changed, and that now he was being called upon to be a sword for the gods. He had been hardened by tragedy, tempered in blood; fat and old and slow though he had become, he finally had within him the clear-burning, ruthless flame that he needed to be wielded by an eternal hand. Vincalis would have been satisfied with his qualifications.

In his heart and in his soul, he could hear the bell-clear ringing of metal on metal. He had been unsheathed.

He wondered who the true enemy could be.

Chapter 21

Snow-blind, half-starved, freezing, and sick, Danya Galweigh pushed herself to take one more step across the unending tundra. And one more after that. And one more after that. She drifted in and out of awareness; when she was awake, she could recognize the voice that urged her on as the voice of her guardian spirit, assuring her that salvation lay just over the next rise. The voice metamorphosed into dreadful things when she became confused: it became Crispin Sabir coming to torture her again, and it became the chanting Sabir Wolves in the center of a huge circle; it became the voices of all of those she had seen suffer but had not helped; it became her dead grandmother, and a favorite cousin who had died in childhood.

She rose out of the mists in her mind one more time, and into the temporary clarity, and the voice said, *Almost to shelter, Danya. Almost to friends, who will help you take care of yourself and the baby. Just a little farther. Just a tiny bit farther.*

She said, 'Baby?'

Yes. The baby. You knew, didn't you?

She remembered the torture. The rape. The brutal laughter, the cruel stinking faces shoved close to hers, grinning while they hurt her, delighting in her humiliation.

'Baby?'

There could be, would be, no baby from that horrid union. The gods could not be that cruel.

But now that the voice had told her, she could feel, through her magic, the truth of what he said. The vomiting, the weakness, the dizziness, the *wrongness*, were not just symptoms of the Scarring, nor were they entirely signs of her nearness to starvation; a new life grew inside of her. She reached into herself with what little magic she could summon, and felt that life. Small and weak as the flame of a single candle in a drafty room, it pulsed inside of her.

She wanted to hate it, the way she hated whichever of the three monsters had been its father. She wanted to hate it, she wanted to find a way to be able to kill it, yet when she touched it with her mind, something pure and genuinely good reached back and touched her. She pulled away from the first tentative touch of the stranger inside her and stood in the snow, staring down at her feet, sickened. How could anything good come of so much evil? She didn't want to know, and she didn't want the child. But that tendril of goodness – and not a little of her own momentary weakness – stopped her from twisting the growing infant away from its delicate link to her and purging her body of it.

She sensed satisfaction from the one who watched over her. *You have done well, dear child. And you will continue to do well. Only hurry, now, and I'll get you to safety.*

She hurried, for what little good it did her. The promised safe haven did not lie only a few more steps ahead of her. She walked for another half-day before she finally toppled into a hole in the snow and found herself face to face with a Scarred family. The family drew weapons, but she, surrounded by unexpected and marvel-ous warmth, by the rich scents of cooking meat, and by relief that someplace existed away from the endless awful cold and hellish snow, fainted.

She had no way of knowing how much time had passed when she finally woke, but she found herself still in the warmth, lying in the flickering light near a small open fire. The creature that crouched across the fire from her held a long, bone-tipped spear in one hand. He stared into the flames, narrowed eyes almost hidden in the deep fur that covered his face. His flat, glossy gray nose and the narrow slash of his thin lips were the only other breaks in that thick white pelt. His ears, if he had them, were so small they were hidden within the thicker ruff of gray-white fur that circled his face. Danya thought him odd-looking, but his appearance was not unpleasant. When he saw Danya looking at him, he waved the spear at her in a warning fashion and said something unintelligible. What he said didn't sound as if he had hostile intentions, though. His voice held kindness, and reason. And only the gentlest of warnings.

She imagined him saying, 'Don't do anything stupid. I want to help you, but I can't if you attack me.'

Close enough, the voice in her head whispered. *Given time, I can make sure you can talk to them. For now, eat the food he's made for you.*

She sat up slowly and held out her hand to show that she carried no weapons. None other than her claws, in any case.

The creature said something else, and pointed to the large fired-clay cook pot that hung over the little fire. Danya reached forward slowly and took it, carefully trying to look as unthreatening as possible.

He'd cooked some form of stew. She said, 'Is this for me?' She didn't understand his reply, and she couldn't read the expression on his fur-covered face, but his tone furthered her belief that he meant her only good.

She reached into the pot and speared a cube of meat on

her claw. She knew she didn't dare eat too much or too quickly, but aside from the few hares and snow-pigeons she'd managed to catch and eat raw, she had not had food since her last meal, the night before she became a sacrifice. She ate the meat cube, wishing she could lower her muzzle straight into the pot to lap out the contents in a few quick gulps. She didn't want to be sick, though. So she forced herself to take dainty little bites, and to hand the pot back to her host even before it was empty, because she could feel uncomfortable pressure in her stomach.

The two of them sat looking at each other across the fire. She recalled the others that she'd seen in the house before, but she could not hear them or smell them or get any sense that they were still present.

He made his family leave. They went to one of the other homes in the village until he could be sure that you weren't dangerous.

Danya considered that for a moment. *Why didn't he just kill me when I fell into his house? Why take any chance on me at all?*

Among his people, apparently strangers are always taken in and made welcome. I've seen similar things before . . .

But I'm not of his people. I'm a completely different kind of . . . of monster.

A soft chuckle in the back of her mind then. *You aren't in human lands anymore, Danya. Beyond Ibera, people are usually considered people no matter what form they take. With a few exceptions, the humans are the only ones who refuse to recognize that.*

Danya didn't respond to that. She couldn't think of herself as human anymore, but she had to admit that on the inside she was the same person she had been before; at least, if she was different, she hadn't discovered how yet.

You . . . you brought me to these people. How did you know they were safe?

She felt rather than heard the sigh. *First, now that you are fed, and sheltered, and for the time safe, let me tell you my name again. I've never cared for being called 'You.'*

You've told me your name before?

Certainly. But it proved an exercise in pointlessness when you were in and out of delirium. My name is Luercas. I am . . . or rather was . . . a Wolf like you. I was killed in a situation I'd rather not discuss now, but for some reason my body was trapped in the Veil, and I haven't been able to move forward or back. Until now. Something happened when you were . . . ah . . . sacrificed . . . that released me from the prison that had held me for – well, I honestly don't know how long I was trapped. But I found myself inside of your mind, looking out of your eyes, and I think perhaps the reason I was released was because I could help you and no one else could. Luercas fell silent for a moment. Danya waited.

At last he said, *In my current state, I can sense things that are at a distance. I can feel potentials – and while I couldn't be sure what we would find when we got here, I did sense that in this direction lay safety for you, and your one chance of survival.*

Danya lay back and let her eyes drift closed. The food, the warmth, and the hardships of the last however many days all conspired to push her toward sleep. She did ask, *Why did my survival matter to you? I can't understand that.*

Because, Luercas said, *I can sense potentials. You have something important to do. Something vital and good. Something that is going to change your world. And I am, in some way, a part of that. And I believe that you must achieve this goal before I am released to pass through the Veil to whatever awaits me beyond it.*

Danya nodded. Across from her, the Scarred man ate the stew she'd left. He contorted his face, but she couldn't read the expression. She tried to respond with a smile, but realized her own facial muscles were no longer designed for such nuances. She sighed again, and closed her eyes.

I'm glad you're helping me, she told Luercas.

That was her last coherent thought for a long time.

* * *

Kait sat in the ship's parnissery in the darkness before the dawning of Embastaru, the Day of Hours, and listened to the sweet, high voice of the ship's parnissa reading the old words. She had been a month aboard the *Peregrine,* and the rhythms of ship life had dulled some of the pain of her precipitous exit from Calimekka.

'The *Book of Time,* third of the five sacred books of Iber, says, "Number neither your days nor your hours, lest they pass by you quickly while you count them. Instead, name them as friends, and bid them tarry awhile, and you will know long life and happiness." So we greet each station of the day by name, and with reverence, acknowledging all both as friends returned to visit and as strangers to be made welcome – strangers who have come into our midst briefly, and who will never return.'

The parnissa wore the white robes traditional for the day, and the candlelight reflecting off the robes and her pale skin and equally pale golden hair made her look more spirit than flesh. The ship creaked and rocked, and the sounds and rhythms soothed. Kait was close to sleep, but she remembered her duty as one of the Familied to uphold Iberism in all places and at all times, and so she sat on the hard bench in the candlelit parnissery and fought to keep her eyes open.

'Morning approaches – blessed morning.'

The parnissa paused, and Kait and the other attendees said in unison, 'We honor the Stations of Morning.'

'We honor Soma,' the parnissa intoned.

Everyone replied, 'Soma, who is the bringer of first light.'

Kait let the familiar words drift over her. The service was both womb and wound, cradling her in its ties to the past at the same time that it hurt her with its reminder that the future could never be as bright or warm. In the past days, she'd kept to herself. She'd burned candles for her parents and brothers and sisters, for her aunts and uncles and cousins; she'd prayed for the success of her journey, while never quite believing that the artifact she sought could truly exist. She'd tried her best to give herself a measure of peace, but inner peace eluded her.

The parnissa walked along the edge of the pedestal at the front of the parnissery, lighting candles. 'We honor Stura.'

'Stura, the singer of morning songs, the lively child.'

'We honor Duea.'

'Duea, fair daughter who dances the sun to midday.'

Kait recalled sitting in her parents' parnissery on a dozen occasions, repeating the same words in the same sleepy tones, giving half-aware honor to gods neither she nor her family really believed in, comforted by the presence of her sisters and brothers on the bench beside her. Her father had kept them all quiet with hard looks, her mother had bribed them with treats afterward.

The same words, the same tones, the scent of beeswax sweetened with lavender that the candles gave off, and this year the hurt in her heart that would not go away.

'And following on the heels of morning,' the parnissa continued, 'the Stations of Aftering.'

'We honor the Stations of Aftering.'

'We honor Mosst.'

'Mosst, master of heat, creator of fire.'

Thought of her Family brought their killers to mind, and chasing the thought of Sabirs came the thoughts of one specific Sabir. Her gut knotted, thinking of the Karnee in the alley, and suddenly she realized she held him in her mind not because of memory or the random drift of thoughts from one thing to the next, but because some part of him had already been there.

Waiting. A tantalizing glimpse of a dream fragment flitted through her mind and out again before she could catch hold of it, but she had it long enough in mind to realize that at some point, she'd dreamed of him.

'We honor Nerin.'

'Nerin, whose gift is long light and clear vision.'

She shivered and tried to push him from the place he held in her thoughts; she wanted to find her way back to the service honoring the gods of the hours. Instead, she discovered that she could reach out and touch him with her mind.

He slept. She held so still she almost didn't breathe, and let her eyelids drift shut.

He slept aboard a ship. He was some distance from her.

He followed her.

'We honor Paldin.'

'Paldin, who blends the worlds of light and dark, and illuminates the world after the sun has fled.'

He followed her, in a ship filled with his men; he hunted her. She could feel in the lightness of his sleep some of the edge of his determination to catch her. She could feel a sense of loss in him, though she could not fathom what he had lost. She felt his hunger, and felt it directed at her. Even in his sleep, he came after her.

'As we honor the times of light, we honor the darkness.'

'We honor the Stations of Night.'

'We honor Dard.'

'Dard, the first true darkness, who greets the White Lady.'

'We honor Telt.'

'Telt, the middle darkness, who conjoins the White Lady and the Red Hunter.'

The White Lady, who had once been mortal, had fled the Red Hunter in life. He had hunted her from the time she came of age and became very beautiful until the day when, weak and weary, she ran into a passageway between cliffs in a forest she did not know, and discovered that the only way out was the way she'd gone in. Trapped, she prayed to Haledan, the goddess of beauty and truth, asking that she be spared the fate the hunter planned for her. Haledan came to her, and offered to protect her from the hunter if she would pledge herself into Haledan's service forever. The girl agreed, and Haledan turned her into the most beautiful star in the sky, the White Lady, and thus she escaped both the hunter and death.

But the hunter called upon his patron god, Stolpan, the god of craftsmen and workers, and begged not to be cheated from the hunt when he was so close to catching his quarry. Stolpan could not undo what Haledan had done, but he could let the hunter continue his hunt. The hunter agreed that he would serve Stolpan forever, and in exchange, Stolpan made him the Red Hunter, the star that was as dark and frightening as the White Lady was bright and pure, and in that guise, he chased her across the sky every night. He would never catch her, but he would hunt her forever.

Realizing that her enemy, the Sabir Karnee, pursued her, and that he somehow knew where she was, Kait felt a sudden kinship with the White Lady. The only difference was that she didn't have the protection of a goddess – she had no guarantee that the one who hunted her would not catch her.

'We honor Huld.'

287

'Huld, singer of the last darkness, who waits to embrace the rising of the sun.'

'Wait in silence, for the new day comes, and the new hour with it. Hold Soma in your heart, and all those stations that follow after. Be blessed, this day and every day, and rejoice in each moment, for all are sacred, and none will come again.'

'We bless you; we bless each other; we bless ourselves, this day and every day. *Desporati sajamis, tosbe do naska.*'

The words of the final benediction, which in the ancient parnissas' tongue meant, 'In our humanity we unite, body and spirit,' signaled the end of the service. The movement of the people on either side of her pulled Kait away from the link she'd shared with her hunter. That change, in turn, woke him. She felt him open his eyes. She could, for just an instant, see through them; he occupied a cabin more lush than her own, and larger, but he shared it with others. She caught just a glimpse of a hard-eyed man with a lean face who sat across from him on the edge of a bunk, and another, pale-haired and almost sweet-looking, who slept in the bunk above that man. The lean man seemed to look into Kait's eyes. He frowned and said, 'What's the matter, Ry? You look . . . sick.'

Then she felt the Sabir realize she was there, and instantly the tie that linked them broke, and hurled her consciousness back into her own body, into the parnissery. Most of the rest of the worshipers had already filed out, and the parnissa stood looking at her with a curious expression on her face. Kait rose quickly, before the woman could come over to ask her if she had something she wished to discuss, and followed everyone else out onto the deck of the ship. At that moment, the sky, which along the eastern horizon wore rich veins of deep purple and ruby red above a widening line of pink and yellow, erupted in gold, and the sun broke free of the sea that had hidden it.

The alto bell welcoming Soma began to ring, and all the worshipers on deck faced east, dropped to their knees, and welcomed the new station and the new day.

'If you're finished, I need to speak with you.'

She had knelt with the others; she twisted around and looked up, and found Hasmal standing behind her, studying her with an expression that was a curious mix of determination and fear. He hadn't been in the parnissery for the service; she wondered if he'd just happened upon her, or if he'd sought her out.

Still shaken by the contact with the Sabir – with *Ry*, as his companion had called him – she rose and shrugged. 'Maybe later.'

Hasmal smelled afraid, but he lifted his head and stared at her. Without doing anything that she could see, he surrounded himself and her with the same wall of peace that had first caught her attention at the party. In that instant, she felt Amalee protest, then fall silent, cut off in mid-yelp. And a faint weight that had tickled in the back of her mind, and that she only noticed by its sudden absence, also vanished. 'What I have to tell you won't wait any longer. I've put it off much too long as it is, and I've . . . er, I've been told . . . that by doing so, I have put us into unnecessary danger.'

She didn't want to deal with him right then. Later, but not right then. But he'd managed to intrigue her. She nodded. 'We can talk in my cabin, I suppose. Unless you have someplace else . . . ?'

'No. Your cabin will serve.'

She led. He followed.

* * *

'You know where she is, then?' Shaid Galweigh sat in cool near-darkness in the Cherian House private meeting room, at the head of a long cast-bronze table older than

289

memory. The Wolves of Cherian House, untouched by the disaster that had wiped out the Galweigh House Wolves because they had not participated in it, lined both sides of the table.

The head of the Wolves, a plump, jovial-looking woman named Veshre, nodded and smiled. 'We're certain. We've located her aboard a private ship currently heading east-northeast, somewhere along the Devil's Trail. We think they put in for supplies at one of the islands about a week ago, and since then the ship has been moving steadily again.'

'Have you divined her destination?'

The Wolves glanced at each other. None were sure how to give the paraglese the news they had uncovered. Veshre finally shrugged and said, 'There are some complications, Shaid. We've linked a number of . . .' She frowned, not liking the melodramatic terms that came first to mind, but unable to frame what she had to say in any terms less sensational. 'A number of . . . well, deities, I suppose I'd have to say, to her movements. One has somehow attached itself to her, others watch her, there is some sort of blocking force that until now has been near her but seemingly unrelated to her, but now that seems to have involved itself as well, and just before Soma she disappeared entirely. That blocking force . . . it, ah, engulfed her . . . and she has not reappeared.'

Shaid rose halfway out of his seat, his face livid, but Veshre waved him into it. 'She's still aboard the ship. She had no place else to go. That last problem is one we can work with. The involvement of unknown deities is more problematical. She could have acquired powerful defenders.'

'Deities.' Shaid shook his head in disgust, leaned back in his seat, and templed his fingers in front of him. 'Deities. Why has a deity attached itself to her?'

'It is a *lesser* deity,' Veshre emphasized. 'They all are.

None of them is recognized in the pantheon, none of them came from anywhere vital.'

'They came from somewhere, didn't they?' Shaid did not enjoy the company of Wolves, a fact he usually kept to himself. But this morning, his edges showed. 'They've attached themselves to the woman I want dead. Their presence must mean something.'

Veshre nodded. 'Only one has actually attached itself to her,' she reminded him, 'but yes, of course they mean something. We feel we're going to be able to divine their intentions before too long. Obviously we have to be subtle – we don't, after all, want their attention focused on us. That could be . . .' She didn't finish the sentence. *Bad* was such an understatement for the possible consequences of alerting unknown deities to the Wolves' spying presence. *Disastrous*, on the other hand, would make Shaid less certain of the control she and her Wolves had of the situation, and at the moment, the power balance in the Family was unsteady. His lack of faith in her ability to carry out his program could be the deciding factor in his seeking outside assistance. The Wolves were already aware of his clandestine courtship of the Sabir Family. They needed to walk carefully indeed to maintain control of their situation, at least as long as Shaid was paraglese. 'We're dealing with the problem,' she said at last. 'It's unique, and we'll let you know as we make progress. However, if we told you that we could kill the girl right now, we'd be lying. We'll deal with her as soon as we understand the situation completely.'

Shaid didn't look happy, but he did at last meet her eyes. 'Very well. Keep me informed of what you discover, and come to me before you kill her. I want –' He smiled slowly and stopped.

Veshre didn't like the look in his eyes, or his vulture's smile, but she rose, gave him the quick, shallow bow appropriate for one of her rank, and said, 'The moment I have news, you will have it as well.'

The other Wolves rose at her signal, made their obeisance, and followed her out the door.

* * *

The Veil parted and a final brilliant sphere of pale pink light erupted from the void. It spiraled down into the midst of a swarm of similar spheres – perhaps twenty in all. These danced around each other within the confines of an imaginary bubble, their subtle movements and shifting colors conveying at incredible speeds information that, had it been in the speech of mortals, would have translated into the following conversation:

We gather in freedom at last. Welcome, brethren of the Star Council.

We aren't all met, Dafril. One of our number has not responded to the call.

Who is missing? Dafril touched minds with those present, then recoiled. *This fills me with unspeakable dread . . . What has become of Luercas? Has his soul suffered annihilation since our release from captivity?*

Nereas answered. *We've lost him, but he is not lost. Before you arrived, we sought him even as we sought you. You confirmed your approach; he . . . did not. He hides himself; those of us who sought him cannot find him, but his soul line has not been extinguished. He has not fallen – therefore we must assume that he has . . . strayed.*

Then Luercas must be the first item we address. Does he actively oppose us, do you think?

All of us thought he stood with us. Since he expends such effort in evading and eluding us, we must suspect he only pretended agreement so that he could completely understand our plans and aspirations, the better to destroy them.

Why? Why would he stand against a new golden age? Why would he resist us?

A pause fell then – in real terms, it lasted no longer than the time a single bolt of lightning needed to flicker from one cloud to another, no longer than half of the blink of an eye, but in the context of those who participated in the conversation, it seemed to drag on forever.

Finally, one of the spirits of the Star Council offered the possibility all of them dreaded.

Perhaps he seeks to create for himself an empire on Matrin, with himself as god-emperor. Perhaps he wants the golden age we desire, but for himself alone instead of for everyone.

Another pause, pregnant with the distress of all those present. General agreement followed, but became a confused babble as those present tried to press their recommendations for dealing with Luercas on each other. Finally, everyone calmed down enough that Dafril could ask for suggestions again.

We should destroy him when we find him, Mellayne suggested. *We should obliterate his soul line.*

Werris disagreed. *We should force him through the Mirror of Souls into a mortal body incapable of responding to him. He will be trapped while he lives, and when he dies, he will be pushed through the Veil. But the death of his soul will not be on our consciences.*

Vaul found even that excessive. *Perhaps banishment would be sufficient.*

Others offered other suggestions, all of them contradictory, varying in severity and duration. Some only wanted to find the missing Luercas in order to try to bring him to reason through discussion; others wanted his soul destroyed without any question or trial – his absence, they thought, was condemnation enough of his motives. None could think that his absence from this first meeting of the Star Council in over a thousand years was irrelevant. All wanted to take action immediately, but none could agree on the action to take. The babble rose again, and threatened to break into heated argument, and Dafril could tell that her colleagues would accomplish nothing further on the issue right then. Their hypothetical determination of punishment for Luercas remained pointless until they found him, in any case. So she changed the subject.

Have all of us chosen suitable avatars among the mortals?

Everyone had.

Excellent. Dafril shared a feeling of delight with her colleagues. *My avatar is on her way to rescue the Mirror of Souls from its resting place. Events worked into my hands very nicely – she didn't require much pushing at all to undertake the journey.*

Sartrig said, *Mine follows her, in case she cannot complete the mission. He would follow her whether I prodded him or not – he is under other compulsions besides mine. But these compulsions, which come from within, are to my benefit. They allow me to remain in the background, where most of the time he is not aware of my presence. Just as well – he could banish me from his mind if he chose to do so; his magical training has progressed already to that point.*

Other reports followed in quick order: a paraglese encouraged to pursue a path away from the interests of his Family and toward the broader interests of the Star Council; a princess of the Gyru-nalle royal line of Feelasto led to speak of making an alliance with the Families of Ibera; a Dalkan pirate-king just beginning to think of suing for peace with the Iberan Families.

With such encouraging reports to buoy them, the Star Councillors separated to return to their avatars, agreeing before they parted to watch for Luercas and to think until they met again on what should be done about him.

Chapter 22

Hasmal refused the chair Kait offered him; instead, he sat on the floor of her cabin and insisted that she sit across from him. When they were settled, he added to the shield he'd cast around the two of them. He spun through it the 'don't notice us' spell he had prepared so carefully in advance. Kait watched his finger tracing through the powder he scattered on her floor and said nothing. More interestingly, her face gave away nothing that she was thinking. He almost smiled then – her years of training in diplomacy might serve him almost as well in what he needed to do as if she had been brought up from childhood to be a Falcon.

When the shields were strengthened and he was sure the activities in the room would not draw any attention from anyone on the ship, he brushed his powders into a neat pile, scooped them into one hand, and scattered some on himself and some on her.

Her expression still didn't change, but when he'd finished, she did ask in an even, polite tone, 'Religious ritual?'

He shook his head, and now he did smile. 'No. Something that would get both of us condemned to death anywhere in Ibera, and probably here as well, for all of Captain Draclas's liberalism in other areas. The completion of a magical spell.'

He did see a flicker of expression cross her face then, but it never touched on fear. Instead, in the brief instant before calm neutrality removed that tiny spark of visible emotion from her eyes, he thought he saw resignation.

And he thought, Resignation? What a bizarre response.

'It seems that I am born to be a heretic,' she said, and gave him a sad smile that he did not understand. 'No matter how pure my motives or how dire my need or how great my love of Family, every road I travel takes me further from the True Path.'

'I don't understand.'

Now one of her eyebrows arched and the start of a smile quirked at one corner of her mouth. 'You don't understand that if this wall of peace you build is built with magic, and if I desire to learn how to build it as well, that doing so will make me a heretic? Please. How long did you live in Ibera? And how did you keep from being drawn and quartered in the public square?'

He shook his head. She'd missed his question. 'I understand that what I do is . . . heretical. In Ibera, in most places in the world, to most people. I know that. What I don't understand is why you act as if this is only the latest heresy for you.'

'Ahhh. *My* heresy.' She glanced around her cabin and shrugged. 'The walls listen, Hasmal, and the keyholes watch, and I would be doubly damned if my secrets got out. Even here.'

'The spell I cast around us protects us. No one will notice you; no one will listen. You and I are alone.'

That eyebrow flickered upward again. Then she smiled and shrugged, and said, 'Are you a brave man, Hasmal?'

'No.' He didn't even have to consider the question. 'I am the basest of base cowards.'

Her smile grew broad, and hinted at merriment. She leaned forward and rested a slender, long-fingered hand over his, and said, 'You are honest, and I can't remember the last time I met an honest man. We're all cowards, I think. Those who would deny that are simply liars into the bargain.' Her hand squeezed his. 'I'll show you my heresy, and that way we'll be even. You've given me the power to have you hanged aboard this ship, if I ever wanted to betray you; now I'll return the favor, so that you'll be able to sleep at night.'

And then she added, with a final, gentle squeeze, 'I won't hurt you. I promise.'

While he still wondered what in the world that enigmatic statement could mean, a surge of dark, wild magic erupted from her and her body began to twist. Her smile became a feral beast-grin as her mouth and nose and jaw stretched forward and tapered into the lean, muscular muzzle of a killing machine. Her eyes, their rich brown unchanged, moved back in her skull and apart; her forehead angled backward, growing deeper as it flattened. Ears stretched upward, pointing and belling into wolfish erectness, though that was the only part of her face that made him think of a wolf. Her body altered, too, so that she went from being two-legged to four-legged, and the breeches and tunic that had fit her so fetchingly in human form hung weirdly on her in this other shape, stretched almost to bursting across the rib cage and haunches, hanging slack at waist and wrists and ankles.

'We all have our secrets, you see,' she said, and she still spoke in the cultured accents of a woman of Calimekkan Family. Her voice, though, was the voice of a creature of nightmare, one that stalked through the endless forests of sleep.

Sweat broke out on Hasmal's forehead and his upper lip, and when he said, 'So I see,' his voice broke on the word *see*, squeaking as it had when he was fourteen and not since.

Her reversion to human form took longer, though the

process he thought of as melting began the instant she spoke.

When at last she sat before him as a human again, he said, 'What *are* you?'

She closed her eyes and sighed. 'I was born under a curse. We are called Karnee, my kind ... though I have met only one other Karnee in my entire life, and he pursues me even now.' She shrugged. 'I'm a monster. A heretic. An evil beast that most times masquerades as a woman. If my parents hadn't hidden me and taken another baby in my stead before the parnissas on Gaerwanday, the Day of Infants, I would have been slaughtered in an offering to the Iberan gods. As it is, my survival was a threat to them every day that they lived. Had anyone ever discovered what I was, not only I but every member of my immediate family and most – if not all – of the household staff would have been killed in one of the public squares of Calimekka. My existence threatened the lives of every person I ever loved, and I didn't even have the courage to destroy myself so that I could know that they would be safe.'

Her smile was bitter. 'We're all cowards in one way or another.' She shrugged it off. 'Now that you and I have traded our awful secrets, tell me why you suddenly needed to talk to me, when you've been avoiding me since I came on board.'

'I'm to teach you. I'm supposed to ... to initiate you. Into the Falcons. Make you a Warden.'

'Initiate me? You're supposed to?' Kait looked intrigued by that news. 'Who told you that?'

'I consulted spirits.' He felt his face flushing as her eyebrow twitched upward in almost-concealed disbelief. 'I did. It's part of the magic that I must teach you. I have to introduce you to the Secret Texts, and train you to Ward, and –'

She held up a hand. 'The Secret Texts of Vincalis?'

His jaw dropped, and for a moment he could find no words. 'You've read the Secret Texts?' he asked her at last.

'My uncle told me he'd give me a copy when we got back to the House. After the wedding. He couldn't, because he and my cousin and the pilot were killed when we landed, and I escaped. He was going to teach me that wall trick you do, too . . .'

She quickly described the events of that day, finishing with her escape from her uncle's House.

That explained much. 'They're still coming after you,' Hasmal said softly.

'Coming after me? I know.'

Perhaps that shouldn't have caught him off guard, but it did. 'You knew your uncle and the Wolves of his House were after you? I'm surprised. You were marked by Wolf magic, but it was very subtle. I blocked their marker with a spell of my own.'

At that, she *did* look surprised. She shook her head. 'No. The Sabirs are following me. Not my Family.'

'The *Sabirs*? No. I found no sign of that.'

They stared at each other, confusion on both their faces. Then Kait said, 'You're certain my Family is after me?'

'I stake my life on it.'

'And I know that a man named Ry Sabir and his men pursue us by ship. I know this as surely as I know I breathe, or that you and I sit on this floor.'

'Both Sabirs and Galweighs after you. Why? Of what importance are you?'

She stared down at her hands. 'You must know something else. The spirit of an ancestor of mine came to me when my Family was killed. She told me that I could bring them back to life if I obtained the Mirror of Souls. So I am going after it.'

Hasmal buried his face in his hands. The Mirror of

Souls. The Ancient artifact that the Secret Texts promised would be linked to the return of the Reborn. Kait Galweigh, his doom, was on the ship that had been intended to take him away from her, and she was a monster, and they were seeking the Mirror of Souls, and the world as he had known it would be coming to an end at any moment.

He wondered, if he jumped into the ocean, how far he would have to swim to find land. Then he wondered if finding land even mattered; drowning might be preferable.

'You don't want to find the Mirror of Souls,' he said.

She arched an eyebrow. 'I do. I want to have my Family back.'

Hasmal shook his head. 'That isn't the way it will work. Listen. You and I are linked together. Spirits told me that you would be a danger to me, and that by being together we would somehow effect the return of the Reborn, so I did everything I could to get away from you – thinking that you would be coming for me in Halles – and terrible things happened to me but I managed to survive, and I thought I was well away from you on this ship that would sail to the ends of Matrin. *Then* you show up on this very ship, of all the places where you could have gone. And now I find out that we're going off to retrieve the single artifact mentioned in the Secret Texts in reference to the return of the Reborn. This has nothing to do with bringing your Family back, Kait. The gods have their hand in this, and if we keep going, we're going to die.'

Kait tipped her head to one side and stared at him. 'You're actually quite a nervous man, aren't you?'

He almost wept. 'No. I'm the most sensible man in the world. I had work I liked. I spent time with my parents. I knew what I wanted; I was going to take over my father's shop when he wearied of the work, as he did from his father. I was a Falcon because my father taught me, but I didn't expect to have to do anything except pass on the teachings to my son or daughter. I *never* wanted to be one of the tools Vodor Imrish used in returning the Reborn to the world. The tools of the gods end up broken. And I don't want to die, and I don't want my parents to die, either.'

She patted his leg. It was a condescending little pat. A 'don't worry, silly man' pat. She said, 'I'm not doing anything for the gods, Hasmal. And I don't even know who the Reborn is – but I'm not doing anything for him, either. So this terrible future you foresee isn't going to happen. No death, no destruction, no horror. I'll get my Family back, and you'll go back to your shop and be a shopkeeper like your father and his father before him.' She smiled when she said it.

He gritted his teeth. 'I only wish that were true. You keep your optimism because you don't know what is happening. The Reborn,' he said, speaking slowly and clearly, as if he were dealing with a particularly stupid child, 'lived during the time of Vincalis, more than a thousand years ago. The Reborn was a wizard of tremendous talent and perfect goodness named Solander. He created the Falcons to stand against the evil wizards commonly known as Dragons, who used magic as a weapon and people's lives as fuel. He did his best to prevent the Wizards' War, but the Dragons captured him and killed him as a dissident. Vincalis, who was a prophet for the Falcons as well as Solander's student and biographer, put aside the plays and poems he wrote for his living, and cast oracles for one thousand one hundred days. Each day, he wrote the future he saw in the Secret Texts. He correctly predicted the Dragons' self-destruction, and the falling into disfavor of magic. And he also predicted that the Reborn would return when the Dragons rose from their own ashes. And that the

Mirror of Souls must be found and taken to the Reborn to prevent disaster. And that only after terrible destruction and a second Wizards' War would the golden age the Reborn had promised come.'

Kait finally looked like she understood the danger. 'But magic is still forbidden, and forgotten.' She thought of her dead uncle Dùghall, and his claims of magic, and sighed. 'Well, *mostly* forgotten.'

Hasmal laughed. 'You don't believe that, surely. The Falcons kept the Reborn's magic alive for all of the thousand years after the Wizards' War. Your Family's Wolves and the Sabirs' Wolves have been scouring Ancient cities for the texts and artifacts of the Dragons for more than four hundred years. In the Wolves, the Dragons have risen. And now the horrors begin.'

'I'm working for the return of my Family. Not for your god and your wizard.'

Hasmal shook his head. 'The gods use who they will. And they never ask for volunteers.'

'Fine. So you come to me and you tell me that you have to speak to me, and this is because you want to commiserate with me, that you and I have been chosen by your god as . . . sacrifices? Is that it? Well, you've told me. Now you've done your duty and you can leave. Forgive me if I don't choose to go along with your god's plan.'

She was an exasperating woman. 'I came because I need to give you the Secret Texts to read. You need to know what we face. And I need to teach you the magic of the Falcons. I need to make you a Falcon.'

She snorted. 'You didn't want to have anything to do with me, and now suddenly you want to be my mentor? How fortunate for me.'

'I don't want to be your mentor. And I don't want to have anything to do with this destiny, any more than you do. I never fancied myself a hero. I want to teach you so that I'll have someone who can back me up if we get into trouble.'

Kait shrugged. 'Well, teaching. That's a different matter altogether. I won't serve your god – I'm not even sure who Vodor Imrish is. But learning is never a mistake. Teach me whatever you know.'

* * *

Anwyn Sabir rubbed one clawed hand along his horns. They'd gotten longer since the abortive attack on the Galweighs. He crossed his legs and glowered at the twin cloven hooves, flat and broad as dinner plates. His human leg – the last thing he'd had to remind him of the time when he'd been a man instead of a monster – had vanished in the backwash of magic and the simultaneous overflow from the Galweigh attack. He missed the leg; missed the smooth flesh and the foot that, if he looked at it, reminded him of the days when he looked into mirrors readily and with pleasure. Walking was easier, though, with legs that matched and that both bent the same way.

'Aren't you ready yet?' he growled.

'Quiet, unless you want me to shift the damned *rewhah* to you. Maybe next time you'll grow a tail.' Crispin glared at him. Andrew gripped a girl-child of about five under one arm; Crispin held her hand over the little fire he'd started in the cauldron on the stone table. He slashed across her palm with his knife – blood spattered and the girl shrieked and managed to kick Andrew solidly in the shoulder.

Anwyn laughed, but didn't say anything out loud. He was still recovering from the effects of his last Scarring, and didn't want to find himself in the way of any more rebound magic for a while.

Crispin let go of the child's hand and focused on the spell he was casting. It was a tiny spell, really – not one that would require the girl as a sacrifice. Anwyn thought he'd probably use her as a sacrifice anyway, both as a

304

precautionary buffer – they'd all gotten leery of unexpected magical rebounds since the disaster – and because he took pleasure in the suffering of his sacrifices. But if he wasn't greedy, they might be able to get another use or two out of her before she died.

Crispin finished casting the spell, and Andrew and Anwyn both looked into the dancing flames in the cauldron. At first, nothing appeared.

'Maybe the bitch's son really is dead,' Andrew suggested.

Anwyn laughed. 'Not even we're that unlucky. He made it look like we'd killed him for a reason, and it wasn't so someone else could do it and get away with it.'

'Maybe someone else made it look like we'd killed him.'

'We've been over this before –'

'Silence,' Crispin said.

Images began to form in the flames. A square of white, then water ... these resolved gradually into a high-prowed Rophetian ship moving across open sea.

'A ship?' Andrew frowned and leaned farther forward. 'Why would he be on a ship?'

'Silence.' Crispin never looked away from the flames, but the growing exasperation in his voice sounded clear enough to Anwyn.

They'd suspected from the moment the bloody mess in Ry's room was discovered that he wasn't dead. They'd been sure of it when the magical pointers and traces had all marked them as the killers; they knew they hadn't killed the little bastard, though it would have been a good idea. They were at a loss, though, as to *why* they would be set up as the killers. Ry couldn't return to claim leadership of the Wolves after faking his own death; his mother couldn't hope to benefit from the sympathy he'd generated for her or the hatred his death had generated against them, since she was Sabir only by marriage; and for any of the other Sabir Wolves who might have eyed the position at the head of the pack, the removal of Ry and the blaming of the three of them for the death wouldn't help to secure their ascension.

So what benefit did anyone gain by the stunt?

The three of them had discussed the matter, carefully secured a sacrifice, and after a month of avoiding any activities that might have made them look guilty of what they'd been accused of, they found both the time and the place to work their divination without drawing any attention to themselves. By the end of the month Anwyn was healthy enough to participate, too. The paths were finally clear for them to discover what Ry was up to.

Now it looked like he was on a ship, and sailing away from Calimekka.

And who did that benefit?

'Can you bring in any more detail?' Anwyn asked.

Crispin wore his frustration on his face. 'He's well shielded, and has shielded the people with him, too. I can't even get a look at the captain or the crew. He's been very careful.'

'You're certain he's aboard that ship?'

'The blood and hair we got from his room would not form links to anyone but him. He's there.'

'Mark the ship, then. Sooner or later, he'll cease to be so vigilant. Sooner or later, we'll be able to see what he's doing, and what he's hiding.'

Crispin nodded. Andrew dragged the child back to him – this time she started screaming before he touched her, and kept screaming when he nicked the artery in her neck and the blood began to spurt into the cauldron. The three of them focused on the spell they cast, to mark the ship and everything in it magically, so that they could locate it again wherever it might be. Then they braced for the rebound, for the marking spell was bigger and fiercer than the divination spell. They funneled the backlash, when it came, into the dying body of the child. She shimmered and glowed and began to melt into a fur-covered, bat-winged monster, and at the same time she began to cry – pathetic little mewlings that grew weaker and weaker as her blood spurted into the cauldron to sizzle and hiss and smoke.

Anwyn watched Crispin without seeming to watch him, and saw the weakness there that he saw every time they sacrificed a girl child. Amused, he looked away to keep from betraying himself to his brother. Handsome, arrogant Crispin had few weaknesses, but the one he did have was for little girls; he'd had a bastard daughter by one of the threesome's toys, and kept her safely hidden from everyone. Anwyn suspected she was in the hands of a caretaker family somewhere in the New Territories, or possibly even in New Kaspera. But not even he knew.

He did know that she still lived, and thrived, and that Crispin, for all that he thought he hid it well, remained squeamish about the sacrificing and killing of little girls. Which was a useful thing to know. Knowledge was power, and Anwyn had decided long ago that where his older brother was concerned, he would take any power he could get.

The child went limp in his arms, but not before the backlash had spent itself in her frail body. Anwyn said, 'Here, Crispin, I'll get rid of that for you.'

Crispin handed the little corpse to him. Andrew giggled, and said, 'Give it to me to play with first, won't you?'

Both brothers turned to study him with distaste. Anwyn grew wearier daily of his cousin – Andrew's perversions had been amusing when first he and Crispin discovered them, and the two of them had even, from time to time, participated out of curiosity. But Andrew seemed to be both defined and encompassed by the lusts that drove him, and Anwyn thought that no matter how deep he and his brother dug into their cousin's soul, they would find nothing but more layers of the same muck and scum beneath the surface. Which made Andrew tiresome company.

'Not this time,' he said, and watched Andrew's face pinch tight. 'Crispin's roses need fertilizer. If you want a toy, get one of your own.'

Anwyn turned back to Crispin. 'What do you want to do about Ry?'

Crispin brushed the wavy golden hair Anwyn so envied out of his face and shrugged. 'Not much we can do until we can uncover his reasons for leaving, for staging his own murder, and for destroying his own chance to ever lead the Wolves. We'll watch him. When we can prove he's alive and on that ship, I suppose we'll expose him. Then . . .' He smiled and glanced down at the cauldron. 'Then I imagine we'll kill him. Without making ourselves to blame for it.'

Chapter 23

The *Peregrine* slipped past another island in the Devil's Trail. Smoke curled from a tall cone in the center of the island, and a thick black trail of new rock drove down to the shore between the burned skeletons of trees that forested either side. Kait thought that Joshan, the goddess of the high places, of solitude, and of loneliness, would feel right at home there.

Kait paced the port deck, staring at the island, smelling the things that still lived there. The *Peregrine* ran close in, close enough that Kait could pick out the herd of deer that grazed at the edge of the burn line, where new growth had already started to come back. She growled softly and flexed her hands, and stared at them with hungry yearning.

Forty days since her last full Shift. Forty days – that had always been the outside limit between Shifts for her. Her little demonstration for Hasmal had given her a tiny reprieve, but she needed to be able to let go. She wanted to run, to hunt, to chase, to kill, and prey was within her reach, and she couldn't let herself go after it. She needed to give herself over to the other for a full day, and if she jumped over the side and swam to the island to hunt, by the time she could excise her demon for another two months the ship would be eighty leagues to the northeast. She turned away from the deer.

She had to Shift. The need burrowed under her skin now,

an unceasing and ever-worsening itch. She couldn't leave the *Peregrine*, because she would never be able to rejoin it if she did. She was terrified to Shift aboard ship, though. She had no doubt that if she was found out, the crew would kill her. And how could she keep from being found out?

She growled again, as the rich scent of the deer on the island swirled out to her one final time. Already the island lay behind them instead of beside them. Even knowing that she would be trapped if she jumped overboard, Kait almost couldn't restrain herself.

The hunt. The chase. The kill.

Her fingernails dug into the palms of her clenched fists, and she realized that she felt points digging into her flesh, not crescents. She stared down at her hands in horror. She had claws now, not fingernails, and her smooth human skin wore the first faint down of beast fur. She looked around her, frantic. Perry the Crow, one of the ship's lookouts, hung in the rigging at the top of the mainmast, staring ahead. Ian's second-in-command, the dour Rophetian navigator Jhoots, stood at the wheel, also with his back to her. A few of the crew checked the coils of lines, or climbed through the rigging, shifting or tying sails at Jhoots's command. So far, none of them had paid any attention to her. Thanks to the moonless darkness, if she could get off the deck before she Shifted from two legs to four, perhaps no one would.

But where could she hide?

Not her room. Rrru-eeth would be by in the morning to clean it. The door had a lock, but Kait didn't trust Rrru-eeth's hearing, which she suspected of being keener than her own. The Scarred girl would catch the change in her Shifted voice, or her breathing, or gods only knew what else.

Down below, the crew slept. But below them lay storerooms. And below that, the bilge.

Moving casually, so that she would not draw attention

to herself, Kait went below. She paused halfway down the gangway. Most of the off-duty crew slept in hammocks strung from the cross braces, hammocks that swayed with every rise and fall of the ship. Their snores played an interesting counterpoint to the slapping of water outside the hull and the creaks of the ship's timbers. She would have no trouble at all getting past the sleepers. But along the far bulkhead, close to the doorway that led to the storerooms and gave access to the bilge, four people played a game of hawks and hounds, and one of the players was Rrru-eeth.

Kait felt her clothing loosening and tightening. She swallowed hard and stared through the forest of posts and strung hammocks at the players bent over their game board. She had so little time. She tried to hold her fear in check; Rrru-eeth, predator that she was, would notice fear as quickly as Kait would have in a similar situation.

Calm, then. Calm.

She dropped the rest of the way down, and stood as straight as she could. Then she walked through the swinging hammocks as if she belonged among them.

She made one reassuring discovery. Rrru-eeth wouldn't smell her as she passed. As Kait moved farther away from the gangway, the fresh night air succumbed to the miasma created by more than a dozen poorly washed bodies and their various gases. The cloud of belches and farts and sweat and dirt was thick enough it was almost visible. Kait thought she could probably herd cows through the common room without anyone being the wiser, if she could just keep them quiet.

Rrru-eeth's ears swiveled toward her as she moved nearer the doorway; Kait kept her steps confident and steady, and prayed she would be able to maintain her form human enough to walk on only two legs until she was out of earshot.

'That's five to you,' one of the men said, and Kait heard the rattle of dice.

'Six. I go again . . . Nine . . . Again. Eleven.'

'You've missed your point three times. Do you want to stand hounds or hawks?'

Rrru-eeth said, 'If it were my play, I'd demand to see those dice. You haven't made your point once tonight.'

Kait was almost to the door. They were paying her no attention.

A steady voice tinged with annoyance. 'Maybe he's just unlucky tonight.'

Rrru-eeth again. 'Maybe. Though I've never seen him so unlucky before.'

Kait stepped through the door, and almost breathed a sigh of relief, and behind her heard, 'I'll let the three of you settle this. I'm for the head.'

Kait's heart leaped for her throat. The head – what she had mistakenly called the water closet until a few of the amused crew had corrected her – lay at the lowest level of the *Peregrine*, and all the way aft. The exact way she'd hoped to go.

The shock of fear pushed her heart faster, and her breath hissed in and out, and she heard the growl starting in the back of her throat. Felt the fizzing in her blood, and the red-hot animal rage, and she Shifted into the beast . . .

. . . darted into the deep shadows as the man came around the corner . . .

. . . huddled there as he strode past her, close enough for her to touch . . .

. . . and all the while, in her mind, she felt the fury of the other, that she should hide instead of attacking, that she should cower like prey when she could easily kill the man who endangered her.

Kait, small and weak in the back of the other's mind, still somehow kept the beast chained until the man was past. Until she could slip through the patchy darkness, lit only by two storm lanterns, to the narrow trapdoor that opened into the bilge. She dropped down into the bilgewater, ignoring the stink, and let the trapdoor drop shut above her. She curled up on a timber brace, and let the rats come to her, and when they did, she killed them, snapping their spines with a single toss of her head.

In a day, when the Shift passed, she would have to come up with an excuse for her absence from her room. For her enormous appetite. In a day, she would have problems, and the crew would wonder about her, and Ian would have cause to distrust her. But had she stayed, even if she had been able to keep everyone from her room, Rrru-eeth would have heard the change in her voice, would have heard the clicking of her claws on the plank floor, and she would have known something was wrong. She would have *known*. This way, as long as she wasn't found out while she was still in Shift, the worst they could all do was wonder.

* * *

Crispin Sabir strode into the Hall of Inquisitions prepared to face his accusers. He wore his formal clothing – silk breeches and velvet cutwork tunic both dyed forest green, the finest white Sonderran lace at his throat, cloak of cloth-of-silver with an enormous Sabir crest in the center, the two trees worked across the back in thousands of tiny drilled emeralds. On his right hand the golden wolf's-head ring, the tourmaline eyes glowing in the dim light as if the beast lived. On one hip his sword, on the other his dagger, both bearing his insignia. His soft black boots gleaming with polish, his silver cloak pin burnished to a sheen.

Andrew and Anwyn had already been questioned. Both had been able to provide independent alibis for their whereabouts the night of Ry's supposed murder. Crispin intended to do more than that.

Grasmir Sabir, majestic in simple silk, with the emerald-studded chain of the paraglese around his neck, sat ready to condemn Crispin for the murder of his cousin Ry. To either side of the paraglese sat half a dozen members of the Family, none Wolves. In fact, no other Wolves had been permitted in the room for any portion of this trial, not even as observers. This fact pleased Crispin, and worked in his favor. He noted the predominance of the trading branch, who had for years tried to oust the Wolves from any positions of power and tried to eliminate their influence in the Family councils. Today, Crispin intended to deal their faction a crushing blow. He had his alibi, and his proof, and something else. As he took his place in the low seat beneath the dais, he smiled a tiny, secret smile.

'This inquisition into the murder of Ry Sabir, son of Imogene Valarae Sabir and Lucien Sabir, deceased, is reconvened. This is an ongoing investigation into the means of his death, and the guilt, implied by both the dead man's letter and physical evidence within his room, of Crispin Sabir. Before we bring forward the evidence against you, Crispin, have you anything to say for yourself?'

'I have.' Crispin stood, knowing that he looked regal; he was easily a match for the paraglese, and far outshone the rest who stood against him. He heard the murmurs of approval from the onlookers, all Family who had few or no dealings with the Wolves. He smiled, this time for everyone to see, and from beneath his cloak produced a device of glass and metal – a long spindly framework of the Ancients' unrusting steel built to reveal a glass globe within. The device had several levers and switches on it, and a gear train running from the switches to the globe.

'May I bring this forward for your inspection?'

'If it has anything to do with this investigation, you may. What is it?'

'My alibi,' Crispin said, and carried the device forward and set it on the dais. 'If you would switch the blue switch at the base to the right, you will see what I mean.'

314

All of the Board of Inquisitors gave him suspicious stares.

'It's a device of the Ancients,' Crispin said. 'One the Wolves discovered some years ago which we have made use of from time to time.'

The paraglese toggled the blue switch, and a faint light began to glow within the glass sphere. Nothing else happened.

'Very pretty,' he said, 'and I could see where it might be useful at night, when I wanted to read at my desk instead of by the fire. But I fail to see how it proves your innocence. Or even suggests it.'

'You have some of Ry's hair, and some of his blood. Don't you?'

'You know we do. Both were found where he was murdered.'

Crispin nodded. 'Take a single hair, and slide it into the slot at the base of the device.'

The paraglese narrowed his eyes and said, 'I fail to see the purpose of this.'

'Please. I promise I'm not wasting your time.'

The paraglese called for the evidence box, and put on a pair of fine white calfskin gloves, and opened the small metal casket with care. He pulled out one of the silver boxes inside of it, and from that box withdrew a hair. Crispin showed him where to put the hair, and when it was in place, said, 'Now, in order, and counting to five in between each switch, toggle the green, yellow, and orange switches to the right.'

The paraglese toggled the green switch. 'One . . . two . . . three . . .'

The sphere began to turn a dull blue. The change was visible throughout the room, and Crispin heard scattered gasps.

'. . . four . . . five . . .' The paraglese toggled the yellow switch. '. . . one . . . two . . .' A cloudy dark spot began to resolve itself within the blue. '. . . three . . . four . . . five . . .' The paraglese toggled over the final switch, and immediately the dark shape in the center of the sphere resolved into a clear image.

The image of Ry Sabir, very clearly alive and moving. He was speaking, though the person to whom he spoke remained invisible.

'That's my alibi,' Crispin said quietly, though his voice carried through the stunned chambers as loudly as if he had shouted. 'Ry isn't dead.'

'Where is he?' and 'What happened to him?' mingled with 'Who is responsible for this?' among the onlookers and the council. Crispin pressed his lips into a grim line, and in response moved the two dials that worked the gears within the device. The view moved away from Ry so rapidly that no one could get a clear view of anyone who was with him, though it was clear he was with many people. Not until Crispin had a ship fixed cleanly within the glass did he remove his hands from the dials.

'You tell me where he is and who is responsible,' he said.

The paraglese leaned forward, and gradually his expression hardened into cold rage. He looked up from the glass and then to the councillors on either side of him. 'He's on a ship,' Grasmir said. 'One of our ships. One of our trade ships.' The paraglese looked down at Crispin and said, 'It would appear that you, your brother, and your cousin have been the victims of conspiracy between the Traders and your cousin Ry. And perhaps his mother. I revoke the charge and rights of this council and find you innocent myself. And I apologize that I cannot ask you to sit on the council that will begin investigating the conspiracy that tried to implicate you in a crime that wasn't even committed. That your enemies sat on the council that would have tried you was an unfortunate accident – I cannot, though, knowingly appoint you to sit in judgment against them. Though the idea strikes me as ultimately fair, I cannot overlook the bias you will have against them for what they've attempted.' He rested his head in his hands for a moment, then pushed his fingers through his receding and graying hair. 'However, if you have anything that you would ask of me as paraglese, I will be inclined to look favorably on your request.'

Crispin nodded. 'I do have a favor to ask, one that will cost you very little. The Wolves have been without a leader since the death of our beloved head Wolf, Lucien. Our efforts on behalf of the Family are weak and scattered. I would, with my brother and my cousin, lead the Wolves forward for the good of all the Family. I ask only that you support our bid for leadership, and then only if you feel we would be worthy of that honor.'

Grasmir smiled. 'It would seem, from the letter that Ry wrote to me before leaving on the trade ship, that one point of this exercise was to prevent the three of you from doing just that. I don't like conspiracies, and I don't appreciate being lied to or made a fool of. It is my right to override the autonomy of any branch of the Family if I feel that doing so is in the best interests of the Family as a whole. I feel that way now. Therefore, there will be no bid among the Wolves for leader. I declare you leader of your people, and your brother Anwyn and your cousin Andrew your assistants. Nor will I brook any disagreement with my decision.' He stood. 'Go, with my blessing. I dismiss this council. Traders – stay within the walls of the House. You will answer for your actions on this same day next week.'

* * *

They had almost torn the ship apart looking for her when she finally crawled out of the bilge and dragged herself up toward her cabin. Hasmal found her as she fought her way up the gangway toward the main deck. Ian and Rrru-eeth and Jayti were right behind. Hasmal, bless him, had spent the time that he searched for her in thinking, because the first words out of his mouth were, 'You had a seizure again, didn't you?'

Seizure. The falling sickness. That frightened people, but not to the point where they felt they needed to kill the victim. Not like the Karnee curse.

So she nodded. 'I think so. I don't remember. The last thing I remember, I was in my cabin reading. And the next, I woke up in the bilge.'

They helped her up onto the deck, talking about fresh air and sunlight. It didn't help. She still felt like a week-drowned corpse. She stood, having a hard time keeping her feet under her.

Ian stood in front of her, backlit by the setting sun, and his eyes narrowed thoughtfully. 'You have the falling sickness.' A statement, not a question.

She nodded.

'How often?'

'Not often. Once every couple months.'

'But often enough that your Family couldn't hope to make a good marriage for you?'

'Once would have been often enough to prevent that.'

'Damaged goods.'

'That's the way it is with Family.' Which was true. No one could hope to arrange a marriage for a woman with falling sickness – her dowry would be forfeit but she'd be sent home after the first episode; everyone knew that the falling sickness passed from mother to child. So Kait's story about taking the book gained another layer of realism – an unmarriageable daughter would end up doing something hideous like translating dead languages in a windowless room for the rest of her life. Further, she had a rational excuse for her absence, and for any future absences. Thank all the gods for Hasmal. She could have hugged him. Would, she thought, when she was clean again, and fed. When she'd slept. She'd eaten rats when the hunger grew

318

too great, but even in her beast form she didn't like rats. They weighed on her stomach as she stood there.

Ian was nodding, and his eyes bore an empathy that surprised her. He was silent for a long time. Then he said softly, 'I know all about the Families and their damaged goods. I do indeed.'

Hasmal said, 'We were afraid you'd fallen overboard.'

Kait said, 'I'm glad I didn't.'

And Rrru-eeth, standing off to one side, said, 'How did you get all the way down in the bilge without anyone seeing you?'

Kait shrugged. 'I don't remember. I don't remember anything.' She wished that were true. She wished she could at least forget the rats. Weak from hunger and exhausted from the Shift, she staggered, and as the ship rode over the crest of a wave, the deck rose beneath her and she fell.

Suddenly the movement was too much for her. She was wretchedly sick. She crawled to the rail and threw up into the sea.

That put an effective end to the questioning. When she was done being sick, Ian and Hasmal carried her into her cabin, and Rrru-eeth assigned herself to nurse her.

For the next two days, she decided she would do nothing but eat and sleep.

* * *

'So what did you do with the bodies?' Crispin still wore his formal clothing, though he'd gotten rid of the cloak as soon as he came through the door.

'In the garden, beneath your roses. Of course.' Anwyn chuckled. 'I trust we didn't disturb the roots too much.'

Crispin didn't smile. 'I trust you didn't. I have some very delicate hybrids taking root out there right now.'

Andrew sat playing with the switches of the contraption they'd put together to amuse the Inquisitors. 'They like our toy?'

'The paraglese did. The Traders sitting on the council thought it was fine until they saw the ship.'

'Making it a Trader ship was a nice touch,' Anwyn said.

Crispin shrugged. 'Doing it that way eliminated two of our problems at the same time – Ry's disappearance and the Traders' power.'

Both his brother and his cousin smiled. 'Eliminated the problem,' Anwyn mused.

Andrew giggled.

'Eliminated.' Crispin pulled out a chair and sat astride it, facing backward. He draped his arms along the back and said, 'I wish you could have been there. It was beautiful.'

'If we'd been there, who would have worked the magic to make your pretty pictures?' Andrew was frowning.

Both Anwyn and Crispin looked at him with annoyance. 'He didn't mean it literally,' Anwyn said. He turned his back on Andrew and said, 'Tell me, how beautiful was it?'

'You know how we'd hoped to have Grasmir support our bid for leadership of the Wolves?'

Anwyn nodded.

'He went one better than that. He declared us leaders. Rather, he declared me leader and the two of you my assistants. We don't have to win over anyone the pro-Lucien faction might field. We're in charge, and the rest of the Wolves can't do a thing about it.'

Anwyn studied him thoughtfully, too clever to point out right then that they had agreed the three of them would share power equally. But Crispin could tell he was thinking about it. It would come up later – not as an argument, because the paraglese had said Crispin would be in charge, and Anwyn wouldn't be able to prove his brother had manipulated events to make that happen. But it would come up.

Meanwhile, however, all Anwyn said was, 'Well, things are certainly going to change now.'

Andrew tittered, evidently already imagining *how* they were going to change.

Chapter 24

Three weeks of reading the Secret Texts preparatory to learning any actual magic. Three weeks – twenty-seven days – of pondering the history of magic and the future of her world as told through the prophecies, aphorisms, and asides of a man who was undoubtedly brilliant, but sometimes perversely vague. Three weeks of sitting in her cabin from before the sun rose until long after dark, trying to fit what she knew of the events of the past and the present to the complex puzzle Vincalis had left behind – and Kait had finally reached her limit.

When Ian Draclas knocked on her cabin door, she opened it gladly.

'You haven't come out of your cabin for anything except meals in so long,' he said, 'that poor Rrru-eeth is certain some form of sea-madness has overtaken you and that you are pining away from grief in there.'

Kait already felt the pressures of Shift growing inside of herself again, and thought that would make a convincing enough form of sea-madness for Rrru-eeth when it materialized, but she managed a sincere-sounding laugh. 'I've been studying,' she said.

'Something fascinating, no doubt.' He leaned a bit past her so that he could peer around the cabin.

'History,' she said, moving unobtrusively to block him.

'I want to be very sure of the location of the city and its treasures.'

'Of course,' he said. 'I hadn't considered that you might not have finished translating your book when you st – I mean, when you . . . bought it. Of course you hadn't translated all of it. Buying it, how could you have?' He flushed.

His awkwardness amused her. She moved closer to him, hypersensitive to his warmth and to his scent, which was musky, sensual, and very male, with unmistakable overlays of fresh air and sunshine. He was handsome – she hadn't permitted herself to think about that, but now she caught herself smiling up at him just to see him smile.

And his return smile disarmed her; in it, she could see surprise and hope and a faint shadow of her own growing hunger.

'You seem different tonight,' he said. She couldn't help but note the touch of wariness.

'I *feel* different. I'm lonely, and tired, and I want to enjoy an evening *not* thinking about lost cities or Ancient artifacts.' She rested a hand on his forearm, and lightly stroked the soft furring of golden hairs.

'Really?' His eyebrows rose; his voice dropped. His smile this time was much more overtly sexual.

She brushed past him and pulled her door closed behind herself. 'Yes. Somewhere outside of that room.'

She'd managed to push all thoughts of sex out of her mind since boarding the *Peregrine*. It made for complications she didn't want to face. But she knew she would never manage celibacy through two complete Shifts, and she would be better off picking a partner rationally than in the midst of the raging fire of Karnee lust. She'd considered Hasmal as her desires got stronger; he attracted her. She knew there would even be an advantage in taking him as her mate – he knew what she was. He, however, was one of

323

the few men she'd ever encountered who was not compelled by her accursed Karnee blood to think he loved her.
In fact, he had clearly stated, when she made a tentative
overture, that he bore no interest in her at all.

For all her complaints to Amalee about the men and
women who were drawn to her, and how humiliating it
was to know that they were not drawn to *her* at all, but to
her curse, Kait found it even more humiliating to run across
someone who was immune even to the curse. That
immunity suggested to her that she had nothing genuinely
lovable about her; that without her curse, she would have
been invisible to men.

Ian was not immune, even after his experience with her
bout of 'falling sickness,' and at the moment she took
comfort from that.

He rested fingertips lightly on the small of her back. 'If
you don't want to spend any more time in your cabin,
would you enjoy visiting in mine?'

'I would love to.'

Neither of them said anything else until she followed him
to the door to his cabin and let him usher her inside.

He lit his lamps, and only when the golden glow bathed
both of them did he ask her, 'Are we going to reconsider
being friends now?'

She leaned against his chest and raised up on her toes to
kiss him lightly on the lips. 'We're going to be even better
than friends, I think.' Her heart pounded and her blood
surged through her veins. She'd wanted this – she'd needed
to feel desirable, beautiful, wanted. She could see in Ian's
eyes that she was all of those things. She kissed him again,
and loosened her tight control over the passion that boiled
inside of her; she submerged herself in the touch and taste
and scent of him, in the feel of his arms around her and his
hands touching her.

She let herself pretend that he wanted her for herself.

And at the same time, she managed to bury her forbidden

hunger; she pushed the enemy Karnee, Ry Sabir, away from the center of her thoughts, where he had occupied her free moments while she was awake, and her dreams while she slept.

* * *

Rrru-eeth listened outside the captain's cabin for a long time. She'd been listening out there every night for more than a week, ever since the first time the captain had taken Kait to bed with him. When she left at last, she joined Jayti in the little corner of one of the storerooms that they had appropriated for their trysts.

She complained to him about what she'd heard, finishing with a bitter snarl. 'I can't believe the captain sleeps with her. I cannot believe he wants her.'

Jayti, lean and dark and easygoing, pulled her down onto his lap and laughed. 'Well, be happy for him. He's been alone for a long time.'

'No.' Rrru-eeth snarled as he started unbuttoning her blouse. She pulled back and said, 'I've told you before, there is something wrong with her. She isn't normal.'

'Ruey, how could you of all people possibly care about that? Who's normal? You and me?'

Rrru-eeth said, 'She has things wrong with her. She talks to herself in her room, and she hides things. She and that Hasmal meet in her cabin early in the morning, before the watch shifts. As soon as they go in there, I can't hear a word they say, but I can still feel them talking. It's . . . unchancy.' She whispered, 'And she has an animal smell to her. I've thought that since even before she was sick . . . but since then, I've noticed it even more.'

'An animal smell!' Jayti laughed at Rrru-eeth. 'You're jealous of her, aren't you? Because she's pretty and the captain wants her. She treats you better than any human woman who's ever been aboard this ship, Ruey. I've watched her. She never asks extra work of you, and she talks good to you. Real good.'

He pinched her buttock and Rrru-eeth growled at him.

'Don't you dare,' he said, still laughing. 'You've fancied the captain ever since he gave you a place on this ship. And now some woman of his own class wants him, and you've realized you'll never be captain's lady. Isn't that it? Hmmm? Isn't it?'

Rrru-eeth shrugged and nestled against his chest. 'You can think what you want. But I don't trust her. And I don't like her. She'll turn the captain. You just watch if she doesn't.'

* * *

In Kait's dream, they danced. At first, her partner's face stayed hidden in shadow as they spun and floated over an otherwise deserted dance floor. She felt the music but she could not hear it. All she could hear was his breathing, deep and slow and steady. And his hands burned on her bare shoulders.

In Kait's dream, they danced, and she began to recall that they danced this way every night. She looked around, feeling as if she had been trapped by the chains of day and had just regained her freedom. The silent music moved quicker, and his breathing grew faster with it. Yearning, and the pounding of her blood in her veins; that was the music to which she danced.

Touch me.

His voice made her very soul tremble. She brushed his skin with her fingertips, and discovered that he was naked. As was she. Magic. This was magic, but not the magic of wizards; this was the magic of man and woman, of lust and desire. This was the dance of sex, and the heart-pulse drumbeat quickened yet again.

Touch me.

In Kait's dream, they danced skin to skin, floating across an open meadow, and the shadows fell away from his face and his eyes were a pale, beautiful blue, dark-ringed, and his smile burned its way into her heart, and she loved him.

Gods help her, she loved him. In her dreams she danced with Ry Sabir, whose Family had murdered hers, who might have had a hand in killing her loved ones himself, and in her traitorous dreams she welcomed his embrace, and she opened her heart to him. In her dreams she knew she loved him – she, who had never loved a man.

In her dreams, they danced, and because he was her enemy, and because in her dreams she was too weak to kill him, she woke.

And found herself in Ian Draclas's bed.

Disappointment seared her, stung her, cut her until she bled. She bore its sulfur-bitter taste without letting her emotions show.

'Did you sleep well?'

I slept with my enemy. She kissed Ian lightly, playfully, and did not answer his question. 'Time for me to go, while it's still dark.'

'You don't have to leave. Stay with me.'

She nibbled along the nape of his neck, trailed her fingers down his spine. 'I have to go. For now, I have to. But if you want, I'll be back tonight.'

By the return of night, she would have banished Ry Sabir from her thoughts. She would have convinced herself that she hated him, that she wanted to see him dead. She would have made herself believe that she could feel genuine passion for Ian Draclas, and in Ian's bed she would prove to herself that her dreams didn't matter.

Until she slept.

In her sleep, she could not lie.

Chapter 25

Kait made it back to her cabin just before Hasmal arrived. So far, she'd managed to keep him from knowing about her relationship with the captain, just as she'd managed to keep Ian from finding out about the time Hasmal spent with her. Another week had passed, and she'd finished her solitary study of the Secret Texts, and begun learning basic magic.

He knocked on her door, and she let him in, acting as if she'd just woken.

He glanced at her bed, where she'd rumpled the covers and made it look like she'd just climbed out of it. He gave her a cold look and said, 'You didn't have to mess them on my account.'

Kait felt heat flushing her cheeks. 'I . . .'

'You need to learn not to lie. Not to your colleagues, anyway. I already knew about you and the captain. It isn't as if it were any great secret.'

That was news to her. 'When did you hear?'

'Two weeks ago. I probably knew not long after you did.' His tight smile told her she'd been foolish to hope to keep the relationship secret. 'How are you doing on your shielding?'

'The dreams aren't bothering me as much. Most times I can wake up from them when the dance starts now. And

I don't have the feeling that he's looking over my shoulder during the day – not like I did at first.'

'You still think he's following us?'

'Yes.'

Hasmal sighed. 'I think you're right. I wish we could get rid of him. I've thrown *zanda* half a dozen times in the last few days, and I get nothing at all.'

Kait tugged the blankets on her bunk straight, then sat on top of it. 'That seems like a good sign.'

'No. "You've lost him" would be a good sign. "He's still back there" would be a neutral sign. "Sorry, I have no information regarding your question" is a very bad sign.'

'Why?'

'Because it means he has access to magic powerful enough to make himself and his whole ship disappear to the *zanda*. I couldn't do that. I and my father together couldn't.'

'Oh.' Kait knew that only she could feel Ry behind them, and the feeling connected to her through her Karnee senses. Hasmal had said that as far as he could tell, no one was following them physically, though he insisted the Galweighs from Goft still tracked them magically.

'We'll deal with the problem when it arrives,' Hasmal said. 'Now, what has your spirit said about our destination?'

Finally Kait felt that she had good news to give him. 'She told me that we'll find a chain of islands tomorrow. From that point, we only have another two days or so to reach the continent, depending on the weather.'

'The weather has been good so far.' Hasmal didn't look happy, though.

'What's wrong?'

'Once we reach the continent and find the city, we'll also find the Mirror of Souls.'

'Exactly. That's why we've come all this way.'

'As soon as we have the Mirror of Souls, we become a target both for the Sabirs who are following us and for the Galweighs who are waiting for us to come back to them.'

'Amalee assures me that we're going to survive this, Hasmal. You'll see.'

He nodded. 'So she says. But I did a divination last night. The Speakers say the Reborn has already been conceived. If that's true, your ancestor may be guilty of wishful thinking. Once the Reborn is conceived, disaster is imminent. So tonight you're going to help me with a ritual to see if what they say is true.'

'I can't help you with a ritual,' Kait said softly. She glanced around the tiny cabin as if expecting the ship's parnissa to rush in with a lynching crew. 'I barely know enough about magic to maintain a shield.'

'Even that will help. With you adding your strength to the shield, I'll be able to use more of my energy to seek the Reborn. The ritual is dangerous and difficult, but we have to know.'

Kait didn't think they needed to know at all.

I promise you the Reborn isn't going to figure into your future, Kait, Amalee said.

Kait had learned to answer her without speaking. *Perhaps not. But I'll never convince him of that. The least I can do is help him with his ritual so that he can see for himself that he's exaggerating the dangers we face.*

'Your ancestor doesn't like my idea, does she?'

'You can hear her?'

'No. But I've gotten better at reading your expressions. I can always tell now when you're discussing something with her. You get a faraway look in your eyes, and your mouth tightens. Tell her I want your help whether she thinks I need it or not.'

Kait didn't need to tell her. Amalee heard perfectly

well. And responded scathingly. Kait didn't pass on her comments word for word. She just said, 'She still doesn't like the idea, but I don't care. If you need me, I'll help you.'

'Then meet me in the aft food storeroom tonight when Telt rings.'

*   *   *

Kait knelt on the hard storeroom floor, behind the bags of yams and flour and the casks of beer, and beneath the dried meat that hung, swinging with every movement of the ship, from hooks overhead. In the darkness, the silhouettes of those homely things loomed like monsters rising from the sea; she could almost feel their hot breath against the back of her neck. With every creak she was certain that she was about to be discovered. The sounds of rats scrittering along the enclosed shelves suddenly unnerved her, and every stray step that echoed across the deck above her head set her heart pounding like a war drum.

The darkness had never bothered her. But she discovered that she feared her pending introduction to real magic, and as much as that, she feared being discovered.

Across from her, Hasmal cupped a blood-bowl to his chest and closed his eyes and offered up a quick, whispered prayer to Vodor Imrish, that they might not be interrupted as they sought across the leagues for the Reborn. That done, he lit a tiny candle and crouched over it, and by its light drew his own blood and poured it into the blood-bowl. Kait watched his facility with the tiny knife and the tourniquet and thought she would be practicing very little magic. She hated the idea of piercing her flesh or drawing her own blood. Though Hasmal insisted very little of the *farhullen* magic involved bloodletting, Kait felt any amount was too much.

As soon as Hasmal had a little puddle of blood in the bottom of his bowl, he pinched out the tiny flame. He leaned, shivering, against a bag of yams beside him, breathing hard. 'Now we begin the actual spell,' he said. 'Keep your shields around both of us until I tell you to let them drop.'

'You're sure I have to drop them? The Galweighs and the Sabirs will be able to see what we're doing . . . and where we are.'

'The shield that keeps others out would trap us in.' He shrugged. 'You cannot send out a spell while shielded. Nor can you send a spell through a shield someone else has placed over you. That fact is part of what makes magical battles so deadly. But back to what we were doing. Just be ready when I tell you.'

Kait already felt queasy, and the idea that she would be exposing herself to those who followed her only increased the sick feeling. But she nodded, and focused herself the way Hasmal had taught her.

Meanwhile, he shook several packets of powders into the blood-bowl and murmured an incantation that she recalled reading in one of the later parts of the Secret Texts.

'*He'ie abojan treashan skarere*
Pephoran nonie tokal im hwerat . . .'

[*I who wait in the long darkness*
For the coming of the light,
Seek now the quickening spirit
Of the Reborn; you who were once
Master of the Falcons,
Our teacher, and our guide;
You who were stolen from us before your time
And who promised to return to lead again;
You who taught love and compassion,
Humility and responsibility,
Integrity and honor above all virtues.

I call out to you.

The world needs you, and
Your Falcons have not forgotten.

Kind Solander,
Shall I be blessed to hear your voice?

I offer myself as your protector
While you are weak,
Your teacher while you are young,
Your servant always,
That you may return
To heal the pain of the people
And bring love and the fulfillment of hope
To the hollow shell of the world
You left behind.]

The powders within the mix of blood began to glow.
Kait shuddered. She could be brave in the face of the
most terrifying physical dangers, but in the face of magic,
she wanted to cower and flee. She could feel the spell
beginning to work; she could feel it in her bones and in
her blood, and though she didn't experience Hasmal's
magic as being painful or 'greasy' the way she had the
magic Dùghall had identified in the airible, she still
became increasingly uncomfortable. As if she were
standing near a fire and the fire were growing bigger and
hotter. She knew she wasn't in danger. But she could
sense the *potential* for danger.

'Drop the shields now. If the Reborn was truly
returned, the blood itself will begin to glow,' Hasmal had
told her before they started. Now, in the silence and the
darkness, Hasmal's blood proved the truth of the message the spirits had given him. It began to glow softly, its
white light a radiant nimbus that started as a thin skin

around the bowl, then spread to envelop his hands, his arms and shoulders, and finally all of him.

Then it spread farther, covering Kait in its warm, comforting cocoon.

Once within the sphere of the light, she felt the tenuous awakening of the Reborn. Far away, the infant stirred in his mother's womb and reached out to embrace the feather touch of magic. He was full of love; he *was* love. Hot tears welled in Kait's eyes and slid down her cheeks, and she embraced the fragile connection. While his spirit touched hers, her fear of magic dissolved, and she felt whole. More, she felt accepted in a way she had never been in her life. Even with her parents, she had always known that they loved her in spite of what was wrong with her. But the Reborn loved her just as she was, and accepted her because in his eyes, she was as perfect as he was.

In the instant that their souls touched, she felt that a pain that had always been inside her had healed. And when she looked at Hasmal, and saw the tears running down his cheeks, she knew that she was not alone. Kait could not believe that she had been so blessed that she had been chosen to assist the Reborn when other, worthier people had lived and died waiting for his arrival, and had never seen their hope fulfilled.

Peripherally, she sensed that other Falcons like Hasmal had come to offer their services and fulfill their oaths, and had come, as well, to witness the private beginning of the wonder and the joy that was promised to all people. So many minds, all strange to her and yet all unified in purpose and in love, brushed against hers and did not pull back in revulsion. She was what she was; they were what they were; gathered around the soul of the Reborn like men who had been lost in the desert and who had found a spring at last, all they could do was love each other and rejoice together.

Kait stretched herself farther, and touched the Reborn's mother – and got a shock. All she could feel from her was rage and pain and hatred. She sensed that the woman had suffered horribly at the hands of her enemies. The mother seemed blocked off from the love her unborn child offered; her pain and anger locked her into her own mind and prevented her from being healed in the way that Kait had been healed. Then Kait received a second shock. Flashes of the other woman's thoughts and memories reached Kait, and she discovered that the Reborn's mother was her cousin Danya.

She wanted to shout, *You're still alive!* Someone she loved had survived the Sabirs' treachery. But she couldn't make Danya hear her. She wanted to say, *You aren't alone. I'm here, and I'll come help you.* But Danya was deaf to her offered comfort, too.

Kait lacked the magical skills to make herself heard. But that would change. She would learn whatever she needed to learn, because in the moment that Hasmal brought her into his circle, her world had changed for the good. She had so much to live for, and so much to do. The Reborn was real, and would be the son of her beloved cousin, who had not died at the hands of the Sabirs. Kait would do whatever she had to do to keep them safe, and to help the Reborn's love restore the world.

* * *

Rrru-eeth's diffident tap at the cabin door woke Kait, who had spent the night alone.

'Come in.' She yawned and stretched. In spite of the increasing tension caused by her need for Shift, she felt good. Lighthearted, full of hope, certain for the first time that the future would be better than the past. Danya, mother of the Reborn. She grinned at Rrru-eeth when she peeked her head in the door.

'What shall I do for you today? Do you have any

laundry, or does anything in your cabin not meet with your satisfaction?'

Kait grinned at her. 'Do you have something else you'd rather do today? Spend time with Jayti, maybe?'

Rrru-eeth shook her head. 'Perry the Crow sighted the islands you described, and until they've made sure we won't ground on a reef, Jayti will be on deck working.'

Perry the Crow was a sociable crewman named Perimus Ahern, who had a liking for heights and whose eyesight was as sharp as Kait's. During meals, he told amusing tales of his life before he'd joined the *Peregrine*, when he'd been a Calimekkan barrister prosecuting cases of patent theft among the city's inventors. In his last case he'd made the mistake of winning the case for the actual inventor who had accused a minor member of a major Family (though he refused to say which one) of the theft of his idea. Perry discovered to his chagrin that he needed to make both a career and location change the very next day. He said, though, that he had come to love the sea, and his trial against the Family 'inventor' had turned out to be his luckiest one.

'I'll be glad to reach land again,' Kait said. 'I'm tired of the sea.'

Rrru-eeth's smile had an edge to it. 'The ship can be confining for even a short time. Imagine spending your entire life on it.'

Kait thought of living in a tiny world built of wood bounded by nothing but water and sky. She shook her head. 'I can't imagine that. But surely you only spend some of your time on the ship.'

Rrru-eeth's dark eyes narrowed, and she said softly, 'I wouldn't think of leaving the decks of the *Peregrine*. As long as I'm on board, I answer only to Captain Draclas. If I were to leave, well . . . there are those in Ibera and the Territories who have reasons to want my neck in a rope.'

Kait sensed the other woman's pain as a change in her

scent, a tensing of her body, a shift in the pattern of her breathing. All those things came to her clearly – the Karnee senses were growing more acute as she neared her next Shift. She leaned forward and said, 'I can't believe you earned that fate.' She shook her head. 'You're a good person.'

Rrru-eeth clasped her hands together and said, 'Yet by Iberan law, I've earned death in any Iberan land.'

'How?'

'It's not important.'

'If it's your life, how can it not be important?'

Rrru-eeth laughed – a sharp, angry bark. 'My life is important to me. To Jayti, I suppose. Certainly not to you – you're Family.'

Kait shook her head. 'Not anymore. My neck is, I'm sure, marked for the rope, too.'

Rrru-eeth sighed, and Kait pointed to the chair across from her bunk. 'Sit. Talk. We have some time, surely.'

With obvious reluctance, Rrru-eeth took the offered chair and said, 'My people were from the mountains to the southeast of Tarrajanta-Kevalta, what you would maybe know as Lake Jirin in Manarkas.'

Kait nodded. The Galweigh Family had holdings in the New Territories south of Lake Jirin, which was one of the lakes the Wizards' War had created.

'I lived there until I was about six, I suppose. Maybe a little younger. Then diaga came to our town, and claimed all the people in it as their slaves.'

Kait said, 'The diaga? That's humans like . . .' she was going to say *me*, but at the last instant, she changed that to 'the captain? And Jayti?'

'Yes. Our people were good fighters, and they stood against the diaga, but your people's weapons were better. Most of our fighters died. This left the injured, and the old, and the young, and a few of the women who were pregnant at the time and not able to fight. The diaga gathered all of us and took us to the New Territories. We went first to Old Jirin, then to Badaella, then to Vanimar, and finally – for me, at least – to Glasmar. At each stop, the diaga sold such of us as they could. No one had much interest in a child as small as I was until we reached Glasmar, and there, at last, a buyer found me.'

Her voice had grown harsh at those last few words; Kait had the idea that the buyer had not been some kind family who needed a companion for their young daughter. She was right.

'A man named Tiroth Andrata bought me. He also bought my younger sister, who was the only other member of my family to survive, and two other little girls from our village. We'd been acquired to be trained as concubines for those among the upper classes of Glasmar who had ... exotic tastes. Tiroth Andrata apparently had a thriving business in exotic concubines; he became wealthy from his trade, and met his own needs at the same time. He trained us all himself, you see. He was very fond of small children, and perhaps fondest of all of little Jerrpu girls.'

'Jerrpu?'

'My kind of person. As you call yourself human.'

Kait swallowed and nodded to show she understood. 'So he ... trained you ...'

'*Trained*. A weak word for what he did.' Rrru-eeth smiled thinly. 'Oh, yes. He trained us regularly. We learned all sorts of techniques for pleasing those who would one day be our masters. Bagga, which is what he had us call him, was especially fond of teaching us to take pain and humiliation, which he said was the ultimate form of giving pleasure.' She looked away and her eyes narrowed again. 'We spent long years with him, my sister and I. The other two from our group he sold, and all of those children that he bought afterward, as well. The two of us he kept until we were no longer little girls at all –

338

but you see, we had become very good at taking pain and humiliation, and he spent a great deal of time and effort finding new ways to give it out. He told us he kept us because we were stronger than the little children that he could sell for a better price, and he didn't want to risk breaking one of them while developing new training when he could practice on us.'

Kait closed her eyes and rubbed her temples. She felt sick. She'd taken the existence of servants and slaves for granted all her life; they were the silent faces in the hallways, bringing things or taking them away, making sure rooms stayed clean and beds had fresh linen and food came on time and tasted the way it was supposed to. They'd never had voices to her before. They'd never seemed entirely *real*.

Now she thought of the slaves that belonged to her own Family – they were different because in Ibera they had to be human, of course, not Scarred, but they were still slaves. Among the Galweighs, she could think of several men who bought child slaves regularly and sold them to their associates when the children reached adolescence. She'd never given much thought to the purposes those children served, nor to where they had come from or what became of them when they grew up. There were things Family didn't discuss, and how relatives used their slaves was one of them.

She looked over at Rrru-eeth and bit her lip. She was ready for the happy ending, the one in which Rrru-eeth won her freedom and found love. 'So what happened? How did it all end?'

'During training one day, Bagga hurt my sister more than she could take. She died.' Rrru-eeth's voice was flat. 'I saw him kill her, so I killed him. I hurt him first, using everything I had learned from years of torture. Then I killed him very slowly. Then I took the children he was training to sell, and dressed them, and stole as much of

Bagga's money as I could find in his house, and marched the children through the streets of Glasmar down to the docks. I could find only one captain who would take us aboard without the children's papers.' She jerked her chin in the direction of the ship's helm. 'Ian Draclas. He wanted a lot of money – more than I had. It's risky transporting slaves if you don't have a slaver's seal or slaver's papers, and of course neither of us would be able to prove that the children were free, because they weren't. So I offered myself without wages for as long as it would take to pay for their passage to safety. He hired someone who made papers for all of them. And for me. He took them someplace where they could live as free children, and found them families. I found my own family here. I found love here, and freedom from pain and humiliation and torture. And as long as I never step on land ruled by a Family again, I should be safe enough.'

Sick, Kait closed her eyes and covered her face with her hands. 'I'm sorry,' she whispered.

'You don't owe me an apology.'

'I'm sorry you suffered. I'm . . .' How could anyone make restitution for the pain Rrru-eeth had suffered? How could she be marked for death, when the ones who had deserved death had been the men who killed her family to take her as a slave, and the men who had sold her, and the man who eventually bought her? Where was the justice that would champion such an outcome?

The Reborn would free the slaves, Kait realized. He would bring peace, and justice, and he would remove Rrru-eeth's pain.

'I'm sorry that someone could do that to you, and leave you to blame.' Kait stood and rested a hand on Rrru-eeth's shoulder. 'That's all going to change. All of it.'

*　*　*

Ry paced along the deck, forward, then aft, then forward again, in no mood to talk with anyone. She was

340

out there. Still far ahead of him, getting closer to her goal.

He tasted the salt spray on his lips, and stared out at the sea. Clouds built along the southern horizon, a line of black that looked for the moment like a distant mountain range. The sun dropped closer to the western horizon. A pod of whales had run alongside the *Wind Treasure* for nearly two days, until sometime after midday they had either tired of their game, or lost interest in the humans and their ship, or had been lured away by schools of fish; in any case, they had veered off and Ry had seen nothing alive in the ocean the rest of the day.

The captain said the clouds looked like the leading edge of trouble. He'd set the ship's course more directly northward and added extra sails. The change might move them toward safety, but it moved them away from Kait.

Ry grew impatient. He wearied of the waiting, of the bleakness of the sea, of wanting her and not having her. She was a drug, and the longer she was out of his system, the more he lusted after her.

In their cabin, Valard and Yanth played querrist, and Jaim wrote a long entry in his journal, and Karyl played his guitarra and wrote another of those sad love songs he used to lure women into bed with him. Only Trev had been out on the deck since the evening meal, and he kept his distance, watching Ry without saying anything.

He stalked forward, then aft. Lately, the visions he saw through her eyes when he closed his own had changed. Now, late in the night, he saw a man – oddly familiar-looking, whose presence in her bed was somehow more infuriating for that tantalizing familiarity. They were lovers, Kait and this stranger.

Ry knew about the Karnee drives. He'd subsumed his own by the use of magic, but at a fierce cost. When the lusts were worst, he quenched them with a spell – but when he did, he burned inside, and suffered terrible

341

rages, and blinding headaches, and Shift came at him harder and faster. Still, he did not give in to the lust, which was why, when his mother demanded he serve in his father's stead, she could not trot forward half a dozen of his little bastards for him to legitimize.

Kait showed no signs of knowing Wolf magic. So she couldn't know the spell that suppressed the lust. Her Karnee desires ran unchecked.

Ry didn't care.

She was *his*. He'd claimed her, his magic had marked her, she did not belong with another man. And when he closed his eyes in the night and saw her touching that stranger, and kissing him, and bedding him, he made himself a promise.

When he caught up with Kait and claimed her, Ry intended to rip out that stranger's heart and crush it in his hand.

Chapter 26

Danya twisted in her sleep and cried out, and in doing so woke herself. Another nightmare, another return to the dungeon and the Sabirs, to her Family's abandonment of her, to torture and horror. Waking was no better, for as she shook off the nightmare, the reality of unending touching by invisible fingers became stronger. Invisible eyes spied on her; invisible strangers reached inside of her and caressed the child she carried. Those strangers promised lies – love and safety and security, concern, compassion, joy. She fought them off when they tried to smother her with their false comfort; she was unable to push them away from the bastard babe.

Their presence had been constant for days. She couldn't stand it. She wanted to scream, to destroy things, to hurt someone, but as before, when she had been the Sabirs' prisoner, she was helpless. She shivered beneath the fur robe, but not from cold.

Gently, child, Luercas said. *Gently. Your fear won't help you, and it won't change anything. Let them have their moment, and don't spend yourself in wasted resistance. Your moment will come. For now, get up and come with me; I want to show you something wonderful.*

'Who keeps touching me?' she asked.

Hush. Not here, not now. Be satisfied that they won't hurt you. We can discuss who they are and what they want soon. Soon. In the meantime, come. What I have to show you will bring you joy.

Luercas didn't understand the sense of violation that those constant touches brought back. He said the things that had killed him had been much like what had happened to her, but for him to tell her to accept – to quit fighting – he proved to her that he didn't really remember.

Nevertheless, doing something would be better than lying there in the darkness with nothing to think about but the unending probings of the strangers. She rose and let the robe fall to the floor. She pulled on the fur chaps her host's wife, Tayae, had made for her, and the modified fur tunic that had been a gift from the women in the next house over – the tunic that made room for the spikes erupting from her spine and joints, and somehow emphasized her hideous deformities – and she tugged on the straw-insulated fur boots that kept her feet warm but still permitted her claws to project. She listened to Tayae and Goerg and their children sleeping in the loft; she made no noise as she crawled down the passageway that led from the main room, where she slept, to the outdoors. Her hosts woke easily, and though they would never question her activities, she would feel obligated to give them some sort of explanation, in her still-halting Karganese, of where she was going and why.

Outside, the long night of the arctic winter still reigned. The stars glittered with cold brilliance, close and malevolent. The snow crunched beneath the flat, hard skin soles of her boots, the only sound other than the wind whistling across distant drifts.

Set out along the main path. Follow it to the river. When you reach the river, cross and turn right along the bluffs.

She was coming to know the area well enough. Because she didn't know what else to do, she'd offered her services to the villagers – after a few days, and with some nervousness, the Kargan women had asked her to help them carry stored food from the village's outlying caches back to the underground houses. She'd accepted, and had been on her way back to the village with them, loaded with food, when a pack of lorrags attacked.

The lorrags were Scarred monsters that might have started out as wolves or bears, but might as easily have been rabbits before the Wizards' War twisted them into nightmares. They burrowed beneath the snow where they could and, where they could not, moved on top of it on four wide, well-padded feet, nearly invisible in their heavy white winter coats. They were terrifying beasts, cannier than wolves though a bit smaller, lean and fast and tough. The four lorrags that erupted out of their tunnels in the snow had given no warning of their presence beforehand, and had Danya not been there with teeth and claws at the ready when they struck, one or more of the Kargan women would have died.

That none had, and that the village had lost none of its food, either, had won Danya both gratitude and complete acceptance. No one cared that she bore different Scars than they. She became a part of every food-carrying expedition; she became an invited companion during hide preparation and sewing sessions, though her hands were not capable of holding the tiny bone needles or of threading the sinews through the little eyes. She was more physically suited to hunting, and the Kargan men welcomed her, too, and took her with them. Her nose was better than theirs and her speed over short distances allowed her to run down game that would otherwise have escaped. She added to the wealth of the village in measurable ways, and the Kargans showed their appreciation at every turn. The women gave her gifts; the adults brought her into their council circles. The village adopted her as one of its own in a smoke-hut ceremony, and the boys who were too young to hunt and the men who were too old or injured were renovating an abandoned house for her as they did for their own children who reached adulthood and stayed within the village. Until they finished the renovations and purified it with ceremonies, she continued to live with Goerg's family, and to collect her welcome gifts, and to alternately hunt with the men and work with the women.

She remained bitter. She did not forgive her Family, she did not forgive the Sabirs, and she could not forget the Scars that made her a monster, or the unborn child that had been forced upon her. Acceptance into the Kargan clan made the sting more bitter, because she could not forget that the Kargans were monsters like her. She could not forget that she could never go home – that she was outcast forever from the society of humans, and that the people who *should* have welcomed her never would again. Yet . . . if she could somehow make her way through Ibera without being killed for being an abomination, and if she could reach the Galweigh Wolves, they would take her in and set her in the circle with the rest of their Scarred to work magic. She would have to hide in the darkness, her only contact with the world she had once loved through the eyes of the young Galweigh Wolves who had not yet been set in circle and who therefore remained free.

Every human from her past, though, had been taken away from her, and nothing she could do could ever win even one of them back. She was dead to them, and they to her.

Accompanied by such thoughts, she crunched through the darkness over the shell of compressed snow, breaking through occasionally, and quickly reached the river. The Kargans called it the Sokema, which meant 'Our Blessing.' It cut like a raw wound through the rolling white-on-white tundra, a darker line of black in the darkness.

Wind blew thin curvettes of snow across its mirror-slick black-ice surface, but the snow didn't stick. She walked out onto its surface without hesitation, not worried about it holding her weight. She'd helped the village women chop ice to reach the running water beneath – they used the holes both to draw up cooking and drinking water and so they could set the live lines that gave them fresh fish to supplement the dried fish and smoked meat and the occasional fresh game. She knew from that experience that the frozen surface was thicker than she was tall.

The novelty of ice, like the novelty of snow, had worn off quickly. It became just another obstacle to contend with – its slickness offered little purchase to her boots, and would have offered even less to her bare, hard-scaled feet. She scrabbled with claws splayed out; she kept her arms out for balance; she wished once again that she could master the art of skimming across the surface on the narrow carved-bone blades that the Kargans used, but her unwieldy, Scarred body seemed unable to accommodate itself to the graceful, flowing movements required.

Reaching the bluffs on the far side took both time and effort, and she was panting by the time she arrived.

She didn't remember the directions Luercas had given her. 'Which way now?'

Turn to your right. Climb the bluffs, but not all the way to the top. Follow along them just below the ridge so you won't show against the skyline, should anyone decide to look for you.

Danya wondered why Luercas thought anyone might care to look for her. The villagers' sense of privacy, from everything she had so far seen, was acute. If she went out for a walk, they refrained from asking anything about her destination or what had happened while she was out; they did not ask her where she was from; they did not question who she was. Early on, they had offered her their own names, but did not ask for hers. When she eventually told them, they treated her name as a gift. She couldn't imagine them looking for her unless they thought she had come to grief. She suggested as much to Luercas.

The surprise I have for you is something the villagers are aware of, though only in a distant way. None of them has ever seen it; none of them would ever dare. Their superstitions make them fear this place, though neither they nor their parents nor their grandparents nor their great-grandparents have ventured to test those superstitions against reality. If they realize you have gone to In-kanmerea, their name for the place, they will fear for your life, and for your soul. He paused, then added, *In-kanmerea means 'House of the Devil Ghosts.' I could give you their beliefs about it, I suppose, but they have no basis in fact, so why bother? Better you see the place for yourself.* She felt his next pause as a sigh. *I don't know that any of the Kargans would be brave enough to attempt your rescue if they knew you had entered . . . but I would not gamble against that; you seem to have made yourself beloved in a very short time.*

She said nothing. She clambered along the bluffs and considered the idea of the pragmatic Kargans being superstitious about any sort of wonderful place. Such an idea seemed to run counter to everything she'd seen of them so far. Their fears seemed to be of those things that offered real danger to them, like the lorrags, or like the sudden ice storms that had already killed one young man since she arrived. But people were contradictions. It was their nature. She assumed the fact would be true even about almost-people like the Scarred.

Like me.

The bluffs carried her around a bend and out of sight of the village. Immediately, Luercas told her, *Now climb*

348

up to the ridge. Stay along the river – In-kanmerea will be easy to miss otherwise.

It was almost easy to miss in spite of her following his directions exactly. She almost walked by the entranceway that lay at arm's length to her left. White on white in the starlight, with the same delicate glitter as the snow all around it, it could have been a large, oddly formed drift. The snow that did drift into the corners of the long curve of stairs burrowing into the snow-glazed tundra furthered the illusion.

Go down. Slowly; the stairs may be icy. A warming spell cast on them prevented that once, but if snowdrifts can accumulate, the spell must have fallen apart.

Danya looked down into the darkness, uneasy. The Kargans feared things that were dangerous; they waited to discover the danger of the unknown before fearing it. Had they acted in any other way, she would have died when she fell through the roof into Goerg's house. At the mouth of the House of the Devil Ghosts, she hesitated, and presented Luercas with a plausible excuse for her hesitation. 'If the spell ever worked, it should still work. According to the law of Magical Inertia, spells in force tend to remain in force unless acted on by an opposite force.'

You quote your teacher well enough. You simply aren't applying the rule. Remember the spell that Scarred you and threw you all the way from Ibera to here. The energy of that spell sent shock waves across most of Matrin, if not all of it. When it did so, it stirred any number of latent spells, and stilled any number of active ones. I would almost wager that In-kanmerea's spells were active until you arrived. Otherwise, these steps would have cracked and weathered centuries before this.

Still she stood at the top of the stairway. Hesitant. Afraid.

Luercas grew impatient. *Hurry, girl. The wonders of an age await you.*

Did she want to see the wonders of an age? She put one foot on the first step and stopped. She didn't hesitate beyond that point, however. She'd come this far already, and the architecture of the stairway and the smooth white material it was made of gave her subtle reassurance; such stairways filled Galweigh House. The stairway led down into one of the homes of the Ancients, she guessed. Or perhaps a public building. In either case, it would offer her an opportunity to surround herself, however briefly, with things that reminded her of home.

She descended steadily, allowing her eyes to adjust to the increasingly impenetrable darkness. By the time she estimated that she'd made three complete turns around the spiral, however, no light remained, and even she, with her incredibly sensitive vision, was blind.

'You want me to keep going?'

You'll find accessible light within. You haven't much farther to go in the darkness, and you're in no danger.

She didn't know that she believed him, but it didn't really matter. She trailed a hand along the wall to her right and held the other out in front of her face to keep from stepping into a solid wall, and she felt for each step below her before committing her weight to it, and in that manner traveled what seemed to be another full spiral.

The hand in front of her face proved unnecessary. The soft, slightly hollow sound she made in descending the stairway changed in both volume and tone as she neared the end, warning her, and she felt the door in front of her with hearing and her sensitivity to pressure and the movement of wind before she felt it with her fingertips. 'I'm here,' she said.

Yes. Open the door and go in.

'Are there any traps set?'

Intelligent of you to ask. However, no. The door will

open as any of the outside doors at your Family House would open. You might have noticed –

She cut him off. 'That this is an Ancient place. Yes. I'd noticed.' She ran her fingertips across the front of the door until they reached its midline. From the midline, she let them slide up to the cold, slick curve of the latch. She pressed upward on the latch with one hand and rested her palm firmly on the pressure pad just beneath it.

After a brief hesitation, the door swung inward. She stepped in, and warm, stale air filled her nostrils. Everything smelled of dust and long-closed spaces. She could feel the immensity of the room in which she stood, but she could not see anything; absolute darkness offered her no markers by which to guide herself.

'One step into this and I could lose my way completely,' she said. 'I could become turned around, could lose sight of the door, could be trapped in here until I died . . .'

You could, I suppose, if you didn't activate the lights. You'll find the pressure pads for them on the wall to the right of you. Just reach out.

She did. Her hand brushed through something soft that crumbled to dust at her touch, and came to rest on a series of raised pads. She pressed them, and thousands of warm, shimmering lights sprang to life overhead and down long corridors that spread away in half a dozen directions. The lights reflected through sparkling prisms as numerous as the stars, and covered the floor with uncountable rainbows. The floor was done primarily in a rich, dark blue stone speckled with gold; inlays of white marble and a stone as pale as green seafoam in the shape of waves turned the entire vast expanse into an ocean. The reflected sparkles gave the scene a life that made her feel she was walking across water.

She gasped.

'It's beautiful.'

The Ancients could not have intended In-kanmerea as a private residence. Its vast lobby could have held ten thousand guests at one time, and was designed to direct traffic toward the broad branching corridors. Fountains shaped like delicate ships dotted the immense floor. No water spouted from them, but Danya expected that they worked as the fountains in Galweigh House worked, and that if she felt along their bases for hidden panels, she would be able to locate the pressure pads that brought them to life.

She was tempted to do so, but she refrained. Luercas wanted her to see something, and she didn't think he would have been so insistent about bringing her to In-kanmerea to see the pretty fountains. He had something bigger in mind.

And in fact, he said, *Go to the first corridor on your left. You're going to follow it back until it ends in a terminal intersection. When you reach the place where you can go either right or left, go right. You want to enter the last door on the right in that corridor. Do hurry – we have much to do.*

She would have time to explore the rest of the place in the future. For the moment, she did as he asked her and hurried.

The corridors ran for unbelievable distances. She must have passed a hundred doors to either side of her before she reached the end of the first. When she turned to look behind her, she could see nothing but corridor – no sign at all of the vast lobby she'd left behind. And as she looked to the left and the right down the intersecting corridor, she couldn't see any sign that either of them ended.

She felt small and young and temporary, overwhelmed by the great age and vast expanses of the Ancient place. She picked up her pace, anxious to reach a part of the building that was built to a scale she felt comfortable with. By the time she finally got there, her lope had become a hard trot that had in turn metamorphosed into a dead-out, panicked run. She leaned against the last door on the right, breathing hard, until Luercas told her to open it. His voice held a condescending chuckle that she didn't like.

She let herself in, and found the pressure panel that illuminated the room. She looked around. Unlike the lobby and the corridors, this room had not been designed for beauty. It was large, circular, sunken into the ground in tiers. In the center of the lowest circle a raised dais sported a round stool beneath a dome on pillars. None of the room's appointments – neither the rows of utilitarian seats in the surrounding tiers, nor the plainness of the central seat and dome, nor the flat, too-bright lights overhead, said anything but that this was a place where people came to work.

What sort of work?

Go down to the dais. Sit outside the edge of the circle, but allow your head to rest beneath the dome.

Odd instructions. Danya shrugged and carried them out.

The reason for them became immediately and shock-ingly clear. The sensation of being touched or spied on by the unknown, unwelcome watchers vanished immediately. She could still feel, though only as if from a great distance, their connection to the child she carried in her womb, but even that felt impersonal and not threatening.

Can you still hear me?

'Yes.'

Good. Don't move – if you pull the rest of your body under the dome, the criminals who have been spying on you will realize that they've lost their contact with you. As it stands now, they're so tied up with your baby that they don't notice you've escaped their spying. But if you give away the fact that you've managed to escape them,

353

however temporarily, they'll move the stars in the heavens to force their way back. They might already be strong enough that nothing you could do would stop them.

'Who are they?'

A cabal of wizards who have hidden themselves and their goal of world overthrow for over a thousand years, while waiting for the return of the wizard who led them the first time. They've found their leader now, and they'll do anything they have to do to get to him.

'And what does this have to do with me?'

You're carrying this wizard in your belly, Danya.

She didn't want to hear that. Bad enough she was pregnant. Bad enough the horrors by which she had gotten pregnant. Now a pack of rogue Wolves had claimed the bedamned fetus she carried as their savior-to-be-born, and had found a way to control it, and to watch her.

'There are herbs that will end a pregnancy,' she said.

There are. But that would be the wrong choice. If you tried to take such herbs, these wizards would see you as a threat and stop you from taking them. Further, they might wipe your mind entirely – they don't need your mind in order for your body to bring forth their hero. That is why I had to get you here so quickly; you were beginning to make your resentment of their intrusion too clear, and you might have done something to fight against them before I could safely tell you the danger they pose to you. And they would have destroyed you. I won't let them destroy you, Danya. Not if I can stop them.

She felt sick. 'Why this baby? Why me, Luercas? Haven't I been through enough?'

That's precisely why you. The infant you carry inside of you is the product of the mating of a Sabir Wolf who is also Karnee, and a Galweigh Wolf – a mating that would have created tremendous magical potential under ordinary circumstances. But the circumstances of your early pregnancy were anything but normal. You were the channel through which one of the largest focused bursts of magic since the days of the Wizards' War grounded – the magic that Scarred you also Scarred the unborn infant. His Scarring may not show on the outside, but it will make his body the perfect house for the returned spirit of the long-dead leader of these monsters who seek to control you. And the world.

'What do I do, then?'

For now you do nothing. The time will come when you'll be able to regain complete control of your body, and perhaps wrest the baby away from them. You probably have no way to save the child, even if you wanted to. But you can save yourself if you're careful. Pretend you don't notice them, and in those times when their presence is so obvious that you can't pretend you don't notice them, pretend you don't mind – or even that you welcome them.

And never forget they're dangerous.

Danya closed her eyes. It would be like trying to pretend that she hadn't minded being raped. Would she be able to do that, even to save her own life?

Luercas broke into her reverie tentatively. *There's something else I need to tell you now.*

'What?'

I'll be near you, and I'll be watching over you, but the only time I'll be able to speak to you is when you come here.

So she was to be robbed of her guardian spirit and protector at the same time that she submitted to the invasion of her body and mind. She shouldn't have been surprised.

'Why?'

Because I can only protect you if my presence remains

secret. Once your enemies know of me, they'll attack me – and weak as I am, they'll destroy me.

'They'll never find out about you from me.'

Then we'll win against them. Eventually, at least.

* * *

Light split the Veil, and spiraled inward like a galaxy being unborn, and the Star Council reconvened.

This time, however, the excitement and enthusiasm of the first meeting were absent. Dafril brought the meeting to order with ritual greeting, but immediately said, *Has anyone found Luercas?*

Above the babble of negatives, one voice said, *We would find him more easily if we could compel our avatars instead of simply suggesting.*

Patience, Dafril said. *My avatar is close to the Mirror of Souls, and mere months away from returning it to civilization. Sartrig's avatar pursues, believing himself to be capturing the Mirror so that he can re-embody Sartrig, whom he believes to be his dead brother. If my avatar falters or fails, Sartrig's will take over. We have a larger problem than our powerlessness or Luercas's continued absence – that problem is why I've called this meeting.*

What could be worse? Werris asked.

Solander has returned.

The councillors greeted that statement with dead silence.

Finally one ventured to ask, *Are you certain?*

As certain as I am of my own existence. Dafril thought the question stupid and impertinent.

But we destroyed Solander. Banished him to the outer Veil.

Time passes, Dafril said, *and he has found his way home. The Falcons are not extinct, either, and have located him, and are beginning to answer his summons. My avatar had contact with him. He is not yet born, but he is already embodied.*

That horrified silence again. This time no one broke it. So Dafril said, *With Solander present, we face the possibility of our own demise. Therefore, before we panic about the missing Luercas or worry about our own weakness, we must find a way to destroy Solander. No other priority must come before that.*

Chapter 27

'I think I could stand beside you for the rest of my life,' Ian said.

Kait smiled up at him, and reached up to brush a strand of hair from his cheek. They stood on the foredeck of the *Peregrine*, watching as the ship moved out of the narrow channel between two islands and into the clear water beyond. 'You'd tire of me before long,' she said. She kept her voice light and playful. 'I wear on everyone after a while. Too many quirks.'

'I haven't seen any quirks,' Ian said. He slid an arm around her waist and squeezed.

She refused to give in to the sadness of knowing that if he knew what she really was, he would be repulsed. Pretending that he loved her, or that anyone like him *could* love her, made such a pleasant fantasy that she wanted to hang on to it as long as she could. 'No,' she agreed. 'You haven't.' Then she changed the subject. 'I've never seen anyplace as beautiful as this.'

She wasn't exaggerating at all when she said that. The islands that rose behind and to the sides of the *Peregrine* were like uncut emeralds rising from a glass-smooth surface of sapphire. Onyx cliffs and beaches that glittered like black diamonds only emphasized the lushness of the terrain. The island forests grew densely at the bases, leaving pillars of stone to jut above tree lines. In the softer, gentler light of this latitude, a slight breeze set the leaves of the trees trembling and sparkling so that the trees appeared to be decorated with silver coins.

'It is lovely,' Ian said, but his brow creased and he frowned thoughtfully. 'But I don't like the stillness of the water.'

The breeze was enough to keep the *Peregrine*'s sails filled, and to keep her moving steadily. Kait said as much.

'It isn't the wind. It's the islands. And the water. I've seen something similar once . . .' He pulled away from her and moved to the rail; he looked down at the water, then back at the islands again. 'Crow!' he shouted.

Perry the Crow answered from his nest in the high riggings. 'Cap'n?'

'Are we out of this chain of islands yet?'

'We look to be.'

'Then can you tell which way the chain runs to either side of us?'

Perry shaded his eyes and turned first left, then right. 'The line of the islands curves north-northeast to the north of us and south-southeast to the south of us.'

Kait noticed that the crewmen all over the ship had grown still; she felt as if they had drawn in a single simultaneous breath and were, unaccountably, holding it. 'What's wrong?'

Ian didn't even look at her. He shouted, 'Describe the curves.'

A pause. Then, 'Haw, *shit*! We're inside a circle, Cap'n! A big one!'

Ian's response was immediate. 'About! Bring us about and get us out of here! Now!' And the crew moved with similar terrified speed.

In the center of a circle. Two possibilities existed. The first was that the cone of an enormous submerged volcano lay beneath them, its broken rim rising out of the water to form islands. That was the harmless possibility.

The deadly possibility was that they had sailed into an uncharted Wizards' Circle.

Kait yearned in that moment for just one god to whom she could cry out. But what god would have ears for the prayers of the cursed? If they were in a Wizards' Circle . . .

The ship failed to come around. The *Peregrine* seemed to have grown a will of her own; she sailed straight on across the glass-smooth water, heading straight east. 'Turn her, damn you!' Ian screamed. 'Turn her, if you love your lives!' He bolted for the great wheel, leaving Kait standing alone on the foredeck, staring down at the water from which a mist now began to rise. Soft and pale, opalescent, reflecting colors from soft pink to pale green and blue, gently swirling, it formed along the surface of the mirror-smooth ocean in little cloudlets.

One of the human crewmen was yelling for the parnissa; some of the Scarred had prostrated themselves on the deck and were praying in their own tongues.

Immune to the labors of the captain and the crew, the *Peregrine* kept to her course, as if guided eastward by the invisible hands of the gods themselves. But Kait knew the guiding hands belonged to nothing as benign as gods.

The parnissa raced out onto the deck, her hands full of the sacred implements of her calling. While men and women, both Scarred and human, swarmed around her, she laid out an altar on the ship's deck and dropped to her knees on the planking. Then, in a trembling, singsong voice, she began to chant 'Lodan's Office for the Lost.' Lodan was the month-goddess of love and loss, and her office was one of grieving for those already dead and beyond the reach of the living. Kait decided the parnissa was a pessimist.

But their situation, already grave, worsened quickly. The mists grew out of the surface of the sea like ghosts rising from their graves, billowing upward and expanding outward into an ever-expanding, ever-thickening sea of prism-tinted white. The sails fell slack and hung flat and empty, but the ship's forward speed increased. And Kait picked up a knife-edged keening, clear at the upper range of her hearing, and felt her skin prickle and her heart begin to race.

The crew had ceased trying to turn the ship. Some stood on the deck watching, as she did, too transfixed by the impending disaster to move. Most knelt and wept, or prayed. Ian stood behind the ship's wheel, berating the gods in a loud voice, and alternately threatening them and bargaining with them.

A Wizards' Circle. One of the places where the worst and largest of the spells cast during the Wizards' War had fallen. Most likely a city had once stood where the *Peregrine* now sailed; a target for the vengeance of power-hungry madmen. Where unfathomable ocean lay, humans had once worked and lived and loved and hoped, in houses built on hills or plains – solid ground, now gone. And gone with it the lives of those who had lived there, and everything they held dear.

Humans outside the range of total destruction when the spells fell had become the Scarred, and the viable offspring of those poor damned creatures were Scarred still; monsters born of evil not of their own making. Within the hell-charmed circles, land, buildings, and people had vanished. And what had become of them, no one knew. The circles remained potent. And to Kait's knowledge, no one who ever went into one came out again.

Mist wraiths blotted out the sky and closed the ship in on all sides as if they had packed it in cotton. Kait heard a series of splashes, followed by voices coming through the fog. The magic-born cloud had thickened to the point where day became night; only if she looked straight up could she find any proof that somewhere the sun still burned and somewhere light still existed. The fog changed the character of sound, making everything seem equally distant, or perhaps equally near. The praying crewmen on deck and the parnissa mourning the souls of men and women not yet dead sounded neither nearer nor more distant than the liquid, gobbling, gurgling cries that almost formed recognizable words. Because they were hidden within the embrace of the fog, Kait's mind created images of the owners of those horrible voices: corpses long gone to rot, their vocal cords shredded and their bloated lungs almost full of water. The fear she'd felt when she faced Hasmal's magic paled next to the formless dread that washed over her at that moment.

The mist began to move onto the ship then; light tendrils dropped down from overhead and crept up onto the deck from below. In the mist-born darkness, these looked solid, like white vines, or the tentacles of the corpse of some sea monster. The gibbering voices grew louder.

But the mist fingers did not reach out to anyone or touch anyone. As soon as they came within reach of the ship, they lost all form and condensed into mere drops of water.

Kait watched that happen again and again, and let out a breath she didn't realize she'd been holding. She almost laughed. Something about the ship kept the horrors at bay. Hasmal, perhaps, working some great shielding spell from deep within the heart of the ship. Or . . . it didn't matter. The ship continued to speed on its course, and the animated mist continued to dissolve before it could attack, and soon – soon – they would have to sail beyond the reaches of the Wizards' Circle.

She watched others realize that the magic of the circle was impotent. She listened as the weeping stopped, as the prayers changed from terrified pleading to gratitude, as imprecations to the heavens became nervous laughter at death narrowly averted. A few of the crew members embraced.

A light breeze caught the sails and they filled slowly, and the ship, already moving quickly, picked up speed. At that, the *Peregrine*'s crew sent up a jubilant cheer. All they needed to make their joy complete was to see the fog lift and the islands on the other side of the circle come over the horizon.

Perry the Crow yelled, 'So much for the legends,' and danced across the deck.

Through a growing puddle of water.

Which rose up to embrace him as he touched it.

Crawled over his body lightning-fast, covering him with a bubblelike film.

Inside of the film, he began to dissolve. Liquefy. As he melted, he wept and cried out, his voice increasingly indistinguishable from the voices echoing out of the fog. Several of the crew members tried to help him. Tried to dry him off, to free him of the thing that killed him. As they touched him, the bubble whipped across the bridge of their arms and coated the would-be rescuers.

They glistened in the darkness – glistened, and screamed. Their anguish and their fear infected everyone, including Kait. Shift surged through her blood, and in spite of every trick of mind control she'd ever learned, her body betrayed her and altered into its Karnee form.

She looked around for a place to hide, where she could die unseen, away not just from the danger but from the crew. Both the human and the animal parts of her cowered at this horror that she could not understand – mist that hunted, water that devoured its prey. She feared death, and she didn't want to die as a beast. More than that, though, she didn't want anyone to see her as a beast, to know that she was as Scarred as any of them, but in ways that made her an outcast wherever she went.

363

But then Ian shouted, 'Off the deck! Get below, everyone, and close the hatches. We'll seal the doors with wax. Hurry.' In the stampede that followed, one of the growing puddles of water enveloped the parnissa. Ian lunged for her without thinking.

Kait was faster. Across the deck in two bounds, she catapulted into Ian's chest, preventing him from touching the dying, dissolving parnissa. She growled and sank her teeth into his upper arm and dragged him toward the hatch down which the rest of the crew fled.

'A monster has the captain,' someone screamed, and others took up the cry.

'Kill it!' Kait heard. 'Kill it!' And interspersed with those cries, one voice that yelled, 'It's too late to save him. Just don't let it in here.'

One voice cut clearly through the rabble. Rrru-eeth yelled, 'She saved the captain! Don't touch her!'

Kait dragged Ian to the hatch and tried to shove him in, but hands reached up and grabbed both of them and pulled them down into the gangway.

Already the crew had gathered the ship's stores of candles and wax, and when the hatch closed, men and women were already shoving tapers lengthwise along the space between door and doorway, and melting the wax into place with the flames from oil lamps. Kait had no hands, and so got herself out of the way. She found a dark corner and huddled there, miserable, ashamed of what she was and humiliated to have been found out.

No one paid her any attention – they all were too busy sealing the door and checking belowdecks for leaks.

She wondered if they would kill her when they finished taking care of their own safety. The humans among the crew would surely want to, and the Scarred were no more likely to want her in their midst – she knew of no people in the world who did not revile skinshifters. The fact that her sort could appear to be one thing but in truth be something entirely different made them universally hated, or so it seemed to Kait.

The wax in the doorway seemed to work. Nothing came through, no one else screamed or began to dissolve. Silence reigned belowdecks – everyone listened for some sign that more danger came, or that, conversely, the danger had passed and they could return to the deck and their work. The voices of the sea still cried out, their anguish muted by the barriers of wood all around the survivors. Kait heard them without difficulty, and knew that Rrru-eeth did, as well. Rrru-eeth took it upon herself to keep the rest of the crew informed that they were still out there – the sounds were apparently too faint for human ears to pick up over the creaking of the ship and through the barriers of wood.

Kait fell asleep while still in Karnee form, her head tucked beneath her paws, her hind foot along the tip of her nose, her tail held close to her belly. She woke in human form, aching from the inhuman posture she'd retained even after she Shifted back. Ian sat beside her.

'I wanted to thank you for saving my life,' he said.

She nodded dully, in no mood for thanks or kindness. Post-Shift, the depression and the hunger overwhelmed her, and the fear of attack, now that everyone knew what she was, gnawed at her. She wanted to eat, and hide, and sleep. Nothing more. Outside, she could still hear the lost-soul wailing of the sea; it had taken on more ominous tones, and the ship rocked and heaved from side to side, tossed by the angry water.

'Are you sick?' he asked.

'Hungry. One of the symptoms of my . . .' She paused for thought, then said, 'Of my curse. I get hungry . . . after.'

'Go down to the storeroom and get something to eat. Whatever you want, as much as you want. I'll be here when you get back.' As she nodded and rose, he added,

'Be careful. If the water can get in anywhere, it will be down there.'

'I'll be careful.' She felt dull, slow, dim-witted. She thought if any of the deadly living water had leaked aboard the *Peregrine*, she would be too sluggish and stupid to evade it. But hunger overrode any dim sense of self-preservation she could muster; she went past the crew, who stared silently at her, and climbed down the narrow gangway to the deck just above the bilge.

She knew her way to the storeroom; that was, after all, where she and Hasmal had magically touched the Reborn. When she thought about the Reborn, her mood lifted a little; that in itself seemed like a miracle to her. She considered him and found hope within herself, even in her worst moment.

She should have realized earlier that she hadn't seen Hasmal. Only when she found him sprawled on the floor of the storeroom, bled white, did she realize she hadn't seen him since the fog began to build. He'd been doing magic. His implements lay in disarray on the deck beside him; mirror, empty blood-bowl, tourniquet and bleeding knife, and several objects she hadn't seen before and thus didn't recognize. At first she thought he was dead. But she saw the faint rise and fall of his chest, and felt the breath barely moving from his half-open mouth.

She shook him, but he didn't respond.

'Hasmal! You have to wake up! Hasmal!'

Still he made no sign that he could hear her – no sign that he was anything but a man one breath away from death.

She closed her eyes in resignation, gathered his things together in his bag, and hid them among the bags of yams. If the ship escaped the Wizards' Circle, she would retrieve them for him. She didn't think she would have that opportunity; nevertheless, she was not so sure of their demise that she would let anyone else see what he had so carefully kept hidden. Once his magical tools were out of the way, she rolled him over on his stomach, then worked her way beneath him so that she could line up his shoulders with hers. She thought she heard scuffling as she was trying to get to her feet, but when she held still and kept silent, she could hear nothing but the creak of the ship and the moaning of the ghost-damned sea.

With Hasmal's head draped over her right shoulder and his arms pulled like a stole around her neck, she struggled to her feet and, bent double, half-carried, half-dragged him out of the storeroom and to the gangway. She called for help, and several crewmen appeared above her.

'I found him in the storeroom. He's breathing, barely,' she told them, 'but I don't know what happened to him. He looks pale to me.'

Without a word, they lifted Hasmal up and carried him away.

Kait didn't try to follow; she saw no need to attempt to offer an explanation for what she'd found. She knew what had happened to him – at least in part – but anything she might say would only further incriminate her and cause problems for him, too. She had no reason to know why he was in the storeroom or what had happened to him. Let the crew come to their own conclusions.

She returned, instead, to the storeroom, and ate. She gorged on salted pork and dried fruit and beer. Only when she finally felt full – and so sleepy that she wondered if she would be able to make the trip to the deck above – did she pull out the yam sacks to make sure Hasmal's belongings were safe.

She moved bags back and forth; at first she'd been sure which one she'd hidden the little bag behind, but her certainty faded as they all began to look alike. She frowned, and began from one end of the yams, working her way methodically to the other. And only when she had moved every single bag did she allow herself to believe the disaster that had befallen her and Hasmal.

Someone had stolen the bag.

* * *

Outside, the wind screamed and rain slashed the ship and the waves tossed it as if it were a child's toy. Ry stayed below through the worst of the storm; he discovered, to his dismay, that he got seasick – something he had been sure would never happen to him – and that only lying still in his bunk kept him from feeling his death was imminent. From time to time either Karyl or Yanth, both of whom proved to be immune to the ship's heaving, would come in to check on him and Trev and Jaim and Valard, and tell them how much their course had changed, and offer them food. Ry suspected they offered food out of some mild impulse toward sadism, since at the very word, the four men in the makeshift infirmary turned green. He hoped he would live long enough to repay the favor. Sometimes. And sometimes he just hoped he would die before the storm could get any worse.

His one consolation was that his connection to Kait had grown stronger during the storm. She was in the middle of troubles of her own, and he supposed he could be grateful that his ship had been forced to sail north to miss the worst of the weather. They would have a huge amount of distance to make up, but they would not end up in the middle of a Wizards' Circle.

The wizard who traveled aboard the ship with her – the one whose shields had made sensing her presence and her location such a difficult proposition – had dropped his shields to cast some sort of immense spell. Ry didn't know where he'd gotten the power for it, but he seemed to have single-handedly conjured a wind that was blowing Kait's ship through the Wizards' Circle toward

368

the safety of the water beyond. Ry had felt the other wizard casting the spell, and he'd been both fascinated and horrified by the amount of personal energy the stranger had put into it. That amount of energy, drawn from his own body, should have killed him, but though the stranger had drained himself to the point that he was near death, Ry could feel that he still lived. He wondered what coin the other wizard had paid for the spell he'd cast.

Something I can discover later, he decided. Not something to lose sleep over now

The wizard's secrets were secondary to the artifact Kait hid – the artifact she was crossing the ocean to find. *That* he would have to claim at the same time that he caught up with her; she was his ultimate prize, but he intended to claim her prize, too. He'd paid a tremendous price to come after her – the price of his Family, his honor, his own life, and the lives of his friends, which could never afterward be the same as they had been. His dead brother Cadell whispered in the back of his mind, in the rare moments when Ry dropped his shields, that the artifact she sought was worth any amount of effort and any sort of sacrifice. Ry believed him. Still, he found himself hungering for some proof that he had not chosen a fool's path, and at that moment, knowing he was declared dead at home, he felt certain that only a massive prize would repay him for all that he had lost.

Chapter 28

We've all discussed this, Cap'n, and we want some-thing done about her.' Rrru-eeth stood at the head of the small cluster of crewmen, all of whom stared at Ian Draclas with an intensity he found disconcerting. Gone was the mild, diffident young Scarred woman he'd known for so long, replaced by someone who resembled a frightened animal. 'We don't have to have one of her kind aboard, and we won't.'

He understood the fear. In the moment that Kait had changed, he'd felt it himself. The gods had not intended skinshifters to live in the midst of men, or they would not have made the creatures so terrifying. He thought about the nights she'd slept beside him, and tried to imagine waking to find that mad-eyed, long-fanged beast at his throat instead of the woman he found so compelling. His skin crawled. Nevertheless, he did not intend to give in to the demands of the crew; they wanted him to let them unseal the door and shove Kait out on the deck to act as an offering to whatever demons inhabited the Wizards' Circle.

'She saved my life,' he said. He didn't bother to mention that she'd caught his imagination or that just seeing her set his pulse racing; that wouldn't help his cause, which was keeping her on the ship.

'And when she turns into that monster again and eats

one of the crew, will you remind us of that again?' Rrru-eeth had no tolerance for anyone who fell outside of her definition of normal. He'd known this for years, but her prejudices had never bothered him. Now they became a problem, because the crew liked her and she would stir them up if she didn't get what she wanted.

He said, 'I'd think you would consider a woman who carries a death sentence on her head because of an accident of birth an ally, not an enemy.'

Rrru-eeth curled her lip in a disdainful snarl. 'You think you can compare us because neither of us would be welcome in Ibera? You cannot. I am exactly what everyone sees – no more and no less. I have never masqueraded as a human for the benefits of privilege and Family that doing so could give me. *She* is a liar, a blood-hungry monster who moved among us pretending to be a friend. And worse, she is in collusion with Hasmal.'

'You don't like Hasmal, either?'

'He's a wizard.'

Ian looked at her to see if she was serious; then he burst out laughing. 'A *wizard*? He's a competent enough shipwright, and evidently he used to be a shopkeeper of some sort. But a wizard?' He laughed again, but Rrru-eeth didn't respond to his merriment with a smile of her own. Instead she shoved a cloth bag at him.

He took it and studied it. It was made of fine leather, carefully stitched; inside it were a silver-lined wooden bowl, a mirror, a variety of powders in packets, all labeled in a language and script he didn't recognize, a bloodletting kit, and other oddities. And a book. The Secret Texts of Vincalis. He'd never heard of the book, and didn't know what to make of the bag and its contents.

'That's a wizard's bag,' Rrru-eeth said, and behind her, glowering Manir the cook nodded.

'Saw one just like it at the executions in Calimekka

once,' he said. 'Had the same things in it, and the parnissas used it to prove the wizard done 'is magic. Nasty business. And now we have a wizard among us. Or two, p'haps, since that skinshifter hid those things before she brought him to us, so we wouldn't know what he was. And we find oursel's in a Wizards' Circle, and like enough to die with our crewmates before we get out.'

Murmurs of agreement moved through the quiet cluster of crew like the rumbling of the earth before a volcano erupted, and those murmurs had much the same feel to them.

'So we say, throw them to the sea,' Rrru-eeth said.

Neither Kait nor Hasmal was anywhere to be seen. Ian looked at his crew, realized he had a problem that could turn dangerous, and weighed his options, all in a split instant. He leaned forward and sighed. 'I didn't want to tell anyone what we were going after until we actually found it. But Kait has a manuscript – in a language I can't read, so don't ask me to take the manuscript and throw her to the sea – and her manuscript tells where we will find an Ancient city that hasn't yet been discovered by anyone else.'

The stillness of the crew changed in character. Greed invaded where a moment before only hatred and prejudice had been. He could see it in the faces of the men and women before him – in the way their eyes shifted, in the way their mouths tightened, in the way they suddenly looked at each other, obviously weighing options on their own.

He sighed and said, 'You would have found out when we arrived, and discovered you were cut in for your regular shares. But I didn't want to tell you what we were looking for, in case we never found it.' He paused, clasped his hands together, and said, 'We have to keep her on the ship, and because they're friends, we have to keep him, too. Without them, we have no hope of ever finding that city. And I want to be rich as a paraglese. Don't you?'

They murmured among themselves, and stared thoughtfully at their feet. 'You're sure she knows where such a city is?' Rrru-eeth asked.

'No.' Ian shrugged. 'I'm taking a chance, because I think the rewards will be worth it if she does know the location . . . if, of course, we live to find it. I'm taking a risk. You signed on under my command; I assumed both the risks and the chance of reward on your behalf. But I didn't come this far to throw away my only chance at this opportunity when we're almost there.'

He waited. They looked at each other, and he could almost see their thoughts. *Wait. We can get rid of the skin-shifter and the wizard once we've found the prize.*

Rrru-eeth crossed her arms over her thin chest. 'So we find this city and claim it. And then . . . ?'

Ian met her eyes and kept all expression from his face. In a flat voice, he said, 'What do you think?'

She saw what she wanted to see. Her arms uncrossed, she nodded with satisfaction, and said, 'Then we'll wait.'

* * *

In the ship's infirmary, Kait sat next to Hasmal and held a mug of beer to his lips. 'Drink,' she said. 'It will do you good.'

He looked like a corpse. Black circles ringed his sunken eyes. His lips were blue, his skin chalk-white and waxy. 'I don't . . . think I can drink . . . anything,' he whispered.

'Drink. You're going to need your strength.' She sighed. 'Maybe sooner than we could wish.' She slid one arm under his neck and lifted his head enough that he could swallow. When he managed a long swallow, she let him lie back.

'What do you mean, sooner than we could wish?'

Kait wasn't looking forward to telling him the bad news. 'I hid your bag of implements before I took you out of the storeroom. Then, as soon as you had help, I went back to get it. In the meantime, someone else had already found it. It's gone, and your secret is probably now as well-known as mine.'

Hasmal frowned weakly. 'Your secret? How?'

He didn't need to be more specific. Kait said, 'I got scared when the people started dying. The water . . . it ate them. When I saw that happen, I Shifted. I couldn't stop myself. Almost everyone saw.'

'Not good. And they found my bag?'

'Yes.'

'Not good.' He groaned. 'Though I don't even know why I'm still alive. I . . .' He closed his eyes and licked dry lips.

Kait raised his head and gave him more beer. 'Don't talk. Just drink and get better.'

He pulled his head away from the mug after a moment and said, 'I need to tell you this. It's important, and I don't think I'm going to live.'

'You're going to live. Don't talk like that.'

'Shhh. Just listen.' He let her force another swallow of beer down his throat, then said, 'The water is alive.'

'I saw –' Kait started to interrupt.

'*Alive*,' Hasmal said a bit more loudly.

Kait could see that the effort cost him strength, and fell silent, letting him tell her what he needed to in his own way.

He looked at her, then nodded faintly. 'I did a divination to find out the danger we faced. A city once stood here, filled with more people than I can imagine. It was greater than Calimekka, perhaps ten times greater. The spell that the Dragons attacked it with devoured city, people, and land and dropped the edge of the continent into the ocean. And when it did, it trapped the souls of every living creature in the basin that it carved. Water flowed in and the magic that permeated the crater

374

poisoned it. The magic bound up the souls of the dead in the water, and souls and magic combined imbued it with life. And memory. The sea beneath us remembers each of the millions of lives that ended, because each of those lives was, in effect, its life. It has died horribly millions of times. It wants revenge.'

Kait felt sick.

Hasmal continued. 'The Reborn needs at least one of us. And you are the braver. And the one more likely, I thought, to be able to survive. While I was the one who had the magic to get us to safety. So I made a deal with my god, Vodor Imrish. I offered my life and my soul to him if he would get you safely to the city and to the Mirror of Souls, and he accepted. I think. He told me he accepted. Except I'm still alive, so perhaps he didn't.'

Kait held the hand of the man who'd told her he was not brave and thought about him offering his life in exchange for her safety. *Brave*, she thought, was a relative term. In her eyes, no one could have been braver. She told him that, but he only shrugged.

'I think it takes more courage to live than to die sometimes. I thought I had the better end of the bargain, considering the trouble the world will see before the Reborn overcomes it.'

Kait could still hear the many voices of the sea crying out. 'How will we know if we're safe?' she asked.

Hasmal looked at her with disbelief. Then he closed his eyes and began to laugh softly. 'I have no idea,' he admitted. 'I forgot to ask for a clear sign.'

* * *

Ian yearned for the comfort of his own cabin, and for the pleasures of fresh air and daylight, and for the sight of the sea that he loved. But the survivors huddled together belowdecks – captain, crew, and passenger – leaving the ship to tend to itself, because attempting to sail it while fighting the living water of the Wizards'

Circle would be certain death. So they hid and prayed that the ship wouldn't hit a reef or a cliff and sink, taking them all with her; only that course of action might permit them to survive.

A day passed. Then two.

Ian woke on the third day to find sunshine blazing through the deck prisms, and to hear nothing but the lapping of water on the sides of the ship. He asked Rrru-eeth if she heard voices outside, and at last, after two days of gloomy answers in the affirmative, she told him, smiling, that she did not. The crew cheered her acute hearing and her news. Ian cheered with them.

Then he drew a deep breath. 'We have to take the wax from the hatch. And we have to go up on deck. I'll go first, but I'll need volunteers to go with me.'

Jayti volunteered, as did Rrru-eeth. Hasmal and Kait both offered. Ian accepted all four, and the five of them began peeling the wax away from the bottom sill. Everyone else stood well back. A few crew members left completely for other parts of the ship. Ian understood. His heart felt like it had risen into his throat and would choke his breath at any moment. Still, he was as eager to be out of the confinement of belowdecks as he was terrified of what he would find when the hatch opened.

Nothing came in between the hatch and the sill; Kait had stood with wax and flame at the ready to stopper the gap again, but she didn't need to use it. When the last of the seal came down, Ian said, 'I'll go first. Then the rest of you, in whatever order you prefer.'

Kait made a face. 'And if something happens to you, who will get this ship back to Calimekka?'

Ian grinned. 'I have one of the best crews sailing. Even if I'm dead, they'll get you back home again.' If he were dead, they probably wouldn't, he thought. He was going to have the hells' own time convincing them to take her back with them as things stood. But they were a superb

376

crew, and they were people he'd known for years. Some of them were even friends. He'd make them understand.

He hadn't given up his dream of marrying his way into the Galweigh Family through Kait – but he liked her more than he ever thought he would. He thought, in spite of her . . . well, her affliction . . . that he might even love her. Funny, that. He'd been certain until she walked into his life that he was immune to love.

With thoughts of love and possible imminent demise on his mind, he climbed up the gangway and out onto the deck. Into the sunshine. He looked around, and gasped.

'What?' someone from below asked. The hatch started to swing shut.

'The city,' he said wonderingly. 'The city is right ahead of us.'

Below, he heard Hasmal say, 'Vodor Imrish did it. He actually did it.'

'Did what?' Kait asked.

'Gave us wind for the sails and got us all the way to the city. It was what I . . . ah. What I asked for. When I prayed. But I didn't think he would give us all of that and still let me live.'

People poured out onto the deck then, and shot up into the rigging to get better looks, and leaned against the rails. Ian Draclas stood where he was, staring up at the cliffs ahead of them. Tangled greenery couldn't completely hide the lean white spires of Ancient architecture, or the occasional pillar or buttress. It lay there, all right, waiting for him for more than a thousand years, like a jewel in a pile of rubbish. Just waiting, untouched, ripe, and rich. He could feel it. He could feel his fortune, fame, power – all of it tucked away behind sealed doors at the end of long-forgotten streets.

His palms itched, and his mouth went dry. The gods had to love him, to deposit him and the *Peregrine* safely in that beautiful bay, on a sunny day in the month of

Drastu. Fitting, he thought. Drastu was goddess of fertility, of the egg and the womb – and, by correlation, the goddess of the conception and birth of new work, new ideas, and new wealth.

'You'll have a shrine from me, Drastu,' he murmured before he turned to direct the dropping of the anchor and to select the crew that would first go ashore.

They took two of the *Peregrine*'s three longboats and rowed to the rocky shore.

'This first day, we'll do a preliminary exploration,' he said. 'Never go anywhere alone, never let yourself out of calling distance of one other group, never put your weapons down.' He cleared his throat. '*Especially* never put your weapons down. We have no idea who, or what, we'll find here, and we have to assume that if we find inhabitants, they'll be hostile. Be careful. Things you can pick up and carry in one hand you can bring out today. Bigger things will have to wait. If you find something that is both good and big, mark the spot and we'll go back to it as soon as we can.'

'Do we get to keep what we find?' Jayti asked.

'If you find something that you especially want for yourself, mark it. Small things shouldn't be a problem. However, we divide the treasure by shares, and the only way we'll be able to figure shares is to sell everything when we get back to Calimekka. Or Wilhene.' He didn't like the idea of Wilhene, which was a Sabir city, but the brokerages there sometimes offered better prices than those in Calimekka.

The whole time he was giving them the rules, he was trying to figure out how he could make sure none of them walked off with something irreplaceable, and at the same time he was wondering how he could get more than his share. And he knew that most, if not all, of them were thinking the same thing.

Kait and Hasmal stood together. There, he thought.

Right there was the money crop. Kait knew where the city was, and presumably had an idea of what might be found in it. Hasmal had bargained with his god to get them out of trouble and to the city. (Ian needed to find out more about Vodor Imrish, too, he decided. A god who would get that deeply involved in his worshipers' lives deserved a few new converts. He had a few favors he thought he would ask of a god who paid attention.) So when groups paired off, he appended himself to Kait and Hasmal, smiling all the while. 'As my passenger,' he told Kait, 'you deserve the attention of the captain.'

'I thought I was more than your passenger,' Kait said once the three of them were alone. 'Though I can understand why that's changed.'

'It hasn't changed,' he told her. 'I love you, Kait. But I've had to work hard to get the crew to agree to keep you on board – they wanted to throw you to the sea when they found out what you were, and they would question my motives if I seemed to be still . . .' He shrugged, at a loss for words. 'Still infatuated. I've had to make some concessions for the sake of appearances.'

He knew he sounded weak-willed to be letting his crew influence his public actions. Intelligent captains, however, did not invite mutiny by ignoring the legitimate concerns of the men and women beneath him.

'I understand. I didn't expect them to welcome me once they knew. For that matter, I was sure you would want to be done with me, too.'

'I don't,' he said. 'I won't ever want to be done with you.'

Her wan smile told him more than words could have. She didn't believe him. He needed to *make* her believe him; his future as he wanted to envision it depended on that belief.

At least he had time on his side.

Chapter 29

Kait stared up the steep cliff, at the tops and sides of buildings that peered out from beneath a thousand years of forest growth and a thousand years of detritus. She could make out no roads or signs that there had ever been roads; no doors or windows; few intact roofs. The remains of the city lay like the half-buried bones of an ancient battlefield – one where both sides lost and no one came along to collect the bodies.

Listening to the wind blowing through the branches, smelling plants and animals unlike any she had ever known, feeling the sun on her back altered by latitude and season, she felt a combination of hope and despair too vast and rich to put into words, even to herself. In that jumble of ruins lay her Family's single fragile magical hope of escape from the deaths it had already suffered. Somewhere, a thousand years ago, in the midst of destruction, the blasting of spells, and the end of the world, someone had left the Mirror of Souls in this city, in one of the buildings above her. Somewhere. And she had no idea what this Mirror looked like, no idea how it worked, no idea how to even begin looking for it. From that depth of ignorance came her despair.

Hasmal rested a hand on her shoulder and whispered, 'Has she told you where to find it?'

'No. I don't think she knows.' Kait frowned; Ian worked

on the rocky beach to the north of them, hiding the longboats with several of his crew.

Amalee told Kait, *I don't know. Things here are very different than I – than I thought they would be. But with you able to sense magic, perhaps you'll be able to track it down that way.* She projected frustration and disgust. *If you can't, you'll just have to hunt through the buildings one at a time. And I thought the hard part would be getting here. I had no idea how difficult things could be when we arrived.*

'She isn't going to be of any help,' Kait said.

I got you here. And I can identify the Mirror when you find it.

Kait ignored that protest.

Hasmal asked, 'Then where do we start looking?'

Kait closed her eyes. She had a faint headache, one that felt very much like the headache she'd had when she attended the Dokteerak party. The headache that Dùghall had later identified as being caused by magic.

Interesting that Hasmal's use of magic doesn't give me a headache like that, she thought. Perhaps his magic is very weak.

She let the thought drop. With her eyes closed she began to turn in a slow circle, trying to find one direction that made the headache worse or better. She found nothing. So she opened her eyes and began to walk, first along the rocky beach toward Ian and the longboats, then away. Again, she could sense no difference in her level of pain. Her headaches let her know something magical waited nearby, but weren't sensitive enough to guide her toward it. Or, she realized, the entire city could be soaked in magic. Or there might be artifacts scattered around evenly enough that no matter which direction she went in she felt the same.

'We're simply going to have to start looking.'

Hasmal sighed. 'There must be an easier way. The city might be larger than it appears to be from here.'

Kait had studied what was known of the cities of the Ancients with her tutors. Some of them had evidently been quite large. And though this one seemed to fit neatly around the rim of the bay, it might run inland. She nodded, and, feeling grim, picked a direction at random.

'If it's any consolation,' Hasmal said, 'the fact that we ended up here together seems to indicate that the gods themselves favor our endeavor. So perhaps we'll just happen upon it.'

'Perhaps. In the meantime, though, try to think of some way that we can find it without luck or the intervention of the gods. I would like to get home while I'm still a young woman, and while I still have hope of saving the people I love.'

'Since they're already dead, I don't see where speed is an issue,' Hasmal said.

Kait's glare sent him hurrying ahead.

* * *

Three days and hundreds of filthy, half-buried, ruined buildings later, Hasmal was willing to concede that his joke about waiting for the intervention of the gods had not been his best. The rest of the searchers had found treasure beyond their most fevered imaginings. Plaques and bits of machinery, precious metals, statues and jewelry and things impossible to identify that would nonetheless draw a nice sum in the market were rowed out to the ship in the longboats and poured into the ship's holds. The crew went through the city in shifts, with half staying on board to recuperate and keep an eye on the accumulated treasure, while the other half did their best to outdo the previous shift in adding to it.

Hasmal had never heard of such a trove as the one accumulating aboard the *Peregrine*. He thought this city was the richest ever found. A thousand young men could spend long lives combing for treasures and do no more than skim the surface. The sheer brutal size of the place stunned him. Calimekka was the largest city in the world. More than a million people had lived within its boundaries at the last census, and it grew greater, in numbers and sheer size, every day. Mathematicians were forever estimating how many times the roads and streets of Calimekka could circle the world, if they were laid end to end. But the ruins of this nameless graveyard in the forest could have swallowed the great Calimekka and another dozen like it, and perhaps more. The buildings around the bay had been only the leading edge of what Hasmal guessed must have been one of the largest cities ever to exist.

Kait grew more and more dispirited as they searched. She and Hasmal marked their share of sites where treasure lay, and already they would be richer than all but the Five Families. But they weren't searching for wealth, so while everyone else grew jubilant and talked about the castles they would build and the slaves they would buy, Hasmal watched Kait draw deeper and deeper into herself.

Ian had noticed her mood, and had done everything he could to find out what was causing it. He'd been solicitous, but Hasmal believed the captain suspected he and Kait were searching for something specific, something of tremendous value, and he wanted to be sure he got his share of it.

Kait remained uncommunicative.

* * *

The torches of the night searchers flickered on the beach. They stood waiting for the remainder of the day crew to ferry the last of their finds out to the ship. Kait stood next to Hasmal at the longboat that would be last to leave.

'I'm staying,' she said.

Hasmal rubbed his eyes. 'Staying? By Vodor's eyes, Kait – we've searched all day. What can you hope to accomplish wearing yourself out?'

She stared up at the hills, then returned her attention to Hasmal. 'I'm not going back to the ship again until I find it.

I have this terrible feeling that we're running out of time. I don't know why – I don't know where the feeling comes from, or if there's any truth to it. But I want to see my mother and father again. My brothers. My sisters. Dùghall. My cousins. I would do anything –'

Her voice broke. She swallowed hard, tasting tears. She knew – *knew* – that if she didn't find the Mirror of Souls within the next day, she would not find it at all. She felt the truth of that in her marrow, in her blood. She had nothing she could point to that would let her say, *Here. This is why I'm afraid.* But that only made the fear worse. She held lives in her hand, hundreds of lives, and among them the lives she valued more than her own. And if she failed them because she hadn't tried hard enough, she would not be able to live with herself.

Better she had died.

'I would do anything to save them,' she said when she regained control of her voice. 'But there are only so many things I can do. One thing I can do is search at night.'

'And when will you sleep?'

'Once I've found it.' She was Karnee. She could drive her body harder than any human if she needed to. Now she needed to. 'Go and get some sleep, and I'll meet you here tomorrow morning. We'll hunt together then.'

'I can't let you do this.'

'You don't have a choice.'

'Perhaps not. But what about the captain? You know he wants to stay with us; he wants whatever we're looking for.'

'I know. So you have to lie for me. Tell him you think I went to the ship in an earlier boat. If he tried to stay with me tonight, he would only slow me down.'

Understanding flashed across Hasmal's face. 'You're going to . . .'

'Shift. Yes. I can cover much more ground that way, and my senses are better. There's something we've been missing, and I have to think this will be my chance to discover what it was.'

Hasmal looked past her shoulder and whispered, 'Then go now. The captain's dragging something down the beach; he'll be here in a moment.'

Kait nodded, and moved toward the trees. 'I'll see you tomorrow. Wish me luck.'

'Luck,' he said.

Kait loped up the hill, unlacing her shirt as she went. She had not taken a torch. Even in human form, her eyes made the most of available light, so that she saw quite clearly. When she Shifted, she would see as well as if she hunted by daylight.

She wanted to avoid the night teams. Like the other crewmen on the *Peregrine*, they didn't like her; she didn't trust them. No matter what good things she'd done for their lives by bringing them to this city, she suspected any of the pairs would try to hurt her if they found her alone.

She stripped out of her clothes, folded them, and left them in a building at the top of the cliff. Then she gave herself over to the inhuman hungers and lusts of Shift, and flowed into the ecstasy of otherness.

To her keener Shifted senses, the night became a thing of unutterable beauty. The stars blazed through the broad leaves of the hardwood canopy, carving the trees into statues of liquid silver and bleaching the ruined buildings into creations of translucent shell. The wind sang in whispers, sweet accompaniment to the voices of insects and nightbirds and the four-legged predators who hunted through the wood. And the scents . . .

As soon as she Shifted, she'd begun running inland, acting on hunches and some subliminal direction that she go east. She and Hasmal had hunted in that direction during the day, and there had been something . . . something . . . something that had excited her, but had been too muted and insubstantial for her to identify. It had tickled the back of her mind during the day, leaving her certain that she headed in the direction of something vital. Life-changing. Essential.

Now, stopping at the top of a ridge and facing into the wind, she caught the faintest whiff of that same pulse-stirring scent. Yes, her mind told her. Whatever it is, you'll find it in that direction.

She ran into the wind, pushing herself hard, hoping that the scent would get stronger. It was probably stupid to be chasing it – after all, what were the odds that the aroma meant anything? She kept running, though; she had no other ideas to pursue.

She ran far beyond the area she and Hasmal had covered, far enough that she broke free of the cover of forest onto a rolling plain. Even in the moonlight, she could see the scars that a fire had left on the remaining stumps of trees. The field had burned more than a year ago, and in its wake grasses had grown in profusion, and exquisite wildflowers, and the first tiny starts of what would, in twenty or thirty years, be the new forest.

Life didn't disappear in the aftermath of disasters, either large or small, though it did change. Uncounted small creatures inhabited the plain. They weren't alone. She smelled and heard a pack of big animals moving northeast of her. Her nose identified the blood-scent on them. Predators, then. She was glad to be downwind.

That other scent – the one she thought she knew – got stronger. Sweet. Beautifully sweet, but under the sweet-ness, the slightest taint of decay. Where had she smelled that scent before? Floral images flashed in her mind, but the scent had not come to her in a garden. Not in the jungle. No place ordinary.

The puzzle nagged at her, but she didn't focus on it. She kept tracking; when she found whatever it was, she would most likely remember where she had run into it before. She lost the scent, doubled back, and began quartering north to south and back until she picked it up. When she found it again, the seductive tendrils of that tantalizing perfume led her far onto the plain, through rows of the ribs of buried buildings, along a stream, and finally into a declivity.

She came to the head of a small falls. Cliffs dropped down to either side, sandstone that jutted at sharp angles from between tangles of vines and scrub trees. A pond at the bottom of the cliffs swirled away into a stream that rolled out of sight around a curve. Whatever she'd been tracking was down there. The scent filled the valley. Sweetness and decay. Both excited and afraid, she worked her way down the rough cliffs, sampling the air for any change that indicated danger. A bird sang beautifully, but fell silent as she neared the water. The insect noises stilled, and she felt the eyes of the darkness watching her, the frightened and huddled prey acknowledging her as the predator she was. She took the silence as her due, but did not break it. She, too, could find herself prey – hunted instead of hunter.

At the bottom of the cliffs, she discovered a path. To that point, she had seen nothing that would make her think humans survived anywhere near the city. But while she could not catch any human scent about the path, it had the look of human work. It was neat, straight, sharp-edged. And it had been kept up. The fur along her spine stood up and an instinctive growl rumbled in the back of her throat. But the path led toward the source of the scent. She flexed her claws and moved forward, trying to focus on all directions at the same time. The path followed the edge of the little pond down to the stream that drained it. It continued to parallel the stream for perhaps two Calimek-kan blocks. Then it veered sharply to the right and uphill into another ravine.

This ravine bore further signs of current inhabitants: the increasingly broad, neat path edged with flowers; thorny shrubs planted to form a barrier hedge along the tops of the cliffs; and finally, a building in good repair built into the stone in the same manner that Galweigh House was built into the cliff.

This building looked small from the outside. The part of it that Kait could see was about as big as the gatehouse back home. Or perhaps as big as one of the shrines to lesser gods. That thought occurred to her because in its form, it reminded her of those shrines. One doorway, no door, no windows, an elaborate roof, and within the shrine, an altar on a pedestal.

The altar was different, though. It glowed, radiant as a small sun, its warm golden light illuminating the inside of the shrine, setting its translucent walls ablaze, and spilling welcoming light out onto the pathway and the tumbles of flowers to either side. And from the altar emanated the scent that she'd followed for such a distance.

Honeysuckle, she realized. The cloying sweet scent was honeysuckle. And the place she'd smelled it before had been in the airible, in the instant before magic had overwhelmed her and Dùghall. In the instant before everything changed.

In the back of her mind, Amalee said, *That's it. That's the Mirror of Souls.*

Where? Kait asked, not speaking out loud.

You called it an altar in your thoughts. The glowing pedestal.

Kait stared at it and groaned. *It's too big. I'll never be able to take it back by myself.*

Then get back to the beach and be waiting when your friends get here. And do it quickly. Because that is what you've come all this way to find.

At that moment, the monsters who guarded the shrine chose to attack.

Chapter 30

She'd never smelled them coming, nor heard from them the faintest sound. The honeysuckle-and-rot scent had hidden them from her. They dropped down from the sides of the cliffs and shambled out of the shrine; warped and twisted parodies of humans, naked and snarling, carrying hoes and long-handled trowels and rakes in their knot-jointed hands. Their ancestors had surely been human, but they were not. They smelled only of leaf mold and damp earth and dark, hidden places, and they whispered as they moved toward her, wordless whispering that mimicked the rustle of leaves. They came at Kait from all sides. In spite of her wariness in her approach, in spite of her strength and speed, they cut off her route of escape, and she discovered how well they had planned the protection of their shrine.

She had the low ground, and nothing to guard her back. She couldn't seek refuge in the cliffs, nor could she attempt escape in any direction but the one by which she'd come. She counted twelve of them, and doubted that they'd sent their full complement against her in the first wave. She still saw too many good hiding places like the ones out of which these attackers had materialized.

They weren't armed well, and they moved awkwardly, their bodies poorly designed for speed or fighting. Those two advantages she held. Against the monsters' advantages of position, numbers, familiarity with terrain, and surprise, her two strengths would not, she felt, be sufficient to save her life. She felt fear as a force that pressed the air from her lungs and sat atop her shoulders and back, pressing her down. Making her slow. Weak.

So close. She stood so close to success, to triumph. She'd come from half a world away, and now crouched less than a stone's throw from the magical device that would restore her beloved dead to her, and neither she nor they would have their chances. Kait howled her rage and her anguish, and attacked the nearest of the monsters.

Kait.

They shrieked and swung their gardening tools, catching her in the face and across the shoulders and ribs. She leaped and slashed with teeth and claws, and those she attacked fell back. But others moved in at her sides, and more blows fell. She slashed one of the monsters and blood spurted from its belly; at its screams, more of the creatures appeared from above her, behind her, in front of her. All of them carried tools, or sticks, or clubs.

Kait!

At last she heard Amalee shouting at her, and realized she had been doing so since the monsters first surrounded her. 'Not now!' she snarled. 'Can't you see I'm busy dying?'

You have to be human.

Kait killed one of the creatures, but even more appeared. She guessed that more than thirty now surrounded and attacked her, though she couldn't be sure – they were all around her and she was too busy fighting to try for an accurate count. For every one she killed, a dozen managed to connect with their makeshift weapons. They wounded her faster than she could heal. They would kill her in pieces, dragging life from her a little at a time, tearing her into a slow, gruesome death.

You have to be human! Amalee insisted again, shouting it into Kait's mind so fiercely that she could no longer ignore her dead ancestor.

'Pity I'm not, then, isn't it?'

Listen. You have to Shift into human shape. They'll kill anything and anyone not in human shape. They're the guardians of the Mirror, and if you're human, they'll let you walk on the path safely. They'll even let you take the Mirror. Your arrival is what their kind have waited almost a thousand years to witness.

'I have no weapons in human form,' she said. 'No clothes. I'll be completely helpless.'

You have to be human. Or you'll die. If you're human, they won't hurt you.

Kait didn't believe her ancestor. Five of the monsters now lay dead, and she didn't believe they would forgive that slaughter if she Shifted back to her human form. They would, instead, kill her all the faster, and with no further loss.

But she was dying. Slowly. She would, in her Karnee form, kill more of them before they completely overcame her. Nevertheless, she would still die.

I have to be human, she says.

They won't kill a human, she says.

She's a fool, I say.

Well, if I must die today anyway, I'd rather die as a human than a beast.

Snarling, fighting, in pain, she struggled to find the still place within herself, the place that was all blues and greens and placid water and silence. Fear, rage, and anguish buried her humanity deep. The red-hot bloodlust nearly drowned it. Years of effort to keep herself human in the worst of circumstances rose to her assistance, though, and she found that place after all. Touched the

391

silence in her soul. Felt the battle hunger die slowly, even though the monsters still attacked her, even though she no longer attacked, but only attempted to ward off the blows that rained on her from all directions.

She Shifted, and felt her blood cool, and her skin grow heavy, and her senses dull.

She stretched and reformed, and all around her the monsters backed away, mewling, as she rose from four legs to two, and stood over their hunched and twisted forms. They dropped their weapons, and some began to weep, and all of them prostrated themselves at her feet. She stood over them, bleeding from a hundred burning cuts, dizzy with pain, and slowly she stepped over and around them. Not toward the Mirror of Souls. Away from it. Back the way she'd come. She had to get back to the beach by the time the morning crew arrived. She had to bring Hasmal and Ian and one or two others to help her carry the Mirror back to the ship. The journey, which in Karnee form she could run in one night, would take humans several days. And time was precious. Time was everything.

Once out of the ravine and well away from the Mirror's guardians, she forced herself into Shift again, though it drained her body's resources. Her body devoured itself to complete the Shift, and would consume even more of her own tissue when she had to become human again upon reaching the beach. She stopped her headlong rush several times to kill and devour animals unlucky enough to end up in her path. They would only keep her from starving to death before she reached the ship; she would need a massive meal when she arrived.

That was a minor detail. *Everything* else was minor detail. Against all odds, she had found the Mirror of Souls. Her Family and the Reborn would triumph.

* * *

Ian stepped out of the longboat onto the beach, the

mists of dawn wrapping around him like a cloak. He met the night crew as they dragged the last of their finds down to the rocky shore.

'Where's Kait?' He kept his fury in check, and held his voice to a semblance of reasonableness intended to prevent the crew from discovering how completely her betrayal the night before had shaken him.

Everyone he asked shrugged and looked surprised. Their answers varied from, 'Day shift, I thought,' to 'I figured she'd run off sooner or later,' but not a single other person had seen her.

Hasmal had insisted that she would be on the beach waiting for the two of them when they arrived. Ian had accused him of lying, and morning had proved him right.

When the night crew finished loading and rowed back to the ship, and the day crew scattered to find more treasure, he turned on his shipwright. 'Now you can tell me what the two of you have been looking for all this time. What is it that she's found? What did the two of you really come here for?'

Hasmal hooked his thumbs into his belt and glared up at Ian. 'You've been bedding her, Cap'n. You're the one she'd share her pillow talk with.'

'I didn't share . . . my . . . pillow talk with . . . anyone,' Kait said. She staggered out from the cover of the forest, and Ian gasped. All he could recognize of her was her voice, and that was uncharacteristically harsh. She was skeletally thin, so that her clothes hung on her like unpitched tents on a tent pole. Scars in various stages of healing covered her face and every other piece of skin he could see. Her hair tangled in her face, matted with clots of blood and dirt. Her ashen color and the waxiness of her skin would have convinced him, had she not been upright and speaking, that she was already dead.

His anger dissipated, as if it were fog beneath a blazing sun. 'Kait? By Brethwan, what's happened to you?'

'I . . . I found it,' she said to Hasmal. Then she turned to Ian. And smiled. And sagged.

She managed to catch herself just short of collapse. She breathed like she'd been running. 'We need to . . . get started now. I figure . . . the place where it's hidden . . . is . . . about three days' walk. Plus . . . three days back.'

Ian almost couldn't breathe. 'Hasmal, get her into the boat. We've got to have the physick look at her.'

Hasmal said, 'The physick is out hunting for treasure with the rest of them. He didn't want anyone to question his share.'

'Damnall.' He put his head down, thinking. 'Then we'll get her out to the ship and ring the bell. By the time the physick gets back, we can have something done for her.'

'I'm fine,' Kait said. 'But we . . . have to hurry.'

'You aren't fine!' Ian found himself terrified for her – terrified that she might collapse and die at any moment.

Kait gave Hasmal a beseeching look. 'Tell him I'm . . . fine, Hasmal.'

'You aren't fine,' Hasmal said. 'You're damn near dead.'

'I just need . . .' She sagged again, and Ian could see she had more difficulty preventing her fall.

He picked her up and kissed her once. She felt like a bird in his arms, too light and fragile to survive. To Hasmal he said, 'Back to the ship. We'll figure out what happened to her and what we're going to do about it when we get there.'

Ian's emotions took him by surprise. He didn't *need* her anymore; he had the city that would make him rich and powerful beyond measure, and if she were to die from her injuries, he would be able to claim primary possession of it. But as he and Hasmal rowed her out to the *Peregrine*, he discovered that he *wanted* her, and that the wanting went deeper than any amusement she provided in his bed. He wanted to argue with her again about the relative merits of the philosophies of Farellhau and N'stanri. He wanted to sit in front of a great fire in a great House with her and recount the adventures that had brought them to that place of wealth and power and happiness. Or, he realized, he would be happy to spend the rest of his life sailing across Matrin's great seas with her at his side. Ian Draclas stared at the gaunt, dying woman in his arms and discovered to his dismay that somewhere between deciding to claim her city for the wealth and determining to marry her for the Family power, he had fallen irretrievably in love. In doing that, the wealth and the power that could undoubtedly be his fell by the wayside, and his only concern became her life.

By the time they reached the ship, she was barely breathing. Ian tried to keep her awake and talking, while Hasmal brought in water.

'Until the physick gets back, we can try to get some of this into her. She looks dehydrated.'

Ian nodded. He cradled her head in one arm and helped her swallow the water Hasmal poured into her mouth by stroking her throat. Before long, the two of them noticed an improvement. She began to swallow without assistance, and finally she opened her eyes and reached for the cup and began drinking on her own.

When she spoke again, her first word was, 'Food.' And it was her only word for quite some time. Hasmal brought things from the storeroom and the galley and Kait devoured them and requested more. The food helped faster than Ian could have imagined. Within two stations, he could see where she had actually put on weight – she went from being skeletal to being merely frail. Further, her wounds healed themselves as he watched. She ate constantly, not speaking at all except to ask for more. In his entire life he had never seen one person consume so much food.

Finally she pushed her plate back. 'We have to go after the Mirror now,' she said. 'We'll need help. It's much larger than I expected. The two of you, me, maybe two other people. Some sort of travois or sledge to drag it back on. Supplies for three days out and three days back. Probably weapons. I crossed paths with predators that would have found me tasty in human form, though.'

Ian said, 'We aren't going after anything. You nearly died today –'

She cut him off. 'I found the single artifact that I claim as my portion of our treasure. I renounce my claim to everything else.'

Ian froze for just an instant, as greed briefly reasserted itself. Then he shook it off. 'Tell me what you found.'

It took her a while, but she did.

Finally, he managed to take it all in. 'An artifact that brings back the dead. And you're going to revive the Galweighs. Once you learn how to use the thing, anyway.'

'Yes.'

It sounded like madness to him, but the Ancients knew more about everything than anyone had since rediscovered. Perhaps the reason the Wizards hadn't been worried about destroying the world was that they knew a way to bring everyone back afterward – at least everyone they liked. He guessed that the person or people who knew how to do it must have been killed, though.

He took Kait's hand in his own. If the Mirror of Souls did work, then he would gain quite a bit of favor with his future in-laws. If it didn't, he gained the greatest share of the wealth of the city. In either instance, he won. And he would have done it without hurting Kait in any way.

'We'll go after it tonight,' he said. 'I'll help you in every way I can. I'll even help you get it to your House so that you can revive your Family.'

Her brow creased in puzzlement. 'You will? But why?'

He stroked the soft skin on the back of her hand, and felt the delicate bones beneath. She needed to eat more before they left, he decided. He wouldn't risk her running herself to the brink of death again. 'Because I love you,' he told her.

It felt funny to know that was the truth.

* * *

'He kissed her,' Rrru-eeth said to Jayti. At Rrru-eeth's request, the two of them had waited in the trees above the beach; Rrru-eeth said she was concerned about the captain's behavior.

Jayti had grown used to her concern. Every day when Ian Draclas went treasure-hunting with Kait and Hasmal, Rrru-eeth complained about him being in the clutches of the skinshifter and the wizard. She mentioned at least once each day that she thought she and Jayti ought to get Kait and Hasmal off by themselves and kill them, so that the captain would be able to break free from their spell. She fretted that he would forget he had promised to leave them behind. Now, spying on them from the cover of the trees, Rrru-eeth radiated anger.

'I can't say I like it,' Jayti said, 'but as captain, he can do as he pleases.'

Rrru-eeth's eyebrows rose. 'Do you think so? Tell me, do you really?' Her voice was a dangerous growl, laced with scorn.

As much as Jayti adored Rrru-eeth, his first loyalty was to Ian Draclas, who had saved him from hanging ten years before, when Jayti, at the age of seventeen, had been accused of touching a paraglesa. He'd been an assistant to the cook in the Sabir House in Wilhene, and the wife of the paraglese had taken a fancy to him. She'd specifically requested him to bring a tray of confections and a carafe of wine to her room 'for a small party.' He'd discovered when he arrived that she intended the party to consist of only the two of them, and she had more in mind than confections for her dessert.

He – thinking the paraglese would have him drawn and quartered if he touched the man's wife – refused to participate in her party. She – with no appreciation of his care for her honor – immediately called the guards and accused Jayti of accosting her.

Ian Draclas had somehow heard of his plight, and had spirited him out of the Sabir House dungeon. Jayti still had no idea how he had managed the trick, or why he had. But he never forgot his rescue, nor the debt he owed the man who had accomplished it.

If the man found a woman he liked, Jayti thought he deserved to keep her, for however long he could.

'Rrru-eeth, even if he takes them with us when we sail, he'll leave both of them in Calimekka. They'll be out of your life forever in just a few more months.'

'He *kissed* her. What if he wants her to stay aboard the ship with him?'

Jayti snorted. 'She's a parata. You can see Family in her very bones. She won't give up House and power and riches to tramp around the sea in the *Peregrine* with him. You mark my words – she'll vanish from the captain's life the second we make landfall.'

Rrru-eeth said nothing. But the look in her eyes sent ice down Jayti's spine. He thought he would be wise to stay close to the captain for a while.

* * *

When the storm finally ended, the *Wind Treasure* lay far north of Kait's position. Ry Sabir felt her presence as a fixed mark, south and east. Knowledge of Kait's position meant nothing at that moment, however. The *Wind Treasure*'s sails were rags, her hull leaked dangerously from half a dozen places, and she'd lost nearly a third of her crew. The captain said the Rophetian ship would be days under repair at best; he also said Ry could spend his time pacing or he could help with the work, but that if he and his lieutenants didn't help, they would be weeks instead of days in the barren northern harbour where they'd come to rest.

Sabir Wolves did not do manual labor. Ever.

So I'm lucky to be declared dead, he thought. Mother won't have to die of shame.

Ry put himself to work, discovering when he did that he was less skilled than the least of the crew. He knew nothing of the shipwright's tools, nothing of the builder's techniques, nothing of the captain's needs. He fumbled at the simplest tasks, and at first he irritated the men and women who made their livelihood from ships and the sea. In his favor, he had only his tremendous strength and stamina, and his willingness to learn. He applied both to the tasks he was given, determined that he would do whatever he had to do to get to Kait. He struggled, he ached, and he learned.

I'm coming, Kait, he thought as he worked.

You're mine. You're mine. You were born to be mine, and you belong to me and me alone.

And I'm coming for you.

Chapter 31

Kait led the party up the walk to the shrine. No sign of her battle with the guardians remained. The path was perfectly groomed again, the trampled flowers replaced, the bodies removed. Even knowing that the guardians kept watch all around the shrine, and even knowing where they hid, she could not see a single one of them.

Ian and Hasmal, and Jayti and a sailor named Turben – who had both volunteered to help bring the Mirror back to the ship – followed her up that perfect path to the shrine. She crossed the threshold first, and got the first unobstructed look at the Mirror.

It had been made by someone with an eye for beauty. Its sleek, unornamented lines called to her mind lilies and orchids. It had both a 'flower' and a 'stem.' The 'flower' consisted of a ring of five connected petals of luminous platinum-white metal, the largest of which bore colorful incised markings. The base supporting this ring mimicked the smooth curve of three long, swordlike leaves, also of that glowing white metal. The 'stem' was the most amazing part of the entire artifact – a column of flowing golden light that began at the ground, rose between the three leaves, and spiraled outward in the center of the ring to disappear at last when it touched the petals. Kait stood watching the movement of the light, mesmerized.

Ian came to stand beside her, and rested a hand on her

shoulder. 'I doubted you when you told me about this,' he said softly. 'I didn't think such a device could exist. But when I look at this, I can see its value. It's worth more than everything else we've found so far. And it will be worth even more than that when it gives you back your parents and sisters and brothers.'

She nodded, too full of emotion to even speak. She reached out a hand and touched one of the petals, and through her fingertips felt the Mirror humming with a life of its own. She felt that stirring as a promise, as rich and beautiful in its own way as the love she'd felt when her soul touched the Reborn. The Mirror promised to return her world to her, or at least the part of it that mattered most.

Jayti and his friend Turben put together the travois on which they would strap the Mirror. While they were lacing cord around their poles and through the sailcloth they'd carried with them, Jayti pulled the captain aside. It was clear he didn't intend for Kait or Hasmal to hear what he said. Hasmal wouldn't be able to; Kait, studying the Mirror, pretended she didn't.

Voice soft and nervous, he said, 'Turben and I came with you for a reason, Cap'n. I expect trouble when we get back. Rrru-eeth's scared of yon Kait and the wizard – she wants them left behind, and she thinks you don't intend to do it.'

Ian glanced at Kait and Hasmal, then looked past them as if he were checking out the area. 'She's right,' he said. 'I'm not leaving either of them. I love Kait. And even if I didn't, she's the one who brought us to this city. Hasmal offered to sacrifice himself while working the spell that got us out of the Wizards' Circle.' He turned and looked evenly at Jayti. 'I'm not that disloyal. And I don't think you are, either.'

Jayti shrugged. 'That's why we're here.' He kept lacing the cord, and kept his head down. 'They may need protection on the way back. Rrru-eeth may intend for them to have an ... accident. And if she does, I think she'll be able to get some of the others to help her.'

'Just some?'

'Most. You know Turben and I aren't the only ones who owe you ... but most everyone is afraid, Cap'n. Knowing you're sharing space with skinshifters and magic don't let a man sleep easy at night.'

'Even you?'

He shrugged again. 'I'm no braver than most. But I reckon if you think they're trustworthy, then they are. You've had my life in your hand more than once, and I'm still drawing air.'

The captain patted him on the shoulder. 'I vouch for both of them with my life, Jayti.'

'That's more than enough for me.' He finally looked up from what he was doing. 'We'll get them back safe, me and Turben. I swear it.'

Kait's eyes blurred with tears. That a man would offer his life in protection of hers out of loyalty to the captain stunned her. Ian was a pirate, she knew. She suspected he was *barzanne*, as well – the son of Family ejected, disowned, and declared never born for some sin or imagined sin that he'd committed. But he was more than that. Much more.

She wondered if she would ever find out all there was to know about him.

When the travois was ready, they faced the dilemma of moving the Mirror onto it.

'Can we just pick it up?' the captain asked.

Everyone looked at Kait.

Amalee told her, *Don't touch the light.*

Kait passed that information on. It was harder advice to follow than it seemed. Her own hand brushed very near it when she helped pick the Mirror up, and when it did, her skin prickled and the honeysuckle scent grew

402

stronger. So did the scent of decay. She pulled back, and gagged.

Ian glanced at her face and frowned. 'What's wrong?'

'The smell. It got worse when my hand came too near the light.'

His puzzled expression intensified. 'Smell?'

Now Hasmal looked puzzled. 'The smell. From the Mirror of Souls. Sweet, and a little rotten.'

'It doesn't smell,' Ian said. Jayti and Turben agreed.

'This close, the smell is almost overwhelming,' Kait said.

'I can't smell a thing,' Jayti said. 'And I have a good nose.'

'I don't,' Hasmal said, 'and I could smell the damn thing from the top of the ravine.'

'I followed it here by its smell,' Kait said.

They stood looking at each other, all equally puzzled. Then Hasmal smiled slightly. 'I know what it is.'

'What?' Kait asked.

'The scent is magical in origin. You and I can smell it because of . . .' He winced as he glanced at the other three. 'We're . . . sensitive to magic. They aren't, so for them, there is no smell.'

Kait sighed. 'That makes sense.'

'Then it isn't important?' the captain asked.

'Why would it be? It's just a characteristic of the Mirror. It isn't as if the scent does anything,' Hasmal said, and shrugged.

A little gingerly, they began dragging the Mirror away from the shrine. They passed out of the ravine as easily as they had entered, and with no sign that guardians existed there beyond the flower-lined walk and the carefully tended hedges. Their return took less than three days, perhaps because they were elated by the magnitude of their prize. Kait wanted to shout to the sky that she'd found what she came for. Except for a few times in childhood, and the day that she received her first diplomatic assignment, she could never remember being so happy.

She would embrace her mother again. She would talk with her father one more time about his horse breeding, about his prize stallion and beautiful broodmares. She would hear the voices of young cousins and nieces and nephews racing through the lower floors of the House, playing chase and can't-find-me.

And when she had done those things, she and Hasmal would take the Mirror to the Reborn, wherever he might be. They would give it to him, and then they would witness the birth of an age of love and enlightenment.

Chapter 32

When they neared the bay, the party became cautious. Kait didn't let on that she knew the crew expected an attack against her and Hasmal. She remained on alert with her sword loose in its scabbard and her other hand near her dagger. The lively conversation the five of them had shared during the trip back died to silence – a silence unbroken by any human noises at all.

'They've either planned an ambush or they've done nothing at all and are far afield hunting for treasure,' Ian said at last. 'I don't hear *anyone*.'

Neither do I, Kait thought, and I think I would. She braced herself for the attack.

They kept moving forward through the forest. At last they reached the rise that led down to the bay. Silence. Kait wished they could find a clearing, but the thick forest offered no view of what lay ahead.

Her nose picked up an unmistakable scent, though, and no sooner did she stop and sniff the air than the rest of the party followed her example. The reek of death and decay blew through the forest, and the buzz of flies grew very loud as the five of them put the Mirror of Souls down and carefully worked their way to the bay.

Four bloated bodies sprawled on the rocky beach. Ian ran to them, with his men close behind.

'Daverrs,' Ian called, identifying the first corpse.

Turben said, 'Seeley and Smith's Son.'

'Bright,' Jayti said. 'All the ones with the most reason to be loyal to you.'

Kait had been looking at the bodies with the rest of them, but suddenly her heart thudded painfully in her breast. She looked out over the water and asked softly, 'Ian, where's the ship?'

The five of them stared out at the empty bay, then back down at the bodies.

Ian looked as dead as the corpses. 'Rrru-eeth convinced them to take my ship. My ship.'

Hasmal paled. 'We're the only humans on this continent?'

Turben and Jayti looked at each other and then at the other three. Jayti said, 'We have no supplies besides the little we have left in our packs.'

Kait stared out at the bay and at the thin line of the ocean that lay beyond. 'It doesn't matter,' she said. She lowered her shields, and instantly she felt Ry Sabir, still hunting her, getting closer. 'It truly doesn't matter. Our problems are bigger than that. Night falls, and the hunters are coming.'

About the Author

Holly Lisle, born in 1960, has been writing fiction and fantasy full-time since November 30, 1992. Prior to that, she worked as an advertising representative, a commercial artist, a guitar teacher, a restaurant singer, and for ten years as a registered nurse specializing in emergency and intensive care. Originally from Salem, Ohio, she has also lived in Alaska, Costa Rica, Guatemala, North Carolina, Georgia, and Florida. She and Matt are raising three children and several cats.

VENGEANCE OF DRAGONS

The Secret Texts
Book 2

Kait Galweigh is a fugitive. Her family has been massacred by the Sabir. Her only hope lies with the Mirror of Souls, which she believes will bring her kin back to life. But Crispin Sabir wants it too, believing it capable of making him a god.

Neither Kait nor Crispin know that the Mirror contains the captive spirits of the Dragons who once conquered and destroyed the world with their magic. Neither know that the Dragons are intent on release so that they can wreak vengeance on the world which has kept them prisoners for an eternity . . .

Royal Format
Hardback £16.99 0 57506 868 X
Trade Paperback £9.99 0 57506 869 8

THE JACKAL OF NAR

Book 1 of Tyrants and Kings

John Marco

To his enemies he is known simply as 'The Jackal',
a fearsome warrior in the battle for the frozen
borderland of Lucel-Lor. They taunt him with the
name as they come sweeping out of the woods to
fall yet again on the battered ranks of the soldiers
of Nar.

But Prince Richius is a reluctant hero in a war he
doesn't believe in, fought for an Emperor he
doesn't trust. And when he falls in love with a
woman of Lucel-Lor, 'The Jackal' is torn between
his kingdom, his loyalty and his heart.

Royal Format

Hardback £17.99 1 85798 568 0

Trade Paperback £9.99 1 85798 567 2

THE GRAND DESIGN
Book 2 of Tyrants and Kings

In *The Jackal of Nar* Prince Richius forsook his command in the savage war that was tearing apart the lands of Nar and Lucel-Lor in search of the woman who had captured his heart in the briefest of moments.

But he cannot escape the reach of the war as his king becomes ever more maniacal in his pursuit of victory against the wizard whose evil designs on the world have their own genesis. A genesis which casts severe doubt on the question of which side has right on its side.

'The Jackal of Nar opens with an attention-getting hellhole curtain raiser very reminiscent of Saving Private Ryan. The moral ambiguity is refreshing, with sympathetic opponents and no one whiter-than-white.' *SFX*

'Marco has written a well-crafted military fantasy, fast-paced, and underscored with believable characters and politics.' J.V. Jones

Available May 2000

Royal Format

Hardback £17.99 0 57507 072 2

Trade Paperback £9.99 0 57507 073 0

DAWNTHIEF
James Barclay

'A fantasy legend is born ... an enthralling novel: gritty, down-to-earth and delightful, invoking tears and laughter by turn. The best new fantasy I've read in years'

Maggie Furey

The Raven have fought together for years, six men carving out a living as swords for hire in the wars that have torn Balaia apart, loyal only to themselves and their code.

But when they agree to escort a Xesteskian mage on a secret mission they are pulled into a world of politics and ancient secrets. For the first time the Raven cannot even trust their own strength and prowess, for the first time their code is in doubt. How is it that they are fighting for one of the most evil colleges of magic known? Searching for the secret location of Dawnthief; a spell that could end the world? Aiming not to destroy it but to cast it. All at the behest of a man, cloaked by deceit, with a demon as a familiar and a wild story of a threat so old it has passed into folklore.

Royal Format

Trade Paperback £9.99 1 85798 594 X